## They held the stuff of legend
## in their hands. . . .

"I finally remembered the sapphires. Are you aware the stones are cursed?" Emmy asked.

Joss's lips twitched in what might have been a smile. "You mean that nonsense about the volcano and the prince of Katmandu murdering his wife?"

"You do know the story. The curse says only the owner's true love can wear the stones."

"There's hardly a shred of truth to that story. The fact is, my mother made it up when my father had one of the stones set for her engagement ring. She wanted something interesting to tell her friends."

"Well, your mother can take great satisfaction in knowing that it's become a very famous story. Will you become the Duke of Albrick when your father dies?" Emmy said. He didn't seem to mind her questions, and curiosity had been nagging her since she'd first seen the sapphires.

He shook his head. "I've two older brothers in line ahead of me. Which I count as a blessing, by the way. I don't think I'm suited to being a duke."

"Dukes probably have to keep clean offices."

"Without a doubt. Not to mention being exceedingly more diplomatic than I ever have been. I'm counting on you to introduce me around the town. Escort me to the ball. I can hardly attend a ball without a partner."

"You don't need me for that. This is a very friendly place. It shouldn't be so terribly difficult to find another partner."

"Perhaps I don't want another."

Emmy adjusted her spectacles on her nose and looked at him dubiously. "You're more diplomatic than you think."

# A MATTER OF HONOR

## Mandalyn Kaye

**Pinnacle Books**
Kensington Publishing Corp.
http://www.pinnaclebooks.com

PINNACLE BOOKS are published by

Kensington Publishing Corp.
850 Third Avenue
New York, NY 10022

First Printing: December 1996

Printed in the United States of America
10 9 8 7 6 5 4 3 2 1

*To Guy Williams and Tyrone Power,*
*who made Zorro worth loving,*

*and to Judy, my sister and friend, who not only showed*
*me the many uses of the petticoat, but who laughed in*
*all the right places, cried at all the right times,*
*and taught me the meaning of:*
*"Bloom where you are planted."*

*Everyone, at least once in their life,*
*should have a friend like you!*

# Prologue

The end.

For Joss Brickston, it came by way of a dark, yawning hole of grief and raw despair. The familiar sting of tears, an awful, ever-present pain in his throat scraped away in relentless fury at nerves drawn too tight and emotions too close to the surface. He almost welcomed the frosty bite of whistling December air that chapped his face, and the swirling mists of fog and ice-laden wind that ate at his bones. Mopping away a flood of tears with the back of his gloved hand, he watched as three coffins, one large, two small, were lowered into soft, snow-dampened earth. The life drained from his soul and followed.

He closed his eyes at the first sound of dirt plunking onto pine. The sound found a permanent place in the recesses of his mind.

Just as the haunting sounds of gunshots still plagued his dreams, that sound would claim his soul deep in the night when there was no light to drive away the sorrow. Even now, with his boots sodden from the melting snow, his fingers nearly frozen from the wind that seeped through the fine leather, the sound of three gunshots, of screams and cries of anguish, of betrayal and guilt echoed through his mind with each sickening thud of earth against wood.

In a wash of grief so intense it was almost a physical thing, he turned his back on the yawning graves. The numbness in his limbs did nothing to lessen his pain. Unable to bear the scene any longer, he strode down the hill with his dark cape whipping behind him like a spectre.

# One

*Carding, Missouri, 1851*

"In a feat of unbelievable daring and courage," Pearl Greene read from the Carding *Gazette*, "the Diamond Hawk leapt from the back of his magnificent black horse and attacked both thieves, knocked them unconscious, and tied them to the back of the coach, allowing the driver a fast, harmless escape into town. Marshal Gray Lawford arrested the dangerous, defiled footpads, and they are now in the secure Carding jail awaiting trial. While this was the now legendary Diamond Hawk's third courageous raid, our own Marshal Lawford was unprepared to speculate on who the mysterious man might be." Pearl bent down the corner of the newspaper. Her cornflower blue eyes sparkled as she met her cousin's dubious gaze. "Isn't it just dreadfully romantic, Emmy?"

Emmy glanced over the rim of her spectacles. "You don't believe all that nonsense, do you Pearl?"

Pearl indignantly rustled the paper. "Of course. It's in the *Gazette.*"

Emmy stifled a groan. "Horace Newbury has no business printing those far-fetched stories in that tattle-piece he calls a newspaper. Someone should tell him it's a waste of ink to use so many adjectives in one sentence."

"Must you be so level-headed, Emmy?" Pearl's slight frown marred her delicate features.

Emmy pulled a bottle from the polished desk in her cramped, if exceedingly well-organized, office. "Someone in this house has to be, Pearl, or we'd all fritter away our time with daydreams of the Diamond Hawk." She didn't even attempt to disguise her sarcasm. Horace Newbury, Carding's eccentric newspaper publisher, had made up the name for the dark character who had appeared several weeks ago.

The cloaked figure had managed to single-handedly disrupt a similar roadside robbery, and had started a storm of gossip and speculation. Horace had managed to whip the storm into a virtual tornado with his over-romanticized reports. The foiled thieves, hardly the most reliable of sources in Emmy's opinion, had reported that the mysterious man in black could see in the dark, had the strength of ten men, was a giant of a man with a giant of a horse, and, oddly enough, wore a diamond stickpin in the lapel of his black shirt. Horace Newbury had promptly dubbed him the Diamond Hawk, a name that set many feminine hearts aflutter in quiet little Carding where the town's favorite pastime was predicting the weather, estimating the weight of John Eggle's stud boar, and betting on how high the Mississippi River would crest following the spring rains.

Emmy Greene was far too busy to pay much heed to Horace Newbury. Pearl glared at her as she set the folded paper on the desk. "All the girls are talking about him, Emmy. I heard that Mary Jean Blilough is taking bets on who he could be."

Emmy looked up quickly. "Pearl, really."

"It's true," Pearl said defensively. "You may not be interested, but everyone else is." She rubbed a finger absently over a long, manicured fingernail. "I, personally, think it's Gray Lawford."

Emmy uncorked the bottle, then picked up a cleaning swab. "It is *not* Gray Lawford."

"How do you know?"

"Because Gray Lawford is a decent man with a strong sense of duty to his job as marshal. He is not running about the countryside in some ridiculous costume stirring up trouble."

"I think Gray Lawford is," Pearl paused, "offensive."

"What on earth for?"

"Because he's . . . well, because I do."

Emmy leaned back in her chair. "You don't like Gray Lawford because he ignores you, Pearl."

Pearl's pink skin, the same perfect hue and texture of her precious gem's namesake, flushed. "I have never been even remotely interested in Gray Lawford."

Emmy shrugged. "Perhaps not. That doesn't mean you aren't irked that he's never been interested in you." Pearl was very used to the men of Carding paying court.

Pearl's features grew harsh. "That is not true, Emmy. And besides, even if he were interested, he's a half-breed."

Emmy frowned. It was common knowledge that Gray's father had been a full-blooded Sioux Indian. It accounted for Gray's dark coloring and even darker good looks. It also accounted for his phenomenal success as a negotiator and lawman in the Indian territories, and his rapid promotion to marshal before he settled in Carding. "That's irrelevant, Pearl. Gray is a very respected man."

Pearl stuck her lower lip out in a delicate pout. "I don't know why you need to be so critical all the time, Emmy. I merely said I thought Marshal Lawford was the Diamond Hawk. I can certainly picture him riding about in the dark, dressed in black and foiling bandits."

So could Emmy, but she declined to say so. She decided to ignore Pearl's pout and set about removing the oil and dirt residue from the ruby necklace she was appraising for a client. When some of the cleaning agent dripped onto her fingers, she winced at the slight sting.

Pearl clucked her tongue. "You'll ruin your hands. I've told you before you shouldn't spend so much time with Papa's chemicals."

"I'm helping Uncle Robert, Pearl. He cannot handle all the business on his own, and besides, we need the money."

"I know that, of course, but you should take better care. Your hands will be stained and chapped."

There were worse fates, Emmy thought. Like starvation. "As I'm not planning on attending any of your garden parties or balls this year, you needn't worry that my hands will embarrass you, Pearl."

"Well-bred ladies don't have calluses on their hands." She made no effort to disguise her disapproval.

A flash of anger got the better of Emmy's hold on her tongue. She laid aside the cleaning swab. "Well, then, perhaps you'd like to tell me how else we're to put food on the table and clothes on our backs. With Uncle Robert's gambling debts, and . . ."

Pearl's gaze darted anxiously to the door. "You know we're not to speak of Papa's gambling."

Emmy brushed aside a stray tendril of her lamentably red-blond hair. How she wished it was the same fine, summer gold as Pearl's. "I'd like to do a good bit more than just speak of it, Pearl. Just last week I was forced to ask Avery Brooks for an extension on our credit."

At Avery's name, Pearl patted her soft golden ringlets. "Surely that wasn't so terrible a burden. I'd like to ask Avery for a few things myself."

Stifling a frustrated groan, Emmy forced her attention back to the necklace. She attacked the tarnish with renewed vigor. Avery Brooks was the owner of the mercantile in Carding. His shock of blond hair, handsome face, and tall good looks, made him the most eligible and available bachelor in town.

"Avery was very kind about it. He even referred the customer with this necklace to me. I hope I will earn enough with its cleaning and appraisal to repay the money we owe him."

Pearl flicked her delicate hand in absent dismissal. "I wouldn't worry about the money. Avery can afford to lend it."

Emmy looked at her sharply. "That's not the point, Pearl."

"Of course it's the point. I don't know why you insist . . ." Pearl's voice trailed off at the sound of the firm knock on the door.

Emmy glanced up in surprise. She expected no visitors this afternoon. "Come in?"

The heavy wooden door groaned in protest when Avery Brooks shoved it aside. He entered with a stranger who virtually overwhelmed Emmy's small office in Robert Greene's house. For the first time in longer than she remembered, Emmy completely ignored Avery Brooks.

The stranger was tall and broad-shouldered, his crisp white shirt and navy blue cotton kerchief only emphasizing the width of his chest. Tan breeches hung casually on his lean hips and muscular thighs. They disappeared into a pair of well-worn, dust-covered boots. His thick waves of sun-kissed brown hair were caught at his nape with a leather cord that wrapped the length of the queue. A black patch covered his left eye, but even the ominous-looking scar that ran from beneath the patch in a jagged path to his ear, did nothing to detract from the startling deep purple color and piercing intensity of his right.

His penetrating stare unnerved her. Deliberately, she swiveled her gaze to Avery. He was looking at Pearl. "Good morning, Avery."

Avery reluctantly glanced away from Pearl. "Good morning, Emmy. I've brought you a client." He indicated the stranger with a sweep of his hand. "This is Mr. Josiah Brickston. He has just arrived in Carding and has a piece or two he needs appraised for insurance purposes." His gaze returned to Pearl. "You look lovely this morning, Pearl."

Emmy felt suddenly self-conscious in her denim trousers and faded, oversized shirt. She stood and looked back to the stranger. Cautiously, she extended her hand. "It's a pleasure to meet you, Mr. Brickston."

He enveloped her hand in his warm grasp. "And you, Miss Greene. Mr. Brooks assures me you can be of assistance."

Emmy extracted her fingers from his warm grasp with a barely suppressed shiver. That stare again. It was so horrifyingly disarming. There was a certain sadness in his expression, it was true, but there was something else as well. Something that looked suspiciously like rage. Her eyes slid to Avery's. "Avery, surely Mr. Brickston wants Uncle Robert to do his appraisal."

Avery laughed. "Don't be a goose, Em. Robert's down in the saloon gambling away the money I lent you yesterday. I know you're perfectly capable of a simple appraisal."

Emmy's face turned scarlet at the tactless mention of the money. "Avery . . ." She was relieved when Pearl's delicate cough reasserted her presence.

"Avery," Emmy continued. "You haven't introduced Pearl."

Pearl smiled prettily when Avery lifted her hand to his lips. "I was hiding you back here, Pearl. I wasn't certain I wanted Mr. Brickston to meet you and learn one of Carding's best kept secrets."

With a giggle, Pearl extended her manicured hand to Josiah Brickston. "It's certainly a pleasure to meet you, Mr. Brickston."

Josiah Brickston gave Pearl's hand the same business-like shake he'd given Emmy's. "And you, Miss Greene."

"Oh, please, you must call me Pearl." She fluttered her lashes at him. Emmy diverted her attention to the small bottle, still open on her desk. Trying to ignore Josiah Brickston and the way he was looking at her, she recorked the bottle and dropped it in the drawer. She pushed the drawer shut with her thigh. "Avery, I really can't take on another job just now. The rubies were a godsend, but I've still got four chapters of Uncle Robert's book to transcribe."

Pearl laughed. "Emmy, don't be ridiculous. Avery would not have brought Mr. Brickston all the way out here if his business weren't important. Would you, Avery?" she purred.

Avery shook his head "Of course not."

Pearl smiled at Emmy. There was a slightly menacing look in her eyes that clearly said this-is-an-attractive-man-and-you'd-better-not-ruin-my-chances-by-being-rude. "So you see, Emmy, you simply must help him." She turned the full force of her cornflower blue eyes and dazzling smile on Josiah Brickston. "You'll have to excuse my cousin's rudeness, Mr. Brickston. I know Emmy's embarrassed that you caught her dressed like that, as if we couldn't afford any better." Pearl laughed. Emmy wanted to sink into the floor.

Josiah Brickston's gaze grew so cold, Emmy was

tempted to turn around and look for frost on the windows. "I am the one who has been rude, Miss Greene." He glanced at Emmy. She wondered if she imagined the slight softening of his expression. "I should not have come this afternoon without an appointment, but I was hoping you could see me. I'll be glad to come back another time."

Avery muttered something beneath his breath. He flashed a pleading smile at Emmy as he clasped one of her hands in both of his. "Please, Emmy." His thumb rubbed against her hand in a slow caress. "Mr. Brickston is new in town. He only just arrived, and is setting up his business." The way Avery squeezed her hand told her he hoped Josiah Brickston's setting-up would mean a lot of business at the Brooks Mercantile and General Merchandise. "I wouldn't wish to disappoint him." He paused. "Do it for me, Em. Because we're friends."

She concentrated briefly on the soothing feel of Avery's fingers on hers before she drew a resigned breath. "All right, Avery. I suppose I can work it in."

He dropped her hand. "Excellent." Avery looked briefly at Josiah. "I knew she would help you."

Emmy didn't fail to notice that Josiah's only answer was a slight lift of his right eyebrow. She'd always admired men, men like Gray Lawford, who could do that trick with their eyebrows. At times, she'd even stood in front of the mirror and tried to master it by holding down one eyebrow and lifting the other. It was so very, very intimidating. She had thought it would serve her well in her business transactions.

The brief notion of Josiah Brickston standing in front of a mirror and practicing tricks with his eyebrows startled a giggle from the back of her throat. She masked it, badly, with a cough, before she turned her attention back to Avery. "I've finished the rubies, Avery. You can return them to Mrs. Carver."

"She will be delighted I'm sure. I know she wanted them cleaned in time for the Mayor's party tomorrow night." He scooped up the necklace so he could hold the sparkling red stones to the light. "Have you finished the appraisal?"

With a nod, she pulled open the second drawer in her desk. A brief, efficient search through the carefully organized files yielded the papers she sought. "It's all here."

Avery accepted the papers and studied the top sheet. Tiny creases marred the handsome perfection of his forehead. Emmy took the rubies from him and dropped them into a soft leather pouch. "Is something wrong?" she asked.

Pearl made a small, exasperated, sound. "What could possibly be wrong, Emmy? You've been in this dingy little room pouring over those stones all afternoon."

Avery ignored her. His earlier flirtatious manner gave way to a brisk, businesslike efficiency as he examined the numbers on the appraisal. "It's a bit low, isn't it?" he asked Emmy.

Emmy shrugged uncomfortably. "Three of the stones are flawed, four more are inferior quality. There's only one of any real value, and a good number of the diamonds are paste."

Avery frowned. "You should learn to be a bit more diplomatic, Emmy. It wouldn't hurt you tremendously to turn a blind eye every now and then. You know Rosalynd won't accept this."

Emmy's lips pressed into a tight line. She and Avery had argued over this issue before. She found his insistence in the matter incongruous with his otherwise benevolent nature. While she knew customers like

Rosalynd Carver were difficult to please, she could not assign the stones more value than they had. "I checked all the figures against the Carrollton Guide. They are correct."

With a shrug, Avery dropped the leather pouch into his pocket. "No matter, I suppose. I can always adjust the figures when I transfer them onto your uncle's account sheets. Mrs. Carver needn't know."

"Yes, Emmy," Pearl said, placing her hand on Avery's forearm. "You'll be certain Mrs. Carver doesn't know. Won't you?"

She opened her mouth to tell Pearl her opinion wasn't wanted, but thought better of it. "Mrs. Carver never speaks to me," she evaded. "I will have no cause to tell her."

"That's a good girl," Avery said, folding the appraisal and slipping it into the inside pocket of his jacket. "Your fee on this, plus the work you're doing for Mr. Brickston should just about cover your extended credit. We'll have to work out something on the other charges. I'll see that the rubies are delivered to her this afternoon."

"Thank you, Avery," she whispered past a knot of mortification. How she wished he'd refrained from discussing their financial situation in front of the strange man in her office.

Avery didn't seem to notice her discomfort. "I knew I could count on you, Em. I always can." He turned his gaze back to Pearl. With a sweep of his hand, he lifted her hand to his lips once more. "I haven't had the opportunity to ask you to Mayor Slinkton's party, Pearl. You will go with me?"

Pearl beamed at him. "Why of course, Avery."

"I was afraid," he said, "you would have another escort."

With a laugh, she patted her carefully arranged ringlets. "I have. I will simply cry off."

Avery pulled her hand through the bend of his elbow. "Walk with me to my horse and I'll let you tell me about your gown, Pearl."

Her fingers caressed the soft fabric of his jacket sleeve. "Why, Mr. Brooks. I shall be delighted."

Avery nodded briefly at Emmy, and again at Josiah. "Good day, Mr. Brickston."

"Good day, Mr. Brooks."

Emmy looked at Josiah in surprise. Was that distaste she heard in his voice? Avery didn't seem to notice. "I'm certain Emmy will do a fine job for you."

"Pearl." Emmy pointed at the discarded newspaper. She'd lost what remained of her patience. "You've forgotten your paper."

Pearl snatched up the paper to toss it into the small waste bin. "Really, Emmy. I don't think it's necessary to be so critical. I'm sorry I upset the excruciating order of your office. I would think you could learn to be less demanding."

Josiah Brickston slanted a look at Pearl. "I have to sympathize with your cousin, Miss Greene. I have learned that an orderly office is the best and most efficient way to conduct business."

When she saw Pearl's frown, Emmy knew Josiah Brickston had just slipped into the same category as Gray Lawford. "Emmy could stand to be a bit less efficient and a bit more feminine, Mr. Brickston."

Emmy barely stifled a hurt gasp by turning to silently rearrange the books on the shelf next to her desk. The remark had stung and Pearl knew it; had meant it to.

Josiah Brickston fixed Pearl with a hard stare. "There's nothing unfeminine about efficiency, Miss Greene," he said quietly.

Pearl visibly withdrew. Raising hurt eyes to Avery she pleaded, "I'm ready to go, Avery."

Josiah ignored her. "I must thank you again, Mr. Brooks, for tending to my dilemma so directly. I'm sure you've left me in capable hands."

His voice held a trace of an accent, Emmy noted, as she analyzed the effect the warm tone was having on her. Deliberately, she slid a heavy volume on rock formations between her Carrollton Guide and her Harkwell Treatise on the source of diamond tints. Just as quickly, she removed it to return it to its original place. She was aware that Josiah was watching her again with that disarming stare, and she moved the book once more before she realized it and put it in its proper place.

Avery cast Josiah a speculative look before he nodded a final time in Emmy's direction. "I assure you that I have," he said. "Emmy will know what to do about my fee." He slipped through the door with Pearl hanging on his arm.

Emmy finished replacing her books before warily looking up at Josiah Brickston. He looked awfully tall towering over her desk. "Won't you sit down, Mr. Brickston?"

He studied her a long moment, then lowered his large frame into the chair across from her desk. It suddenly seemed a very fragile, shabby chair to Emmy. Dozens of clients had sat in it before, and it had never seemed to bother her. She wondered why this stranger had managed to so thoroughly disconcert her.

Josiah crossed one long leg over the other as he leaned back in the chair. "Please," he said. The cadence of his voice was so soft, so pleasing, it reminded Emmy of a brook tumbling over water-smoothed pebbles. "I would prefer that you call me Josiah. Joss, if you prefer."

Emmy looked at him closely. Something in his gaze sought her trust. She sensed a brooding unease beneath his lazy countenance. The way his hair tumbled across his forehead made him look almost boyish. Had it not been for his underlying intensity, he might have appeared at ease. As it was, the tension in him intrigued her. This compelling stranger, she suspected, was about to somehow turn her world upside down. With a quiet sense of resignation, she met his gaze across the desk. "Very well, Josiah. Now perhaps you will tell me what brings you to Carding, Missouri."

# *Two*

Josiah searched Emmy's face as he watched her across the desk. Avery Brooks's description of a bespectacled, red-haired, too-serious, twenty-six-year-old spinster who spent her days poring over books and treatises on the science of gemology, had failed to prepare him for the contradictory bundle of expertise and undisputed femininity that sat before him. Emmy Greene was indeed unique.

Her hair, a warm, reddish gold, reminded him of spun birch honey. The afternoon light made her unruly curls look glossy. He wondered if they'd be soft to the touch. The bewitching scent of polished wood and brass, oil soap, and something he suspected was hers alone gave the cramped space an unexpected warmth. He found himself inhaling deeply as he committed the scene to memory.

On the surface, she was all professional. Her instruments and cleaning fluids lay in neat order. But a closer look revealed a tenderness that made him uneasy. A spray of freckles tickled the bridge of her nose. Her full, generous mouth seemed always poised on the edge of a smile. Worse yet, Joss had the uncomfortable notion that the woman's figure carefully disguised beneath her ill-fitting work clothes, hid similar secrets.

His reaction to her shocked him. Something in her pleasant expression made him want, almost, to befriend her. He sensed a loneliness in her that seemed to echo his own. The very idea stunned him. Since his wife and two sons had been killed, he had existed in a small, cloistered world of work, survival and guilt. He generally saw strangers as intruders into his own private hell. He would do well to remember he had but one purpose in Carding, Missouri. Emmy Greene could not, must not, distract him.

She was busily avoiding his gaze by rubbing a fingerprint off the polished surface of her small, cheap desk with the cuff of her shirt. "I'm in Carding doing survey work for Continental Shipping," he said in answer to her question.

She met his gaze so abruptly, he almost flinched. "The English firm? Out of St. Louis?"

Her eyes seemed to brighten, as if she'd seized on the answer to a puzzle. "Continental is headquartered in London, but we do have a significant operation in St. Louis." That was an understatement, he knew. Continental Shipping's operation was global in scale. They controlled nearly half the Mississippi river traffic in and out of St. Louis.

"Are you originally from England?"

"Yes. I grew up there."

"Ah. That explains your accent."

"My accent?"

"Oh, it's just the barest hint. I noticed it when you first came in." She shrugged. "In my work, I meet people from all over the world. I'm fascinated by accents."

Her intelligent eyes held his gaze. In their depths, he saw a frank inquisitiveness that made the knot of unease in his stomach begin to expand. He hadn't reckoned on finding Emmy Greene such a challenge, but years of building an English-based shipping company in the United States had taught Josiah Brickston how to adapt. "I've been working with Continental

Shipping's American operation so long, I thought I'd lost most of my English manners."

"You have," she said frankly. "I doubt most people would notice. As I said, it's a curiosity of mine." She seemed embarrassed by the train of the conversation, and abruptly diverted the subject. "So you are here on Continental business? Are they thinking of moving some of the operation upriver to Carding?"

He shook his head. "We're looking at Carding as a possible railway extension, not for shipping."

"Hence the survey work," she said.

"Hence the survey work."

"I see." She scooped a stray paper off her desk, then placed it carefully in the second drawer.

He sensed her reticence. "Do you not approve of the railways?"

"No, it isn't that," she said. Again, her frankness surprised him. He was accustomed to the kind of girlish flirtation that demanded evasive answers and coyly prodding questions. Emmy spoke to him with an openness he found uniquely disarming. "I just . . . Carding is so quiet. I hate to see the peace disturbed with the bustle of the railways. It's the future, though. The rails have always fascinated me, but I don't think life will ever be the same once they run through."

He studied her for several long seconds, perplexed that her appreciation for the railroads should please him so much. Their brief discussion had touched off an aching memory of his son, Michael. At four years of age, Michael had adored the railways, been obsessed with the locomotives, and with Joss's drawings of prospective track lines and designs. Just two weeks before his death, Michael had tipped an entire pitcher of raspberry juice onto a stack of carefully rendered cartographic sketches. Joss wondered if Michael had known he'd been forgiven before he died.

Resolutely, he shoved the thought aside, and tapped one long finger on the end of his knee. "There are over a thousand miles of track already operational in the East. With the new innovations that are being made, I suspect it won't be long before the entire country, including the western territories, is connected by the railroads."

"So I understand," Emmy said quietly. A tense quiet fell between them as Joss struggled with the memories. As if she sensed his discomfort, Emmy cleared her throat. "If you don't mind, Mr. Brickston—"

"Josiah," he prompted. A wave of unexpected heat washed through him when she leaned farther over her desk. Her breasts pushed enticingly against the fabric of her worn, oversized shirt. The soft cotton did nothing to disguise their fullness. With something of a start, he realized this was the first time he'd felt warmth in months. He didn't want, couldn't afford, to feel anything, especially not warmth. With ruthless determination, he clamped the internal lid back on the seething cauldron of rage and grief in his soul. Once he surrendered to it, there'd be no return.

"Josiah, then," Emmy was saying, "I meant what I told Avery. I am very busy right now. I would like to get on with the business of your appraisal."

"Of course," he said, relieved to have the conversation on sound business footing. If his voice sounded odd, there was no help for it. "I'm sorry to have detained you." He extended a black leather bag to her and placed it on the desk. "There are three pieces. I wish to have them insured against theft while I'm in Carding."

Emmy pulled a soft cloth from the top drawer of her desk and spread it carefully on the polished surface. She then slipped on a pair of white cotton gloves, smoothing them over her long fingers. The laces of the black bag easily yielded. She dumped the contents onto the cloth to examine them. He didn't miss the spark of appreciation in her eyes. The stones, he knew, were magnificent. "I've never seen anything quite like this, Mr., er, Josiah."

He watched as she marveled over the gems. Her eyes sparkled behind her spectacles. "They are family pieces," he told her. "I gave them to my wife on the eve of our wedding." The answer shocked him. He had no intention of telling her about Allyson.

Her swift intake of breath was his only warning before she raised compassion-filled eyes to his. "Your wife is . . . no longer living?" she asked gently.

"No." The answer was deliberately terse.

"I'm sorry," she whispered, and he detected a genuine empathy in her tone so unlike the usual response. People, he had learned, failed to understand that a mumbled apology was insufficient in the wake of his revelation that his world had all but ended with Allyson's death. Emmy, on the other hand, said the words with a depth of compassion that left him oddly breathless.

As if she understood that the depth of his grief could not be salved except in private mourning, she gave him what he needed most and turned her attention back to the necklace and earrings. The sapphires, he knew, were amazing. A deep, unmistakable shade of purple instead of the usual, more common blue, they were almost priceless. The necklace consisted of just four marquise-cut stones. A ring of tiny pearls surrounded each sapphire. He'd always liked its delicate design. It had looked perfect against Allyson's soft skin. Emmy held the necklace to the light, then laid it aside to study the earrings. They matched the necklace, each had two pearls and a similarly cut sapphire.

With a soft sound of dismay, she met his gaze. Behind

her wire-framed spectacles, her tawny eyes held a stricken look. "They are magnificent stones, Mr. Brickston."

"But?"

"But one of the pearls is a fake."

Joss stifled a pleased smile. She was as talented as Avery Brooks had promised. "Are you certain?" He feigned surprise.

She picked up the earring, then held it across the desk for his inspection. "Look." She pointed to the surface of the genuine pearl. "Do you see the pinkish cast?"

"Yes."

She pointed to the fake. "This one's color is too pure. Pearls are natural phenomena. They are never completely white like this. One of their most intriguing features is the way they reflect the color of their surrounding gems, background, or even a wearer's skin."

"I shall have to have it replaced," he said. "I had no idea." And I certainly didn't expect you to be quite this adept, he thought. The stone had been replaced as a measure of Robert Greene's talent as an appraiser. It was an excellent fake. A less talented gem appraiser wouldn't have detected the switch.

Emmy continued to stare at the stone, frowning indignantly. "It's scandalous that gems this fine should be set aside artificial ones, even good artificial ones. Were the stones set by a credible jeweler?"

Joss thought of Robert Farrell and wondered what the old man would say if he knew Emmy had questioned his credibility. The jeweler had been setting gems for the royal household, and a good number of the members of peerage in London, for over forty years. "I imagine they were," he said smoothly. "They belonged first to my mother. I cannot imagine that my father would have taken them to anyone he did not implicitly trust."

Emmy stared at the stones for several long seconds before she removed her spectacles. She retrieved her loupe from the top drawer of her desk. Fitting it to her eye, she studied the gems more closely. When she glanced at Joss with the large loupe still fitted to her eye, he almost smiled at the comical picture she made. "And what is your prognosis, Miss Greene?"

She let the loupe drop into her palm. "They are beyond price, Mr. Brickston. I'm not qualified to appraise them. Perhaps my Uncle Robert . . ."

"Ah, yes, Uncle Robert. I have heard a good deal about him."

"Uncle Robert is one of the leading gemologists in the world. I'm sure he would be delighted to help you."

"I do not want him to help me," Joss insisted, beginning to think perhaps there was a great deal more to Emmy's business partnership with her uncle than met the eye. "That is why I brought the gems to you."

Emmy shifted in her chair as she fingered the priceless gems. "I don't think you understand," she said. "I have a special arrangement with Avery Brooks. He will charge you according to the value I place on the stones. The higher my appraisal, the higher his fee."

"How do you get paid?"

"He pays me out of his fee."

"That seems a bit backwards."

She shrugged. "I wouldn't get much work otherwise. Few clients are willing to trust their stones to a woman gemologist with no credentials other than her family relations. Most of our clients believe my Uncle Robert does the appraisals."

"And what does Uncle Robert do?"

She diverted her gaze. Joss watched the way her down-soft eyebrows drew together in a perplexed frown. He had an insane notion to rub the tip of his index finger over one winged tip and test its texture. What the bloody hell was the matter with him?

"He's terribly busy with his books," Emmy explained. "He writes papers and such for the geology society. The research requires a good bit of his time." She brushed a lock of red-gold hair off her forehead. "I can assign a price, but you will be forced to pay Avery a rather steep sum for the appraisal, and because I'm not qualified to appraise the stones, I cannot even guarantee that the price will be correct."

"What if I simply paid you directly for your time?"

Her eyes widened. "That would violate my agreement with Avery."

He found himself strangely uncomfortable with her misguided sense of honor. It made his plan more difficult. Perhaps. "Do you believe he will pay you a fair commission after he marks up the figures on Mrs. Carver's ruby necklace?"

She flushed. "Mrs. Carver is difficult to please, and she's a good client. Avery has to be careful with her."

"I'm certain he does," said Joss dryly, remembering that Rosalynd Carver was the voluptuous wife of Carding's banker, Jason Carver. Absently, he rubbed a finger along the outline of his black eye patch. "But he will not increase your commission simply because he increases the value of the necklace?"

Emmy shook her head. "No," she said quietly.

Joss's nod was brief. "I thought not. Very well then, Miss Greene, with your permission, I will tell Avery Brooks that you were unable to evaluate the stones for me."

She released a relieved sigh. "Thank you. I cannot see my way fit to letting you pay Avery a fee for an appraisal I'm not qualified to give. I will be delighted to clean them for you if you like."

Joss nodded. "I will wait if you don't mind."

It took her less than fifteen minutes to clean the gems. When she finished, they were even more striking than before. She traced a gloved finger over one of the facets. "They really are lovely," she told him. "I hope you'll have that pearl replaced. It seems a shame to have their beauty marred by the fake."

"I have always admired them. Even as a child, they were my favorite of my mother's gems."

Emmy wrapped them carefully in a soft cloth before slipping them back into the leather pouch. "I'm sorry I could not be of more help."

"On the contrary. You have told me exactly what I wished to know." He'd brought her the stones to test her capability, not the value of the gems.

She tipped her head and studied him. "What do you mean?"

"I suspected that the stones were irreplaceable. You have confirmed it."

"I would take very good care of them if I were you. They clearly have significant sentimental value for you as well."

"Yes. They do." He pocketed the black pouch. "Now, you must tell me what I owe you."

She shook her head. "I could not charge you just for the cleaning. It was a pleasure to handle the stones."

"As I said," he insisted, "I consider the appraisal to be complete. I have every intention of paying you for it."

"I don't normally charge for a cleaning. I wouldn't feel right about it."

"I insist, Miss Greene. I've taken your valuable time. You must allow me to compensate you for it."

She frowned. "I suppose, I could charge you a nominal fee for the cleaning."

He nodded. "Quite right. Is one hundred dollars sufficient?"

Emmy's breath came out in a strangled cough. "One hundred dollars? Oh no, no. My fee is nowhere near that high. Avery pays me five dollars for the appraisal and the cleaning combined."

He found her shock disarmingly appealing. He knew from town gossip that the Greene family was in desperate need of the money. Emmy's reticence to accept it won his grudging respect. "I assure you that Mr. Brooks would have charged me at least that amount had you assigned an appraisal for the stones." He removed several bills from his wallet and laid them on her desk. "Are you certain that's enough?"

She stared at the money. "It's more than enough. Mr. Brickston, I think you should reconsider. This is way too much money."

He shrugged. "I do not know why you feel compelled to argue over it."

"Because I didn't give you a professional appraisal. You will still be unable to get the gems insured without the papers. You are, in effect, paying me for nothing more than my opinion and some cleaning fluid."

"An opinion that is worth a hundred dollars to me."

"But I didn't even do an account sheet," she persisted. "I would not wish for you to feel cheated. Please consider bringing the stones back for Uncle Robert to evaluate."

He shook his head. "No. I consider the matter settled."

"But, Mr. Brickston, are you completely certain—"

He cut off her protest with a wave of his hand. "I never do anything unless I'm completely certain, Miss Greene."

"I, well, I suppose it's all right. If you insist."

"I do." Joss made a rapid decision. His meeting with

Emmy Greene had changed his perspective, but certainly not his goal. "Now, perhaps I can persuade you to do me a small favor."

Emmy looked at him warily. "What did you have in mind?"

"I would like for you to accompany me to the mayor's party day after tomorrow."

Night came to Carding with the gentleness of a lover's caress. In a robe of darkness, the small town sleeping to the humming rhythm of the Mississippi river. From his hiding spot at the edge of town, a cloaked figure stepped from the shadows. The whir of crickets harmonized with the hum of bees to disguise the slight creaking of his boots. The Diamond Hawk paused to listen to the natural lullaby. He had always liked the sound.

Adjusting the black hood that covered his face, he began to weave his way among the buildings and houses in a silent, well-rehearsed pattern. Only the saloon noise, with its raucous crowd and tinkling piano disturbed the still night.

When he reached the small hotel, he studied the shadows for prying eyes before he extended a long, braided whip from his belt. With an efficient flick, he curled the end around the cantilevered edge of the roof and pulled himself up. He landed on the shingles with a soft *thump*.

He remained crouched as he waited to ensure he had not attracted unwanted attention. Only the quiet river-scented breeze seemed to pay him mind. With a soft smile, he coiled the long whip back onto his belt. He picked his way along the roof, seeking the overhang of room 314, the room Avery Brooks kept for his personal use. In silence, he counted the rooms until he found the one he sought. Dropping to his stomach, he leaned over the edge and found, as he expected, Avery and Rosalynd Carver involved in rather exuberant love play.

With a disgusted groan, the Diamond Hawk rolled to his back. While he needed, urgently, the information he sought, he refused to watch the sordid little scene. At half past eight o'clock that evening, just before daylight surrendered to darkness, he'd watched Rosalynd and Avery enter the hotel. He had hoped, by now, they would have progressed beyond their carnal diversion to the conversation he wished to hear. He had not given Avery enough credit, it would seem, as he was forced to listen to several minutes of heated exchange.

"Oh, Avery," Rosalynd purred. "I have missed you so desperately. How do you always know what I need?"

Avery laughed. "I have an excellent memory, Rosalynd." She screamed softly in response to something he did. "I remember," Avery continued, "that you like it like this."

"Yes." Rosalynd's answer ended on a sibilant hiss.

"And this," Avery said.

There was a long pause, followed by another scream. "You like it when I bite you here," Avery said.

Good God. The Diamond Hawk frowned. Was there no end to this?

"Oh, Avery," Rosalynd's voice had taken on a desperate quality. "Now, my love. Do it now."

"Will you give me what I want?" Avery asked.

"Anything," she promised.

"Anything at all?"

"Yes. Yes! Avery, I cannot stand anymore."

"Then hold me tight, darling. I'm coming inside."

There were several more screams, and exclamations of delight, and a great deal of heavy breathing. When it finally passed, the cloaked figure rolled to his stomach to peered into the window once more. He was surprised the glass wasn't fogged.

The two lovers sprawled naked on the bed. Avery's blond head lay cradled between Rosalynd Carver's ample breasts. She caressed his shoulders with her long, painted fingernails. The half-moons and reddened streaks on his back suggested that her soothing strokes were in soft contrast to her earlier zeal. "Avery?" she said, her voice a throaty murmur.

The Diamond Hawk leaned closer to the window to catch the conversation. Avery grunted in response to his name. Rosalynd tried again, tugging on his hair for good measure. "Avery, I want to speak to you."

Pliancy had disappeared from her voice. Rosalynd was all business. Avery pushed himself up on his elbow. He dropped a kiss on her nipple before he met her gaze. "Yes, my love?"

Rosalynd caressed the handsome plane of his face. "Jason will be leaving for Kansas City in a few days."

Avery smiled. "I'm looking forward to it."

She raised her head to kiss him. "So am I. You know how much I hate the way we are forced to sneak about."

The man on the roof almost laughed. Hardly a soul in Carding didn't know about Avery's liaisons, the politest possible term, with the banker's wife. "Anyway," Rosalynd continued, raking her fingers down Avery's chest, "Gray Lawford came to see Jason today."

Avery's posture grew taut. "Do you know why?"

Rosalynd nodded. "I was in the other room working on the books. Gray said he's worried about Jason making the transfer on his own."

"All that gold could be dangerous to transport," Avery said quietly.

"Even though no one is supposed to know the purpose for Jason's trip to Kansas City, Marshal Lawford is concerned that word may have leaked."

Absently, Avery began caressing Rosalynd's breast with his long, slim fingers. She closed her eyes on a rapturous sigh as she leaned back into the pillows. "Do you think he suspects our plan?" Avery asked.

Rosalynd shook her head. "He can't. It's just a precaution . . ." her voice trailed away when she moaned. Avery bent his head and took the peaked nipple between his lips.

"Is Jason adding extra protection?" Avery asked against her breast.

Rosalynd nodded feverishly. "Yes. Yes."

The man on the roof pushed aside his irritation at the renewed loveplay and leaned closer to the window. If the fates were kind, Avery would tell him what he wished to know before the scene culminated in another act of adulterous transgression. "How many extra men?" Avery persisted. Rosalynd didn't answer. He lifted his head.

"How many?" His previous gentleness gave way to a brisk command.

"I . . ." Rosalynd clutched at his head as she sucked in great gasps of air. "I shouldn't, Avery. It's bank business."

Avery's hand moved between her thighs. Without thought to preliminaries, he roughly plunged two fingers inside of her. "How many, Rosalynd?" She screamed in frustration. "I can't give you what you want until you tell me," he insisted.

"Avery!"

He inserted another finger as he loomed over her. "You must tell me, my love."

"Four," she managed to say. "Two more with the wagon, and two along the path. I don't know where."

"Will you find out?" Avery asked, moving his fingers.

"Yes." Rosalynd shut her eyes. Her head dropped against the pillows.

"Do you promise?"

"Yes!"

With a thin smile, Avery bent his head to her breast once more. "You're getting quite good at this, my love," he mumbled.

The Diamond Hawk glided to his feet. He made his way silently down from the roof and back into the shadows. He had what he'd come for.

# Three

"Emmy." Her cousin Ruby looked at her in disbelief. "He asked you to the Slinktons' party? He's a complete stranger."

"I think he's a very nice man," Emmy said, sifting idly through the meager contents of her small wardrobe.

Pearl's laugh was in harsh contrast to her earlier giggling flirtation with Avery Brooks. "You should have seen him, Ruby. 'Nice' is hardly the word I would use."

Emmy bit back an angry retort. Pearl was four years younger than she, but, on occasion, her tongue held the razor-sharp edge of a seasoned old woman. "It isn't true, Pearl. After you left, he was a perfect gentleman."

Ruby raised her eyebrows. "Good heavens, Emmy. He was in the office with you. You were no doubt wearing those awful denim trousers and one of Papa's shirts. Of course he was a gentleman."

Emmy refused to let the barbed comment disturb her good humor. "Well, be that as it may, he asked me, and I said I would go. The matter is settled." She looked at the dismal selection of gowns with something akin to despair. Why hadn't she noticed before how threadbare and hopelessly out of fashion her gowns had become.

Ruby seemed to read her mind. "If you're thinking that you're going to attend the mayor's ball wearing one of those, you're sadly mistaken. We shall have to see if there is something you can borrow. Heaven knows, we'll all be embarrassed beyond belief if you show up wearing a patched gown.''

"Don't be silly, Ruby," Pearl said. "Emmy couldn't possibly wear any of our gowns. She's too tall."

Emmy sank to the bed with a growing sense of depression. It was true, after all. Her cousins all favored their mother. They were petite; the picture of feminine delicacy. But Emmy had inherited her father's stature. At five feet, nine inches, she towered over the rest of them. Jade was the tallest, and even if she could somehow contrive to lengthen one of her gowns four or five inches, it would never fit across the bust and around the waist where Emmy's figure was noticeably fuller. "Perhaps you're right," she muttered.

"Of course we're right," Pearl snapped. "You will simply have to send him a note and tell him you have changed your mind. You know we cannot afford a new gown for you."

Emmy thought of the money he'd paid her yesterday. Briefly, she entertained the notion that surely she could find a suitable gown for a not-too-exorbitant cost. Just as quickly, she squelched the thought when she remembered the large bill she'd paid at Mabel Tattingly's dress shop just that afternoon. Her cousins had spent quite a bit on their spring wardrobes. It had taken all but a few dollars of the money she had left to finish paying her uncle's other creditors.

Emmy forced the glum thought aside as she looked at Ruby and Pearl. As usual, their appearance was the picture of femininity. Suddenly, she was very conscious of her acid-stained hands and denim trousers. When she pictured Ruby and Pearl standing with the rest of her cousins at the Slinktons' party, she cringed. How had she imagined she could stand, even for a night, amidst such a flock of beautiful birds? She'd look like a chicken masquerading as a swan if she even attempted it. Josiah Brickston must have been suffering a brief burst of insanity when he'd asked her.

She deliberately squashed a wave of self-pity. Pouting would do her no good. What was done, was done. "You're right," she conceded. "I've nothing to wear, and even if I did, I couldn't spare the time. I still have work to finish for Uncle Robert. I'll send Mr. Brickston a note this afternoon so he can make other arrangements."

Ruby nodded. "I'm sorry, Emmy. I know you would have liked to have gone. If we'd dreamed you would have an escort, we could have planned ahead."

Emmy met her cousin's gaze with a sad laugh. Dear Ruby. She did try. "Do not fret over it, Ruby. It was a silly notion. As I said, I have too much work to do anyway. When else will I have the house almost completely to myself?"

Pearl gave her wrist an absent flick. "We're all going except the children. You'll only have the two of them to contend with."

"Yes," Emmy agreed. "I should be able to get quite a bit done." When her cousins left, Emmy walked to the window of her tiny room in Robert Greene's attic. As always, her eyes strayed to the west where her father, Jedediah Greene, was somewhere making his way as a trapper. "I hope you are well, Jedediah," she whispered, tipping her forehead against the cool glass. She had stopped praying for his return somewhere between her thirteenth and fourteenth birthdays. Now, at twenty-six, she knew quite well that he was not coming back.

Her unnatural melancholy today disturbed her. She had been unable to dismiss the memory of the saddened look in Josiah Brickston's eyes. She recognized loneliness, knew the feel of it. When he'd spoken of his wife, she'd heard the deep sense of loss. Perhaps that explained the odd effect he had on her. Having once known the bitter despair of losing her parents, she found herself irresistibly drawn to salving his hurt.

She should have known better. With a resolute tug, she straightened the cuffs of her shirt. The sooner the note was written and delivered, the sooner she could have the whole business behind her.

Emmy was still making the same promise to herself an hour and a half later when she entered Josiah Brickston's small office on the second floor of the Post Office in Carding. Based on her knowledge of Continental Shipping's operations, she'd expected to find a large office, filled with activity and clerks. She'd hoped to pass her note to an employee, who could surreptitiously deliver it later to Josiah Brickston. She had known he would not be there, as his survey work would require his presence on the site, but she was completely unprepared for the silence that welcomed her into the cluttered office.

Emmy looked around in distaste. Piles of papers and books covered every available space. A chair sagged from the weight of the papers piled on its seat. In the massive bookcase, books were crammed in at haphazard angles, and tufts of papers stuck out like cowlicks among the leather-bound volumes. Amid the boxes and equipment and furniture, a clear path led to the center of the room where two desks sat facing each other.

On both, stacks of reports and correspondence teetered ominously between piles of drawing utensils, rulers, and ink jars, as if the smallest movement would send them crashing to the floor. More from impulse than forethought, she moved to straighten one of the piles. Her eyes fell on the rolls upon rolls of paper stacked in incongruously neat rows beside the desk. The rest of the office lay in such disarray, the careful stack appeared out of place. Curiosity got the better of her. Emmy gingerly cleared a space on the desk, then picked up one of the rolled papers. It flattened with easy familiarity, suggesting its frequent use.

The map held her spellbound. With certain insight, she knew just as surely as she knew her own name that Josiah Brickston had drawn it. Every line was firm and sure. The contours of the land came alive beneath the solid strokes of his pencil. His markings were clear and precise, giving every measurement and angle in complicated technical formulas, but his attention to detail was far more impressive than his obvious cartographic skill.

He had drawn groves of trees and included sketches of leaf types and shapes with a list of the vegetation he had identified. Tiny drawings of foxes and birds and groundhogs and even a few beetles and a snake or two completed the picture. On one side of a hill, Josiah had drawn a brown-eyed susan, two daffodils and a trumpet vine curved around the rugged contours of a split-rail fence. The stream that traversed the map was complete with leaping fish, and a doe and her fawn drinking from the cool water. He had sketched in the proposed line of the rails to show how they would carefully follow the flow of the land rather than carve a straighter, and no doubt less expensive, route. This wasn't a map, it was a work of art.

With a smile, Emmy traced her finger over the sketched railroad tracks. Josiah Brickston was a man who loved his work because he loved the land.

Joss opened the door to his office, and would have stepped aside to let his assistant enter, but he stopped short at the sight of Emmy leaning over his desk. In

her patched gray dress, with her red-gold hair drawn
back from her face in a braid that threatened to explode into a tangled mass of curls, she looked less like
the self-confident businesswoman he remembered, and
more like a naughty child caught with her fingers in
the pantry. Even her spectacles were perched on the
end of her freckled nose at a precarious, uncharacter-
istic angle. "Miss Greene," he drawled. "What a pleasant surprise."

Emmy nearly leapt through the ceiling at the sound
of his voice. She looked up, guilt clear on her face.
The map dropped to the desk in a flutter. "Mr. Brickston," she said, flustered.

He didn't budge from his spot by the door. "I
thought we settled the issue of my name yesterday
morning. I asked you to call me Josiah."

Emmy didn't know what to say, so she stared at him
without saying anything at all. Sweat had dampened his
hair into a glossy mass of waves. The dust on his loose-
fitting blue shirt and tan trousers spoke of a long morning on the survey site. Even the black patch over his
left eye was dust-speckled. Emmy had a sudden notion
that if she removed it, the skin beneath would be
smooth and white, in startling contrast to the deep
bronze of his face. At the irreverent thought she felt a
blush stain her skin. To disguise it, she began nervously
re-rolling the map.

Joss watched as she attempted to straighten his desk.
He set the equipment he was holding on top of a cluttered trunk, then stepped aside to let a curious Jim
Oaks precede him into the office. Jim shot him a knowing look as he paused to stamp the mud off his boots.

"I really wasn't trying to pry, Mr. Brickston," Emmy
said anxiously. "I shouldn't have looked at the map,
but I was just so intrigued. I didn't stop to think that
perhaps . . ."

Joss held up a hand to interrupt her hasty explanation. "If there were anything in here Jim and I didn't want the world to see, we would have locked the door."

Emmy noticed his companion for the first time. The black man was even taller than Josiah's six feet plus. His clothes were just as dirty, but his smile seemed oddly out of place next to Josiah's sad eyes. Emmy smiled back. "Miss Greene," Joss said, crossing to the desk, "this is my assistant, Mr. James Oaks. Jim, this is Miss Emmy Greene."

Emmy decided she liked the way Josiah said her name. It must be the hint of his British accent she'd noticed the day before. She extended her hand to Jim. He gave her a curious look as he briefly shook her hand. "It's nice to meet you, Mr. Oaks," she said.

"You too, ma'am."

Josiah swept a stack of papers off a sagging chair to clear a space for her to sit. He dumped them in an unceremonious pile on top of a wooden crate. "Now that you're here, you might as well sit."

"Joss," Jim interrupted. "We're expecting that new scope for the transit today. All right with you if I head down to the shipping office to check on it?"

Josiah nodded. "Of course. We've done all we can outside today because of the sun glare. After you pick up the scope, there's no need to come back this afternoon."

Jim's face split into a wide grin. "My Annie will thank you mightily."

"Give her my best, Jim." Joss waved him out the door then indicated the now vacant chair to Emmy. He dropped into his own with a loud, exhausted *thud*. "Now," he said, watching Emmy as she seated herself, "to what do I owe this pleasure?"

"I was so impressed with your defense of my clean

and orderly office yesterday, I had a strong desire to see yours."

It took Josiah several seconds to realize she was teasing him. The banter oddly pleased him. "I said I admired the practice of an ordered office. I didn't say I had one."

Emmy looked around. "I don't think anyone could accuse you of that."

"In my defense, I've been here less than two weeks. I haven't had the chance to settle in yet."

Her look turned skeptical. "If you haven't settled in two weeks, you aren't going to."

He shrugged. "Probably not, but it suits us. Jim and I never have any trouble finding what we're looking for."

"Mr. Oaks seems very . . . nice," she said.

Josiah nodded. "He's the best surveying partner I've ever had. It's pretty damned amazing considering he'd never handled a transit or a Gunter chain until I hired him when I came to Carding to find office space."

Emmy looked at him in surprise. "You hired him. You mean you don't . . ."

"Own him?" Josiah asked, his face hardening slightly. "Good God, no. That's a barbaric practice. The one thing I dislike most about this country."

Emmy sighed in relief. Josiah Brickston climbed three more rungs on the ladder of her esteem. "I'm glad. It's such a divisive issue here in Missouri. Especially following the congressional compromise. I wouldn't have wished to quarrel with you about it."

Joss propped his booted ankle on his knee. "I imagine you're fairly formidable when you argue, Miss Greene."

"Not really." She shook her head. "But I admit, the entire issue does disturb me. I'm afraid the whispers we've been hearing will lead to war very soon."

Joss nodded. "Most likely. In fact, I do not think it can be avoided."

Emmy sighed. "It must be very hard on Jim living in Missouri. I imagine good jobs are hard for a free black man to find in this state."

"He was fairly out and out when I hired him to help me with the surveying."

"Continental didn't have any objections to Jim?"

Josiah shrugged. "Continental lets me do more or less as I please."

Emmy had seen the maps. She believed it. Continental Shipping would be foolish to lose a cartographer as talented as Josiah Brickston, no matter what his relationship with them. "Is he married?"

"Jim? He wants to be. Annie's his fiancée."

"Who is Annie?"

"She works for Mrs. Carver," Josiah said tightly.

"Oh," Emmy said, knowing quite well that Annie was a young black slave the Carvers had bought to serve as cook and housekeeper in their spacious home. "He can't marry her until he buys her papers, can he?"

Josiah shook his head and pointed to a door across the office. "Jim lives in the back room to save money. I offered to give him, or at least loan him, what he needed, but he wouldn't take it from me. They'll have to wait until he's saved enough."

"I think that's awful."

"So do I, Miss Greene."

She smiled at him. "And please, there's no reason for you not to call me Emmy."

"Does this mean I will finally get my way on your use of my given name?"

She nodded. "I suppose it does."

"I think we will get along exceedingly well. I am very fond of having my own way."

Emmy laughed. "Probably as fond as I am of having mine."

Josiah leaned back in his chair. He refused to consider the odd sense of ease he felt with her. "Now, suppose you tell me what brings you into town in the middle of the afternoon."

Emmy looked away. She toyed with the small bottles of ink on Jim's desk. Josiah watched as she put them in order by height. "I hadn't planned to tell you directly," she said quietly. "I was going to give my note to one of your clerks."

He indicated the empty office with a sweep of his hand. "As you can see, there is no one but Jim and me to run the place."

She placed the shortest bottle at the end of the row before she began rubbing at an ink stain on Jim's desk with her gloved thumb. "It's a bit embarrassing."

Josiah captured her hand. Her gloved fingers felt very small enfolded in his large grasp. "Tell me what's wrong, Emmy?" he persuaded.

His voice had dropped several decibels. She remembered thinking it sounded like a mountain brook. "I . . . I cannot go with you to Mayor Slinkton's party."

"Why not? Are you crying off for a better offer?"

"Oh, no." Emmy looked stricken. Almost as upset as she'd been when she'd told him about the artificial pearl in his mother's necklace. "It's nothing like that."

"I didn't think it would be," he said. "You didn't strike me as the type. Then why can't you go?"

She tugged her hand free and began lining up the pencils on the desk so they rested in a neat row, end to end. "I haven't anything to wear." She stifled a small, hysterical giggle. "This is, in fact, the nicest dress I have. Imagine what a stir that would cause at Mayor Slinkton's."

Josiah had a sudden memory of Pearl dressed in pale

blue organdy silk seated in Emmy's office. He frowned. "Why?"

Her fingers snapped a pencil in two at the abrupt question. She put it down carefully before she turned to look at him. "Because I don't think Mayor Slinkton expects his guests to wear gray serge." She flipped the edge of her skirt to show him a patch. "Particularly not patched gray serge."

Josiah shook his head. "That's not what I meant. Why is this the nicest dress you have? Surely you've earned enough money with appraisals and cleanings to afford a new one." He didn't think it would be polite to point out that one hundred dollars should have purchased a complete wardrobe.

"There were bills," she said hesitantly. "And my cousins . . . well, it just wasn't possible."

"Cousins? I thought Pearl was the only one."

"Oh, good heavens no. I have nine cousins."

"Nine?"

Emmy nodded. Before my Aunt Clare died, she and Uncle Robert were very, well, close."

"Are they all like Pearl?"

Emmy heard the slight note of distaste in his voice. "Pearl is not really so bad."

"No?" he asked, his eyebrow arching skeptically.

Emmy shook her head. "Just this morning, Pearl and Ruby both were trying to think of a way I could borrow one of their dresses for the party tomorrow night." She decided it would be disloyal to tell him that she'd been forced to spend most of the one hundred dollars at the mercantile and the dressmakers to cover the expense of her cousins' wardrobes.

"Why couldn't you?" he asked.

"All my cousins are petite, like Pearl. Jade's the tallest, but even then, the gown would be a good four or five inches too short."

Josiah tipped his head to one side. The movement sent a lock of hair tumbling over his forehead. Emmy had to stifle the urge to brush it into place. "Ruby, Pearl, and Jade," he speculated. "What are the other six named?"

Emmy smiled sheepishly. "You must never tease them about this. They're very sensitive."

"You have my word as a gentleman."

"Well," she hesitated, "it's only because Uncle Robert loves his work so much."

"I understand."

"Topaz is the oldest. She's a year younger than I am. Then Ruby, then Pearl." She ticked off the names on her fingers. "After Pearl, there's Jade, Garnet, Coral, and Opal. And then Gem, he's the only boy and he's eleven. Alex is the youngest. She's nine."

"How did Jim and Alex get so lucky? Did Robert run out of names?"

Emmy shook her head. "It's Gem, not Jim. G-E-M. Alex is short for Alexandrite."

Joss felt a rare smile tug at the corner of his lips. "You must feel very fortunate to have escaped such a disastrous fate," he said.

She blushed to the roots of her hair, but not before she noticed that his smile didn't quite reach the piercing intensity of his eye. "Not quite," she whispered. "My uncle was never very creative, you see, and I'm afraid my father gave him the idea."

"Gave him the . . . Emmy. It's short for Emerald?"

"No. It's short for Emerelda, and not after the stone, either. After Emerald Lake in Tennessee where I was born. And don't you dare call me that."

"Emerelda Greene," he drawled. "It does have a certain ring to it."

"Yes, well, I don't know that my father intended for me to become a spinster. He married my mother when she was sixteen. I think he believed the problem of the last name would take care of itself."

Joss heard the hint of melancholy in her tone when she spoke of her parents. "Did your parents die? Is that why you live with your uncle?"

She shook her head. "My mother died when I was nine. My father didn't think he could handle the responsibility of a young girl in the wilderness, so he asked Uncle Robert to take me in."

Joss frowned. "He abandoned you?"

"Not precisely. He was supposed to come back as soon as he made enough money to stop trapping for a living."

"Your father was a trapper?"

"He still is. Perhaps you've heard of him. He's quite famous. His name is Jedediah Greene."

Josiah's breath came out in a low whistle. "Well, I'll be damned."

"Do you know him?"

Joss shook his head. "I know of him. His explorations in the West, and his journals, are used in cartography laboratories around the world. I fell in love with America because of Jedediah Greene."

"Many people do. Still, I'm surprised you came to America given your family's ties to England."

"What do you know of that?" he asked cautiously.

"The sapphires," she explained. "I finally placed the sapphires."

"Placed them?"

"I knew I had read about purple sapphires somewhere. They're such a phenomenon, they were bound to attract attention from the scientific community. It was only a matter of time until it came to me."

"I should have known."

"Are you aware that legend has it the stones are cursed?"

Josiah's lips twitched in what might have been a smile. "You mean that nonsense about the volcano and the prince of Katmandu murdering his wife?"

"You do know. The curse says only the owner's true love can wear the stones."

"There's hardly a shred of truth to that story. The fact is, my mother made it up when my father had one of the stones set for her engagement ring. She wanted something interesting to tell her friends."

"Well, your mother can take great satisfaction in knowing that it's become a very famous story. I found it in one of my books."

"The stones are so rare, I imagine they would attract some attention. There are only two sets in the world, I believe. One belongs to the Queen of England, and the other belongs to my father."

"Since you look nothing like the pictures of Queen Victoria I've seen on English pound notes, I assumed you must be the Duke of Albrick's son."

"Thank you for the compliment. Even if I am a traitor to my homeland for saying so, no one should look like Victoria. And you are right, my father is the Duke of Albrick."

"Which makes you part owner of Continental Shipping."

Josiah nodded. "I see you've done a thorough job of investigating. My Uncle Tryon is the primary owner. My cousins Mark, Morgan, Ben, Kalen, and I bought our way in."

"As I understand it, Continental has offices all over the world."

"That's right. Ben is my only blood cousin. He runs Continental's London office. Morgan oversees our European operation, Mark handles the Caribbean, Kalen is responsible for Asia and the East. I chose America."

"What does your uncle do?"

"Gets rich off the rest of us and lives like a prince in London."

Emmy laughed. "How very generous of him."

"He's quite a man, my uncle. It's hard to believe he never married. There was a woman once, I think, but he rarely speaks of her. I believe that's why he's taken us on as his personal projects. He hasn't got any children of his own."

"Will you become the Duke of Albrick when your father dies?" she asked. He didn't seem to mind her questions, and curiosity had been nagging at her since she'd first seen the sapphires.

He shook his head. "I've two older brothers in line ahead of me. My brother Jarred is the marquess." At her blank look, he clarified, "The oldest. Duncan is a year younger than Jarred and two years older than I. He's next in line should anything happen to Jarred. Which I count as quite a blessing, by the way. I do not think I am well suited to being a duke."

"Dukes probably have to keep clean offices."

"Without a doubt. Not to mention being exceedingly more diplomatic than I have ever managed to be."

Emmy remembered the hundred dollars and thought perhaps he was much more diplomatic than he thought. "Do you have sisters as well?"

"Two. My sister Cana is the oldest in the family. She's married to Curtis Rain."

"The explorer for the London Geographical Society?"

"Yes."

"You have a very interesting family."

"That whole story is extremely long and complicated. Remind me to tell it to you one day. My sister Katy is the youngest, and she's presently driving my father mad with her antics and flirtations in London.

Is there anything else you wish to know with this interrogation?" The question was, perhaps, more blunt than he'd intended, but he feared she would soon begin asking about his marriage.

Emmy blushed. "I'm sorry. I shouldn't have pried."

He shook his head. "You weren't prying. I don't mind answering your questions."

Emmy didn't tell him she wanted to ask about his wife. She suspected he'd mind answering those questions very much. Instead, she said, "I'm curious by nature. It's one of my most regrettable faults. It's going to get me into terrible trouble someday."

"I wouldn't worry about it if I were you. In my experience, curious people are much more interesting than non-curious ones. They know a good many more things."

Emmy shifted uncomfortably. It was very close to a compliment. "Well, I've no doubt taken up more than enough of your time. I merely wanted to let you know about the party so you could make alternative arrangements."

"I was counting on you to introduce me around."

"You don't need me for that. Carding is a very friendly community. I'm sure the mayor would be delighted to introduce you to people."

"I can hardly attend a ball without a partner."

"It shouldn't be so terribly difficult to find another."

"Perhaps I don't want another."

Emmy adjusted her spectacles on her nose as she looked at him dubiously. "You're more diplomatic than you think."

"If you had a gown, would you go with me?" he asked.

"I hardly see that—"

"Would you?"

"As I don't, it isn't a matter of—"

"But would you?"

Against her better judgment, Emmy relented. My but he looked handsome. Even covered in dirt and in need of a bath, Josiah Brickston was a striking man. "Yes, Josiah. I would."

# Four

"Oh Emmy," Jade wailed. "You simply must go with us. It isn't fair for you to stay behind."

Emmy looked up from her desk to give Jade a reassuring smile. Of all of her cousins, Emmy was fondest of Jade. At nineteen, Jade was just coming into her own among her older sisters. Although she lacked Pearl's beauty or Ruby's self-confidence, her kind heart and gentle spirit had turned more than one masculine head in present weeks. Emmy suspected Jade would soon be knocking away suitors by the score. With a name like Jade Greene it was probably a good thing, she thought with a wry smile. "It's all right, Jade. I really need the time to finish transcribing Uncle Robert's manuscript."

Jade pulled her companion forward. "Tell her she must go with us, Grant. We don't care about your dress, Emmy."

The young man tugged nervously at his collar. "Really, Miss Emmy. Jade and I would be delighted for you to accompany us."

Emmy almost laughed. Grant Lewis's boyish face had turned redder than beet stew, and the poor man looked ready to crawl under the floor with embarrassment. She knew from experience he was painfully shy. It had been nearly a miracle when he'd mustered the courage to ask Jade to walk out with him. Emmy was certain the very last thing Grant Lewis wanted that evening was a spinster chaperon. She made a mental note to ask Jade her opinion on Gray Lawford. The handsome marshal was more man than poor young Grant Lewis would ever be. "I wouldn't dream of intruding on your evening, Grant, though it's very nice of you and Jade to offer."

Jade slapped her fan down on Emmy's desk and dropped into the chair. "Then we're not going either. Grant and I will stay here and help you with Papa's book."

Emmy picked up Jade's fan, dusted it carefully with a soft cloth, then handed it back to her cousin. "It's very sweet of you, but I really don't mind staying home. You and Grant have a good time tonight."

Grant looked relieved. Jade frowned. "I just feel awful, Emmy. I don't want to leave you here over this silly issue of a gown. I wish we'd found one of mine you could borrow. Are you certain you don't want to try the one with the lace? I'm sure we could lengthen it."

Emmy shook her head. "I'm certain." She stood up and walked around the desk to clasp both of Jade's hands in hers. On impulse, she leaned down and kissed her cousin's cheek. "You do look lovely tonight, Jade. That soft blue crepe de chine suits you perfectly."

Jade gave Emmy a hug. "Garnet wanted me to buy the green silk, but I thought I, of all people, would look ludicrous in a green gown."

Emmy laughed. "I'm glad you showed better sense."

Jade slipped a hand through the bend of Grant's arm, then looked closely at Emmy. "Are you sure you won't reconsider? I know we'd have a much better time laughing with you than listening to Topaz' stuffy comments all evening."

"Jade, really," Emmy exclaimed.

"Well, it's true and you know it. Sister or not, Topaz is about as interesting as overcooked oatmeal."

"Jade, that's enough," Emmy said. She gave Grant an apologetic smile. "Try to keep her from getting in too much trouble tonight, Grant."

Again, he tugged on his collar. "I will, Miss Emmy."

She winced. For all his boyish charm Grant had a way of making her feel a hundred years old. She decided Jade would never make it to the Slinktons' without help, so she began bustling the young couple toward the door. "Now, go and have a wonderful time. There's no need to rush home."

Jade paused a final time when Emmy had them nearly out the door. "I'm sorry, Emmy."

Emmy smiled sadly. "So am I, Jade," she said, giving her cousin a final push through the front door and out into the warm night. "Take care of her, Grant."

He nodded. "Good night, Miss Emmy."

"Good night." She shut the door with a soft click, then walked back to her desk, grateful for the diversion of her work, and the long quiet hours it would require.

Although her cousins didn't know, Robert Greene had not actually written a treatise in over three years. Emmy did the bulk of the writing, and, occasionally, Robert would review her work for accuracy. Even that had stopped during the last year or so. It was her work, published under Robert's name, that the geological community reviewed. It was her work on ruby discoloration and the effect of carbon deposits under heat that had earned world-wide recognition.

She sank down in her small chair, rubbing a hand wearily through her tangled curls, and stared dismally at the stack of papers on her desk. Usually, her work with the gems enthralled her. She'd been known to disappear into her office for hours on end, hardly surfacing for anything other than the most pressing of physical needs. At first, the books and writing had been merely a source of income to keep pace with Robert's gambling debts, but it hadn't taken Emmy long to fall in love with the chore.

When she handled a new stone, or made a particularly startling discovery, she felt an exhilaration unlike anything else in her life. She likened it to her days as a child when Jedediah Greene had allowed her to trail behind and watch as he laid beaver traps. The first time he'd helped her catch and clean her very own fish came close to the rush she found when she handled the stones.

When she dared spend the money, she would send to Boston or New York for used copies of the more famous monographs into the science and study of rare gems and decorative stones, then, spend months poring over the books until they nearly disintegrated.

But not tonight. Tonight, the moon outside was too silver, and the soft breeze too pleasant. The quiet hum of the crickets punctuated the night air. Emmy slid open her window and leaned forward on the sill with a wistful sigh. She'd already managed to get Gem and Alex into bed. Even they had seemed to take pity on her by retiring without the usual arguments. The unnatural quiet in the house was almost oppressive. From somewhere in the shadows of the velvet night, a giggle of laughter carried on the wind and reached Emmy's ear. She wondered briefly which of her cousins had delayed their arrival at the party in favor of a walk with her suitor.

Resolutely, she slammed the window shut. She still had four more chapters to complete before she could send her latest work on polishing methods for coral and shell deposits to Robert's publisher. She managed to work steadily for nearly two hours, despite the frequent intrusion of purple sapphires and Josiah Brickston's sad expression on her concentration.

The tear coincided perfectly with the start of her second chapter. It plopped, heedless of the damage it caused, onto the fresh sheet of paper. She tried to ignore it, but a second followed, leaving a ragged water mark on her page. Emmy sniffed as she waged a war against the threatening torrent for several long seconds. When four more tears slipped through her defenses and soaked the paper, she gave up.

"Oh, why not," she muttered and tossed her pencil onto the desk. Dropping her head onto her crossed arms, she began to cry. The longer she cried, the more reason she found for the tearful outburst. Shortly her sleeves were soaked through, and her chest hurt with the effort to breathe.

She cried because her mother had died. She cried because Jedediah had left her with Robert Greene. She cried because he'd never come back for her. She cried because Robert Greene's debts were beginning to get ahead of her. She cried because the roof needed mending, and two of the shutters leaked, and the front porch was missing a plank. She cried because Alex needed new shoes, again, and that meant more credit at Avery Brooks's mercantile. And she cried because she had desperately wanted to walk out with Josiah Brickston, and everyone had thought it a silly idea. Just because it probably was silly, made her cry all that much harder.

When she'd cried so long she was exhausted from the sheer effort of it, she lifted her head and tugged open a drawer for a handkerchief. Her nose was running something fierce. Her swollen eyes stung from the effort to hold them open. A brisk search through the desk yielded no handkerchief. Left with the possibility of blowing her nose on her cleaning cloth, or finding a better solution, Emmy swiped at her face with her cuff. It didn't help. Her nose continued to run. Tears continued to flow.

With a small moan of frustration, she flipped up her skirt and grabbed the hem of her peach-colored petticoat. As cumbersome as petticoats were, the damned things had to be good for something. She pulled up the edge, grasped it in both hands, buried her running nose between an embroidered flower and a worn cotton patch, closed her eyes, and blew.

"I hope I'm not disturbing you," the quiet voice said from the doorway of her office.

Emmy's eyes flew open, and with her nose still tucked into the folds of her petticoat, she gasped, "Oh! It's you."

The man they called the Diamond Hawk stepped inside Emerelda Greene's tiny office. She was looking at him with the most horrified expression. Her fingers still held the hem of the peach cotton petticoat to her nose. He reached in his pocket and withdrew a black silk handkerchief. "I didn't mean to startle you." He gave her the handkerchief. "Please allow me to come to your assistance."

With a startled gasp, she dropped the petticoat and quickly brushed her gray serge skirt over it. "Don't you think a black silk handkerchief is taking the matter of a disguise a bit to the extreme? Surely you could have used white cotton like everyone else."

The corner of his mouth twitched. "I could not help but notice your petticoat was not a common white."

Emmy blushed. She'd made the undergarment from one of Coral's discarded gowns. "I had the material left over."

He shrugged. "So did I."

Something about the notion of the tall man sewing his own handkerchiefs eased her mortificaton. Emmy wiped her swollen eyes with the square of black silk and motioned for him to sit down. "Who are you?"

He took the small chair across from her desk. His black cape swished around him. Black trousers hugged muscular thighs. A loose-fitting black shirt did nothing to disguise a strong chest and arms. The infamous diamond stickpin in his lapel winked at her in the lantern light. "Don't you read the papers?" he inquired.

He held her captive with his penetrating stare, visible even behind the black mask that disguised his eyes if not their shimmering intensity. His mask and hat completely covered the top of his head. Only his firm mouth and chin were visible. It was a very firm chin, she noticed. "I . . . of course. You're the Diamond Hawk."

He waved a gloved hand in absent dismissal. "I didn't choose the name, I assure you. I would not have picked anything nearly so dramatic."

Despite herself, despite the disarming presence of the man in her office, Emmy laughed. "The reason for your rather flamboyant appearance, I suppose?"

"I don't suppose you'd believe me if I told you I have a very good reason for this disguise?"

Emmy shook her head. "Not likely. I do know, however, that Horace Newbury has an overactive imagination." She pulled open her top drawer to replace her pencil in the slot where two more, already sharpened, lay side by side. An uncomfortable silence fell between them. To mask her nervousness, Emmy rearranged the bottles of cleaning fluid in her desk.

When it became apparent he wasn't going to speak, she finished stacking her cotton swabs bottom to top before she looked at him. "So, Mr., er, Hawk," she ignored his amused look, "are you in the habit of breaking into people's houses in the middle of the night?"

"I didn't break in. Your front door was unlocked.

You should have the plank fixed on your front porch, you know? Someone might get hurt."

His mocking insolence made her frown. "I know the door was unlocked. That is not the point. You nearly scared me to death when you walked in here unannounced. I was . . . too busy to hear your approach."

His shoulders lifted in what might have been a shrug had it not been so gracefully executed. "As I said, it was not my intent to frighten you. I did knock, but you evidently didn't hear me."

"I suppose I should tell you now that if you've come for money, I haven't any to give you."

Beneath the mask, she saw his eyes narrow. "You don't believe I'm here to rob you, do you?"

"What else am I to think? Why would you be running about the countryside dressed in that ridiculous costume if not for the sake of ill-gotten gain?"

"I prevent robberies. I don't initiate them."

Emmy remembered the way Josiah Brickston had lifted his eyebrow. She wished she'd taken the time to ask him how he did it. Now would be a most appropriate moment to try the trick for intimidation purposes. "How charming." She injected as much condescending sarcasm into her voice as possible.

To her dismay, he seemed not to notice. "I see you are properly skeptical."

She frowned. "You must forgive me, Mr. . . ." Emmy bit off the sentence in frustration at the ludicrous notion of his name. Her patience, and her temper, were exhausted. It had been an extremely trying day, and she had little energy to spare on this self-appointed Robin Hood. "What do you want?"

"I came to ask for your help." His bluntness matched her own.

"My help? What on earth could I do for you?"

"More than you know."

"You cannot seriously think that I will assist you in this," she indicated his costume with a sweep of her hand, "charade?"

"I'm deadly serious."

She didn't like the way he said that. She didn't like it at all. He certainly wasn't mocking her now. "What do you want from me?" she asked warily.

He held up a hand and leaned forward. "Please, do not be alarmed. I give you my word I don't mean you any harm."

"Why should I believe your word? You are hardly the most credible of characters."

He slowly removed one of his gloves. Delving into his pocket, he pulled out a leather pouch. She recognized the stamp of a prominent St. Louis jeweler on the side. He set it on the center of her desk. "Look inside."

She hesitated. The gems were probably stolen. If she saw them, she'd be obligated to report them to Gray Lawford. As if he sensed her indecision, the man pointed to the pouch. "Go ahead. Open it," he said.

Emmy removed a soft white cloth from her top drawer. Carefully, she spread it on her desk. She slipped on her cotton gloves, then gingerly untied the leather laces. When the mouth of the bag spread open, she looked at the stranger once more before she dumped the contents onto her desk.

Emmy gasped. A large pile, perhaps thirty-five carats in diamonds, tumbled onto her desk. Even though the gems were inferior quality, some of them even fake, it was still an impressive amount. "Where did you get these?"

"I lifted them off of two footpads last week. Are they artificial?"

Would he be angry, she wondered, if she told him

his ill-gotten gain was hardly gain at all? "Do you think they are?"

Again that graceful lift of his shoulders. "That's why I brought them to you."

Emmy turned her attention back to the stones and began sorting through them with her fingers. She made three neat piles, leaving any unidentified stones in the center. When she'd done what she could visually, she pulled out her loupe. A brief inspection allowed her to sort the remainder of the stones. She dropped her loupe into her hand, then looked up at the stranger.

"There are basically three types," she said, indicating the separate piles. "These," she pointed to the first and smallest pile, "are the genuine diamonds. Admittedly, they are very poor quality, but by strictly technical definitions, they are natural carbon diamonds." She waited for his reaction.

There didn't seem to be one. He pointed to a larger pile. "What about these?"

"Those are well-cut, polished crystal. They are very good imitations."

"And these?" He pointed to the third pile.

"Paste. Some of the very best I've ever seen."

"What would you say is the net worth of the entire lot?"

"It's difficult to say. Their value depends greatly on their use. For inexpensive jewelry, their value is fairly high. The quality of the stones, compared to the usual artificial, is exceedingly high. To a jeweler, they are worth quite a bit, perhaps five or six hundred dollars for the lot if he plans to set them."

"But loose?"

"Loose, they are worth less than fifty dollars, and that's a generous estimate."

He watched her scoop the stones back into the

pouch. "Then why," he asked, "would a thief, who is known for his rather expensive taste, trouble with them?"

Emmy met his gaze. "It's true, then, that you up-ended Gentleman Mack last week?"

He nodded. "Gray Lawford immediately transferred him to St. Louis. He was afraid Carding was too small a town to hold him."

"Gentleman Mack has never been this far north before. Surely it can't be profitable for him. He is used to much more sophisticated heists."

"Unless there's a shipment of diamonds involved."

"Fake diamonds?" she asked.

"Perhaps he didn't know." He stroked his chin thoughtfully. "Still, it is odd. Gentleman Mack himself was on that road. He must have been anticipating something very big indeed to take such an enormous risk."

Emmy finished returning the stones to the bag, then pulled taut the ties. "Do you think he was after the diamonds?"

"Undoubtedly. How much would that bag of diamonds be worth if the stones were genuine?"

"Even if some were flawed, they would still be worth several thousand dollars." She removed her gloves and placed them carefully in the drawer before handing him the leather bag.

He accepted it. "As I thought." Standing, he dropped the bag into a pocket of his cape. "I cannot thank you enough for your help, Miss Greene. I suspected the stones were not genuine, but I needed an expert opinion."

Emmy watched as he slipped his long fingers back into his black glove. She couldn't seem to take her gaze from the movements of his large hands. "What are you going to do with them?"

"I'm unsure. I will have to give the matter more thought."

"Why are you . . ." she hesitated. How did one simply ask a character as mysterious, as legendary, as the Diamond Hawk, why he'd chosen such an odd course of action?

"Who I am?" he asked.

Emmy nodded. He circled the desk to sit on the corner beside her chair where he swung one long leg idly back and forth. "I have excellent reasons for my actions, Miss Greene. I did not simply decide one day that I had an excess of black silk at my disposal."

"But surely Gray Lawford could . . ."

"Gray Lawford is doing all he can." His answer was terse.

"He is the marshal," she insisted. "If you are working for, and not against, the law as you claim, then certainly Gray . . ."

"Miss Greene," he interrupted, "while I appreciate your help this evening, I am not prepared to offer you any explanations for my actions. They do remain my own."

"I did not mean to sound rude, sir, but you startled me. You must admit, you are rather odd."

He brushed a dried splatter of mud off his polished black boots. Emmy noted the action with a smile. He appeared to be quite fastidious about his flamboyant appearance. "I will admit," he said, rubbing at the caked dirt with his glove, "that odd is the very least of my faults." The mud wiped clean. Once again, he met her gaze. The hard line of his jaw seemed to gentle as he studied her in the lamp glow. "Now that you have done me a favor, perhaps you will allow me to return the compliment."

Emmy's eyebrows rose in surprise. "What favor could you possibly do me?"

"Never underestimate the power of a man who can see in the dark and has the strength of ten men," he quoted from Horace Newbury's article.

Emmy laughed. "You shouldn't believe all that you read. Horace Newbury has a tendency to exaggerate."

He laid a hand over his heart. "You wound me, madam. You do not believe I am a mystical character of the night."

Emmy slowly took in the impressive figure he cut clothed all in black and casually leaning against her desk. Mystical might not have been the word she would use, but she was prepared to credit him with any number of things she might have doubted before his appearance in her office. "I believe you stumbled into a shipment of black silk and could not resist the appeal of playing at masquerade."

His firm mouth twitched. "Perhaps you are right. Now, I have two reasons to return your favor. I am in your debt, and I can see I certainly have my honor to defend."

"My fee for an appraisal is five dollars. Although lately," she said dryly, "I've been commanding a bit more. That will be more than sufficient to repay the favor."

He shook his head. "I will gladly pay your fee, but the debt I owe you certainly warrants much more than that."

"What do you mean?"

"I entered your home unannounced and uninvited. I frightened you. You could have refused to help me."

"But you gave me your handkerchief," she said.

"Quite so, and I insist that you keep it as a remembrance of this evening. Nevertheless, you must allow me to repay the debt as I see fit, and the indubitable pleasure of possessing my handkerchief cannot begin to measure up."

With some effort, she feigned ambivalence to his splashy show of false arrogance. "What did you have in mind?"

"I shall consider it in due course. In the interim, I would have a promise from you."

Emmy wondered if he was trying to distract her from the five dollars he owed her. As if he'd read her mind, he pulled a black purse from another pocket in his cape, produced a gold piece, and laid it on the desk. "This should more than cover the cost of the appraisal," he said quietly. "May I have your promise now?"

She raised startled eyes to his. "What promise?"

"I was very careful to approach your house without being seen. I cannot be certain, though. Should my presence here this evening cause you any . . . discomfort, you will promise to alert me so I can right the situation. I would not wish to burden you unnecessarily."

"What am I to do," Emmy asked, unable to keep the taunt from her voice, "fly your handkerchief from my chimney?"

"A rather romantic notion, isn't it? But, no, I would not require anything nearly so dramatic."

"What then?"

He fingered a lock of her hair with the gloved fingers of one hand while he delved into yet another pocket with the other. He extracted a black satin ribbon. "If you will secure your braid with this ribbon and wear it into town, I will know. I promise."

Standing, he dropped the ribbon onto her palm. She stared at it, wondering at the bizarre conversation and even odder request. He wasn't really serious, was he? Why on earth should she need his help? And if by some strange twist of fate she did, he didn't really expect her to believe he would come rushing to her defense like some knight from a medieval fantasy. That was simply too much to credit. Her fingers tightened on the black satin. She thought to demand an explanation from the mysterious stranger.

But when she raised her eyes, the words already on her tongue, the Diamond Hawk was gone.

Emmy stared at the door for several long seconds and tried to decide if she'd imagined the entire encounter. The black ribbon in her fingers, and the silk handkerchief and gold piece on her desk declared she had not.

Gingerly, she slid open her desk drawer, and hesitated briefly, then reached inside to release the spring on the secret compartment. Carefully, she dropped the ribbon and the handkerchief on top of the lock of her mother's hair. Recalling the intense gaze, the broad shoulders and strong thighs of the man they called the Diamond Hawk, she wondered where Marshal Gray Lawford was spending his evening.

# Five

Josiah stepped back into the crowded ballroom with a wary glance around. He barely resisted the urge to sigh in relief. Coral Greene had been rather avidly clinging to his arm for the better part of the evening. He had finally managed to detach himself long enough for a much-needed escape into the mayor's lush gardens. Now, he was relieved to see that Coral had redirected her attentions toward Cleavis Dunn.

From his vantage point by the door, Joss used the respite to survey the inhabitants of the room. He had been unpleasantly surprised by the opulence of the Greene family wardrobe when they had descended on the party in a wave of high-pitched giggles and affected flirtations. His marriage to Allyson had taught him a good bit about women's clothing, and the memory of Emmy's dark serge skirt, with its two worn calico patches, caused his brows to draw together when he contrasted it with the pink and yellow tartan of Topaz Greene's satin skirt and matching bodice.

Robert's ivory brocade waistcoat, with its elegant embroidery, only added to Joss's ever-growing dislike of the man. His gaze narrowed on Robert's yellow head. He watched as the man moved his ample girth about the room with undiluted glee. His pale skin was flushed from the heat. Joss had the suspicious notion that Robert's clothes would swish and creak when he walked

from the over-padding of his jacket and trousers.
Robert's attempt at a more fashionable silhouette had
failed miserably, however, and he looked considerably
more like a stuffed sausage than an athletically en-
dowed gentleman.

Joss's fingers tightened into a fist as he continued to
watch the man who was responsible for his arrival in
Carding.

He had not really needed to do the surveying himself, although he did enjoy the work, but no power on
earth could have kept him from Carding. After Allyson,
and their two sons, Michael and Adam, had been murdered on the highway road outside St. Louis, Joss had
spent three months locked in a prison of grief and
guilt. Nothing, not the frequent inquiries of his staff,
the letters from his family in England, nor the slow
decay of his health, had been powerful enough to
rouse him. Nothing until Gray Lawford's visit.

As marshal for the St. Louis territory, Gray Lawford
was leading the investigation into the murder of Joss's
family. He found Joss that afternoon, locked in the library of his spacious St. Louis home, surrounded by a
scattered pile of whiskey bottles, slowly trying to kill
himself. He'd been too much of a coward to do it the
honorable way and put a gun to his head.

It had taken several dunkings in a bathtub of frigid
water before Joss was coherent enough to discuss the
murders. Gray had been willing to wait. The facts were
sketchy and scattered. There were too many unanswered questions, but one thing had been certain, the
trail led directly to Carding. And to Robert Greene's
door.

That the murder might not have been a chance robbery on a darkened highway, and that Robert Greene
might have stolen Allyson and Michael and Adam from
him to cover a larger crime, had been all the incentive

Joss needed for his trek to Carding. The disturbance of the mysterious Diamond Hawk had begun two weeks before Joss moved to the small town. It was rumored that Gray Lawford was nearly at his wits' end trying to piece together the truth.

Joss was not nearly as distracted. He had plotted a course of action and would stick to it at any cost. That Emmy Greene had proved to be an unexpected pleasure only made the task easier. Joss Brickston was going to ruin Robert Greene, force him to acknowledge his guilt, and then kill him. And nothing would stand in his way.

He muttered a disgusted oath when he saw Robert slip through a heavily curtained doorway with young Enid Carver. When they disappeared from view, Joss tugged sharply at the edges of his black evening jacket to settle it more firmly on his shoulders. He forced his breathing to return to normal.

"You don't look like you are having a pleasant evening, Mr. Brickston," a soft voice to his right captured his attention.

He squelched an irritated groan at this latest interruption to his reverie. Jade Greene stood watching him with wide, inquiring eyes. At least, he thought, it was Jade who had arrested his progress. She was the least objectionable of Robert Greene's daughters. Had circumstances been different, he might have enjoyed the young lady's company. With the exception of Alex, Josiah had endured the unpleasurable experience of tedious introductions to the Greene sisters that evening. All, it appeared, were in the market for eligible men to finance their extravagant tastes, and, Joss suspected, Robert Greene's mounting gambling debts.

Jade, at least, seemed the most reasonable of the lot. A noticeable lack of hardened edges on her beauty, appealed to his sense of the extraordinary. "Good evening, Miss Greene," he said. "I trust you are enjoying yourself."

She nodded. "I am. Your expression's more sour than three-day-old goat's milk, though. I'd hasten to say you don't appear to be enjoying the mayor's hospitality."

"I'm sorry. I sustained an injury in my knees sometime ago. They still pain me when I am on my feet too long."

Her expressive face registered her concern. "Would you like to sit down? I'd be happy to fetch you some punch."

"To be absolutely proper, Miss Greene," he said, his voice conspiratorial, "I am supposed to do the fetching."

Jade's genuine laugh warmed him. She had failed to master the flirtatious giggle of her cousins. "I've never held much account for proper. Proper people are almost always boring." She glanced past his shoulder. "Mrs. Dillbalm has just vacated the two chairs by the door if you'd like to sit down."

"How can she have vacated two chairs?"

"You obviously haven't met Mrs. Dillbalm." She grabbed his hand and began tugging him toward the door. "Are you certain you don't want punch?"

He shook his head. "Just a seat will do nicely. Thank you, Miss Greene."

They nearly reached the chairs when Jade had to scare away two young ladies with a fierce frown. "There," she said, as she sank down in one seat. She patted the one next to her. "Do sit, Mr. Brickston. I cannot tell you how delightful it feels. My feet are aching from all this dancing."

With a wince, he took the adjacent chair. More weary than he'd thought, he tipped his head back against the wall. Damn, but his knees hurt. "I have noticed you have been rather popular this evening."

Jade gave him a wry look. "Isn't it the most amazing thing? Not a boy in the whole of Carding so much as looked my way until this last summer."

Joss slanted a glance at her. On the edge of womanhood, Jade was indeed transforming into a swan. He suspected any number of boys would be looking in her direction before too much longer. He rubbed his left knee and wondered how Emmy would respond to her cousin's suitors. He suspected she would have a soft spot for Jade. Something in her expression when she'd told him about her cousins had sparkled when she spoke of Jade. "How old are you, Jade?"

"Nineteen. Almost twenty," came the artless reply.

"Does your cousin approve of your escort this evening. What's his name? Neil?"

"Grant." Jade laughed. "And Emmy approves I suppose. Although she has been throwing Gray Lawford's name in my direction a good bit lately."

His question answered, Josiah thoughtfully rubbed at the pain in his knee. Gray Lawford had little in common with Neil, or Grant, or whatever his name was. If Emmy were matchmaking between the marshal and her cousin, she did, indeed, take Jade's matters of the heart quite seriously. "Perhaps you should pay attention to her. Marshal Lawford is a fine man."

"Oh, it wouldn't matter a speck if I did. Gray's never had eyes for any of us despite Emmy's best efforts. She's the only reason he stays in town."

His eyes popped open. "What?" His voice sounded a bit sharper than necessary. He hadn't reckoned on Gray's interest in Emmy. This could prove an unexpected complication. He didn't like complications.

Jade didn't seem to notice his sudden tension. "Gray

is very fond of Emmy. In fact, she's the reason he lives
here in Carding instead of in St. Louis."

"I haven't seen Gray tonight. Have you?" he said
warily, wondering, for the first time, if Emmy had indeed stayed home.

"He was here earlier. He usually doesn't stay around
long, though. I don't think Gray Lawford is very so-
ciable, if you know what I mean. Hello, Jeannie Lou,"
Jade called, waving to another girl about her age.
"How's your mama doing?"

Joss ignored the conversation about Jeannie Lou's
mother and her bout with croup. Instead, he thought
about Gray Lawford and Emerelda Greene. It simply
wouldn't do to have her—

"Mr. Brickston," Jade interrupted his thoughts.

"Yes?" He frowned at her. Her young escort was tugging on her hand.

"I—I promised Grant this next dance, but I wanted
you to know, well, it may not be the most proper thing
for me to say, but Emmy really did want to come this
evening. Really she did."

"Then why didn't she, Miss Greene?" he asked.

Grant looked sheepish. Jade gave Joss a stricken look.
"Because we were all too selfish to notice that Emmy
hadn't bought herself anything to wear. I told her that
you wouldn't mind if she wore her serge skirt, patches
or not, but she was afraid you'd be embarrassed."

Joss lifted the eyebrow above his eye patch. The girl's
candid reply surprised him. "I do not embarrass easily."

"I told her that." She laid an imploring arm on his
sleeve. "I even tried to convince her to add a ruffle to
one of my gowns, but she wouldn't." She looked at her
companion. "Would she, Grant?"

He shook his head. "No, sir. We both tried."

Joss gave Jade's hand a reassuring squeeze. "I shall

endeavor to call on your cousin tomorrow. Perhaps I can persuade her that I'm somewhat partial to gray serge."

Emmy woke to the persistent, nagging sound of a hammer pounding away at a hapless nail. With a frown, she wiped her hand through her disheveled hair as she sat up. What on earth was going on?

A brief glance at the window confirmed that the time was barely past dawn. Her first thought was that Gem was building yet another contraption to clutter up the hen house. Last time, it had been an automatic egg collector, designed to scoop the eggs into a bucket and relay them on a rope to the kitchen. After the first six eggs had shattered on the hen-house floor, Emmy had made him dismantle it.

This morning, she could already hear her Uncle Robert's disgruntled complaints wafting down the hall. She hurried to pull on her robe, hoping to stop Gem's racket before he brought the wrath of the entire household down on his young shoulders.

She didn't bother with her slippers, as they were worn nearly through to her toes anyway. Instead, she tied the belt of Robert's discarded dressing gown at her waist to cover her forest green silk nightdress—another of her cousins' many cast-off gowns made over for a more utilitarian function.

"Gem!" she called as she raced down the stairs. "Gem, saints a mercy, what are you doing?" She pulled open the front door. "You're going to wake the . . ." Emmy's voice trailed off when she found herself staring down at the top of Gray Lawford's dark head.

He was on one knee, hammering a new plank into the front porch. He glanced up with a warm smile despite the six nails he held between his teeth. "Mornin', Em."

"Gray! What are you doing here?"

He positioned another nail, then drove it into the wood with three firm blows of the hammer. Emmy was impressed. "I was out here to talk to your uncle last week when I noticed the plank needed fixing." He placed another nail. "I hadn't been able to steal the time until this morning." That nail only took two blows.

Emmy pulled her robe a little closer around her before she sank down onto the small bench by the door. Not for the first time, she admired the way the sun glistened on Gray's glossy dark hair. There was no good excuse whatsoever for that man to be so by-God attractive. His red shirt had faded to pink from many long days under the hot sun, but it draped casually across ridiculously broad shoulders, and tucked into pants that were entirely too tight in the rear to be decent. Emmy couldn't fault the view, though. She really ought to talk to Jade about this man. "There was no need for you to do this, Gray. You know I would have gotten to it eventually."

With a nod, he plucked another nail from between his teeth. "I know. Sorry it's so early. I won't have time later today." Emmy watched in silence while he pounded the nail into the new plank. He must have hit a knot. It took four blows.

"Emmy." He paused from his hammering to look up at her. His white teeth, she noticed, looked all the brighter in contrast with his sun-bronzed skin. "You'd tell me if you'd had any trouble around here, wouldn't you?"

Wary, she avoided meeting the penetrating look in his black eyes. "Trouble?"

"Yeah, trouble. You know, strange visitors, problems, difficulties."

She unconsciously pulled the lapels of her robe tighter. She didn't have to ask to know that Gray was referring to the Diamond Hawk. "What do you mean, visitors?"

Gray studied her with a shrewd expression. "Just people passing through. Any problems they might be giving you."

The coincidence of Gray fixing the plank after the stranger had brought it to her attention last night was too great. But, instinctively, she knew that Gray was asking out of concern, not because he wanted her to betray the Diamond Hawk. So she nodded. "If there were any danger, you know I'd tell you, Gray."

He studied her for several more seconds before he returned his attention to the floorboard. "I hope so, Emmy. I hope you, of all people, have learned to trust me." As if he sensed her reluctance, he let the subject drop, and they chatted amiably for several more minutes while he secured the plank.

The morning would have passed quite nicely, she later thought, if Gray hadn't been on his knee looking up at her when Josiah Brickston rode up to the house on his bay gelding. With her in her underwear and bare feet, and Gray looking for all the world like he was paying court, it was almost too much to bear.

"Good morning, Mr. Brickston," she called, doing her best to sound like she entertained men on her front porch wearing nothing but her nightdress and robe every day of the week. Josiah's fierce frown wasn't making it any easier.

He arched that very arrogant eyebrow. "Good morning. I was afraid perhaps I was calling too early." His voice held the slightest hint of accusation.

She shook her head. "No. Marshal Lawford was kind enough to come fix this plank for us."

Josiah dismounted. She noticed, belatedly, that his horse was heavily loaded with equipment and supplies. His expression didn't change as he approached her. "So I see," he drawled. "And you were kind enough to receive him in your nightclothes?"

Her lips pressed into a tight line. There was something about him that always made her feel just the slightest bit out of focus. She wasn't used to the feeling, and was finding she didn't like it at all. It didn't help that he looked so handsome all the time. How any man could look that intimidating in a snow-white homespun shirt and dark blue trousers was beyond her. It must have been the combination of his black hat and the black patch, she decided. She, however, refused to explain herself to him. If she chose to entertain Gray Lawford in her undergarments, that was her business. She resisted the urge to tug the lapels of her dressing gown together as she squarely met his gaze. "As it happens," she said loftily, "I did."

Gray looked from Emmy to Josiah, then back again, before he leaned back on his heels with a slight grin. "Well, I'll be damned," he said beneath his breath.

Emmy fought a losing battle with a blush. She gave Gray a sharp look to disguise her embarrassment. "Marshal, do you know Mr. Brickston."

Gray winked at her before he looked at Joss. "We've met. Mornin', Joss."

Josiah's nod was brief. "Good morning, Gray."

Emmy coughed as she stood. "If you two will excuse me, I'm going to dress, and I'll put on some coffee."

Feeling disgruntled, and oddly petulant, Joss looped the reins of his horse through the hitching post. He felt like a fool with Gray Lawford standing on Emmy's porch, staring at him. He felt like an even bigger fool for his reaction. But damn it, he hadn't been prepared to find the marshal kneeling at Emmy's feet at six o'clock in the morning.

When the door banged shut behind Emmy, Joss turned back to Gray with a narrow look. "I didn't realize you were such good friends with the Greene family," he said.

Gray hammered home another nail. "Only Emmy. She patched me up once when my gut got laid open by a bear. I was too far out to make it back to town."

Joss propped one booted foot on the first step of the porch so he could rest his forearm across his thigh. "How'd she find you?"

Gray placed another nail, then tipped his head in the direction of the enormous palomino mare hitched next to Joss's gelding. "I sent Agisah galloping ahead. I'd hoped she would make it to town. She found Emmy instead." He hammered home the last nail before he shifted to sit on the same bench Emmy had vacated. "I don't know how many of the women out here would ride into the woods to stitch up the half-breed marshal, but Em did."

Joss shoved his hat back on his head. "I'm not surprised."

Gray raised his eyebrows. "I wasn't aware you were such a close friend of the Greene family, either."

"Only Emmy," Joss said, well aware the tables had been turned.

"What'd she do for you?"

Gray Lawford's tone was almost an accusation and Joss leveled his gaze on him. "If I didn't know better, Lawford, I'd take offense at that."

"Emmy mostly has to look out for herself. I used to be that way. Still am. I guess you could say I take the debt I owe her fairly seriously."

Joss decided it was best to play out the hand. "You

know why I'm here, Gray. I told you before I was coming to Carding."

"I also know I told you to keep your hands out of this business."

"Would you do that if you were in my place?"

Gray paused, briefly, then shook his head. "Hell no."

"I didn't think so."

Gray picked up his dove gray hat and settled it on his head. "But I'm going to do my job. You get involved where you don't belong, and somebody might get hurt."

"What have I got to lose now?" Joss asked, his voice turning bitter.

"Emmy could lose everything, Brickston. I aim to see that doesn't happen. I owe her that."

Emmy stepped back onto the porch with the pot of coffee in her hand. She'd changed into worn work clothes while the coffee was brewing. When she saw the scene on her porch, she stopped short. The two men stood assessing each other with a casual wariness that made the hairs on the back of her neck stand up. The tension was uneasy, thick. They looked like two stallions sizing up their competition. At the thought, she giggled.

Both men turned to look at her. Gray took the three cups from her hand. Joss reached for the pot and held it while she sat down. "What are you chortling about?" Gray asked, putting the cups down on the bench.

"Well," she said, settling down next to Gray on the narrow bench, "it isn't every morning a lady awakens to find two such fine men standing on her doorstep."

Gray accepted a cup of coffee from her. "Thanks for the coffee."

"Seemed the least I could do for your trouble." She glanced at Joss. "Sugar and cream, Mr. Brickston?"

He shook his head. "Black is fine." When he took

a sip of his coffee, it rolled pleasantly on his tongue. She'd flavored it with cinnamon. Somehow, the sweetened spice reminded him of her. What seemed plain on the outside, always held a surprise. "You shouldn't flatter the marshal, Emmy," he said smoothly. "His head might swell too big for his hat."

She rewarded him with a throaty laugh that made his skin tingle. Gray finished his coffee and set down the tin cup with a decisive *thunk*. "I'd best be going, Em. I've got a shipment coming in from Kansas City today, and I want to make sure we don't have any mishaps. You'll remember what I said?"

She nodded at Gray. "I won't forget. Thank you for fixing the porch, Gray."

"My pleasure." When he settled his hat on his dark hair and looked at Joss, his cool, black gaze sent a silent warning. "Good to see you again, Joss. I know you'll keep me informed if anything should shake out?"

Joss nodded. "Of course, Marshal. I gave you my word."

Gray hesitated, then finally strode to his horse.

With Gray's departure, a tense silence fell between Emmy and Joss. She swirled the coffee in her cup and tried to decide how best to ask Josiah Brickston what he was doing on her porch at six o'clock in the morning. When she met his gaze, the question died on her lips. Saints a mercy but that gaze of his could heat the bristles off a porcupine.

Joss was watching the way her fingers twisted in the thin apron that covered her full green skirt. She was rubbing at a tiny stain as if her life depended on getting it out. Despite his best efforts not to, he also didn't fail to notice the way her tan blouse fitted a good deal better than the loose-fitting shirt she'd worn when he'd first met her. He had been right about her figure.

The thin cotton gave her full breasts and narrow waist the faintest suggestion of emphasis. A suggestion he found considerably more alluring than the stiff, unyielding corsets he'd seen on her cousins. He'd bet his last dollar Emmy wasn't wearing one, and the thought of all that soft, warm flesh with nothing but a faded blouse and a cotton chemise for cover was having one hell of an effect on him. "It's promising to be a warm day," he said, feeling like a fool all over again for not thinking of something better to say.

She nodded. More silence.

"I missed you last night at the party," he said.

Emmy's eyes widened. "Did you? Did you really?"

She sounded a little too young and a little too innocent to make him entirely comfortable, but then he remembered that Michael and Adam had been young and innocent, too. "Yes. That's why I stopped by this morning. I have to ride over to the bluff and chart the slope for the track lines. I knew I'd come right by your house."

It was not a very good excuse and Joss knew it. He could tell by the way Emmy was looking at him that she knew it, too. She looked awfully pleased with herself and it made him uncomfortable. "How long will it take you to do the charts?" she asked.

He shrugged. "Depends on how much detail I want. I could do it in a day or two, but it'll more likely be next week when I'm done."

She ran the tip of her pink tongue along her lower lip. Did she dare ask him if she could go along for the day? She wanted to. Oh, how she wanted to. She had been cheated out of his company the night before, but surely he wouldn't mind her faded green skirt and tan work shirt if he was just going to work. She screwed up whatever courage she still had and faced him square on. "Would you—" She hesitated, losing some of her nerve when Joss's eyebrow arched above his patch.

"Would I what?" he prompted.

"Would you mind if I went along?" she blurted. He stared at her in surprise and she rushed out, "I just want to watch. I won't be in your way."

Joss was amazed. The business of mapping charts was slow and tedious. "It will likely be boring," he said, doing his best to caution her.

"Oh, no," Emmy said a little too quickly. "It could never be boring out on the bluff." *With you.*

"Are you certain you want to go? I can't promise to be much of a host. I have to concentrate when I'm mapping."

She nodded. "I saw the map you had done in your office. You do beautiful work."

Joss knocked his hat back on his head a few inches as he considered the change of events. Well didn't that just beat all? Here he was worrying about how to get the lady's attention, and all he'd needed was a map.

He shoved aside the wedge of guilt that intruded on his satisfaction and smiled at her. "I would like the company for the ride if you're certain you won't be bored."

Emmy shook her head. "I won't be. I assure you I know what it means to be absorbed in a task. I'm very much that way when I work with the stones." She pushed a stray tendril of hair off her forehead and tucked it into her neat braid. "In fact, I've still two more chapters of Uncle Robert's book to transcribe. If you won't mind, I'll bring them along."

"I won't mind at all."

Before he could change his mind, she leapt to her feet and took his empty coffee cup from him. Scooping up the pot and Gray's discarded cup, she called over her shoulder, "I won't keep you waiting."

When the door banged shut behind her, Joss leaned back on his heels, trying to convince himself the progress was pleasing. He'd confirmed yesterday that Robert Greene would be virtually helpless without her. He would likely learn today whether or not she was really transcribing Robert's book or, as he suspected, writing it herself. She seemed pleased with his visit, and eager for his company. It should be no trouble at all to persuade Emmy to play into his hand. And that was, after all, what he wanted.

A picture of Allyson sitting beneath a tree, laughing at Michael while he chased butterflies, and holding Adam to her breast, burst into his memory. He curled his fingers into a tight fist until the knuckles showed white and his wrist ached. He didn't need any other reminders that Robert Greene was his enemy. So why did he feel like such a cad?

# Six

"Will you explain what you're doing?" Emmy asked an hour later, watching as Joss unrolled his maps and laid out his equipment.

He looked at her in surprise. "Are you interested?"

When she nodded, her spectacles bobbed on her nose. "Very much so."

He hesitated, studying the way the sun kissed her red-gold hair and highlighted her tawny eyes, and tried to decide if she was truly interested in the rather tedious process of surveying and mapping, or just flirting with him. He wondered for the hundredth time if it had been a mistake to let her accompany him to the bluff. He couldn't deny that he had appreciated her company on the long ride. She didn't chatter overly much, but asked intelligent questions, and supplied intelligent answers to his own. It would be boorish to refuse her simple request for a lesson in cartography. "All right" he nodded, almost reluctantly. "Come over here."

Emmy dropped her leather notebook to the ground and hurried over to where he stood. She had already watched in avid fascination as Joss set up the tent he would use as office and temporary shelter until he finished his work on the bluff. His portable desk and mapping instruments all folded neatly into a tiny little box with an enchanting number of drawers and spaces. She sank down beside him and watched as he spread out a large map. "This one," he said, "is the largest. It's the overall survey."

Emmy pointed to a series of figures in the corner. "What's this?"

"Those are survey marks. When Jim and I survey an area, we take standard measurements so the maps will be accurate. Railway surveys are more complicated than flat maps."

Emmy pushed her glasses up on her nose as she leaned over his shoulder. The intricate lines criss-crossed and swirled on the paper in an intriguing pattern. "All these numbers are measurements?"

"Yes. I have to include the grade of each hill, the depth of each river, and any other variation in the shape of the land."

"That seems like a terrible amount of work for just two people."

He nodded. "Technically, we should have at least six or seven men. A full survey team includes the front flag-man and his corps of at least two ax-men to cut away trees and bushes; the transit-man who records the distances and angles of the line; a chain-man who handles the Gunter chain; and the leveler who takes and records the levels. Sometimes the leveler has his own rod-men to handle the equipment and ax-men. In really big parties, there is generally a chief engineer, a cook, and a topographer as well."

"Then why on earth do you and Jim do all that work yourselves? Surely Continental can afford a bigger team?"

"It's not a question of cost."

She frowned. "But doesn't it take a lot longer for you and Jim to work alone?"

"We have to split the responsibilities. I'll spend this

week mapping the final survey while Jim is out laying the preliminary line at our next site."

"Why are you doing it this way instead of hiring a larger team?"

Joss gave her a meaningful look. "I can't find many engineers who are willing to work with Jim."

Realization was slow to come to Emmy. When it did, she muttered an angry oath beneath her breath. "Because he's a free black you mean?" Joss nodded briefly in confirmation. "That's absurd. Didn't you tell me Jim was one of the most talented transit-men you'd ever had on a team?"

"Yes."

With an angry swipe, Emmy smoothed her hands over her full green skirt. "I haven't much use for people who hold to those types of notions."

"Neither have I."

"You're making a big sacrifice by doing the survey this way. Aren't you?"

He shrugged. "Not really. It will take longer, it's true. But ultimately, it will cost the same. By the time you factor in what Continental is saving in wages, the cost is negligible."

"But you have to do more of the work than you would under normal circumstances." She pointed to the map. "It takes longer and the work is harder."

"It's probably good for a man to work hard every now and then."

Emmy tilted her head to study him, deciding she liked the way his dark hair curled slightly over his forehead. He'd discarded his hat long ago. The wind had lifted several locks from his neat queue and left his hair unruly and mussed. She had to stifle the urge to smooth it for him. "But if you got rid of Jim, you wouldn't have to?"

"I wouldn't do that." His answer was blunt.

Emmy smiled. "I know. I'd think less of you if you did."

"The arrangement Jim and I have works very well. Because of the reduced cost, I'm able to pay him handsomely for his work. He appreciates the extra money and works very hard for it. I appreciate not having to cope with the aggravation of a large survey team."

"You're a nice man, Josiah," she whispered.

As if uncomfortable with her praise, Joss returned his attention to the map. He ran a long, bronzed finger over a series of numbers. "This indicates the approximate line. After Jim finished clearing the site, I do the overall survey and plot the approximate line." He stopped for a minute as he sifted through his maps for another. "This," he said, pointing to an intricate set of tracks, "is the final line. After we do the survey, I replot it."

"So they will know precisely where to lay the track when they begin building?"

Her quick grasp of the subject pleased him. "That's right. After we measure gradients and obstructions, sometimes the approximate line changes."

"Why?"

"Until recently, the track had to be laid straight. That made the surveying far less important. The rails went whichever direction the engineer chose, but when John Jervis invented the swiveling truck, it changed the way we do things."

"What's a swiveling truck?"

Joss found a clean piece of paper and drew a quick sketch. Emmy liked the way his strong hands glided over the paper. She watched in fascination as the intricate diagram took shape. "When Stevenson invented the locomotive," he explained, "it had a stationary truck. That meant the front wheels of the engine moved in one direction." He drew an arrow on the paper.

"How did they go around corners?"

"They couldn't turn a steep corner without overturning the engine. Hence the need for so much blasting. The locomotive couldn't go around the mountain, so they had to cut a hole through the mountain."

She pointed to the second diagram he'd drawn. "This changed that?"

He nodded as he drew several arrows. "The swiveling truck allowed the front wheels to pivot on the track. The most sophisticated locomotives have swivels on front and back." He drew another sketch. "Incidentally, that's why the rails are now standard at four feet, eight inches apart."

"Why?"

"Because only one manufacturer makes the swivels and he only makes one size."

Emmy picked up the large map he'd first shown her. "Is that also why your track lines curve in and out so much?"

"There are two reasons for that. First, it is less expensive to build a track that traces the contours of the land instead of altering it."

"I can see that. I imagine blasting through mountains is a very tedious process."

"And dangerous."

"What's the second reason?"

Joss traced a finger over the track lines. "Aesthetics. It simply looks better when the railroads follow the land."

Emmy smiled at him. "Would you have done it this way even if it hadn't been a matter of cost?"

"Most likely. It seems a bit presumptuous to alter the land too much."

"But they're doing it everywhere," she said. "Just

last week I read an article in *Scientific American* about how they're building the Suez Canal in Egypt."

"You read *Scientific American?*"

Emmy laughed. "I know I'm supposed to keep my nose buried in *Godey's Ladies Book,* but I suppose I'm not the well-bred young lady I'm supposed to be."

Joss shook his head. "I imagine you would find the engineering of the Suez Canal considerably more interesting than methods for storing up pickles."

"I find a great many things interesting. What's happening in the world, right before our eyes, it's so amazing." She straightened her spectacles. "You can cross the Atlantic Ocean now in fifteen days on a steamship. And with the gold strike in California and Mr. Morse's telegraph machine, folks are moving all about like never before."

Joss looked out over the bluff. "The railways are going to be a big part of that. Before long, people won't need the treacherous wagon trains. They'll be able to travel all the way from Boston or New York to California in less than two weeks on the railways. It's only a matter of time before we can build locomotives that go even faster, cutting the trip down to just a matter of days."

Emmy saw the tiny lines that edged his eyes when he spoke about the future of the railways, and she asked, "Is that why Continental Shipping is so interested?"

He looked at her in surprise. "How do you mean?"

"The man who connects East to West is going to make a lot of money."

Joss swept his hand out to indicate the verdant valley that spread like an apron beneath the bluff. "It's never been about the money for me. My uncle thought I was crazy when I told him I wanted to expand our operation into railroads. We already control such an enormous share of the water traffic on the Mississippi and the Hudson, it seemed foolhardy to risk an expansion."

The sudden vibrance she saw in his face entranced her. His features were always so drawn, so intense, but now, he looked very much like a little boy watching a toy boat in a mud puddle and dreaming of pirate treasure. "Then why take it?" she asked, eager to keep him talking.

"It's difficult to explain. I saw my first locomotive when I was eight years old. I accompanied my father on a business trip to Manchester, north of London, where they had one of the first working railways in the world. I was enthralled. In love."

He leaned back on his hands, though his gaze remained steadily focused on the view. Emmy wished she were sitting on the other side of him so his black patch didn't block her view of his expression. "I never gave up that special place in my heart for the beauty of a locomotive. Then," he went on, "after I bought my claim in Continental, I started to appreciate the power of transportation, and what the steam engine meant to the way we live."

"And you saw the future of transportation in the railways."

He glanced at her, then, and Emmy saw a light in his eye she'd never seen before. It was magnetic. Addictive. Enslaving. "We can already move things over water at such a great pace," he said. "You've pointed out that the ocean can be crossed in just fifteen days. If we could move things over land with the same efficiency, think what it would do, of the effect."

He was completely caught up in his dream now. "And I want to be a part of that, a part of building history." He stopped abruptly, his look almost sheepish. "Does that sound very ridiculous to you?"

Emmy reached out to touch his sleeve. "Oh, no. I don't think it sounds ridiculous at all."

He started to roll up one of his maps. "Those dreams belong to an idealistic young man, not very grounded in reality, I suppose."

Emmy tightened her grip on his arm until he looked at her again. "No, Josiah. Only very brave people have dreams like that. It takes so much courage to dare."

"It also takes a fool," he said.

"They thought Galileo was a fool, and Aristotle, John Watt and, well, probably even that Jervis fellow you mentioned. You're a free spirit. That doesn't make you a fool."

She sounded so wistful that Joss stared at her. "You really do understand, don't you?"

Emmy nodded. "Oh, yes. I understand perfectly."

"What's your dream, Emerelda?"

Suddenly wary, she caught her breath. She hadn't realized she'd drifted so far. "What makes you think I have one?"

"Only a dreamer understands another dreamer's heart."

She began folding her skirt into meticulous pleats to avoid looking at him. "You'll laugh," she said.

Joss reached out and caught her chin so he could turn her face toward his. "I've just told you I want to lay three thousand miles of track and connect the United States from east to west. What could you possibly say that would give me cause to laugh at you?"

Her smile was self-deprecating. "It's different for you. You were born to do something magnificent."

"Is that really what you think?"

"Of course. Your father is a duke. You told me so."

"And I also told you I was the third son, which meant I was worth little more to the noble world I was born in than a passing mention at afternoon tea."

She frowned at him. "That can't be true."

"Of course it is. My oldest brother will inherit the title, and all the estates and money. I had the endowment from my mother to make my way in the world. It took every penny to buy into Continental. It was a huge risk."

"But—but you've made it work."

"With a lot of hard work, yes. I've been very fortunate. My wife's father was none too pleased, though, when she announced that she was tossing away her chance to marry a title so she could live in America with me. Imagine their shock that she should choose to be a working man's wife rather than marry a duke or an earl or some other equally important social dilettante."

Emmy's jaw dropped open. "That's terrible."

He tucked a curl of red-gold hair behind her ear in a gesture that seemed, at once, comforting and intimate. "So you see, we're not so very different you and I."

Unable to hold his gaze, she turned her attention to the thick, fluffy clouds that floated overhead. "I did have a dream. It was a childish one, though, so I put it away."

He lay back on the grassy slope and clasped his hands behind his head. "Dreams have a way of refusing to stay where we put them."

She began pulling the weeds out of the patch of grass around her skirt. "Do you know how diamonds are made?" she asked quietly.

"They form under the earth from the heat and the pressure, from coal, I think." He watched as she laid aside a handful of weeds in a neat pile and started plucking clover.

She nodded. "That's right. Do you also know they are the hardest substance on earth? Nothing can cut a diamond except another diamond."

"I had heard that. When they cut the gems, they have to use diamond-tipped chisels."

Emmy put down a handful of green clover before she met his gaze. "Then why do you suppose, no one had thought to harness that strength for purposes other than ornamentation?"

Joss looked at her closely. "What kind of purposes?"

"They are limitless," she said, beginning to warm to her subject. "The thought came to me several years ago when I was examining a stone a colleague had sent Uncle Robert. It was severely flawed, and lacked the fire that is so valued for an ornamental gem. The outside was tainted by boart and calcite, and even after I cleaned it, it was apparent that its decorative uses were virtually nonexistent. Still, I could not bring myself to dispose of it. I managed to borrow a diamond-tipped chisel and I sharpened an edge of the flawed rock."

"Like a knife?"

She shrugged. "I used it for weeks when I was examining coral samples. It cut the coral so easily, so precisely, I saved hours of time by not using standard tools. The cuts were cleaner, too, and more exact."

"And that led to your conclusion that diamonds could have any host of other uses?"

"Well, yes. Think for a minute about using the strength of a diamond and the power of a steam engine in tandem. Why, you could carve your way through a mountain in half the time it would take with explosives, maybe less. And because diamonds are so remarkably consistent in gravity and hardness, the accuracy and cleanliness of a cut are almost immeasurably exact."

Joss looked at her in amazement. "That's incredible. Has anyone done any experimentation?"

"Only a bit, and never on a grand scale. I simply do not think an engineer has come along with the clarity and breadth of knowledge to make the connection."

"You would like to be the one to do that, wouldn't you?"

"Well, not exactly. I haven't the knowledge nor the expertise to know all the practical applications. I would like to be the one to suggest it, though."

Joss nodded. "And you should. You most definitely should. Why, if you wrote this up for the London Geographic Society, or even for *Scientific American,* I'm certain you could get the idea heard."

She started pulling clover again. "No one would take me seriously. Someone would simply steal the concept and put their name on it."

"Someone like Robert Greene?" he asked quietly.

She looked at him in alarm, her hands stilling. "Why do you suggest that?"

"Isn't it true that you do most, if not all, of his writing now?"

"That's not true, I . . ."

"Emmy, please don't lie to me."

She drew a deep breath. "No one is supposed to know that."

"Only a fool couldn't have guessed."

"I—You won't tell him. Will you?"

Joss shook his head. "I would not betray your confidence. Is he the reason you haven't developed your notions about diamonds?"

"Among other things. I don't have any formal education, and I don't have any credentials. My father was a mountain man, for heaven's sake. I could never get the geological community to pay any attention to me."

With a sigh, he sat up. "What if I help you?"

She stared at him in surprise. "What do you mean?"

"I have excellent connections in the engineering field and among academia. I'll help you."

She shook her head. "No, Josiah. I couldn't. I—"

"Why not?"

"Because, I, well, just because."

"Because people would suspect perhaps Robert is not all he appears to be?"

"You don't understand."

"No, I don't."

She held out an imploring hand. "It's about never belonging anywhere. I've never had a place that belonged to me alone. I'm an intruder in my uncle's house and I owe him a great deal. He took me in. He gave me a home and a family when no one else would. I can't destroy his career simply because I have some far-flung idea that may or may not have any merit."

Joss felt his anger brewing. It took so little to work him into a rage at Robert Greene. The more he learned, the more often the anger threatened to undo him. "It's not right, Emmy."

She gave him a pleading look. "Please. It was just an idea, a fantasy. It never needs to be."

"But—"

"Promise me you won't interfere in this."

He hesitated for long seconds before he finally nodded. This was none of his business. In this, he could promise. "I promise. It's not my place, but if you change your mind, all you have to do is ask."

Emmy found herself suddenly wishing very much that it was his place. Josiah Brickston was a kind, caring man, one she longed to keep as a friend. "Thank you," she said.

"For the promise?"

She shook her head. "For sharing your dream with me. For not laughing at mine."

Joss smiled, a rare warm smile. It had a breathtaking effect. "The pleasure was mine, Emerelda."


After that first morning, Emmy visited Joss on the bluff every day for the next week. They generally

worked in companionable silence. Often, they'd talk
only when they stopped for lunch or at the end of the
day. By week's end, he had almost finished his maps of
the area. He estimated he would need two or three
more days at most before he and Jim could begin surveying a new plot. A part of him admitted that he would
miss Emmy's company. In the past few days, she'd pro-
vided a rare companionship he'd found comforting.

Another part, however, the stronger part, was glad
for the coming reprieve. Emmy was becoming more
and more of a distraction for him. It was beginning to
worry him.

Late one afternoon, he knew for certain that the
situation had escalated well beyond his control. The
sun cast ever-lengthening shadows on the ground when
he slanted a furtive look at Emmy. He began rolling
up his maps while he watched the ominous clouds that
had been moving down the river for the past two hours.
"Emmy," he called.

She was seated beneath the tree where she usually
worked. With her feet tucked beneath the folds of her
faded blue skirt, she looked very young and very vulnerable. "Are you through for the day already?" she
asked him.

He shook his head. "No, but I'm quitting." He
pointed at the storm. "I should have warned you earlier, but I was so absorbed, I didn't really notice until
now. It looks like a bad one."

For the first time that afternoon, Emmy noticed the
thick, dark clouds. Storms moved very quickly downriver, she knew. She wondered if she'd have time to
make it home before the deluge started. She began
tugging on her boots. She'd slipped them off earlier
for comfort. When the laces caught in a knot, she muttered a soft oath. "I'll have to hurry if I want to outrun

it," she said. "I didn't see it either." The knot refused
to yield to her fingers.

Joss gave the clouds a final assessing glance, then
scooped up his maps. A raindrop splattered on his
nose. "You won't make it. You'd better wait it out in
the tent with me."

Her fingers stilled on the laces. It was such a logical
suggestion. So sensible. Why did she feel as the world
had just stopped spinning? She pulled harder on her
boot. "I wouldn't want to trouble you." The laces
snapped in her fingers. She groaned in frustration
when several raindrops landed on her spectacles.

Shaking his head, Josiah strode over to her just as a
crack of lightning split the sky. The immediate rumble
of thunder shook the ground. Emmy jumped in surprise. Joss picked up her notebook and thrust it inside
his shirt. Grabbing her hands in both of his, he hauled
her to her feet. "We're going to have to run for it."
He was having to shout now so she could hear him
above the wind.

Emmy nodded. The tent stood over a hundred yards
away. Joss took her hand, and they started running at
the same instant the sky bottomed out as the rain began to fall in torrents. They were still several yards from
the tent when Joss dropped one of the maps he'd been
juggling. He would have run on without it, but Emmy
stooped to retrieve it.

They dove through the tent flap, breathless, soaked,
and laughing. Joss secured the flap by threading the
straps through the buckles. He used his shirtsleeve to
wipe the rain off his forehead. When he finally turned
to Emmy, he nearly fainted. Any traces of humor disappeared in the sudden vapor of heat that poured
through him.

Emmy had unrolled the sodden map and was looking at it in consternation, her eyebrows drawn together

in a sharp frown. She evidently had no idea that the rain had soaked her clothes. Her ivory blouse was plastered to her skin. The wet fabric made her nipples harden and press against the shirt in the most tantalizing fashion. She stood bent over the map. The slight tilt of her body gave him a lush view of the outline of her full breasts, and the tiny rivulets of water that ran down her neck and disappeared into the dark, feminine valley between them. Despite the damp air, the inside of his mouth went desert dry.

Emmy clearly had no idea of his reaction to her, else she wouldn't have begun spreading the map on the small crate he used for a desk. When she leaned over, he could not keep his eyes from straying to the hem of her skirt. Beneath the faded blue folds, he saw the edging of honey-colored silk petticoats. Even the clunky work boots, one laced, one half-undone, could not disguise the curve of exquisitely turned ankles and calves. Visually, he traced the progress of a droplet of rain as it plopped from her hem onto her calf to run in a slow, sinuous path along her leg.

His body at once grew heavy and heated. Desperate, he wiped a hand over his face, sucking in a mouthful of rain water. Dear God but he hoped the storm would pass soon.

When Emmy looked up at him, her face wrinkled with concern. "It's so wet, Josiah."

He teetered for a minute. Standing, as he was, on the brink of insanity, her words threatened to topple him over the precipice. Surely he could not have heard her right. "What?" Was that his voice? He sounded like he'd swallowed gravel.

"The map," she waved it at him. "The ink ran, and it's gotten all wet. I'm afraid you'll have to do it over."

Her practical words broke the spell that had held him in thrall. He nearly collapsed into his chair. "Oh."

"Josiah, are you all right? You look a bit pale."

He concentrated on breathing. "Of course. Just out of breath I suppose." He managed a weak smile as he bent to light the small lantern. The storm had caused the tent to grow quite dark. He hoped the glow of the lantern would dispel some of the sensual tension he felt building in the cramped quarters.

Emmy felt suddenly uncomfortable. Josiah had the strangest expression on his face. It made her feel exposed, somehow, vulnerable. She pulled at the soaked fabric of her cotton blouse. When it sucked back to her skin with a noise that was almost obscene, she drew in a startled gasp. She'd been so concerned about his map, she'd failed to notice the dismal state of her clothes. The noise of the sodden blouse seemed to rend the tension in the tent. Josiah's gaze met hers. At the dark look in his eye, Emmy swallowed. "I'm soaked," she said lamely.

He nodded, but did not quit staring. "So am I."

Nervous, she looked back and forth as she tried to think of something, anything, to say that would take her mind from the appealing picture he made with his damp hair and wet clothes. "Do you think it will last long? The storm, I mean?"

God, he hoped not. "I don't know. These afternoon storms rarely do."

"Do—do you have a jacket I can put on?" She ignored the sudden suffusion of heat in her face. "I'm cold."

Joss seized on the idea. He should have thought of it before. Anything to keep her covered, out of reach, would be blessed relief. He practically dove for the small duffel at the end of the bed. He rummaged inside and pulled out a clean shirt for her. "This is the best I can do, I'm afraid. I have to carry the barest of necessities, or my horse would rebel."

She accepted the shirt without comment. "Could you turn around for a minute?"

Joss mentally began figuring multiplication tables as he turned away from her. If he did not occupy his mind with something other than the sounds of her wet blouse being stripped away from her skin, he would surely lose what little of it he had left. Long moments passed. He searched in vain for an excuse to go back into the rain.

"You can turn around now," Emmy said quietly.

He managed to face her. "Warmer?" he asked.

She nodded, then cleared a space on the second crate so she could sit down. In her lap, she clenched her fingers together to keep from wringing them. The tension in the air bothered her almost as much as the strange look in Josiah's eye, but she would not turn the simpering fool. She was practically a spinster for heaven's sake, a woman of science. Having reached her age, she should be able to interact with him quite normally despite the unusual circumstances.

Outside, the rain continued to beat against the tent and sluice down the side in steady sheets. Cracks of lightning cast eerie shadows inside the close confines of their shelter. Rumbling thunder shook the ground and rattled the glass panes in the lantern.

Uncomfortable, she searched her mind for a topic of conversation. Her gaze fell once more on the ruined map. She picked it up and studied it. "I'm sorry about your map," she said.

He sat down on his small cot. "It's not a great loss. It was only a preliminary sketch. I won't even have to redo it if I don't want to."

Wistfully, she traced her fingers over the smeared image of a family of rabbits. "These are the rabbits we saw yesterday."

Joss nodded, grateful for the inane conversation. "I sketched them after you left."

Emmy glanced at him with wide eyes, and Joss felt his chest constrict. "Why did you draw them?" she asked quietly.

"Because they made you laugh," he blurted, not even realizing until that moment that it was true. The previous afternoon, she had been delighted with the antics of the baby rabbits. After she'd ridden back down the bluff, Joss had paused to sketch them. He'd captured their image, and their burrow, in the appropriate location on the map.

The map dropped from Emmy's fingers and she stared at him. "Josiah . . ."

It was the way she said his name, that half-whisper, half-reverent groan, that proved to be his undoing. A tiny drop of rain had settled in the cleft above her lip. Joss's gaze riveted to it. He had a clawing, irresistible, irresponsible urge to kiss it away. Desire and good intentions warred. Desire won. With the tiniest groan of surrender, Joss wrapped his hand around her nape.

Emmy reached for his shoulders to regain her balance. Joss licked away the drop of rain water with the tip of his tongue. At the explosion of breath that burst from her lungs, he pulled her completely off the crate and onto his lap. His mouth settled on hers in a hot kiss that completely outshone the power of the storm.

Leaning into him, Emmy arched her neck to give him better access. Joss seized on the tiny capitulation with the eagerness of a starving man. He thrust aside his doubts, forced himself to think only of this moment with this woman. Gently, he plucked her steamed spectacles from her nose with a slight smile. "As cute as these are, I think it will be easier without them," he whispered. Tossing them aside, he slanted his lips over hers, caressed them with his firm mouth, laved them with his tongue.

"You're so sweet." His voice sounded rough and tender all at the same time. Emmy melted against his chest with a soft sigh. He paused to suck a droplet of rain from her chin before he claimed her lips again. Of their own volition, his hands slipped beneath the voluminous folds of the oversized shirt to settle on the still-damp skin of her midriff.

With no small amount of pleasure, he realized that she'd stripped off her chemise when she'd removed her sodden blouse. Nothing stood between him and the exquisite sensation of touching her skin. The rain had cooled her flesh. A shudder coursed through him when his fingers encountered the tiny goose bumps that had spread across the smooth, soft plane of her stomach. "Open your mouth for me," he whispered.

Emmy started to ask him why, but the instant her lips parted, his tongue slipped inside. She knew, then, exactly why, and was so desperately thankful that he'd asked.

Her hands still rested on his broad shoulders. She slid them along the rock-hard curves and around his neck. She plunged her fingers into the damp, soft hair at his nape. Josiah groaned against her mouth as he stroked his tongue in and out in a sensual foray that left her clinging. She didn't pull away until his big palm settled over the naked curve of her breast. With a tiny exclamation of shock, she pushed at his shoulders. For the first time, she realized that he was stretched on top of her on the small cot. He was rushing her too fast toward an unknown destination. She felt panicky. "Josiah—Josiah, wait."

Joss sucked air into his lungs as he mentally chastised himself and scrambled away from her. What in the name of hell had come over him? For all the world, he was behaving like a randy adolescent unable to keep his hands to himself. With a grunt of self-loathing, he levered off the cot where he could shove his hands in his pockets. How he wished she would move, do something, besides lie on the cot and stare at him with that flushed, bemused look. "I'm sorry, Emmy. I shouldn't have done that."

She pulled the edges of his shirt closer around her as she sat up. She couldn't seem to tear her eyes away from the harsh planes of his face. She retrieved her spectacles from the crate and dropped them on her nose for a clearer view. His features looked harder, more defined in the lantern light. She ran her tongue over her swollen lips, inexplicably hurt by his apology. "Why did you?" she asked quietly.

Joss stared at her in disbelief. If he didn't know better, he would have sworn this was some feminine ploy to bring him to heel. She looked offended. No, wounded. "Because I wanted to." He paused, narrowing his gaze. "Because you wanted me to."

Emmy smoothed her hands over her shirt as she stood. "Yes," she said. "Yes, I did. And I'm not sorry either."

Joss dragged a hand over his wet hair. "I didn't mean I was sorry I kissed you."

"That's what you said."

"I meant I was sorry I let things move so quickly." He decided bluntness was the best strategy. "It would have been easy to take advantage of you, Emmy."

"Not that easy. I was the one who stopped it."

She sounded so indignant, he almost smiled. "So you were."

She nodded abruptly. "I'm a lot of things, Josiah, but stupid isn't one of them."

He shook his head. "I never thought that."

"Then please don't treat me like a naive child who

doesn't know her own mind." She wiped away a drop of rain on her eyebrow. "All I said was 'wait.' You didn't have to stop."

Joss's mouth dropped open. The statement stripped away the fragile, hard-won, threads of control. He was on the verge of hauling her back into his arms despite his better judgment when a shaft of sunlight fell on the tent. He realized, abruptly, that the rain had stopped. "It stopped raining."

She nodded. "Several minutes ago."

He was irrationally peeved that she had noticed when he had failed to. Hell, he'd been kissing her at the time. If she'd been half as caught up as he was, as she should have been, she wouldn't have been thinking about the rain at all. He felt irrationally irritated. It should relieve him that she'd managed to keep her wits. Muttering beneath his breath, he began pulling at the straps that secured the tent flap, trying to think of something coherent to say.

Before he could form the thought, he'd pulled open the flap. Emmy, her sodden clothes clutched tightly to her chest, fled past him into the warm sunshine and called, "Thank you, Josiah. I'll see you tomorrow."

He was left alone to wonder just what in the hell he was supposed to do now.

# Seven

Joss set down his pencil and gave up the pretense of not watching Emmy work. She was seated beneath the large oak, her yellow skirts puddled around her, her leather notebook propped on her thighs, her spectacles perching precariously on the tip of her nose.

He had been a bit surprised when she'd arrived at the bluff that morning. In light of the near-disastrous encounter in the tent the previous afternoon, he'd half-expected her to hide from him. She'd seemed only slightly embarrassed when she'd ridden up the hill on the ridiculous-looking animal she called a mule.

The only tense moment had come when she'd been forced to ask him for her notebook. She'd left it in his tent during her precipitous departure the day before. He had handed it to her without a word. His conscience, something he was becoming surprisingly adept at ignoring, had warned him to tell her that he'd read it during the long night when he'd been unable to sleep. The clarity of her writing, and her obvious insight and understanding into her subject, had impressed him. The slightly anxious look she'd given him as he surrendered the book, however, had warned him against revealing his transgression. So he'd simply given her the notebook, then watched in silence as she took up her usual spot under the tree.

Despite his best efforts, he had been unable to stop

watching her all day. Occasionally, her forehead would crinkle in concentration while she tapped her pencil idly on her knee. A sudden breeze lifted the hem of her skirt, and Joss was afforded an enticing view of an orange petticoat. He had to swallow hard to conquer the resulting tightness in his chest.

He was becoming obsessed with the unsettling notion that all her undergarments, or at least a good number of them, were similarly discolored. Any number of completely unorthodox imaginings followed that notion.

With a groan of frustration, he leaned back on his elbows. He didn't want to be attracted to this woman. It seemed wrong, tainted, with his memory of Allyson still so fresh, but he'd long since passed the point of no return in acknowledging his feelings about Emmy Greene. The heated kiss they'd exchanged in his tent had effectively squashed whatever denial he had managed to muster. The woman enticed him, pure and simple.

As much as he'd like to deny it, there wasn't any help for it. He wasn't exactly sure why it should bother him so much. He'd come to Carding intent on discovering the truth about his wife's murder and destroying Robert Greene. If he should take Emmy in the process, it wasn't such a bad thing. Robert had taken Michael and Adam. There was justice in that. And the lady had indicated that she was certainly more than willing.

So he would amend his plan. Who was to judge him for it? Again, he insistently squashed a burst of conscience. His life had been destroyed. He was owed all that came to him by way of Robert Greene. With the notion firmly settled in his mind, Joss rolled up his unfinished map and stood to stretch the taut muscles in his neck and shoulders.

Emmy watched him warily between half-hooded eyes. They'd been sitting on the bluff for over two hours.

Despite her fascination with the crystalization process of coral, she had been unable to concentrate on her treatise.

With her mind intent on recollections of his kiss, Josiah Brickston was too much of a distraction. And a mighty fine-looking one at that.

Standing as he was on the edge of the bluff, the breeze swirled about his body in a warm caress. It molded his white shirt to his strong torso. Several locks of his brown hair had worked loose from his queue, and Emmy realized it wasn't nearly as dark as she'd first thought. The morning sunlight made the golden lights in it glisten. When he turned, he caught her looking at him. A blush swept all the way over her face and buried itself deep in the roots of her hair, but she couldn't, wouldn't, look away.

He smiled that sad half-smile that made her heart turn over as he started toward her. "Are you getting much accomplished?" he asked, lowering his big body to the ground next to her. He stretched out on one side and propped his head on his hand.

She nodded and lied. "Yes."

Josiah plucked a blade of grass so he could twirl it in his fingers. "I'm not," he said, as he stared at the blade.

"I'm sorry. I'm not disturbing you am I?"

His gaze met hers once more. "Yes. You are."

Emmy was contrite. "I didn't mean to be in your way. I never would have come today if I'd thought I'd interrupt your work."

"Not like you think. It didn't start with yesterday," he said. Two pink spots appeared on her cheeks. "I've been disturbed by you since the first time I saw you in your office."

"What?" Her voice sounded strangled.

Joss watched her delicate flush heighten. He shifted

slightly so he was closer to her legs. Slowly, he ran the blade of grass over the top of her laced boot. "I've been disturbed by the thought of what was under all those loose-fitting clothes."

Emmy's retort was something between a squeak and a moan.

Joss ignored it as he pushed the hem of her skirt high enough to rub the grass along the line where her boot ended at her ankle. "I've been disturbed by what it would feel like to kiss that generous, tempting mouth of yours."

"Oh my goodness."

He looked at her with a smile intended to melt her. His fingers closed on her slim ankle. He pushed the hem of her skirt a little higher until her flame-orange petticoat lay partially exposed. "And now that I know, I've been disturbed by notions of trying it again."

Emmy merely stared at him.

"And I've been very disturbed by the notion of this orange petticoat I've had such tantalizing glimpses of all afternoon."

She gasped slightly. Joss sat up so he could lever himself closer to her. Slowly, half-afraid she'd stop him and half-afraid she wouldn't, he ran a finger over the curve of her lower lip. She swayed toward him in unconscious surrender. He lost what remained of his resolve. He bent his head to capture her lips.

Emmy leaned against him, rested her hand on his chest. When her fingers twisted in his shirt, he wrapped his other arm around her to bring her close. She was warm, and soft, and she flowed into him like a spring thaw. He deepened the kiss.

The feel of his lips on hers was doing the same things to her insides she remembered from the previous day. When he gently pushed down her chin with his thumb to sweep his tongue into her mouth, she wondered a little anxiously if perhaps she'd swallowed a butterfly. It certainly felt like one was loose in her belly.

Joss languidly stroked the inside of her mouth with his tongue until Emmy felt a flush cover her entire body. The warmth of the sun, and the heat of his skin, were nothing compared to the flames licking along inside her blood. When he lifted his head, her lips clung to his in a momentary effort to maintain the kiss.

Slowly, she opened her eyes. He was out of focus. Joss lifted her steamed spectacles off her nose to wipe them with his cuff. She blushed a furious red blush she was certain rivaled the garish color of her petticoat.

He plopped her glasses back on her face. "Well," he said, "that at least settles one matter."

"Wh-what?" She was still stunned by the kiss.

Joss tapped her nose with his finger. "Kissing you when we're both dry is just as pleasurable as it was when we were soaked through."

Emmy's eyes widened momentarily. "I liked it too," she blurted, feeling like a fool as soon as she said the words.

He smiled. "I'm glad."

Emmy couldn't help noticing that the sadness was still there, lurking behind his smile, coloring the deep purple of his eye. Slowly, she rubbed at a tiny crease that had settled next to his mouth. "Josiah," she said quietly, her voice a question.

He raised an eyebrow. "Yes?"

"Why are you so sad?"

His mouth thinned so suddenly that Emmy thought he might turn away from her. "I don't mean to pry," she rushed out, "but I couldn't help but notice. I thought maybe it might help if you talked about it."

He shook his head. "Nothing helps. Not talking, not being angry, not drinking liquor, nothing."

Emmy hesitated. His face had drawn tight, pale. She

longed to lessen the pain. "Josiah," she persisted, "you cannot go on like this." She rubbed her fingers over his scar. "You're torn apart inside."

Joss stared at her for several long seconds before he captured her hand. He kissed the palm briefly before he tucked her close against his side. He owed her at least a partial explanation. "It's very," he paused, seeking the right word. Difficult? Devastating? Life-shattering? "Hard."

Emmy stole a glance at his face. The scar on his cheek had whitened. "You don't have to tell me if you don't want to. I just wanted to help."

"I've never repeated this to anyone." His voice sounded strained.

"I shouldn't have asked. I'm sorry."

He shook his head. "I would like very much for you to know." With something of a start, he realized that it was true. He had not spoken of the events of that awful day to anyone but the authorities. Until now, he had been unable to bear the thought. He still knew he couldn't tell her everything, but it was a bit of a shock to him that he wanted Emmy to know the truth. He drew in a deep breath. "It happened almost two years ago."

Emmy tucked her head against his shoulder and waited. She rubbed idly at the grass stain on his breeches leg. Joss seemed very far away when he spoke again. "My wife and I were returning from a holiday with our two sons."

Emmy ran her thumb a bit more vigorously on the stain. "I didn't know you had children."

"Yes." His voice sounded tight. "I had two sons. Michael was four. Adam was two."

Emmy heard the strain behind the words and began working at the stain in earnest. "What happened?"

"We were just outside St. Louis when our carriage

was stopped. Despite Allyson's objections, I had agreed to make a bank transfer for a close friend of mine. We were carrying a large amount of gold and valuables with us."

Joss swiped a hand through his hair. He felt the sweat on his scalp. In his mind, he wasn't on the bluff with Emmy any longer. He was in the carriage watching Allyson and Adam dragged down into the dirt. "They stopped us on the northern road. Before I had time to pull out my pistol, they had shot my driver and all but ripped the door of the coach off its hinges."

Emmy's hand shook. She stopped rubbing on the stain. She tipped her head to look at him once more. His eye was closed. The lines in his face had deepened to stark grooves. She clenched her teeth to avoid reaching out to smooth them away. "You don't have to continue," she said.

He didn't seem to hear her. "They killed Adam and Allyson first. It was quick enough with them, thank God. They just dragged them down in the dirt and shot them. Allyson first, then Adam."

Emmy sucked in a breath and stared at his face. "But Michael suffered for days," he continued. "Did you know a bullet in the stomach is the most painful way to die?" He looked at her, not really expecting an answer. "They did," he bit out. "That's why they did it."

"I couldn't do anything for him." His voice was raw now. "I just watched him die and prayed to God that I would die, too. God wasn't so merciful to me."

Emmy's whole body had begun to tremble. She was certain, positive, there was more to the story than Joss was telling her. Why had he been spared? She was as sure as the day was long that something had physically prevented him from stopping the murders. Josiah Brickston was not a man who cowered in the shadows while his family was in danger. He would have died helping his wife and sons. It was killing him that he hadn't. He felt responsible. She knew it. She ached for him.

But the pain on his face, the tension in him was so stark, so agonizingly apparent, she didn't need, nor want, the answer to the questions. Nothing mattered more than giving him comfort and assuaging the haggard look. She wrapped both arms around his waist to hug him tight. She didn't care that his shirt was soaked with sweat, or that his body jerked involuntarily at her touch. "Oh, Josiah. I'm sorry. I'm so sorry."

Joss surfaced slowly from the haze of the memory and realized Emmy was crying. No, sobbing against his chest. He caught her close to him and stroked her hair. Somehow, he found solace for his grief from the shared pain. "Please don't cry. I've done enough of that, I think."

She raised her head to look at him through tear-filled eyes. Pulling her glasses off, she dropped them onto the grass. "I can't h-help it." Her breath was interrupted by tiny hiccups. "I can't seem to stop."

Joss wiped his work-roughened hand over her wet cheek. "I didn't mean to make you cry, Emmy."

She shook her head, then pressed a hand to his lips. "I'm very glad you trusted me enough t-to tell me."

"I haven't been able to speak of it until now."

"I'm so sorry, Josiah," she said again, knowing there was nothing she could say that would adequately express the feeling that she'd been ripped in two.

Joss shuddered once before he moved to set her away from him. "I didn't mean to distress you. There's nothing to be done about it now."

Her arms tightened around his waist. "I'd just like to stay here a while longer. If you don't mind."

Joss realized that he wanted it too. Surrendering, he pushed her head back against his chest so he could give and receive comfort. He closed his eyes as his head drifted back against the tree. Despairingly, he wondered if the pain would ever lessen. Would he ever think of Allyson without anguish and rage churning about inside him? Would he ever remember Michael and Adam without wanting to lash out at the world that had taken them from him? Without wanting to cry? Would there ever be an end to the grief? To the guilt?

Only when Robert Greene and his companions were dead, a voice whispered in his head. Only then would the ghosts stop haunting his dreams and plaguing his thoughts.

Joss's arms tightened around Emmy. He didn't want to hurt her. She deserved better than that from him, but there was only one way to lay the demons to rest. And Emerelda Greene, with her sweet spirit and her kind heart, was bound to get caught in the crossfire. He hoped it wouldn't destroy her.

He sat quietly on the rocky ledge and waited. His ears strained to hear what his eyes could not see in the moonless night. It wouldn't be long now. The faintest thrum of horses' hooves carried on the breeze. The Diamond Hawk leaned down from his perch and watched the road.

Men on horseback, their appearance like great shadows against the darkened backdrop, slipped silently from crevices and shrubs along the desolate trail. Only the haunting cry of an owl whistled in the tense wind. A fox darted across the trail and spooked one of the horses. Its loud whinny pierced the charged atmosphere like a strike of lightning.

The sound of hooves drew nearer.

The carriage would be visible in a matter of moments. Beside the road, six shadowed riders waited. The Diamond Hawk assessed the distance from his perch to the first rider while he mentally calculated his options.

It would be tricky at best. He hadn't counted on the extra two riders. Despite his frequent eavesdropping on Avery Brooks and Rosalynd Carver, he had not been able to learn as much as he had hoped. He thought of Rosalynd and Avery and wondered if they were still locked in tryst in room eight. Did Rosalynd know her husband was returning a full day ahead of schedule?

The coach thundered into view at a sharp bend up the road. The Diamond Hawk crouched into position, any lesser thoughts quickly banished by the urgency of the matter at hand. Yes, it would be tricky, but with any luck at all, his good fortune would hold fast.

"He swept down out of the night like a great hu—hu—," Alex looked at Emmy over the top of her newspaper. "I can't read this word, Emmy."

Emmy smiled at her young cousin before returning her attention to the diamond brooch she was cleaning. Alex sat across from her desk, swinging her feet back and forth in agitation. The stubborn word, Emmy suspected, was more excuse to be done with the reading lesson than challenge. "Spell it for me, Alex."

"H-U-L-K-I-N-G."

Emmy almost laughed. Horace Newbury had once again run amuck with his adjectives. "The word is 'hulking.' "

Alex wrinkled her button shaped nose. "What's that?"

"It means large."

"Well, why didn't he just say so?"

Emmy did laugh then. "Because Horace Newbury has too much fun describing the Diamond Hawk to use any word as ordinary as 'large.' Now finish the story, Alex."

Alex's lower lip slipped into a pout. "I don't want to."

"Your teacher said you must begin reading out loud more often or you'll never get better at it, Alex."

Alex gave the newspaper a glum look, as if the fault for her woes lay within its wrinkled pages. "I don't see why I have to read this dumb story."

Emmy continued to scrub vigorously at the brooch. She could only hope that Alex wouldn't question why she had been so interested in the newspaper that day. "Because I'm interested in it. You promised you would read to me for a quarter hour today, and you've only been at it five minutes."

"It seems a lot longer."

Emmy set the brooch on her desk, then recorked the bottle of cleaning fluid. From her top drawer, she removed a polishing cloth. "I'll strike a bargain with you, Alex. If you finish the story, you may go."

"Really?" Alex looked slightly skeptical.

Emmy started rubbing the brooch with the cloth. "Really."

"No tricks?"

"No tricks." Emmy turned to get better light from her window.

Her cousin shifted restlessly in her chair, then picked up the newspaper once more. "Oh, all right. Where did I leave off?"

"Hulking," Emmy prompted.

"Like a great, hulking bird, his dark, vo-lu . . ."

"Voluminous."

"That means big, right?" Alex asked. She waited for Emmy's nod. "Mr. Newbury seems awfully fond of words that mean big."

Emmy wiped at a spot of tarnish. "Yes, he certainly does. Go on with the story."

Alex drew a fortifying breath. "Dark, vo-lu-mi-nous cape waving behind him like a ghost's shadow." She looked up again. "That sounds silly. Ghosts don't have shadows."

Emmy continued her polishing. It was difficult to argue with that. "What happened next?"

"There were six men on the road according to Mr. Jason Carver, bank owner." Alex looked up again. "Why does he say that? Everybody knows Mr. Carver owns the bank."

Emmy's answer was a noncommittal, "Um-hmm."

Alex rattled the newspaper. "Said Mr. Carver, 'If the Diamond Hawk hadn't come along, I would have lost the entire shipment,' " Alex struggled with the word, " 'of gold. As it is, nothing is gone but a par-cel for a bank cl—cl—' "

"Client."

" 'Client.' Mr. Carver would not comment on the con-tents of the parcel, but said it was of very little val-value." Alex slapped the newspaper down on the desk. "Done. Can I go now?"

Emmy finished cleaning the brooch before she nodded at Alex. "Yes, you may go. Remember what I said about your new shoes."

"I won't get them dirty, Emmy. I promise. Can I go with Gem to the creek?"

Emmy hesitated. As sure as the sun was shining that afternoon, Alex would fall in the creek. She was wearing an old dress, though, one she'd almost outgrown. It wouldn't be too much longer before Emmy used the soft green cotton for a chemise. She had a sudden memory of Joss Brickston and his shameless comments about her orange petticoat the previous morning.

"Can I, Emmy? Please?"

Alex's question brought her crashing back to the present. She mentally scolded herself for her unruly thoughts. "Make sure you take your shoes off before you get too close to the water, Alex."

Alex looked indignant. "I will not fall in."

"No, of course not. It's only a precaution."

Her cousin nodded happily and scooted down from the chair. "I will. I promise."

Emmy watched Alex scramble toward the door. She sent up a silent prayer that the new leather boots would not be ruined by day's end. They simply could not afford to buy another pair, but Alex was legendary for ruining her shoes and dresses. Emmy had used what was left of the money Joss Brickston had paid her to buy Alex's shoes, and for the thousandth time that day, her thoughts returned to their morning on the bluff.

After Josiah had finished his story, Emmy had cried for nearly half an hour. She probably should have been embarrassed, but something in his quiet strength had prevented it. It had been the thought of him going through that terrible ordeal that had been her undoing. Even now, she was forced to admit, her feelings on the matter were still tender, still muddled. She wasn't sure exactly what she felt for Josiah, but she did know—

"Hello," the voice sounded from behind her.

With her heart in her throat, she spun around, certain before she looked who stood by her window. "You startled me."

The Diamond Hawk tipped his head in silent apology. "I seem to have formed a habit of that. My sincere apology."

Emmy sucked in a breath of the fresh summer breeze wafting in through the open window. With the sun at his back, the Diamond Hawk looked no less intimidating in the daylight. "Must you sneak about like that? You could have knocked on the door."

He silently moved to sit on her desk, facing her. "I was waiting for the little girl to leave."

"Alex? How did you know she was here?"

"I have been waiting beneath your window."

With a frown, she dropped into her chair. She wished his warm, muscled thigh wasn't so close to her shoulder. "You were spying on me."

"On the contrary. I was waiting until you were alone. I did not wish to place you in a difficult position with my unexpected arrival."

"Then you should not be here in the middle of the afternoon. Someone might see you." She could not seem to keep the disgruntled note from her voice.

"The little girl was the last to leave. We are alone."

She wasn't sure she liked the sensation of being alone with him, but declined to say so. "I assume there is a reason for your call?" she asked, opening the drawer of her desk and carefully refolding her cleaning cloth.

He placed a small leather bag in front of her. "I find I am in need of your expertise once again."

She stared at the bag. "Are these from the parcel Jason Carver reported was missing?"

With a gloved hand, he tipped her chin up until she met his gaze. "I assure you, Miss Greene, I would not involve you in any improprieties."

"How do I know that?"

He dropped his hand. "You don't. I can only hope you will trust your instincts about me."

"Why should I trust my instincts, and why should they be any good about a 'dark, hulking bird with a voluminous dark cape?' "

He waved a corner of the cape at her in a teasing gesture. "Because you are a lady with a kind heart and a keen mind who likes a taste of adventure every now and again. And who knows better than to believe Horace Newbury."

Emmy thought about arguing with him, but her fingers already itched to sift through the contents of the bag. Reluctantly, she took hold of the leather laces. "I should not be helping you with this, you know?"

He watched as she poured the artificial gems onto her desk. "But you will?"

She nodded and began sorting the stones. "I will. But only because you've piqued my interest with these stones. I see there are several colored stones as well."

"Yes. I was surprised."

Emmy needed her loupe for only ten of the over forty-five stones in the pile. They were mostly artificial diamonds, just as before, but there were also four excellent blue glass sapphires; two rubies, both made of paste; and one severely flawed emerald. The opal, alone, surprised her.

She spent a considerable amount of time examining the opal before she dropped her loupe into her hand. She held the oval-shaped stone between her thumb and forefinger and placed it on his gloved palm. "This one is genuine."

He looked at her in surprise. "Are you certain?"

Emmy gave him a sharp look. "Of course I'm certain. Even a twit can tell the difference between an artificial opal and a genuine one. The natural fire in the center is nearly impossible to emulate with any credible appearance."

His mouth kicked into a smile. "Of course. Any twit would know that."

At his teasing tone, she realized that she'd, once again, slipped into the scientific intensity that always had Pearl nagging at her. Uncomfortable, she looked back at the stones. "The rest are as before. The diamonds are a combination of flawed stones, cut glass and paste. The sapphires are glass, the rubies are paste, and the emerald is flawed so badly it is nearly worthless." She scooped the stones up a handful at a time to pour them back into the bag. She wiped a smudge of dirt off the bag before she gave it back to him.

He dropped it in the pocket of his cape. "Thank you."

"You haven't learned anything else about the stones?"

"No. I'm afraid they are as big a mystery as before."

"How did you know the coach would be robbed?"

"Ah, my lady. That is a secret I cannot tell you."

"Well, I don't see why not. You've had no qualms about involving me this far."

"Do not be cross," he said. "It doesn't become you. Besides, surely you can see that my mystery is my greatest weapon."

She brushed aside her irritation with some effort. "You are an awfully odd sort, you know. If I weren't so intrigued, I'd refuse to help you."

He didn't reply. As he stood from the desk, he reached for her hand. The opal dropped from his gloved fingers onto her outstretched palm with a soft *thud*. "I want you to accept this as payment for your efforts."

Obviously, she realized, he hadn't the slightest idea how much the stone was worth. "Oh, no. I couldn't. I—"

"Would you rather have a gold piece?"

"No, no. It isn't that. It's just—"

He clasped her hand in his and closed her fingers around the stone. "Then I insist." Before she could stop him, he leaned down and kissed her fisted hand, scant moments before he leapt out the window and disappeared.

# Eight

"I want to play our game, Daddy. I'm afraid." Joss clutched Michael closer to his chest as he rocked him.

"Not right now, Michael. Just be still."

"But I'm afraid, Daddy." The cough again. That awful cough. "I can't see the light anymore."

Oh dear God, no. "Michael, be still." Joss rocked him faster. "It's going to be all right."

"Is Mama all right, Daddy?"

Joss shifted Michael in his arms, trying to ignore the searing pain it caused in his own legs. He couldn't faint. Not now. "Everything's all right, son. I promise."

"Play our game with me. Please, Daddy."

More coughing. Joss squeezed his eyes tight, but several tears slipped free. The stench. The heat. Dear God he couldn't lose Michael, too. He wouldn't survive if he did. Sweat poured down his back and pooled at his spine. He wrapped the dirty, tattered blanket tighter around his son and clung to him. The game. Michael wanted to play the game. "All right, Michael. You start."

"How did you pick my name, Daddy?"

Joss waited for the coughing to subside before he gave the now familiar answer. "After the archangel Michael."

"Is Michael the strongest angel?"

"He protects all the other angels in Heaven. Just like the angels protect us."

Michael's breathing became shallow, erratic. Tears streamed

*down Joss's face. He clutched Michael to his chest. Michael's cough was weak. His voice had dropped to a raspy whisper. "You protect me too. Don't you, Daddy?"*

*Joss choked out the right answer. "Forever, Michael." It was the end of the game. One they'd played together almost since Michael had learned to talk. Then, his biggest fear had been the dark. It took on a greater meaning now. They'd played it a lot in the last two days.*

*With a sigh, Michael rubbed his face against Joss's shirt front. "I'm not afraid now," he said.*

*Joss smoothed his hand over Michael's back. He tried not to think about the sticky wet stain on the blanket covering him. "Be still now, Michael. Please."*

*"You shouldn't be afraid either."*

*"I'm not," Joss lied.*

*"But I can see them, Daddy. It doesn't hurt anymore and I can see them."*

*Joss's hand threaded into his son's hair so he could cradle Michael's small head. "See who, Michael?" he asked. As long as Michael kept talking, Joss knew he was still alive.*

*There was another long fit of coughing. Painful, deep, wet coughing, before Michael whispered. "The angels."*

"No!" Joss sat straight up in bed. The heavy pounding noise had startled him awake. Several seconds passed before he realized it was the sound of his heart. He drew several ragged breaths as he struggled for control of his shaking body.

Rivers of sweat ran down his bare chest and back and soaked the bedclothes. When he dropped his head into his hands, his hair was wet. He knew from the tight, raw feeling in the back of his throat he'd been weeping. Again. It took almost five minutes of controlled breathing before he gathered his wits enough to swing his feet to the floor. Even so, the room spun, and blurred, and spun again, until he thought he might vomit.

His body still felt weak and flushed when he levered off the bed and reached for his trousers. He had been spared from the dream for the past few nights, but his morning with Emmy had reopened the wound. His undergarments clung to his clammy skin. He shuddered as he stepped into his pants, then tugged the striped galluses over his shoulders.

His breath continued to come in harsh gasps. By the time he found the bottle of whiskey in the dark kitchen, his stomach was churning about in an angry knot. He took four long swallows before he felt steady, calm, enough to sit and think. He didn't even bother with a lamp. The darkness soothed him.

Emerelda Greene.

Why did he allow her to stand in his way? He took another sip of the whiskey. He was attracted to her, it was true. The kiss they'd shared on the bluff had unsettled him. Surely that was the reason he'd told her about Allyson and the boys, but there was something else, a kinship, he didn't want and couldn't tolerate.

After the shattering loss of his family, Joss had shoved everyone and everything aside in his efforts to find the truth about their murder. Once he learned of Robert Greene's possible participation, he had come to Carding intent on ferreting out and destroying anyone who'd played a hand in that dreadful night.

Joss swallowed another gulp of whiskey. The burning sensation in his throat made him wince.

Despite his intentions, fate had played against him. While he had several suspicions, he knew very little more than he had when he arrived in Carding—except that Emmy Greene controlled Robert's career and livelihood in her work-calloused, acid-stained, ridiculously gentle hands. Forcing Robert's hand should be as easy as stealing Emmy.

Without her, Robert would lose his income. He

would lose the respect of his colleagues. He would lose the shelter of his reputation. And desperate men did any number of desperate things. Joss knew.

Without Emmy, Robert would be destroyed. He would have to act. When he did, Joss would be waiting for him. He took one more swig of the liquor before he recorked the flask and set it aside. He'd have a devil's own time not touching her, a fate he figured he deserved. But memories of Allyson and Adam and Michael would be enough. He was sure. What little conscience he had left hated like hell that he'd have to hurt her. Still, the dream had served to remind him, to refocus his thoughts. He couldn't let her stand in his way. He owed his family.

Resolutely, he forced aside any lingering reservations and lit the lantern. It was time to dress.

When Joss strolled into Bug Danboat's saloon an hour and a half later, he hoped the ravaging effects of his evening were not apparent. It wouldn't do to look weak.

Inside, the air was heavy with smoke and the smell of liquor. A player piano, one of the first Joss had seen so far west, rattled carelessly in the background. The tinny sound was barely audible over the buzz of conversation and raucous laughter. Rough-looking characters lurked in the shadows where they watched the prostitutes ply their trade. The clink of coins, and the clatter of shuffling cards, filled whatever cracks of silence were left in the room. Joss removed his black hat and dropped it on the wooden stand by the door.

He had taken care to dress for the night. He wore his finest black cutaway coat and trousers. The button-on collar itched, but he knew the stark white and purple pinstripe of his homespun shirt, set off by the purple brocade of his waistcoat gave him a polished, sophisticated look that Robert Greene would find intriguing. He hoped, at least, that the black revolver belt that hung low on his hips added the necessary factor of intimidation.

He scanned the room with a cold, assessing rake of his eyes until he found Robert Greene. He was seated at a card table, dealing a hand of five-card draw. Judging from his stack of coins and bills, he was having a good night. A rarity, so far as Joss knew. His fat face looked like a ripened tomato, soft and flushed, and full of juice. He twirled a wide cigar between his full lips. A trickle of tobacco-browned drool stained his chin.

As usual, Robert wore expensively tailored clothes. His gray jacket and lime-green satin waistcoat showed fine detailing. Detailing, Joss knew, that came with a high price. He had a sudden memory of the faded yellow calico dress Emmy had worn to the bluff.

Hatred poured through him as he watched Robert Greene win an easy hand. He paused inside the swinging saloon doors, installed for ease of clearing the house in the event of a brawl, and straightened his jacket with a sharp tug. He acknowledged Gray Lawford with a brief nod. The marshal, dressed in black from head to toe, sat at the end of the bar where he watched Joss's entrance through wary, half-open eyes. Gray's colorless clothes made him look as mean as his reputation. Joss suspected that had been Gray's intent. He ignored the implied warning in his eyes as he began a casual descent on Robert's table.

Robert greeted his arrival with a wide smile. "Well, well. Mr. Brickston. We don't see you in here very often."

Joss shook his head. "I've been too busy up 'til now. Thought I'd come out tonight and see what has you fellows laughing until dawn."

A general burst of laughter resounded in the crowded saloon. One of Bug's prostitutes, dressed in a flame red gown trimmed in black lace, rubbed against Joss's arm. "What can I getcha, sugar?" she drawled. Her lips puckered into a deliberate, cherry-red pout.

"Whiskey. Straight up." Joss curled his hand on the back of a chair. He whirled it two and a half turns on its front leg until it landed in front of Robert's table. "Is there room for another hand?"

Robert gave him an appraising glance, followed by a brief nod. "It would be inhospitable of us not to welcome you to Carding by dealing you in." He scooped up the cards so he could shuffle. "Besides, if you can afford to pay so handsomely for a simple, incomplete appraisal on a few trinkets, I reckon you can afford to lose a few dollars."

The bastard, Joss thought. Emmy had evidently told him about the hundred dollars he'd paid her. "I don't aim to lose."

Robert cast him a condescending look that made Joss's hands ache to be around his fat throat. "None of us intends to lose. Do we boys?" Robert asked as he dealt out the hand.

The other men at the table grunted in agreement. In silence, they studied their cards. Joss was glad he had taken the seat directly across from Robert. It gave him an excellent view of Robert Greene's face and Gray Lawford's wary profile.

The first several hands passed uneventfully with a minimum of banal chatter. Joss determined early that Robert Greene was a moderately competent gambler. Only his enormous ego caused his unnecessary mistakes. Joss allowed him to win three hands.

The game didn't turn nasty until Robert started losing heavily. Joss hadn't touched his whiskey. Robert had consumed nearly half a bottle. When Joss took four hands in a row, Robert started grumbling. Two of the other players dropped out.

Joss lost the next hand because of sheer bad luck. Robert immediately upped the stakes. "I think," he said, loosening his black silk tie, "that we should stop toying about like boys and begin playing like men."

Joss raised an eyebrow. "What did you have in mind?"

"Say, twenty-dollar minimum bids?"

The remaining two players looked abashed. "I can't afford anything that steep," Pete Harless said as he scooped up his remaining coins. "I'm going home to my wife."

Flo, one of Bug's highest-paid working girls, was walking by the table. When Pete stood, she placed one hand on her satin-covered hip. "Why, Pete, I didn't know you had a wife."

There was a general chorus of laughter. It was well known that Pete and Flo had a long-standing arrangement. Everyone knew it. Marlene Harless even knew it. Joss curled his lip in disgust.

The other player, a man Joss didn't know, decided to follow Pete's lead and cut his losses. Robert looked across the table at Joss. That same condescending smile curved his thick lips. The room had grown very still. The piano had long since gone silent. No one thought to re-crank it. The laughter had died. Even the clink of glasses and the buzz of conversation had momentarily ceased. "What will it be, Brickston?"

Joss nodded his agreement. "All right."

The room reacted with loud appreciation. Men abandoned their own games to pull up at the table and watch the confrontation. Flo took up residence behind Joss. The flowery, stifling scent of her imported French perfume cocooned him in a haze of unreality. Another of Bug's girls stood close to Robert's shoulder where she rubbed against him. One look at Bug confirmed what Joss suspected: he was satisfied that the girls were ready to take advantage of a potentially highly charged situation.

Only Gray Lawford remained still amid the chaos in the saloon. He leaned back against the bar and made eye contact with Joss. Joss shook his head in an almost imperceptible dismissal. Gray's gaze didn't waver.

Joss reached in his pocket for a roll of bills. I'll need to have some bills converted. All I've got are gold eagles and fifty-dollar Missouri notes."

"Bug!" Robert called. "The gentleman is in need of change."

After Bug supplied the necessary bills, Joss settled in to finish what he'd started. The game moved slowly at first. Joss kept his wins and losses at near even, waiting while Robert's arrogance escalated. The room grew tenser. Robert began to squirm.

"I must say, Brickston," he said, as he wiped at the sweat on his face with a silk handkerchief. "You're damned lucky for an Englishman."

There were uncomfortable sniggers and murmurings in the room. Joss ignored them. "Gaming is virtually the national pastime in England." He dealt the next hand. "Although horse racing is more popular than cards." He plunked the balance of the deck down on the table, then looked at his hand. Two tens, the jack of spades, the queen of hearts, and a deuce. He bet a hundred dollars. The crowd gasped. Every eye in the place now focused raptly on the card game.

Robert frowned at his hand, but he called the bet. "By the time this night is over, you'll wish you'd stuck to track betting." He discarded three cards.

Joss discarded the queen and the deuce, then dealt Robert his three cards. He placed two for himself, studying Robert through half-lidded eyes before he picked up the pair. Two jacks. Full-house. Robert wiped his brow. "Your bet, Greene," Joss drawled.

"One hundred twenty dollars."

"I'll see that." Joss counted out the bills. "And I'll raise it two hundred dollars."

The room seemed to grow smaller. The stakes were beginning to move unnaturally high. Robert drummed his fingers on the table. "All right. I'll see three hundred twenty, and raise to five hundred."

"Call." Joss waited for Robert to turn his hand.

"Two pair," Robert said with a broad grin. "King-high."

Without a flicker, Joss turned his hand to lay the full house on the table. "Sorry, Greene. Tough break. I think it's time we called it quits for the evening."

Robert's face turned a dark shade of red. Gray Lawford stepped away from the bar and began working his way across the room. Joss scooped up the bills in the kitty. He stacked them in front of him as he meticulously turned each in the same direction. There was a moment of charged silence, followed by a bevy of whispers. Flo squeezed Joss's shoulder in silent invitation. The woman behind Robert turned pale.

Robert finally seemed to find his breath. "You have to give me a chance to win that back. I've lost nearly two thousand dollars."

Joss glanced at him. "We should never have let the bidding go so high if you didn't have the cash to cover it."

Robert spluttered. "I had the cash, of course, but you have to let me win it back from you. It's the only honorable thing to do."

Joss continued counting bills. Was it honorable to shoot a woman through the head in front of her two sons? Was it honorable to kill a two-year-old baby because he was frightened and wouldn't stop crying? Was it honorable to murder a four-year-old little boy who'd done what he could to save his family? Joss swallowed his hatred to keep from shooting Robert Greene. He needed proof. He needed to know who else had been involved in that fateful robbery. Determined, he met Robert's gaze. "All right. We'll play one more hand."

Robert sighed. "I thought you'd see reason."

Gray Lawford shouldered his way through the crowd. He gave Joss a hard look. "I'd like a word with you, Brickston."

"Not right now, Marshal," Joss said blandly. "I've one more hand to play."

Gray would have reached for him, but Robert grabbed his arm and jerked him down into a chair. "Sit down, Marshal. You can watch me clean out the Englishman."

The crowd roared its appreciation. Joss's eyes had begun to sting from the pall of smoke. Flo still stood at his back where she trailed her fingers over his shoulders. He wanted her to stop, could think of only one solution. "I think we should consider changing games, Greene. We've been playing five-card all night, and I'm worn out. Seven-card stud is just sheer luck of the draw. What do you say we let Flo deal a hand, and we settle up at the end."

Robert looked at him, his eyes wary. "What did you have in mind?"

"Ten thousand dollars," Joss said. He ignored Gray Lawford's ice-cold glare.

Robert's fleshy jaw dropped open. "Ten thousand dollars? Are you crazy?"

Joss stood up to shrug out of his jacket. With a flick of his wrist, he draped it on the back of his chair. "What's the matter, Robert? Lost your nerve?"

Robert's face flushed. "Of course not. It's just that I don't carry that kind of cash on me."

Joss sat back down and began to roll up his sleeves. "Mr. Carver," he called to the banker, "is Mr. Greene good for the ten thousand dollars?"

The banker looked nervous. Joss knew the man was trapped. If he said "yes," Robert would have to play out the hand to save face. If he said "no," he'd humiliate him, something Robert would never forgive. Jason Carver made eye contact with Robert. A silent message passed between them before Jason nodded. "Yes," he called, "of course he's good for it. I'll stake him."

Joss looked at Robert once more. "There, you see. That's good enough for my taste. We'll even make it simple. Either one of us can call it a draw before the turn of the last card. If I draw out, you get your two thousand back. If you draw out, I get to keep it, but we forget about the ten thousand dollars."

Robert shifted uneasily as he stamped out his fat cigar. "Flo's going to deal?"

Joss picked up the deck, then turned to offer it to her. "Will you, Flo?"

She smiled at him. Joss suspected men rarely asked Flo *nicely* for anything. Taking the deck, she pushed through the crowd so she could sit across from Gray. She started to shuffle. "The game is seven-card," she said, fanning the deck. "I'll deal two face down, and four face up." She bridged the cards and executed another fan. "Since the stakes are already set, we won't stop for betting. Each gentleman is entitled to three changes. The last card will be face down. Before we turn the hands, either of you has the right to call it a draw. Are you ready, gentlemen?"

Joss nodded. Robert coughed in nervous agitation. Flo dealt. Joss didn't pick up his first two cards.

Flo started to deal face up. "A black nine for the Englishman," she said after she'd placed the card in front of Joss. "And a one-eyed jack for the professor."

Robert glanced at his two cards for the second time. Flo continued to deal. She placed the four of hearts in front of Joss. "A double deuces is no help to the Englishman." She dealt Robert's card. "The clubbed eight gives the professor a possible straight." Flo paused. The room was now completely silent. Joss still hadn't looked at his cards.

Robert picked up his discarded cigar and started to bite on it. Flo dealt the next round of cards. She put the queen of diamonds in front of Joss. "The red lady gives the Englishman a partial flush."

"Crooked ace for the professor." Robert's card was the ace of spades.

Joss waited while Robert checked his cards again. Flo started to look nervous. Deliberately, Joss smiled at her. She dealt the next round. "Pair of nines," she said when she gave Joss the nine of hearts. She placed the four of diamonds in front of Robert. "Double deuces."

Joss finally rolled up the corner of his two face-down, hold cards. He handed Flo the jack and the four of hearts from the face-up pile. "Two, Flo."

"The Englishman wants two." She dealt him the cards face down.

Robert looked from his cards, to Joss, to Flo, then back at his cards. Rivers of sweat ran down his fat face. Joss again repressed the urge to strangle him. Robert finally gave Flo his two hold cards. She gave him two more.

Robert leaned back in his chair and picked up his hand to slowly place the cards in order. Joss left his on the table. He didn't look at his hold cards again. Robert was beginning to look arrogant. Joss couldn't decide whether that was good or not. Robert finished arranging his cards and he stubbed his cigar back in the ashtray. "Deal the last card, Flossie," he said.

Joss saw the spark of irritation in her eyes, but she

dealt one card face-down to Joss and one to Robert. Robert picked up his card and whooped. "I've got you now you English bastard. If you don't call it a draw, I'm going to enjoy spending your ten thousand dollars!"

Joss noticed that Gray Lawford's eyes were still beaded on him and the cards lying on the table in front of him. "Play out your hand then, Greene," Joss said. His voice sounded tight, but it couldn't be helped. He couldn't, he wouldn't lose this hand.

Robert laid four eights on the table with a broad smile. The room clamored in appreciation. Joss met Robert's triumphant gaze with a cool, assessing look. He flipped over his last card first. It was an unimpressive seven of diamonds. Robert chortled with delight. Joss allowed a hint of a smile to tug at the corner of his mouth. He acknowledged Gray's menacing look with a slight nod, then turned over his remaining two cards.

"Sorry, Robert. Four nines ups four eights."

Robert stared at the cards in disbelief. "That's impossible," he spluttered. "You must have cheated."

Joss shook his head as he rose to his feet. "If we were in England, I'd call you out for that." He picked up his jacket and shrugged into it, then handed Flo five hundred dollars. "Thanks, Flo. You're a lady's lady."

Robert's face had drained of color. He was still staring at the cards. Joss dropped the roll of bills into his pocket as he strode toward the door of the saloon. In the silence, his boots sounded unnaturally loud against the oak floor. He picked up his hat and dropped it on his head before he turned back to Robert Greene. He made a show of pulling his watch from his pocket and checking the time. "I shall expect you to call on me in my office by noon today with the money. Good night, Mr. Greene."

Only the creaking of the door followed Joss into the pre-dawn morning.

"Oh, Uncle Robert, how could you?" Emmy stared at her uncle in horror as she pressed her hands to the heated skin of her face.

"He provoked me into it, the bastard."

"But ten thousand dollars. You know we'll never find that kind of money." Emmy sank down on one of the dingy sofas in her uncle's parlor and buried her head in her hands.

"Now, Emmy, you're overreacting." Her uncle chewed on his cigar. "You're taking this entirely too hard."

She stared at him. "Too hard? Uncle Robert, we can't pay the debt. You have gambled away everything we have."

"I had hoped my last book would have brought in a substantial amount. If we make a deposit on the debt, I think Brickston will understand."

Emmy shook her head. "I used what little we made from the last treatise to pay our creditors. The farm wasn't yielding enough to feed the children, much less keep up with our debts."

"This household spends entirely too much money. I've said that before."

Emmy tipped her head back against the sofa. She felt ill. "There are eleven mouths to feed, Uncle Robert." She didn't bother to point out that the money he spent on his tailored wardrobe in the last year was more than their entire food budget.

He spit a dirty stream of tobacco juice toward the window. It missed the opening and joined similar splatters on the wall. "I've told you to find a way to trim corners, Emerelda. You'll have to dig deeper."

Emmy rarely lost her temper. In fact, she couldn't even remember the last time she'd done so. But Robert Greene had just pushed too far. She sat up on the sofa and glared at him. "I can't possibly dig ten thousand dollars worth of deeper. Especially not while you gamble away every dollar we have!"

His eyes narrowed into menacing little slits. "That's gratitude for you. I took you in, Emerelda, when that no-good brother of mine couldn't raise his own child."

Emmy ground her teeth. This was Robert's favorite tactic when he wanted something from her. "I know that, Uncle Robert. You've gone out of your way to remind me of it quite often enough."

His mouth dropped open. "I don't know what's got you all horns and rattles, but you'd do well to remember you're a guest in my home."

Her hands curled into fists. "I've more than earned my keep, Uncle, and you know it. If it weren't for me, your last five treatises never would have made it to St. Louis for binding. You were too busy making love to a deck of cards."

Robert's face turned cardinal red. "That's enough!" His bellow shook the globes on the lanterns. "I don't have to take this from you, you impudent chit. You seem to have forgotten your place."

"Thanks to you, none of us may have a place very much longer. If Mr. Carver really staked your bets, we could lose the farm, the livestock, everything, and still owe Joss Brickston money."

"That damned bastard," Robert muttered, raking a hand through his hair. "He cheated. I know he cheated."

"Whether he did or not, you promised him ten thousand dollars in front of a roomful of witnesses. As I see it, we're barking at knots trying to find a way out of this."

Robert seemed to look concerned for the first time. "He seems to like you, Emerelda. Don't you suppose you could talk to him?"

She glared at him. "Why should I talk to him? You got us into this fix."

Robert's eyes softened, and he shifted to sit next to her on the sofa. He took one of her hands and rubbed it between his beefy fingers. "You've always been so good to us. I've always known I could depend on you. You'll be letting all of us down if you don't try."

She felt the heavy weight of responsibility settle in her chest. Despite her anger at Robert, she knew he was right. She could not allow her family to be turned out into the street. She would have to plead their case with Joss Brickston. "All right, Uncle Robert, I'll try."

Robert looked relieved. "I promised him the money by noon today. You'd best get started into town."

Emmy brushed a speck of dust off her blue cotton dress, then frowned at the stain on her glove. Her cousins' gloves didn't fit right. She'd been forced to wear the pair she used for cleaning. They were stained with acid, but Emmy was determined to look as much like a lady as she could in her worn-out dress and clunky boots. The gloves probably looked ridiculous, but perhaps they'd disguise her trembling fingers.

She walked along the planked boardwalk, carefully picking her way around the piles of mud, and any number of other unmentionable hazards, that littered her path. She wished she'd had a bonnet, so she wouldn't be running about bare-headed, but there was no help for the woeful state of her apparel. It certainly wouldn't make it any easier to confront Joss Brickston.

She stepped over a sleeping dog in front of Wade Collie's Tack and Blacksmith. Wade waved to her from

behind the forge. Emmy managed to wave back as she
continued on toward the Express Office. She only
paused once in her progress, right outside Avery
Brooks's Mercantile and General Merchandise. As always, Clem Johnson, Otis Lampton, and Harley Beaker
were playing checkers out front.

"Morning, Miss Emmy," Clem called.

She flashed him a sad smile. "Good morning, Mr.
Johnson. Are you recovered from your gout yet?"

He waved his foot in her direction. "Not completely.
That linseed oil you and Miss Jade recommended is
working a sight better than anything else I've tried."

She nodded. "I'm glad. I know it was paining you
something fierce."

Otis Lampton grinned at her. "I hear there was a
little trouble at Bug's place last night, Miss Emmy."

It would have been too much to ask, she supposed,
for the incident to be kept quiet. "I'm on my way to
see Mr. Brickston right now, Mr. Lampton. I'm sure it
will be fine."

The glass-paned door to Avery's Mercantile swung
open. He stepped onto the porch, as handsome as the
day was long, with Clara May DeFot—with a silent "t"
as she always told everyone first off—clinging to his
arm like she was preventing a case of the vapors.

"Oh, why Mr. Brooks," Clara May crooned, causing
Emmy to wonder how a woman could giggle and talk
at the same time. "You do say the most outrageous
things."

Avery flashed his ten-dollar smile at her as he patted
her hand. "I mean it, Clara May. You let me know if
you're having trouble up there, and I'll be out straight
away."

Emmy rolled her eyes and coughed. Clara May's
trouble, everybody knew, was an overindulgent father
who turned a blind eye to the constant parade of men

Clara May dragged through his house. Clara May did
her best to convince the town that her father was trying
to marry her off to an unwanted husband. But nobody,
not even Avery Brooks, really believed that Sirus DeFot
was responsible for all those men. "Good Morning,
Avery."

Avery looked at her in surprise. "Emerelda. What
brings you to town so early?"

"I've an appointment this morning."

Clara May clucked her tongue. "With Josiah Brickston no doubt. I was so sorry to hear about last night.
Poor little Emmy. Whatever will you do?"

Emmy drew up her full five-foot nine inches and
glared at Clara May. "We'll be fine, Clara May. I assure
you."

The other girl shook her head as she continued to
stroke Avery's sleeve. "I wouldn't want to tangle with
Mr. Brickston." She shivered. "He seems a cold-hearted
lot to me. Almost as bad as Gray Lawford."

Emmy turned beseeching eyes to Avery, but found
him staring at Clara May's dark, chestnut-brown hair.
She'd get no help from that quarter. "I really can't
waste time discussing it right now, Clara May. I have to
be going. It was nice to see you, Avery."

His gaze flicked briefly in her direction. "Yes. Yes.
Do take care, Emerelda." He looked back at Clara May.
"May I assist you into your carriage, Clara May?"

Emmy didn't wait for Clara May's rapturous reply.
She trudged the rest of the way to Joss Brickston's office.

When she opened the door, the cramped office was
empty. Or so she thought. Closer inspection in the direction of a scuffling noise, revealed the presence of a
young man, thirteen or fourteen years old, trying to
sweep the dirt from behind a large wooden trunk. The
office was as hopelessly cluttered as she remembered.

The poor boy had certainly taken on a formidable task if he hoped to set it aright. She rapped sharply on the door. "Good morning."

He looked up in surprise. "Mornin'. Something I can help you with?"

She waited while he looked for a place to sweep the dirt. Finding none, he shoved it back into the corner. "I'm here to see Mr. Brickston."

The young man laid down the broom, wiped his hands on his streaked apron, then pushed a lock of his light brown hair off his forehead. "Oh, Mr. Joss isn't here right now. He'll be back in a minute, though, if you wanna wait."

Emmy picked her way through the room. Joss's chair looked reasonably clean, so she sat in it. "I didn't know Mr. Brickston had hired another employee," she said, hoping the conversation would take her mind off her troubles.

The boy shook his head. "It was Jim who gave me the job. Said this place was dirtier than a passel of cats in a flour mill, and he'd pay five dollars to clean it and a dollar a week to keep it up."

Emmy frowned. "Does Jim pay you from his earnings?"

With a broad, toothy grin, the boy shook his head. "He's saving up money to buy Miss Annie. He makes Mr. Joss pay me."

Emmy nodded. "I'm glad. I know Jim is trying to save his money."

The boy pushed a stack of papers off the extra chair so he could take the seat across from her. "My name's Sam," he said. "Are you a friend of Mr. Joss?"

"Not precisely a friend. More like," Emmy paused, "a business associate."

Sam looked impressed. "Really? Do you draw maps too?"

"Well, no. It's a bit more complicated than that. My name's Emmy Greene, by the way."

Sam leaned back in the chair to prop his feet on the desk. "I've got nothing but time, Miss Emmy. The sooner I get this office cleaned, the sooner I'll have to look for another job. I'd just as soon hear tell what you do with Mr. Joss."

Oh, any number of things, she thought. Today I'm going to beg him. "I work with rocks," she said.

Sam nodded. "I hear they do a lot of rock blasting when they're laying tracks. Didn't know there was many women in it."

She decided it would take longer than she had to explain. "I don't suppose there are. Where are you from, Sam?"

He didn't seem to notice the change in subject. "Knew right off I wasn't from Carding, didn't you?"

"It's a small town. I'd have known your parents I figured."

"My folks were from upriver. After they died, I took my six little sisters to live with my mama's aunt."

"You have six sisters?"

"Yes, ma'am. The youngest is four and the oldest is ten."

Emmy raised her eyebrows. Sam's parents kept busy. "They all live with your aunt now?"

He nodded. "Yes ma'am. She's keepin' 'em while I earn what I can to contribute to the cost."

Emmy patted Sam's hand. He looked embarrassed. "I think that's very grown-up of you, Sam."

He blushed. "A man does what a man has to, Miss Emmy."

She was about to say thirteen-year-old boys weren't supposed to be men yet when the door opened and Joss walked in. She couldn't help but notice that he looked alarmingly attractive this morning.

His rich brown hair was fastened in a haphazard queue that made her fingers ache to unlace the leather strip and smooth the waves into place. From his black eye-patch, to the fashionable Levi Strauss denim trousers that hung low on his lean hips and casually disappeared into the tops of his working boots, he was one of the fittest specimens of a man she had ever seen. His white homespun shirt clung to his broad shoulders in loose folds that did nothing to disguise his solid strength. The purple kerchief she knew he would depend on in the hot sun to protect the sensitive skin on his nape, hung loosely around his neck. She had a brief notion that he looked almost like a pirate stepping from his wind-tossed ship. "Emmy!" he said. "This is a surprise."

She doubted it was a surprise at all, but she didn't want to discuss the matter in front of Sam. She stood up. "If you aren't too busy, Mr. Brickston, there's something I'd like to discuss with you straight away."

He set down the parcel he carried on an already overladen trunk, then shut the door. "I can spare ten minutes or so."

She looked meaningfully at Sam. "I think this is best conducted in private."

Sam's feet landed on the floor with a thud. Joss picked up a leather box and tossed it to him. "Jim's unloading the new equipment down at the landing, Sam. Why don't you take him his tools so he can assemble the new leveling meter?"

Sam clutched the box close to his chest as he scrambled toward the door. "Sure thing, Mr. Joss. Me and Jim will get it workin' by noon."

At the mention of noon, Emmy's stomach flipped over. When Sam scurried out the door, the office fell silent. Why didn't he say something?

Joss waited, wondering how long it would take Emmy

to crack under the strain. Damn Robert Greene, he thought, hating the man all the more for sending Emmy to do his dirty work. It shouldn't have surprised him that the bastard would send his niece to do his negotiating, but Joss had at least credited the son-of-a-bitch with the grit to come begging himself. It was becoming apparent that Emmy wasn't going to say anything, so he indicated the chair with a sweep of his hand. "Why don't you sit down?"

She dropped into the chair Sam had just vacated as if her knees had suddenly given way. "Thank you."

Joss winced at the strain he heard in her voice. He hoped to God she didn't start to cry. He crossed the office, weaving between the boxes and crates, and sat down behind his desk. "Now, to what do I owe the pleasure of your visit this morning?"

Emmy raised her eyes. The sparks of rage that lurked inside the tawny depths relieved him. She wasn't upset, she was madder than a peeled rattlesnake. Had the situation been less serious, he might have smiled. "I think you know very well why I'm here, Mr. Brickston," she said, her voice clipped.

He lifted an eyebrow. "Are we back to using surnames? I thought we settled that on the bluff, Emmy."

She blushed, but didn't back down. "I'd like to get on with this if you don't mind."

"I don't know what you mean," he said, as he leaned back in his chair.

Emmy ground her teeth. Arrogant beast. He knew exactly what she meant. She sat up in her chair. With an angry sweep of her hand, she wiped the dust from Jim's desk. Her soiled glove turned even darker. "I'm referring, of course, to the debt my uncle owes you."

"That is a matter between Robert and me, Emmy. There's no need for you to concern yourself with it."

She stared at him, agape. "No need to . . . You know. Of course you know."

"Forgive me for saying so, but you aren't making even the least bit of sense. What precisely is it that I am supposed to know?"

Emmy stood up and began wiping the rest of the dust from Jim's desk. She refused to look Joss in the eye. "We don't have the money, Mr. Brickston. We'll probably never have the money." She scrubbed at a water stain with her fingertips. "You knew it when you allowed him to bet you."

Joss grabbed Emmy's free hand, then used it to guide her back to her chair. "Emmy, gentlemen do not wager money they don't have. It's not honorable."

She glared at him. "Is it any more honorable to trick them into the wager?"

"I didn't trick your uncle. He simply didn't know when to stop."

"But you knew. You must have known Uncle Robert couldn't afford the bet."

"Robert may not have ten thousand dollars, but he does have something that is considerably more valuable."

Emmy's eyes widened. "You are mistaken, Josiah. We don't have anything. Nothing. I can't possibly pay you the money."

"Your uncle is supposed to pay it, Emmy, not you."

"Will you throw us out on the street then? Is that what you want? Even if I give you the farm it won't begin to compensate for the whole amount."

He shook his head. "I don't want the farm."

"Then what do you want? Because we don't have anything else. You can't get blood from rock."

"I've already told you, your uncle has something far more valuable than his farm. There is only one payment I will accept in lieu of the ten thousand dollars."

Emmy felt the blood roaring in her ears. Why was he being so unreasonable? Surely he understood that they couldn't possibly pay him. She didn't know what her uncle had told him, but she knew for certain they didn't have anything worth ten thousand dollars. She lifted her hands and rubbed her temples. "What do you want?" she quietly asked, her outward calm belying her inner turmoil.

"The only payment I will accept is your hand in marriage."

Emmy's mouth dropped open. "Marriage?"

Joss nodded as he pulled out his watch. "That is correct. If your uncle cannot pay me the ten thousand dollars by noon today, then I will expect you to meet me in Judge Templeton's office at that hour." He glanced at his watch. "It is nine o'clock now. That gives you three hours to make your decision."

Emmy was staring at him in utter astonishment. "You cannot be serious."

"I'm completely serious."

"But . . . but why? Why on earth?"

He shrugged. "I told you. I do not need the farm, so I do not particularly want it. I do, however, need a wife. You know I'm widowed. I have found in recent weeks that I'm a dismal failure at taking care of my own laundry and meals, as well as trying to keep up my home. You and I get on well. I enjoy your company, and I feel you will do very nicely in the role of my wife. It seemed an eminently practical solution."

She felt some of her anger return. "You don't need a wife. You need a servant."

"You may look at it that way if you wish, but I prefer to view it as a partnership. You take care of me, and I, in turn take care of you."

"I don't need taking care of."

Joss leaned back in his chair and studied her. "Is that so?"

Emmy picked up a stack of books on Jim's desk and began dusting the covers. "Of course it's so. I've been taking care of myself for a very long time."

"Then I am to assume that you enjoy writing treatises and publishing them under your uncle's name?"

She dropped a book. That had been cruel, and he knew it. "That's not true. I—"

"I am to assume that you prefer to be the solitary source of income for your family as they wile away their days in more pleasurable pursuits?"

Her face turned red. "Well, no. You don't understand. It's—"

"I am to assume that you find joy in providing your cousins and your uncle with fashionable pursuits and wardrobes while you are left to work away in your dingy office like some serving girl who is worthy only of their cast-offs?"

Emmy slammed the books down on the desk. A cloud of dust ensued. "You don't understand. You have no right to say these things to me."

Joss surged forward in his chair. The thought occurred to him that he should have simply killed Robert Greene and been done with it. As it was, he had succeeded in humiliating Emmy with his casually distributed opinion. He felt like a cad. "I do understand. I understand a great deal more than you think."

Her eyes started to fill with tears. She wiped them away with now-filthy gloves that left a streak of dirt on her face. Joss dug in his pocket to hand her a white cotton handkerchief. She used it to mop at her still streaming eyes. "I'm sorry. I cannot seem to keep myself from crying at the most inopportune times."

He waited while she gently blew her nose. "I am the one who is sorry. I was provoked. Attribute it to a very long night." He drew a deep breath. "I should not have said what I did, but damnation, Emerelda, why do you let that man treat you as he does?"

Emmy lowered the handkerchief to her lap. Her brief emotional outburst seemed to have weakened his frigid control. She hoped now he would listen to her. "Uncle Robert has been very good to me, Josiah. Despite what you might think of him, I would have been alone without his protection."

Joss ran a finger along his scar. Fatigue always caused it to draw tight, and the all-night card game had exhausted him. "I know you feel a certain amount of gratitude for your uncle, but your debt is well-paid I assure you."

She shrugged. It didn't really matter anyway, not when they still had the matter of ten thousand dollars to settle. Though she didn't dare ask, she hoped from the softer light she saw in his gaze that Joss would forgive the debt. "So will you allow me to work something out on the money? I will need time to pull together the sum."

He abruptly shook his head. "No, I'm afraid not. My demands still remain. I will have the money, the farm, or you by noon today."

Emmy twisted her hands in her lap. "How can you do this to me? You cannot force me to marry you."

"I'm not forcing you. The choice is yours to make." He checked his watch again. "Your time has dwindled to two hours, forty-five minutes. I suggest you use what you have left to set your affairs in order."

Her hands curled into tight fists. "What is wrong with you? Why are you doing this?"

"I have already explained."

"You are prepared to marry me simply because you do not wish to do your own wash?"

"No. I should not have said that. I am prepared to

marry you because I believe we will both be well served by it."

Emmy swallowed a gasp. "I thought you were my friend, Josiah. I trusted you."

"And it is my hope that you will do so again. Once you are my wife. I think you will understand, then. I am not trying to hurt you."

"You do not believe this will hurt me? You've humiliated me."

"No more so," he said quietly, "than Robert Greene."

Emmy could no longer bear the cold look in his gaze. In the past week, she had come to admire and trust him. For the first time in her life, she'd believed that someone respected her for her opinions, for her skills. Now it seemed that Josiah Brickston, like her family, saw only her uses and missed her value. Without further comment, she fled the room.

By the time she reached Avery's store, she had begun to cry in earnest. She ran up the steps to the long porch and twisted frantically at the doorknob.

"Whatsa matter with you, Miss Emmy. You're looking like you sucked on a persimmon bush," Otis Lampton called.

"I need Avery, Mr. Lampton. I just need to speak to Avery."

Clem Johnson shook his head. "He ain't here."

"What?" Emmy looked at the door in startled surprise. Avery's CLOSED sign swung on a nail. "Where is he?"

"Gone chasin' if you ask me," Harley Beaker said.

Emmy frowned. "Chasing what?"

"Not what," said Otis, "who."

The three men laughed as they affectionately slapped each other on the back. Emmy's despair sunk another notch. She had wanted to ask Avery's advice, hoping that somehow he would help her find a solu-

tion. With a depressed moan, Emmy stripped off her
dirty gloves and tossed them on the bench. There was
no sense in looking like a lady now.

# Nine

By ten forty-five, Emmy had given up. She was standing back in front of the Express Office, staring at the door. When she told Robert about Joss's demand, he had been ecstatic. "This is a miracle," he had declared. He proved his renewed faith by downing a hefty glass of bourbon. Most of her cousins didn't seem very disturbed that Joss Brickston was about to turn her life upside down. Oh, Topaz was angry that she wasn't being married first. Pearl seemed to feel slighted that Joss had picked Emmy, though Pearl didn't particularly want to marry him herself. Ruby was positively horrified at the thought that she might have to alter her own gowns in the future. Alex started crying and wouldn't stop, but only Jade seemed truly concerned.

Jade had spent a good ten minutes crying over how much she was going to miss Emmy, and that Joss hadn't even allowed her time for a bride's dress. Emmy had told her there was no point in having a new gown when all she was going to do was wash Joss Brickston's clothes and make sure he got fed proper.

When most of the commotion had petered away, Emmy had quietly discussed her intentions. "I'm going directly to his office. There's no need to put it off until noon," she had said.

"Well, for heaven's sake, Emmy," Pearl snapped. "It's a wedding, not an execution."

Emmy ignored her. "We're to be married in Judge Templeton's office, and I'd like you all to be there. You're the only family I have."

"I can't," Opal announced. "I have an appointment with Maylene Parker to have my new hat outfitted with ostrich plumes. She just got them in from Paris, and she promised to save me first pick."

"And I'm supposed to meet Merle Thickens for a carriage ride," Pearl had said.

"Clara May and I are working on our quilt this afternoon," Ruby chimed in.

"I'm going berry picking with Milt Keenan," Garnet had said.

And in a rare burst of conscience, Robert Greene had done one of the first generous things in his life. He had slammed his palm down on the table and demanded that every member of the household be dressed and ready to go within the half-hour. There had been a moment of stunned silence before all the wailing and griping and crying had begun in earnest, and finally, Emmy had bid Robert good-bye, figuring he could handle his own children for once, and fled the house, headed for town.

Now, she stared at the door of the office and fought a growing surge of panic. It took nearly every ounce of willpower she possessed to climb the stairs to Joss's office. When she walked in, she found him seated at his desk, tediously inking in a penciled map. Jim was working over an incredibly complex-looking piece of equipment. Sam was propped on top of a tall chest, swinging his legs and whittling. The wood shavings dropped, unheeded, onto the floor. Emmy fought the urge to sweep them up. "I'm here," she announced.

Joss looked up in surprise. "What time is it?"

"Nearly eleven," Jim said.

"You're early," Joss told Emmy.

"I didn't see any reason to forestall the inevitable," she told him.

Joss dropped his ink pen back in the bottle, then wiped his stained hands on a cloth. The ink smeared across his fingers. "Very well, then. I assume you have made your choice."

"Yes. I'm ready to go with you. I invited my family. I hope that's all right."

He reached for his hat as he stood. "Would either of you care to join us?" he asked Jim and Sam.

Sam glanced up from his whittling. "What for?"

"My wedding." Joss plopped the hat on his head.

Jim dropped the equipment with a loud crash. "What?"

Joss smiled wryly. "I seem to have become rather adept at provoking that reaction. You heard what I said, Jim. Miss Emmy has agreed to marry me this morning. We're going to Judge Templeton's office right now."

"Isn't this a bit rushed?" Jim asked, staring at Joss.

Joss shrugged. "Maybe. We're doing it though. Do you want to come along?"

Sam jumped down from the crate. "I do. I ain't never been to a wedding before." He paused. "I don't have to take a bath or change or nothing do I?"

Emmy started to say, yes, that would be very nice, but Joss shook his head. "No need. It's only going to take five minutes or so."

Jim met Emmy's gaze and held it for several long seconds. There was something in the way he looked at her that somehow made her feel better. "I'd like for you to come too, Mr. Oaks."

Jim brushed his hands on his trousers legs as he stood. "I wouldn't miss it, Miss Emmy."

They walked across the street together while Emmy tried to ignore the strange glances they received from the townsfolk. They passed Gray Lawford on the way.

Emmy paused, despite the insistent pressure Joss was applying to her elbow. "I'm getting married, Gray. Don't you want to come watch?" she asked.

Gray stopped dead in his tracks. He stared at her for five whole seconds before he turned his cool gaze on Joss. "You better damn sure know what you're doing, Brickston."

Joss nodded briefly. "I do."

Gray glared at Joss, but spoke to Emmy. "Do you want to go through with this, Em? You don't have to, you know."

She swallowed. Joss's fingers had tightened on her elbow, and suddenly, perhaps because the sun was shining warm on her head, or the cool breeze was blowing, or the feel of his strong fingers made her skin tingle, or maybe just because Robert Greene had finally pushed her too far, she realized she really did want to go through with it. She wasn't marrying Joss Brickston because of the money. If Robert had really been determined, he could have found a way to pay the debt or get Joss to forgive it. Even if they'd given up the farm, there still would have been somewhere they could have gone.

No, she'd made the decision to marry this man long before Robert had resigned her to it. She'd made it before the explosive conversation in his office that morning. She'd even made it before the card game. In truth, she realized, she'd made it when they'd sat together on the bluff, and he'd told her about Allyson and Adam and Michael. Joss Brickston was a man who loved deeper than most folks even thought about. While the Robert Greenes of the world were wading about in shallow creeks and stream beds, Joss Brickston was floating in the ocean. Yes, she did want to go through with it. She wanted it very much.

She looked at Joss. "Yes, Gray. I do."

Joss's face registered a brief flash of wary amazement. He wasn't quite sure what to make of her change of heart, she thought, but given time, he'd understand. He dropped his hand. "Emmy," he said quietly.

She laced her fingers through his with a soft laugh. "Second thoughts, Josiah?"

Joss blinked. When his eye opened, the strange look was gone. "No," he said. "Let's go."

Judge Templeton's office was in bedlam. Emmy's cousins, decked out in their go-to-meeting clothes, were packed inside, weeping and wailing and complaining so much, the whole room was buzzing like a beehive. Only Robert sat quiet and subdued.

Joss rolled his eyes in irritation. "Your family seems distressed."

Emmy shrugged. "They had other plans."

"I dislike public spectacles." His voice sounded frozen.

She stared at him in astonishment. "And you want to marry into *my* family. We practically invented public spectacle."

Joss was about to retort when Jade came rushing down the steps and planted her hands on his chest. "Wait right there, Joss Brickston. Don't take another step."

The sight of tiny little Jade trying to prevent Joss from doing anything was so ludicrous, Gray choked out a laugh. Sam's mouth dropped open. Jim winked at Emmy, and Joss glared at Jade. "You're not stopping this wedding," he said. "So there's no sense in embarrassing yourself over it."

Jade shook her head. "I'm not trying to stop the wedding. I'm waiting on the flowers."

Joss stared at her ominously. "What flowers?"

Jade didn't budge. "You cheated Emmy out of a new gown and a proper wedding. You're not going to cheat her out of flowers. Anne Lingson is bringing over a bouquet, and you can just stand yourself right there and wait until she gets here."

Emmy laid a hand on Jade's arm. "It's all right, Jade."

She shook her head. "No, it isn't. He said you had 'til noon to make up your mind, and he can just wait." She glared at Joss. "It's only decent."

Joss hesitated. Emmy's family was making so much noise, they were drawing the attention of the whole damned town. Before long, every gossip and ne'er-do-well in Carding would be jockeying up for a place inside Judge Templeton's office. Instinct told him to get the matter over with, but the feel of Emmy's small, work-roughened hand in his changed his mind. He had a sudden memory of the soiled gloves she'd worn to his office that morning. Jade was right. He'd cheated Emmy out of a lot. He could wait a few minutes on a damn bouquet of flowers. "All right. We'll wait."

Jade beamed at him. "I knew you'd see reason. She should be here in five minutes."

Emmy made her cousins line up in height order, despite their grumbling and complaining over it. She introduced them one by one to Josiah. He tried to hide his growing irritation. He'd already met most of the Greene brood, and he certainly had no desire to do so again. He made no effort to hide the contempt in his gaze. His lip curled into a scornful smile when Emmy introduced Robert Greene.

"And of course," she said, sounding more than a little trepidant, "you already know my Uncle Robert."

"Of course." Joss didn't offer Robert his hand.

The older man glared at him. "This is a damned fool thing you're doing, Brickston. I don't know why you think . . ." Joss's glare was so hard, Robert's voice trailed off.

"I'll be the judge of that, Greene," Joss said. He ignored the way Emmy's fingers tightened on his forearm.

Everyone breathed a sigh of relief when, six minutes later, Anne Lingson came rushing up the street with the small bouquet of pansies. Most of Carding's three hundred residents were standing on the street, staring at the spectacle in front of Judge Templeton's office.

Feeling scared, and ridiculous, and sad, and happy, and anxious all at the same time, Emerelda Greene became Mrs. Josiah Brickston to the sound of her cousins' wailing and a whole lot of gossip.

Joss lifted Emmy onto the buckboard seat.

"Be careful of my flowers, Josiah," she said, rescuing her bouquet before it tumbled to the ground.

Her skirts flared around her when he dropped her on the seat. Irrationally irritated at the mix of emotions pouring through him, he knocked the blue cotton down to cover a mint green petticoat. Her family had finally taken their loud complaining and left the town in peace. Joss felt restless. And a relentless, driving need to distance himself from her. "Jim will take you back to your house to pack," he told her.

Emmy's forehead wrinkled. "Aren't you coming?"

He shook his head. "I have a full day's work to do. Once you've collected your things, Jim will see you settled at my place."

"Oh but, I thought—"

"Then you thought wrong." He ignored her stung look and turned to find Jim. He had to get away from her. Fast. When Emmy had slipped her hand in his and reassured Gray Lawford, Joss had momentarily lost sight of Allyson's face. Emmy's warm smile and tawny eyes had dimmed his memories. He wouldn't have it.

He couldn't have it. He had married Emerelda Greene for one reason. Nothing was going to change that.

Jim was watching him with an intense stare that made Joss's frown deepen. "I'd like you to see Miss Greene home, Jim. She'll need to pack whatever she plans on taking with her from her uncle's house. Then I want you to take her up the bluff."

Jim mumbled something beneath his breath as he shook his head. "Reckon I'll take the boy too. We might need help loading the bags."

Joss nodded. "Fine. Samuel can follow along. I've still got last month's books to balance from St. Louis."

Jim's mouth twisted into a skeptical grimace. He motioned for Sam to hop on back the buckboard before he strolled past Joss mumbling something that sounded for all the world like "danged fool."

Jim swung into the seat and stomped on the brake to release it. "If it's all the same to you," he told Joss. "I won't be back to the office this afternoon."

"That's fine. Just see that Miss Greene is safely settled in at the bluff."

Emmy laid a hand on Jim's sleeve. "Wait please."

Jim nodded and Emmy leaned forward, her hand still clutching the bouquet. Joss stood in the middle of the dirty street and stared at her. "What's the matter?" he asked.

"My name, Josiah. It's not Miss Greene any more. It's Mrs. Josiah Brickston, and don't you be forgetting it."

She was gratified at the shocked expression on his face. She gave Gray Lawford a cool, satisfied nod when they passed him where he leaned against a post in front of Judge Templeton's office. She felt fine. Wonderful, in fact. Everything had gone quite well, and there was absolutely no reason whatsoever for her to be upset.

By the time they reached Robert Greene's farm,

Emmy had cried herself silly. It seemed she'd done little else since Robert's announcement that he'd lost everything to Joss Brickston. As much as she resented Joss for doing this to her, she couldn't seem to stop the flood of tears. Sam had torn off a hunk of his shirttail for her to use as a handkerchief. "I'm sorry," she said. "I don't know what's wrong with me."

"Aw, Miss Em," Sam said, patting her awkwardly on the back. "I'm sure Mr. Joss didn't mean nothin' by it." Sam brightened as a sudden thought occurred to him. "He probably just wanted to give you time to get dug in before he claimed his husband rights."

Jim looked over his shoulder to glare at Sam. Emmy cried harder. "Now, Miss Emmy, you listen to me good," Jim said. "I don't much cotton to sticking my nose in where it don't belong, but Joss is a fine man."

She nodded and blew her nose. "I know."

"But he's also got a lot of hurts rolling around inside him. When he lost his wife and boys, well, that'd be hard on any man, but a man like Joss, a man who protects people and cares for people, it dang near destroyed him."

Emmy mopped at her eyes. She felt like a fool. "He told me about what happened."

Jim's nod was brief. "I don't know exactly all the reasons Joss married you, but I've seen the way he looks at you. He doesn't look at any other woman that way, and that's a fact. There's something 'bout you that unsettles that man."

"But, Jim—"

He interrupted her. "No, ma'am. He may have some reasons he's not telling, but you could heal that man's soul, Miss Emmy. You just gotta give him the chance to do right by you."

Emmy looked at Jim through tear-swollen eyes. "Do you know why I married Joss?"

"The bet," Sam chimed in.

He earned another scathing look from Jim. "I swear boy, you got all the subtlety of a rattlesnake."

Emmy shot Sam a watery smile. "It's all right, Sam. I'm not offended."

Sam looked sheepish. "I'm sorry Miss Emmy. I shouldn't have said it."

"Besides," Jim said, "it wasn't the truth."

"What do you mean by that?" asked Sam. "Everybody in town knows Miss Emmy had to marry Mr. Joss to save her uncle's skin."

Emmy exhaled a slow sigh. "I didn't marry Josiah because of the bet."

"Then why did ya?" Sam leaned over the seat of the buckboard.

"Because I'm in love with him," she said quietly.

Sam's face twisted into a disgusted grimace. "Aw, Miss Emmy."

"Hush up, boy," Jim said. He looked at Emmy. "That's what I figured this afternoon in the street. He may have asked you because of the bet, but you don't let it stand in the way of what you know is true."

She nodded, favoring Jim with a trembling smile. "I won't, Jim. I promise."


It took nearly three hours to pack all of Emmy's office into crates. Alex was still crying. Jade was walking about fuming that Joss hadn't given Emmy more time. The rest of the Greene family had disappeared for parts unknown.

After a quick lunch of sandwiches and an apple pandowdy Emmy had made the previous evening, Jim and Sam set about loading crates, while Emmy climbed the stairs to pack up her meager wardrobe. She stuffed everything into a barley sack, taking more care with her undergarments than her worn-out dresses, and hefted it onto her shoulder. The only personal possessions she owned were the beaver pelt her father had given her one year, and the quilt she'd made of her mother's favorite dresses. She wrapped the pelt in the quilt and tucked it under her arm.

When she met Jim and Sam below stairs, the buckboard was loaded. Emmy hugged Jade and Alex, looked inside her tiny office once more, then turned her back on the life she'd known for seventeen years.

It was difficult not to feel melancholy during the ride to Joss's house. She realized with something of a start that she had no idea where he lived except that he'd said something about the bluff. Sam had fallen silent in the back of the wagon. Emmy tried not to concentrate on the memory of Alex's tear-streaked face, or the tender look in Jade's eyes. "Jim," she said, hoping to take her mind off things. "Where does Josiah live?"

"Top of the bluff, in the old watch house they used to use for river boat traffic."

"The watch house? I didn't know there were houses there."

"It's not a house exactly."

Emmy felt a tiny sliver of dread work its way down her spine. "Then what is it? Exactly?"

"Joss lives in the watch house office," Jim said carefully.

Despite herself, Emmy was intrigued. "Really? Is it fit for living?"

Jim shrugged. "It's outfitted with a kitchen, and an indoor bathing closet. There are two water pumps and huge windows. It'd be nice if it was clean."

Emmy swallowed. "It's not clean?"

"You've seen the office, Miss Emmy. Joss isn't, well, he isn't . . ."

Sam sat up in the back of the wagon. "He's slatternly,

Miss Em. The messiest one person I ever did see. Why, that man can clutter up a room faster than you can sneeze a pinch full of snuff," Sam said. Jim glared at him.

Emmy drew a deep breath. "Well, surely it can't be all that bad."

"I'm sure it's not," Jim agreed, but Emmy couldn't tell from looking at him what he was thinking.

Until she walked in the front door of Josiah Brickston's diggings, Emmy thought pig wallows were the messiest places on earth.

Right inside the door, she dropped her bag on the dust-covered hard-board floor and gasped. Her hands flew to her face in dismay. Piles of soiled laundry were everywhere, stuffed into corners, piled on chairs, crammed in bookcases. She would have sworn one pair of trousers was standing up by itself. Mud covered the floor in foot-shaped tracks. The table and kitchen were strewn with dishes, empty bottles and sacks.

Jim picked up her bag. "Do you want me to move this into the bedroom?"

"No!" she said, feeling slightly panicked. "Don't touch anything."

"But what about the crates?" Sam asked.

Emmy wiped a hand through her hair. "Unload them and leave them outside."

Sam looked puzzled. "Don't you want us to carry them in for you?"

She shook her head. "I don't want anything else brought in this house until I set it aright."

Jim set down her bag, then gave her shoulder a gentle squeeze. "I'm sure it's not as bad as it looks." He nodded to Sam, and they went outside to start unloading Emmy's belongings.

"No," she said to no one in particular. "It's worse."

Sam and Jim unloaded the crates that held Emmy's

books and equipment and set them on the front porch. When Jim knocked on the door, Emmy was still standing rooted to her spot just inside. "You gonna be all right up here, Miss Emmy?" he asked.

She nodded without looking around.

"You sure you don't want us to stay and help a spell?"

Emmy shook her head. No, she didn't want help. She didn't want anybody to know the extent of her new husband's shame. As far as she was concerned, that's what it was. There wasn't a man alive who ought to live like this, and if it took a damned week, she'd turn the ramshackle, grimy watch house into a spanking clean and comfortable home.

Jim lifted his hat to wipe a line of sweat off his forehead. "All right then, Miss Emmy. I'll take Sam and head on back to town. You be careful, now. Do you hear me?"

Emmy finally looked at Jim and nodded. "I will, Jim. Thank you." Sam was already seated in the buckboard. She flashed him a smile, waving at him over Jim's shoulder. "Good-bye, Sam."

"Bye, Miss Em."

Jim shot her one more wary look before he pulled the door shut behind him to leave Emmy alone in the hovel Joss Brickston called home. She picked up her bag of clothes and wandered through the great room, carefully wending her way through the laundry and books and paper and dirt. His bedroom was behind the great stone fireplace that dominated the office. The sight of still more laundry and a half-dozen pair of mud-caked boots made her groan.

The pile of sheets in the corner struck her as odd. Evidently, he didn't care about the clutter, but he'd taken time to change his linens. That thought brought to notice the huge pile of towels, nearly as high as her shoulder, stuffed in the wedge between the door and the bathing closet. Emmy dropped her bag of clothes on the rumpled bed. She'd have to change first before tackling the job. The blue gown was faded and worn, but something in her rebelled against cleaning the house in her wedding dress.

She changed into Levi's and a loose-fitting shirt, not caring that her appearance was scandalous. This far up the bluff, nobody was going to be around to see. "First things first," she muttered as she wandered around the old watch house to get a feel for its size and potential. She did have to admit, things weren't nearly as bad as they seemed. Nothing was dirty in an unhealthy way. She was pleased to find that while dishes and discarded bottles littered the kitchen, everything had been rinsed. Judging from the large can of soap flakes, Joss might have even washed them. She'd do it again, just to be sure.

It wasn't until she climbed the ladder to the loft though, that her heart awoke with enthusiasm for the task ahead. One whole wall was made of glass. While the early afternoon light spilling in over Joss's desk made the clutter all the more apparent, Emmy couldn't help but notice there was an extra desk on the opposite side of the large, sunlit room. She smiled at the pleasant thought of sitting above stairs, working on a new treatise, while Joss worked with his maps—just like their morning on the bluff.

The large loft overlooked the river. Emmy suspected it had once doubled as looking post and work room for the boatmen during its day. She worked her way back down the ladder with a growing energy. At least she would have work to do to take her mind off Josiah's strange behavior that afternoon.

"I'll start with the clutter," she said announced, "and then move on to the dirt."

It took nearly two hours to sort all the laundry into piles by color. Some of Josiah's work shirts were downright offensive they smelled so bad. When she picked up one particularly choice faded orange one, she decided the color wouldn't look good enough on him to waste the soap working out the odor. It ended up on the trash heap.

She bundled every pile of laundry into one of the soiled sheets, then tied the corners into neat knots so she could haul them out the back and down the path to the washroom. It would probably take at least a week or two to get the laundry clean. There was no reason to let it clutter up the house in the meantime.

Once all the laundry was cleared away, the place didn't look so bad. She made quick work of washing all the dishes and bottles. They stacked in neat rows inside a large closet she suspected was supposed to be the pantry, although she wouldn't have guessed it from the half-eaten sack of cornmeal and the bottle of whiskey inside.

There had been a salted ham hanging in the washroom, and Emmy was relieved to find a bottle of what smelled like fresh milk, a jug of sugar, and a slab of butter, a luxury indeed, in the icebox. The new hunk of ice suggested an ice house lay in one of the outbuildings. Emmy decided salted ham and corn biscuits may not have been her first choice for a wedding night feast, but Josiah couldn't complain when he'd given her so little to work with.

Once the dishes were put away, the house almost looked livable. The clutter was mostly cleared. Now, only a good, thorough cleaning was needed. Emmy found a clean pillowcase and set about dusting and reorganizing the books and papers on the shelves. When she came across a piece of Josiah's underwear

stuffed between two books, she tossed it on the trash
heap gradually taking shape in the middle of the room.

By five o'clock, she had the whole place dusted. Even
though a good bit of the dirt was now on her, she was
starting to feel better. She stuffed the trash into a
wooden flour barrel. The ensuing cloud of dust made
her cough as she dragged it out onto the back porch.
It was time to start supper. She had no idea what time
Joss would be home, and she didn't want to keep him
waiting.

She fetched the ham from the washroom and set it
in a large kettle to soak. She hoped that at least some
of the salt would soak out by dinner time. Once she
got the dough made, she rolled thick, corn biscuits and
built a low fire in the cast-iron stove to bake them.

With the simple tasks out of the way, Emmy wiped
her sweat-dampened hair out of her eyes, finished off
a glass of cool pump water, and started in on the real
cleaning. The first thing she did was slit open the
musty-smelling mattress and wash all the goose down
in a tub of suds. She'd been surprised and delighted
that Joss had anything as luxurious as a feather bed.
She was bound and determined to make it last by caring for the feathers. When the water ran clear, she
dumped the feathers in a clean sheet and hauled them
upstairs to the loft, where she spread them in the sun
to dry.

The furniture was good quality, she learned while
dusting, all of it solid maple, cherry or oak, and most
of it spool-turned or Sheraton-styled. She promised before too many days passed, she'd give it all a good polishing.

She'd also discovered, to her infinite delight, that
the various fittings and hooks and instruments built
into the wall were solid brass, not the iron she'd assumed from their black color. If she took to them with

a cake of lye soap, she could have them shining in no time.

The puncheon floor, too, was made of oak and birch planks, instead of a cheaper wood. Emmy mixed a bucket of suds with a bottle of lemon oil she dug out from one of her crates. Moving the heavy furniture proved to be no small task, but by seven o'clock, she had the floor mopped and polished until it shined.

She was dumping the filthy water off the back porch when she noticed the low angle of the sun and started to worry about Josiah. She checked her biscuits, then put the fluffy, dry feathers back into the mattress so she could stitch up the seam. She doubted any man would want to come home on his wedding night, no matter what the circumstances, and find his bed dismantled.

When that thought brought with it a whole host of unsettling notions, Emmy hastily shoved the mattress back in place and put clean linens on the bed. Not sure what to do next, and certainly not willing to simply sit and wait for Josiah's arrival, Emmy went about dragging her crates inside. She pushed them over to the ladder, figuring to get her husband to haul them upstairs for her later.

When eight o'clock came and went with still no sign of him, Emmy began to worry in earnest. She'd polished the kitchen table. The dark cherry took to the oil soap. The table gleamed in the candlelight. She carefully laid her quilt over it for a tablecloth. She set two thick mutton-tallow candles in the center and lit them. The place looked almost cozy in the amber glow of their light. Then she sat down in the slat-backed rocker she'd dragged to the fireplace and tried not to worry.

When Joss walked in at eleven-thirty, Emmy was sound asleep in the rocking chair. She sat with her neck tilted at a hazardous angle. Streaks of dirt and dust covered her face. Her red-gold hair was pulled back from her grimy face in a lopsided braid that looked perilously close to exploding. Tiny, damp curls lay against her neck as stark evidence of a back-breaking afternoon.

With a grimace, he dropped his hat on the brass hook inside the door. Damn, but he felt rotten. One look around the place and he knew why she was so exhausted. She'd worked like a slave that afternoon. His makeshift house already looked like an extremely comfortable little home. She'd only been in it for a matter of hours.

Frustrated, Joss walked over to the fireplace. The days had grown quite warm, but the temperature still dropped in the evenings. He felt a pang of guilt that, in addition to all she'd done, she'd been forced to lay her own fire. He threw another log on the dying embers before he turned to look at Emmy. He shouldn't have treated her so poorly. His conscience had been nagging him all day. Oh, she'd disturbed him all right. Damn near scared him to death, but still, he shouldn't have banished her to the house like a sack of potatoes.

Slowly, ignoring the pain in his knees, he squatted in front of her so he could gently lay his hand on the side of her face. "Emmy. Emmy, I'm home."

She awoke instantly. It took several minutes for her eyes to focus, but when they did, she slapped him hard across his cheek.

# Ten

Joss looked at Emmy in stunned surprise. "What did you hit me for?" He gingerly rubbed his jaw. He frowned when he saw two tears brim in her eyes. "Are you crying?"

"No." Emmy buried her soiled face in her hands to try to stem the impending flood.

"You are. You're crying. Why are you crying?"

"Because of you," she told him. "You're wretched."

Guilt stabbed through him. "Emmy, listen to me. I just—"

"No." She shook her head. When she raised her eyes, two tears had wiped clean streaks down her grimy face. "You sent me up here to this dirty, horrid place." She wiped a sleeve over her eyes. "You ignored me all day long. Your dinner is burned because you didn't come home." A strangled sob caught in her throat. "And you didn't even bother to wash your hands."

"What do you mean I didn't wash my hands?"

"Before the ceremony." She pointed to his large hands where the ink still stained his fingers. "You had ink on your hands from your maps. You didn't even wash them."

The accusation carried a world of hurt. Joss wanted to sink into the floor. Feeling like the lowest form of life on earth, he realized that nothing could atone for his abominable mistreatment of her that day. With a weary sense of depression, he stood and crossed to the pump in the kitchen. The clean kitchen, the polished table, the two mutton-tallow candles now burned low, the quilted tablecloth, and the faint smell of slightly burned corn biscuits assaulted his senses. He lifted the edge of a towel to sniff appreciatively at the scent of the warm bread. Even scorched, the biscuits smelled delicious. He soaked a clean towel in pump water, then carried it back to where Emmy still sat in the rocking chair.

Her face remained buried in her hands. Ignoring the pain it caused him, he went down on one knee beside her. He tipped her face up so he could gently bathe away the dirt and tears. She sniffed when he wiped the damp towel over her reddened eyes. "Better?" he asked softly.

She swiped the cloth out of his hand so she could use it to blow her nose. "Where have you been?"

How could he tell her? How could he say that he'd spent the better part of the afternoon trying to forget the look in her eyes when she'd married him; trying to forget the way she'd felt against him the last time they were on this bluff together; trying to convince himself that he wouldn't want to haul her into his arms and make love to her the minute he walked through the door; trying to remember Allyson. "Working," he said.

She glanced at the clock. Its newly washed face gleamed in the light from the fire. "It's nearly midnight."

"I know it's late. I had to finish balancing the books from St. Louis. There were several big discrepancies, and it took longer than I thought."

Emmy wiped her eyes with the damp cloth. She suspected there was a good deal more to the explanation, but didn't have the courage to ask. "I'm sorry I slapped you."

He shrugged. "I'm sorry I gave you cause."

"Your dinner's burnt."

Joss managed a slight smile. "Only the bottoms of the biscuits. I'm hungry enough to muddle through. Besides, it's my own fault." He rose to his feet, then extended a hand to her. "Come eat with me?"

Emmy pushed a stray tendril of curly hair off her forehead before she slipped her hand into his. He pulled her up beside him. She tugged self-consciously at her shirt. "I should change. I'm filthy."

"No." He didn't mean to be so abrupt, but damn, he wasn't ready for the thought of her taking her clothes off in his house. "I mean, I'm dirty, too. It can wait until after supper."

Emmy hesitated, but sensed the fragility of the temporary truce. Without further comment, she led the way to the kitchen. Josiah paused to light the oil lamps. They cast a warm light around the room as Emmy retrieved the ham and biscuits from the stove. "It isn't much," she said. "You were a bit low on supplies."

Joss went to the pump to scrub his hands with the tiny cake of soap that smelled suspiciously like honeysuckle. "I know," he said over his shoulder as he scraped at his fingers with the soap. The incriminating ink stains were stubborn and wouldn't come off. "I'll leave you the buckboard tomorrow if you like. You can go into town."

Emmy set two heavy plates on the table, then fetched a pair of glasses from the pantry. Joss noticed that her small bridal bouquet was nestled in a bowl of water between the two gutted mutton-tallow candles. He felt slightly sick with guilt.

She seemed not to notice his discomfort. "All right,"

she said. "Is there anything particular you want me to buy?"

Joss turned to watch her as he dried his hands on the clean, faded towel. White undergarments, he thought. He'd been tormented long enough with notions of Emmy's eccentric underwear. "Just get whatever you need. I've got accounts at nearly every store in town."

Emmy filled both glasses with milk before she sat down. She waited for Joss to take the seat across from her. He plunked down in his chair with a weary groan. Her hands lay folded neatly in front of her. She looked at him expectantly. "Aren't you going to say grace?" she asked after several long minutes of tense silence.

He coughed. He'd forgotten civilized people, people who hadn't yet stopped living, did such things. Embarrassed, he folded his hands. "Dear Father we thank Thee for these Thy gifts we are about to receive. Bless this meal to the nourishment of our bodies that we may continue in Thy service. Amen."

"Amen." Emmy reached for a biscuit, sliced it open, slathered it liberally with butter, and inserted two thick chunks of ham. She handed it to him, then repeated the process.

Joss ate half his biscuit in one bite. He hadn't realized how hungry he was. "I, ah, see you've straightened up," he said, hoping to make conversation.

Glaring at him across the table, she swallowed a long drink of milk before she responded. "How could you live like this, Josiah? I mean, didn't it bother you?"

He accepted another biscuit from her. "After Allyson died, a lot of things stopped bothering me."

Emmy dropped her knife to the table with a loud *bang*. "Sorry," she mumbled as she scooped it up. "I haven't finished cleaning yet. It will take me a few weeks to get your laundry done."

He shrugged again and downed a glass of milk. "I'm in no hurry." He watched the way her shirt pulled taut over her firm breasts when she poured him another glass of milk. The sight made him swallow, hard, against the growing heat in his body. He should have stayed gone longer. Being alone in the house with her was harder than he'd anticipated.

"If you don't mind," she was saying, "I'd like to set my office up in the loft—next to your desk," she clarified when he gave her a blank look. "I couldn't help noticing there was an extra desk there, and the light will work nicely for me."

Hell no, she couldn't set up next to his desk. How was he supposed to get a damned thing done with the sight of her bent over one of her treatises and that lingering smell of honeysuckle and cleaning acid that did strange things to his insides? "That will be fine," he said. "I'll send Jim out to help you move the crates."

I'd rather you did it, she thought, but buttered another biscuit instead of telling him so. She looked up at him again. "Would you like another biscuit?"

Joss shook his head. "No. I've had plenty. Thank you for making my dinner."

Abruptly, Emmy rose to clear the table. "I'm sorry it was spoilt."

As Joss watched her walk to the sink, he felt dread, and heat, seep through him. The sway of her hips was so damned seductive, so achingly feminine, encased in those loose Levi's. He was going to lose his mind before this was all over and done. Which brought to mind the notion that the sooner he laid things out, the sooner he defined his course of action, the sooner it would be over. The sooner he could finally allow Allyson and Adam and Michael to rest in peace. "Emmy." He barked her name a good deal harsher than he'd intended.

She threw him a startled glance. "Yes?"

"I have one request of you. If you and I are to make this marriage work, then I'll have to insist on this. Otherwise, I think we can work out amicable compromises to whatever differences we encounter along the way."

She eyed him warily. "What is it?"

"I would like you to promise me that you will not visit your family without my permission."

"I can't visit my uncle or my cousins?"

"No."

"Why not?"

"Because I am your husband, and that's how I want it." He knew he sounded arrogant, but saw no help for it. He must have her cooperation in this. For long seconds, he watched the emotions cross her expressive face.

Finally, she said, "All right."

"All right?" He'd expected a fight.

"All right."

Joss released a pent-up breath. That had not been nearly the ordeal he anticipated. She hadn't even asked for an explanation. He sure as hell wasn't going to give her one. He didn't think that telling her that he'd married her for the express purpose of destroying her uncle, would put them on the road to marital bliss. "Thank you." The beseeching look in her gaze threatened to undo him. In self-defense, he rose to walk toward the door. "It promises to be a cold night. I am going to fetch some wood."

"Josiah?"

He stopped, his hat in his hand, "Yes?"

"That is a very big sacrifice."

He nodded briefly as he turned to look at her. "I know."

"Am I not allowed to ask a favor of you in return?"

"If it is within my power to grant it."

"Will you promise me that the next time you are thinking of Allyson, you won't feel compelled to do so away from my presence like you did today?"

He stared at her. She knew. She knew he was wary of her. She knew he was struggling. Dear God, how could he have failed so dismally to control himself. "What are you talking about, Emmy?"

She wiped her hands on a towel as she crossed to his side. A light muffler hung on the hook by the door. She carefully looped it around his neck so she could hold each end in her small hands. "I don't know why you married me, Josiah. I don't know at all. You're hard for me to understand, but I do know why I married you."

Speechless, he merely stared at her. She tugged on the scarf. "Don't you want to know why?"

He shook his head. "No."

"I'm going to tell you anyway. I married you because I love you." She waited, watched the expression in his uncovered eye. Something lurked there, something she couldn't define, and wasn't at all certain she liked. "I know I'm not Allyson. I can't ever be Allyson, but there's no need for you to grieve alone, Josiah. At least let me be your friend. I'd like to share that with you."

His throat constricted. "You can't." His voice sounded oddly hoarse.

"Yes I can. Because my heart beats with yours now. I know why you didn't come home today."

She couldn't possibly. "You do?"

"Yes. You were afraid you'd like being married to me too much." She couldn't quite bring herself to say the words, but she figured he'd probably discern their meaning.

"I am not going to bed you, Emmy." He said, cutting directly to the heart of the matter.

"I know. And in truth, I don't think I'd let you. I

couldn't bear to know you'd be wishing I was somebody else."

He started to say he wouldn't, then changed his mind. It would be a lot easier if she thought that, than if she guessed the truth. He couldn't tell her she was slowly working her way under his skin. He couldn't tell her he was afraid he'd forget what Allyson had looked like, felt like, once he'd held Emmy Greene in his arms and made love to her. He sure as hell couldn't tell her that just thinking about it made his heart ache, and his body hurt, and the blood ring in his ears.

So he stared at her, and she stared at him, and before he had time to think about it, he jammed his hat on his head and stalked out the door, slamming it behind him.

Emmy felt limp as a wrung-out dishrag. The flash of pain in his eye just then had nearly killed her. But it wasn't as bad, she knew, as it would be to lie in Josiah's bed and know he was pretending she was Allyson. Emmy almost wished she'd met Allyson Brickston. At least then, she would have known what she was dealing with. As it was, she'd been left to conjure up pictures of a paragon of virtue and femininity. Someone Joss had known and loved before that cold, haunted look had permanently fixed itself in his gaze.

Wearily, she walked back to the stove and picked up the boiling kettle of water so she could haul it into the bathroom. She hoped there would be enough to at least partially heat the frigid pump water she'd used to fill the tub.

She dumped the water, then peeled off her dirty clothes. She stuffed them in the basket she'd dragged into the bathing closet. When she'd secured her hair in a coil on top of her head, she sank down in the warm water. "I'm going to win this battle, Josiah Brickston. And don't you think I won't."

Joss paused, his axe in mid-swing, and stared at the curtains. Emmy evidently didn't know the thin muslin did almost nothing to disguise the sight of her silhouette as she removed her clothes and prepared for her bath. His body was, at once, sweaty and hard.

When Emmy reached her long, perfectly shaped arms above her head to secure her hair, her breasts stretched, expanded. Joss savagely drove the axe into the frozen block of wood. It split all the way down the center. With an angry curse, he tossed the two pieces onto the growing woodpile, then raised the axe again.

He was still wary over how easily she'd accepted his request about her family. He wondered just how she was going to react when Robert Greene tried to force a confrontation. He swung the axe again.

For now, she seemed oddly content to stay home and clean his house, a thought that made his stomach clench. He was treating her like a maidservant. Had, in fact, virtually told her that was what he wanted. He felt guilty. And hollow.

Always hollow. Before Emmy, all he'd ever needed was a brief memory of Allyson cradling Adam's dead body, or the thought of Michael gasping for breath and dying in his arms, to clear his head and refocus his attention. But Emmy was chipping away at him.

He was losing hold, and he didn't like it. Unwittingly, he raised his eyes again and saw her stand up in the tub, reach for something. The movement made her full breasts gently sway. The curve of her shoulder, and the tilt of her spine, seemed to beg for his hands. When he saw the rounded shape of her buttocks, he groaned, then attacked another log. She was going to be the death of him.

With a slight smile, Emmy settled back in the tub and let her eyes drift shut. She listened intently to the sound of Josiah chopping wood. She was tempted to stand up again, just to give him one more look, but she didn't. It wouldn't do to be overly obvious. She would have to save that for later.

"What the hell are you doing here?" Avery Brooks stood in the doorway of room eight. He stared angrily at his visitor in the hall. From his position by the window, the Diamond Hawk could clearly see Avery's back, but not the other man's face.

"It's important."

Avery glanced over his shoulder where Rosalynd was stretched asleep and naked on the bed, snoring softly. "It can't be this important."

The man in the hallway made an impatient noise. "While you've been in here rutting with that bitch, things are falling apart."

"What do you mean?"

"It's him again. The Diamond Hawk."

Avery swore. "Did he stop the heist at Southfork?"

"Yep. The boys are scared. They don't wanna go out no more."

The Diamond Hawk leaned closer to the window and strained for a glimpse of the shadowy figure in the hallway. Avery's blond head blocked his view. "Well, tell them to get unscared," Avery said. "I pay them enough."

The man in the hallway shook his head. The Diamond Hawk caught a brief flash from a gold tooth. "It'll have to be more."

Avery dragged a hand through his disheveled hair as he glanced at Rosalynd once more. She mumbled something and rolled over. "Look," he said, turning back to the man in the hallway. "We need the next haul. There's one of him and six of you. What's the problem?"

The man shrugged. "All I know is, there weren't no take tonight, and Mace is dead."

"Dead? My God! You mean that bastard actually killed someone?"

The Diamond Hawk tensed. He'd heard the gunshot while he was galloping away from the scuffle at South-fork. He didn't know anyone had died. The man in the hallway was shaking his head. "Not the Hawk. Wade drew on the bastard while he was gallopin' away. When he fired, Mace got in the way of the shot."

From the window, he saw Avery's shoulders draw tight. "Does anyone else know about this?" he asked.

"No. We weren't sure what you wanted us to do with the body."

"Leave it there," Avery said.

"For the buzzards?"

"No. For Gray Lawford." Avery cast a final glance over his shoulder, then stepped into the hall. "Listen carefully," he said, as he pulled the door shut behind him.

The Diamond Hawk levered himself off the roof and dropped to the ground with a soft *plop*. It was time to pay Emerelda another visit.

# *Eleven*

Within the week, Emmy had Joss into a perpetual sweat. Each time he came home, she appeared to have discovered a new way to torture him. First, it had been the rows of her undergarments hanging on hastily strung clotheslines. He'd come riding up the hill to find a rainbow of silks and laces waving in the breeze.

Next had been the bewitching scents he found throughout the house. In his bedroom, honeysuckle and lavender clung to the pillows. In his loft office, the lemon oil furniture polish would slowly permeate the air as the afternoon sun heated the gleaming surfaces. Her cooking filled the air with smells that made his mouth water.

With a certainty born of dread, he realized that day by day, she was wedging her way into a permanent place in his life. That afternoon, he'd passed Robert Greene on the street and barely resisted the urge to slam his corpulent body against a wall. He had known from the beginning that trapping Robert and Allyson's killers would take time. From the day he'd set foot in Carding, he'd been prepared to wait, but his marriage to Emmy had given him a new urgency. Eventually, he'd bring Robert to his knees. He only hoped he could keep his sanity in the meantime.

When he entered the house that night, his temper spiked three notches at the sight of Emmy, clad in a faded dress, standing by the stove. He shouldn't have appreciated the sight as much as he did. Irrationally, he scanned the room, looking for a reason to vent his frustration.

His gaze landed on a pencil drawing she'd tacked to the wall. "What's this?"

She put two plates on the table. In the week since their wedding, Joss had managed to virtually ignore her. On two separate occasions he hadn't come home at all, claiming he'd slept in the office rather than make the long trip up the bluff. She'd been fighting a losing battle with despair for days, and his sudden burst of temper threatened to undo her. "Alex drew it for me. Jade sent it in a letter today."

Joss snatched the drawing off the wall and thrust it at her. "I don't want it on the wall."

"Josiah . . ."

He folded it neatly and offered it to her again. "Take it, or I'll destroy it."

Swallowing, Emmy wiped her hands on her apron so she could take the tiny picture from him. She knew why he didn't want to see the picture, of course. It would remind him of the pictures his own children must have once drawn and proudly tacked to the walls.

Without comment, Emmy slipped the picture between two books on the small bookshelf. When she turned back to him, she laid her hand on his sleeve. He flinched, but she didn't let go. "Why don't you sit down, Josiah? Dinner's almost ready."

He stood stock still for several seconds as he visibly struggled with his demons. She heard his breathing, heard the rasp of the deep even breaths. His gaze met hers in the firelight. She felt a sudden quickening of her pulse when she saw the fire in his gaze. So slowly that it seemed almost unreal, his large hand rose to cover hers on his arm. His lips parted. The scar beneath his patch seemed to whiten and draw tight. The slightest hint of a sigh passed his parted lips and fanned her face. Unconsciously, she swayed closer to him. With a groan, Josiah pressed his lips to hers.

Relief and heat, and something else, something stronger, swamped through her as she clung to his forearm. His lips rocked over hers in a whisper-soft caress. Her fingers fluttered in his. Her heart seemed to stop beating, then take off in a rapid fire pace when he moved his free hand to her shoulder.

His fingers found the sensitive skin beneath her heavy braid, and he trailed the roughened pads of his fingertips down the delicate ridge of her spine. With a gasp, she closed the slight distance between them. "Oh, Josiah."

At the sound of his name, his hands abruptly fell away. She forced her eyes open, found the mix of emotions in his gaze bare seconds before he masked it. With a jerk, he pulled his arm from her grasp. "I'm not hungry tonight. I think I'll go back to the office." Before she could react, he jammed his hat down on his head, then hurried to open the door. "Don't wait up for me."

Emmy sucked in a gasp when the door slammed shut. She wiped angrily at the tears that threatened to fall. How she wished they didn't come so readily. Her lips still tingled from his kiss. Her flesh still felt heated where he'd touched her. The fine hairs on the back of her neck still seemed to prickle from the caress of his fingers. And he'd rejected her. The moment he'd realized he held Emmy and not Allyson, he'd pushed her away from him.

Miserable, she sank into the slat-back rocker to stare at the fire.

In the week since their wedding, she'd done everything she could think of to keep busy. She'd cleaned the house from top to bottom, scrubbed the brass fittings until they gleamed, worked for hours to polish the puncheon floorboards, and scraped away layers of dust and dirt on the walls. She'd cleaned the large windows in the loft inside and out, made curtains for the downstairs windows, shoveled hay and dirt out of the makeshift stable in one of the out buildings where Joss kept the horses, and even finished his laundry.

But nothing had taken her mind off the growing feeling of dread that Josiah was slipping away from her. Oh, sometimes, she would catch him staring at her in a way that made her heart beat faster and her blood start to heat, but he hardly ever touched her—went out of his way to avoid it in fact. And except for her letter from Jade that afternoon, there had been nothing to take her mind off her troubles. Twice she'd asked to visit her family and twice he'd said no. If she wasn't so afraid of pushing him even further away from her, she'd go anyway, just to get a reaction out of him.

Emmy pulled up the edge of her petticoat and mopped at her eyes. One day soon, she was going to have to invest in a handkerchief.

"I see you are in need of my assistance once again."

With a gasp, she dropped the hem of her skirt. The Diamond Hawk lounged in her doorway. "I—I didn't think I'd see you again."

He stepped into the room, shutting the door behind him. "It was difficult to find you, I'll admit."

She nodded. "I'm married." Emmy vaguely wondered why this stranger made her feel so inane.

"I heard." He strolled across the room to lean on the mantel. "Is that the cause of your distress this evening?"

Emmy wavered on indecision. She longed to confide in someone, anyone, after the long days of isolation, but somehow she couldn't bring herself to discuss the matter with him. It was too personal. It hurt too much. "Do you have more stones you want me to look at?"

He shook his head. The ends of the dark mask swished against his shoulders. "It is something else."

Emmy leaned back in her chair. His gaze was no less intense than she remembered, but something about him had changed. There was a new wariness, a tension she hadn't noticed before. "I will help you if I can," she said.

"Why, I wonder?"

Emmy brushed at a stain on her apron. "I told you before, you intrigued me with those stones. I would like to know where all this is leading." And who you are. And why you're doing this.

He seemed to make a quick decision. "There are several pieces in Brooks' Mercantile that I would like you to look at."

Emmy looked at him in surprise. "Do you believe Avery is selling false gems?"

"They appear to be similar quality to the stones I brought you. I'm not certain, though. It could be the light."

"Possibly. It's rather dark in there. It would be difficult to tell."

"But you can do it?"

"Perhaps. When would you like to know?"

"As soon as you can tell me," he said. "Would you be able to look at them tomorrow?"

Emmy thought about Joss. He probably wouldn't care if she went into town so long as she left him out of it. "Yes. I think so."

"How will you let me know?" he asked.

Emmy thought it over. "If I have anything to tell you, I'll wear the black ribbon in my hair. Will that be all right?"

"I'll see it. May I meet you somewhere?"

She hesitated. She had no way of knowing whether Josiah would be home the following evening. It would be risky to meet the Diamond Hawk there in the house. "On the bluff by the river junction. Under the tree," she said.

"I know the place. I'll be there."

"I might not be able to get away."

"I'll wait until dawn. If not, I'll understand." He turned to go, and Emmy held out her hand to him. He looked at her in surprise. "Yes?"

"You—you didn't kill that man two nights ago? Did you?"

His eyes glistened behind the mask. "Do you think I did?"

Emmy met his gaze. "They found a piece of black silk in his hand."

"Black silk is not so uncommon."

"His partner said you killed him."

"But do you think I killed him?"

Emmy hesitated only briefly before she shook her head. "No. No, I don't."

He nodded. "Thank you for that. I would not want you to be afraid of me. I value your opinion." When he turned to leave, his black cape billowed out behind him. "By the way," he said, as he pulled open the door, "my congratulations on your wedding."

"Thank you," she mumbled at the same instant he pulled the door shut behind him.

Emmy was still staring at the door when a knock sounded a full ten minutes later. She frowned. It couldn't be Joss. He wouldn't knock. Neither would the Diamond Hawk for that matter. She walked to the door and pulled it open. "Gray."

He stalked inside the house. "Damn it, Em. Don't ever open the door without checking who's there first."

She frowned at him. "It's nice to see you too."

Gray pulled his dove-colored hat off, wiped a hand over his face. "Is he still here?"

"Is who still here?"

His silver stare hardened. "Don't play games with me, Emmy."

"Joss is in town," she hedged.

"That's not what I meant."

Emmy planted her hands on her hips. "Then what do you mean?"

"You know damn well. Is that bastard still here?"

"Stop yelling at me." She drew a calming breath. "I assume you're speaking of the Diamond Hawk."

"Don't tell me you've taken to calling him by that ridiculous name."

"Well, what else am I supposed to call him? 'That bastard' seems a bit unladylike."

Gray let out a long breath. "Charlie Dopple scared the wits out of me when he told me he'd seen him leaving your place. What was he doing here, Emmy?"

Taking Gray's hat, she dropped it on one of the mirror-polished brass hooks. "Asking my advice."

Gray slanted her a skeptical look as he pulled out a chair from the table. "You know a lot about thieving?"

"No, but I know a lot about gems."

Gray straddled the chair and drummed his fingers on the back. "Is that what he's after?"

"I don't know. He asks me questions. I answer them. That's all."

"Do you know he's wanted for murder?" Gray said.

"Do you think he killed Mace Johnson?"

Gray paused, then shook his head. "No. Somebody sure wanted me to think he did, though."

"Then why are you so worried about his being here?"

"Because I do know he's decided to take the law into his own hands. Men like that can be dangerous." Gray raised his nose and sniffed appreciatively. "Say, Em, what's that you got cooking?"

"Brunswick stew."

He shot a wary glance at the two empty bowls on the table. "Would it be too much trouble?" he asked.

She paused. Josiah wasn't going to eat it. She might as well feed Gray. She'd made more than enough for three people anyway. If Joss did come home, there'd still be plenty for him. She picked up the bowl, then crossed to the stove to ladle out the stew for Gray. "Do you think he's dangerous?" she asked, still intrigued by Gray's concern over the Diamond Hawk.

Gray accepted the bowl and two hot biscuits. "Thanks. I think any number of things. I just don't have any proof yet."

Emmy plunked the catsup bowl and a jar of crushed red peppers down on the table. "What's that supposed to mean?"

Gray liberally laced his stew with catsup and peppers before he looked at her again. "Nothing I'm going to tell you right now, Emmy. So sit down and eat with me. I don't like to eat alone."

"Neither do I," she sighed, picking up her bowl.

Joss trudged wearily up the hill. He felt more sore and more guilty than he had all week. He shouldn't have kissed her, shouldn't have even touched her, but she'd been so damned close, so soft. The minute she'd spoken his name, he'd felt a ripping terror pass through him. He'd hoped a game of cards and a stiff drink would ease his panic, but they hadn't. He led his horse into the paddock. When he saw the fresh bucket of oats and water in the corner of the hastily built stall, he shook his head. Emmy took better care of his animals than he did. He stroked the horse's nose for several seconds as he thought of Allyson.

She'd never liked horses, was scared to death of them in fact. The thought of Allyson shoveling manure and hauling fresh hay was almost funny. She had begged him not to teach Adam and Michael how to ride, but Joss had done it anyway. Even at two, Adam had begun to show an affinity for his pony. Michael, on the other hand, had been his mother's child.

He shut the stable gate and leaned back against the wall to stare at the moon. His gentle wife had worked herself to death during the long week since their wedding. It looked and smelled and felt like a home now, instead of the squalid temporary shelter he'd lived in before. The notion that Allyson would have liked it, found it a bit rustic was true, but liked it all the same, had occurred to him more than once.

But that wasn't the worst of it. He hadn't wanted to want her, had, in fact, told himself he wouldn't, but it hadn't worked.

Every time he looked at her, he wanted her more. He wanted to know if the fire he saw in her hair would translate into passion. He wanted to know if the ripe curves of her figure he could see outlined beneath her faded clothes would fill his hands as perfectly as he suspected they would. Each time he touched her, her body yielded to his with an intoxicating readiness that made his head swim. He had vowed a thousand times to buy her a corset, and had changed his mind a thousand and one. He was becoming addicted to the womanly feel of her, the way she leaned into him when he touched her waist, the quiet yearning he saw in her eyes. Kissing her tonight had brought back memories of their heated kiss the afternoon of the thunderstorm.

He felt his body harden at the thought of what it would be like to fully make love to his wife, to taste her flesh and feel her heat. He wanted to touch her softness, run his fingers over the ripe, satiny peach of her skin, press his lips to her warmth. He ached with wanting it.

In the last week, he'd chopped enough wood to last them through the winter and well into spring.

With a soft groan, Joss pushed away from the stable wall, recognizing the familiar heaviness that had settled in his loins. He couldn't give into it. He just couldn't.

He started up the hill. The light seeping through the windows surprised him. He'd expected her to be in bed long ago, but a brief sniff told him the fire was still lit, and something else. Yes, dinner still sat on the stove. Brunswick stew unless he missed his guess. He decided he'd sit down, have a bowl, then apologize for his surly behavior.

Until he saw Gray Lawford's horse hitched in front of the house.

"What are you doing here, Lawford?" Joss shoved open the door.

Gray swallowed another spoonful of stew before glancing at Joss. "Enjoying your hospitality it would seem. Evening, Joss."

Emmy leapt from her chair and started toward him. "Are you hungry, Josiah? There's plenty of stew left."

He met her gaze with an unreadable expression, then dropped his hat on a shiny brass hook. "I'm half-starved, wife." He dropped a hard, brief kiss on her lips. Damned if he knew why he did it, but something about the sight of Gray Lawford sitting at his table, cozy as you please, while Emmy laughed at something he said, set Joss's blood to boil.

Emmy stared at him in shock. Joss brushed a lock of her hair off her heated forehead. He felt like a heel, and the wary look in her eyes twisted his gut. "Are you going to feed me or not?"

There was a quiet teasing in his voice she'd never heard before. Wordlessly, she brushed a light covering of dust off his shoulders, then hurried toward the stove. Joss frowned when he saw her hands trembling. He'd upset her tonight. Somebody should just shoot him and get it over with. He took the seat across from Gray Lawford. "You still haven't answered my question, Gray. What brings you to the bluff in the middle of the night?"

Gray leaned back in his chair. Emmy put a bowl of stew in front of Joss, picked up his napkin, refolded it, then hurried back to the stove. "I was just calling on Em," Gray said. "You never know who's going to turn up in the middle of the night."

Joss dumped a spoonful of red peppers in his stew. Emmy placed a plate of biscuits on the table, then folded Joss's napkin again before she retreated toward the icebox. "Is that so?" Joss asked. He took a bite of his stew. "You concerned about something in particular?"

Emmy returned with the butter. She nearly dropped it on the table when she heard Joss's question. To cover her discomfort, she refolded his napkin a third time. She would have scuttled off again if Joss hadn't snaked a hand around her wrist and pulled her into the chair beside him. She could barely breathe past the nervous lump in her throat. She had no idea how to read him in this mood. "Isn't this nice, Josiah? Gray is our first guest."

Joss arched an eyebrow at her, then returned his attention to Gray. "Are you?"

"Your first guest? I wouldn't likely know."

Joss frowned. "Concerned about something in particular," he clarified.

Gray shook his head. His expression turned sober. "No. Just looking I guess. Don't suppose you've heard anything you'd like to tell me about?"

The double-edged conversation made Emmy squirm. "What do you mean, Gray?"

Joss squeezed her hand under the table. "I already promised I'd keep you informed, Marshal. You'll have to take my word."

Gray tipped the chair back on its hind legs so he could level his silver gaze at Joss. "I could help you, Josiah. I don't know why you're so determined not to let me."

Swallowing another bite of stew, Joss shrugged. "My choice, I suppose."

Gray righted his chair with a *plunk*. He stood up, nodding briefly to Emmy. "Thanks for the meal, Em. I hope you'll remember what I said."

Emmy nodded. She would have stood up to walk with Gray to the door, but Joss clamped a hand on her thigh. "I will, Gray," she said. She gave her husband a puzzled look. "Be careful going back to town."

Gray strolled to the door where he picked up his hat and dropped it on his dark head. "G'night, Em." He nodded at Joss. "Joss."

"Good night, Gray," Emmy said. She waited until he slipped through the door to glare at Joss. "I don't know why you feel you have to be so rude to him. What has Gray Lawford ever done to you?"

Joss polished off a biscuit, then took a long drink of water. "This stew is wonderful, Emmy. You should make it more often."

She mumbled an unladylike curse beneath her breath as she walked to the door. Slamming the bolt into place, she took several long breaths before she faced him again. "What were you two talking about just now?"

"Things that don't need to concern you."

Emmy stalked back to the table where she sat in Gray's abandoned seat. "Well, isn't that just fine? You get to treat me like your personal slave while you and Gray talk in circles."

Joss finished his stew, then levered up from his chair to walk to the stove. As he ladled himself another bowlful, he looked over his shoulder at Emmy. He waved the ladle at her. "Do you want more?"

"No," she snapped. She brushed the biscuit crumbs on the table into a neat pile before refolding Joss's napkin. "I want you to tell me what's going on."

Joss sat. "Nothing's going on, Em."

"Do you expect me to believe that you and Gray just bristle around each other for no cause?"

Joss laced his stew with peppers before he looked at her. How could he explain that the kiss had left him reeling? How could he explain why her affection for Gray Lawford bothered him when he didn't know the reasons? Much as he'd like to, he couldn't deny that the emotion that had fueled his rudeness to Gray was the streak of jealousy he'd felt when he'd seen the easy way Emmy laughed and talked to him. Frustrated, he decided to tell her the truth, but leave out the more pertinent facts. "Gray thinks I know something about Allyson's murder I'm not saying." He stuck a spoonful of stew in his mouth.

Emmy stared at him. "Do you?" Her voice sounded strangled.

Joss shook his head. "Nothing Gray needs to know. I'll tell him when the time comes."

"Josiah, don't you think . . ."

"Now's not the time, Em."

Anxious, she fell silent as she watched him eat. Joss had not spoken to her about anything beyond the most mundane of details since their wedding. She wasn't sure why, but she was almost certain that the tension between Gray Lawford and her husband was somehow related to Joss's odd behavior tonight.

Joss finished off his stew in silence before he looked at her again. "Why was Gray here, Emmy?" he finally asked her. He wondered if she'd tell the truth.

She started lining up the bottles and jars on the tables. Joss scowled at the telling action. Whenever she was nervous or upset, she invariably went into a cleaning frenzy.

Emmy searched for a coherent explanation for Gray's appearance on the bluff. She didn't want to lie to Josiah, but she didn't want to tell him about the Diamond Hawk either. Somehow, she couldn't make herself concentrate on the issue of Gray's visit, when she wanted, more than anything, to discuss why Joss had walked away from her earlier. Given the unpredictability of his mood, she feared raising the issue with him. If he forbade her to see Gray, then there would be nothing to relieve her growing feeling of isolation. "Gray was worried about me," she whispered. She decided the sugar bowl was fatter than the catsup bowl and reversed their order.

"Why?" Joss asked.

Emmy's fingers stilled on the salter. She looked at him. "He just was. Gray and I are very close, and I haven't seen him since our wedding." She picked up Josiah's napkin and began folding it in minute accordion pleats.

Joss snorted in derision. "I should think Gray Lawford would know it's usual for newly wedded couples to disappear for weeks at a time."

Emmy stood up with such haste her chair tipped over. She scooped up his bowl and headed for the sink. "But then, we're not a usual newly wedded couple. Are we?" She dropped the dishes in the sink with a loud clatter.

Joss swore. He'd deserved that. Hell, he probably deserved for Emmy to throw the kettle at him. "Emmy . . ."

She started pumping water. "I don't want to talk about it right now, Josiah."

"Emmy, listen to me."

She pumped harder. The handle squeaked as water gushed onto the dishes. "No. Please. I'm too drawn out tonight. If we talk about this now, I might make an utter fool of myself and start to cry."

Joss covered his face with his hands. With his elbows propped on the table, he wearily stroked his brow. "Ah, Emmy. What have I done to you?"

She heard the slight note of anguish in his voice. Despite her determination, she couldn't resist its pull. She stopped pumping water, wiped her hands on her apron, then walked to his side.

His big shoulders were slumped over the table. His dark hair spilled through his strong, bronzed fingers. Emmy placed her hands on his back to softly stroke the corded muscles. He flinched, but didn't pull away. "You won't let me be your wife, Josiah. Please tell me what you want."

Her voice cracked on the last word and it proved to be Joss's undoing. He turned in his chair so he could topple her into his lap. To her horror, Emmy started to cry. Joss ran a hand down her spine. "Emmy, please don't cry."

"I'm sorry. I can't help it."

She sounded so thoroughly miserable, that Joss settled her more firmly against him. He tossed her spectacles on the table so she'd be more comfortable pillowed against his chest. "I've acted like an arrogant bastard, haven't I?" he asked.

She nodded. "Yes."

"And I hurt your feelings."

"Yes."

"And I've been mean-tempered and surly since the day of the wedding."

"Yes."

"And I've acted unreasonably rude about your friends."

"Yes."

Joss managed a slight smile over her head. "Feel free to stop me at any time."

"You're not done yet," she said, as she burrowed against him.

"Have I left something out?"

She raised her tear-streaked face from his shoulder. "You treat me like a stranger, Josiah. Even tonight when you kissed me. You almost seemed to resent me for it."

He wavered on indecision. If he bared his soul to her, she'd own a piece of him. "The memories are painful, Emmy. Sometimes they get the better of me."

"Then why don't you share them with me instead of letting them destroy you?"

"Because I can't. I can't share them with anyone."

Joss's voice sounded strained. She mopped her eyes with the hem of her apron. "I'm just the woman who cleans your house, and does your laundry, just like you said I'd be."

He shook his head. "That's not true." Joss fished into his pocket to pull out his white cotton handkerchief.

She used it to blow her nose. "Yes, it is true." She met his gaze. "Why are you doing this to me?" Her voice caught on a sob.

Joss moved his big hand up her spine. "It's not something I can talk about right now. I never meant for you to feel . . ." he searched for the right word.

"Unwanted?" she supplied.

Joss winced. "Is that what it feels like?"

"You needn't fret over it," she assured him. "It's a feeling I'm used to. I've always been an outsider, Josiah. Ever since my mother died and my father left me with Uncle Robert and his family, I've never had a place of my own." She paused and looked around. "Now that I do, I'm not welcome here either. I just need time to adjust."

Joss's stomach turned over as his conscience kicked him square in the head. He had treated her miserably. She was right. Allyson, his mother, in fact just about every decent woman he knew would gladly skin him alive for what he'd done to her. In his thirst for vengeance against Robert Greene, he'd irrevocably, inexcusably, bruised Emmy. "I'm sorry if that's the way it felt, Emmy. I never meant for you to feel unwanted."

He carefully pushed several wet tendrils of hair off her cheeks. "What can I do to make you feel better?"

Make me your wife, she thought. Come to my bed and let me know you're not sorry you married me. "I'm so alone."

"It's very isolated up here, but you're not a prisoner. You can go into town any time you like. I never meant to imply you couldn't."

"But I can't go see my family."

"No." He couldn't allow that. Robert Greene would find a way to manipulate her. He knew it.

"But why?"

"I can't explain that right now. I'll have to ask you to trust me." At her stricken look, Joss exhaled a long breath. "Suppose I arrange for Jade and Alex to come for a visit?"

Emmy looked at him in surprise. How had he known she would miss Alex and Jade most? She could not re-member ever discussing her family with him in any intimate detail and she felt gratified that he'd noticed such a personal preference. She favored him with a smile. "I would like that very much."

He studied her for a minute, feeling like a cad that such a small concession should bring her so much pleasure. Yes, he had treated her badly. Very badly. And just because he was finding it virtually impossible to keep his hands off of her, was no excuse for his behavior. "While we're on the subject," he said, "I think you should know how much I appreciate your loyalty. Many women in your place would have attempted to go behind my back. I know you haven't had any contact with your family, and I'm grateful."

"I'm not most women, Josiah. I hope, one day, you'll see that. I still don't understand why you married me, or what you want from me, but I wouldn't deliberately break my word. You may count on that. I told you that I married you because I love you. If you choose not to accept that, then so be it, but I wouldn't do anything to hurt you, even if your request seems unreasonable to me."

The unabashed honesty he saw in her eyes made him shudder. With a heavy sigh, Joss kissed her forehead. The faint scent of honeysuckle and cleaning acid assaulted his senses. He sucked in a breath, wondering why in the name of God it had to be Emmy and not one of her ugly, annoying cousins, who controlled Robert Greene's fate. When a wash of desire pooled in his groin, Joss frowned in frustration. He couldn't take much more of this.

He eased Emmy off his lap to set her away from him. He found he was not quite ready to stop touching her though, so he straightened her rust-colored blouse with careful precision. He neatly adjusted the folds where they were tucked into her heather gray skirt. "Better?" he asked finally, not trusting himself to say much more.

She seemed to realize his question went beyond the state of her clothes. "Better," she said quietly.

When he stood, he almost toppled her over. One-eyed sight, he'd learned, severely affected his perception. He hadn't realized she stood so close. He had to steady her with a hand at her waist. Instantly, he regretted it. The soft feel of her flesh asked for his embrace. "I think I'll go cut some wood," he muttered.

Emmy scooted out of his way. "Will you be in late?"

He paused, his hat in his hand, and looked back at her. In the firelight, her red-gold hair haloed around her face. The delicate peach flush in her cheeks made him long to touch her. The memory of how soft she'd felt when he'd held her in his lap was too fresh, too easily summoned to mind. He crammed his hat on his head. "Yes. I will." Very, very late. He'd have to chop a hell of a lot of wood if he hoped to sleep any tonight. If he hadn't known better, he'd have sworn that Emmy giggled just before he slammed the door shut.

# Twelve

"Josiah?" Emmy touched his shoulder. He was still dressed, as if he'd fallen on the bed in exhaustion. Sweat soaked his shirt. Emmy could see the moisture beaded on his forehead and upper lip. When she touched him again, he mumbled something in his sleep and jerked away. In the dim light of the fire, she saw the pained expression on his face and it frightened her. "Josiah, what's wrong?"

She had no idea when he'd come to bed, but he'd awakened her when he'd started thrashing about in the throes of a nightmare. He'd said Allyson's name just before his breathing had become shallow and erratic. Emmy shook his shoulder again. "Josiah, wake up. It's a dream."

Joss's eyes flew open. He blankly stared at her. His chest heaved with the great effort it cost him just to breathe. "It's a dream," she whispered again.

The world snapped into focus. He'd been back in the dust, begging Michael not to die. A harsh pain tore through him. His body jerked in reaction. Emmy sat watching him. Her features were barely visible in the dim fire light. Joss was sure she could hear the ragged pounding of his heart.

Emmy's eyes were dark with concern. Her cool hand rested on his sweat-soaked shoulder where her fingers rubbed gentle circles. Her unbound hair streamed over her shoulders in a cascade of golden fire. Joss's chest tightened into a painful knot. Desire, fueled by the lingering images of the dream, and driven by days of wanting her, pooled in his groin and coursed through his body until the blood rang in his ears. And Joss surrendered.

He couldn't fight her and his demons too. He needed her closeness, her softness, her warmth. Her life. Joss stared at her for several seconds while a host of conflicting emotions fought for his attention. He wasn't sure what had brought the dream back, but he sure as hell knew what would make it go away. At least for now, for tonight, he could be free of it.

Not giving himself or her time to think about it, Joss clasped Emmy's head in his hands. Tugging her down across his chest, he whispered, "I need you, Em." He settled his mouth on hers in a kiss that soared instantly out of control.

Momentarily stunned, she lay passively against him while his hot mouth caressed her lips. "Open for me, love," he said. He applied gentle pressure to her chin with his thumb. "I need to be inside."

Emmy was lost. She parted her lips and welcomed him. She didn't even try to pretend she didn't want what he was doing to her.

At her acquiescence, desire roared through Joss's blood in a torrent. Looming over her, he pushed her back against the bed linens with the pressure of his mouth. God, she tasted sweet. "I tried, Emmy." He dragged his lips from hers and ran them along the line of her cheek. "I tried to keep my hands off you. I swear I tried."

She was starting to worry that he might still pull away from her, so she twined her hands around his neck to thread her fingers into the damp hair at his nape. An-

choring him there, she kissed him back as thoroughly
as he'd taught her how.

With a groan, Joss rocked his lips over hers again
and again seeking solace and warmth. He sucked in a
great breath of air when he felt her tongue duel restlessly with his. He coaxed it into his mouth and waited
excruciating seconds for her tender, tentative explora-
tion. He was on fire. The sheer force of emotions raging through him drove away any vestige of his control.

Emmy sighed in pleasure as the heat of him sent
tingling sensations all the way to her toes. The inside
of his mouth was hot and rough, and she whimpered
when she felt his teeth scrape over the sensitive underside of her tongue.

Joss's hands skimmed over her body, unimpeded by
the beige cotton of her nightdress. She arched into
him, then trailed one of her hands over his shoulders
and down the muscled plane of his back. When she
wedged one bare leg between his denim-clad ones to
rub her foot along the hard line of his calf, he gasped
in pleasure. She had a need to touch him, to soothe
the tension away and with it, the pain that had ravaged
his dreams.

Joss tore his mouth from hers. The tiny noises she
was making inflamed him. The way she'd turned to fire
in his hands fueled a desire so fierce and so strong, he
wanted to drown his memories in it. Emmy's softness
was pushing away the demons. Her warmth was melting
the frozen knot of guilt. Guilt. Joss dragged in a ragged
breath and tried to slow down, to give her time.
"Emmy, God, I can't—" His voice ended in a groan
when her wandering hand reached the waistband of
his Levi's.

"Please, Josiah," she whispered. "I have wanted to
be your wife for so very long."

His breath came out on a low hiss. Ruthlessly, he

pushed reality aside. She wanted this. He needed it. For tonight, it would be enough. Bending his head, he nuzzled the side of her neck. When he found the sensitive hollow behind her ear, he nearly went crazy. Her scent, that alluring, honeysuckle scent that had driven him mad for days, was potent and powerful there. Joss licked it with his tongue.

Emmy bucked against him when a current of sensation shot through her blood. "Josiah."

He groaned when she said his name in that low, throaty voice. He stabbed his tongue into her ear. "Touch me." His command was soft. He slid one hand along her arm until his fingers laced with hers. He brought her hand to his chest. "Touch me, Emmy. Please."

Her fingers curled into the soft fabric of his shirt. He licked the sensitive whorl of her ear before he moved his mouth along her jaw once more and captured her lips in a deep, ravaging kiss. The instant his tongue slipped into her mouth, her fingers moved inexorably to the buttons of his shirt.

She'd never seen Joss undressed before. Emmy delighted in uncovering now what she'd only imagined in the daylight. She was concentrating so hard on the buttons, she didn't even notice that his fingers were working the hem of her beige sleeping gown until she felt his warm hand on the back of her thigh. She gasped. Joss sighed her name into her mouth.

Emmy pulled so hard on the buttons of his shirt that several popped off. Greedily, she plunged both hands inside and twined her fingers in the soft springy curls on his chest. "God, Em. You feel so good." His voice sounded ragged.

Emmy squirmed against him. "So do you."

Joss's hand stayed clamped on the smooth skin of her thigh, while his other came up to cup her breast through the thin lawn of her nightdress. He rubbed his palm over the peak, then lifted his head to watch as the nipple hardened. "You're so quick to my touch." He sounded almost awed. "All I have to do is run my hands over you and you start to quiver."

It took a great deal less than that, Emmy thought as she squirmed against him. The flood of warmth in her body was starting to expand into an inferno. She couldn't seem to keep still. She wedged her thigh tighter between his legs. His startled gasp sent satisfaction pouring through her. "You too," she whispered.

Emmy's fingers fluttered over his chest in the barest of caresses until he nearly exploded from the tender torment. She was right. He was shaking like a leaf in the wind. Bending his head, he took her firm nipple into his mouth and circled it with his tongue. He cupped the underside of her full breast in his palm so he could work the nipple through the material of her gown. The peak turned turgid. When he finally pulled it between his teeth and sucked on it, Emmy's fingers clenched in the hair on his chest.

The feel of his mouth through the wet fabric of her gown was nearly more than she could bear. She gripped his shoulders, dug her nails into the bronzed skin of his back. "Oh, Josiah."

Her voice was a gentle breeze in his hair. He lifted his head to drink in the sight of her flushed face. "You've bewitched me, Em."

She tossed her head back and forth on the pillow as she ran her bare foot over the rough fabric of his trousers. "Josiah, please."

His groin tightened at her uninhibited response. He was fast losing control, and he knew it. He had a sudden need, hot and tight and urgent, to feel her naked flesh pressed to his. His fingers moved to the buttons of her nightgown. There were dozens of them. Tiny and stiff and obstructive. He looped two fingers into the neckline of the worn gown and rent it top to bottom.

Emmy's surprised gasp turned into a moan when he pressed his bare chest against her. The sensitized peaks of her nipples pushed against his warm skin. "I'm sorry," he muttered, kissing her once more.

Emmy wasn't. God, it felt sinful. It was so decadent, so deliciously wonderful. She pushed at the fabric of his shirt. She wanted nothing between them. Joss shrugged out of it as he moved his mouth down her neck and back to the peak of her breast. He pulled her ruined nightdress free with a brief tug. "Better?" he asked, when the fabric dropped to the floor, and his shirt was torn free, and her hands were flying over him in eager caresses.

"Yes," she whispered. "Oh, yes."

When he circled his tongue around her tight nipple, without the impediment of her gown, Emmy's hands clenched into his lean waist. She pushed her pelvis against his in unwitting anticipation.

With a groan, he sucked on her nipple. Hard. Emmy's breath came in fitful pants. He felt inflamed beyond reason. When her hands moved beneath the waistband of his trousers, he gasped. Encouraged, she cupped his hard buttocks and pushed into him. "Please, Josiah."

"Emmy, it's too soon. I'll hurt you." He rubbed his fingers over her nipples, across her stomach, then firmly gripped her waist. "You have to let me slow down."

She shook her head. Her hands moved to the buttons of his trousers. If he slowed down, he'd have time to think. If he did that, he might stop. She'd die if he did. "I don't want you to slow down."

"Emmy . . ." his voice trailed off when her fingers

brushed against the hard ridge of his pulsing shaft beneath the constricting fabric of his trousers. He pulled in a deep breath and tried again. This time, he reached for her hand. But she curled her fingers against him, and there was no chance whatsoever he could deny the heat raging in his blood. "Ah, Emmy. I surrender. Hold on, love."

Joss tore open the buttons on his trousers and shoved them past his hips. He didn't have time to remove them, didn't even have time to finish removing her gown. His groin ached. He was fast reaching the realization that he might not have time for more than one or two thrusts before he spilled his seed in her womb.

His fingers found the springy curls at the apex of her thighs. He twined his hand through them until it settled on the damp flesh at the core of her feminine desire. Soft. So indescribably, intoxicatingly soft. The moist heat, the tight, slick opening, was all the incentive he needed. He slipped his hands beneath her buttocks and lifted her hips, then buried his lips on hers. He plunged inside and past the fragile barrier that marked her femininity.

Emmy gasped in surprise at the brief flash of pain. She hadn't expected it. It made her feel slightly panicked that he would think something was wrong and withdraw. She forced her eyes open to stare at the harsh lines on his face. His jaw was set now with determination and desire. His uncovered eye was clenched shut. His hair lay in unbound waves on his shoulder. She slid her hands up his back. The way his skin jumped beneath her touch amazed her. She twined her fingers through his hair.

"Hold still, Emmy," he groaned when she moved against him.

She wasn't sure, but she didn't think it was supposed to be like this. "Did I—did I do something wrong?"

Joss opened his eye. He sucked in a deep breath when he saw the flushed look on her face. "No. God, no. I don't want to hurt you. Are you all right?"

She didn't want to tell him he'd already hurt her, so she arched her neck to kiss him instead. With a groan, Joss swept his tongue into her mouth. He stroked it in and out in a blatant imitation of what his lower body clamored for. With a pleasured sigh, Emmy rotated her hips against him in unconscious seduction.

The movement hurtled him over the edge. Joss pumped into her with a barely controlled urgency that stole her breath. Her body was tightening, coiling, spiraling toward some unknown destination. She felt his body grow taut. His head reared back. The muscles of his back clenched. He exploded inside of her in long streams of wet heat.

Emmy clung to him until he collapsed on top of her. His weight pushed her into the bed. His ragged breathing fanned over her face. He stayed deep inside of her while his whole body continued to shake. She trembled as she sent up a silent, anxious prayer that she hadn't disappointed him.

And she would have asked him except that he wrapped his arms around her, rolled to his side, then promptly fell asleep with part of his body still buried in her tight warmth.

Emmy tried not to feel disappointed at his sudden withdrawal. She'd wanted the closeness to linger. Wanted to talk to him, tell him again that she loved him. Wanted him to tell her it didn't matter that she wasn't Allyson.

The thought brought a tender smile to her lips. She stroked her fingers through his hair. It hadn't been Allyson's name he'd shouted at the last.

* * *

Joss felt sick. Sunlight poured in through the window of his bedroom. He stared at the bloodstain on the white sheets, on his own groin. He'd awakened to any number of realizations, none of them pleasant.

He was alone in bed, in the house, and he had no idea where Emmy had gone. When he'd sat up and seen the blood on the sheets and smeared across his thighs, he had remembered why. He'd made love to her during the night, although he applied the term loosely, thinking perhaps 'ravaged' would have been a better description.

He was painfully aware that Emmy had found no satisfaction in the act. He'd been too aroused, too out-of-control, too damn selfish to bring her along with him, and, to make matters worse, he'd hurt her. She'd been a virgin, and he'd plowed into her, treating her little better than one of Bug Danboat's whores.

Not only had he betrayed his memory of Allyson by seducing Emmy, but he'd betrayed Emmy's trust. The sudden raw knowledge that she had not said she loved him at any time during the long night sank down on him like a lead weight. He buried his head in his hands with a disgusted groan. It should not have been as important as it was.

"Josiah." She walked into the room with a basket dangling from her hand. "Look what I found."

He raised his head. Her warm smile momentarily disoriented him. "Emmy . . ."

"Blackberries." She plucked one from the basket and popped it in his mouth. "If you have a few extra minutes, I'll make blackberry preserves for your biscuits this morning."

He stared at her as he swallowed the sweet berry. "Emmy—"

"You can wait, can't you? These are the best berries I've found all season." She ate one herself, then ran her tongue over her lips in greedy appreciation.

Joss watched the small, unconsciously seductive action. He felt his body harden. He bit off a curse of self-loathing. Even with the light of day casting a harsh glow on the truth of what he'd done during the night, he couldn't control his own desires long enough to apologize to her.

It didn't help any that she was hiding her bitterness and anger terribly well behind that bright smile. If he hadn't been sure she was upset, he never would have known it. "Emmy, I think we should talk."

She dropped the basket. "What?" Several fat berries rolled out on the floor. Emmy ignored them when she felt a sudden wash of anxiety at his grim tone.

Joss reached for his trousers. When he didn't find them by the bed, he grunted in frustration. Emmy crossed to the chest by the door and pulled out a fresh pair for him. "I put your soiled ones in the laundry basket," she explained as she handed him the tan trousers. She hoped he didn't notice how her hand was trembling. He was going to say something awful and ruin the warm feeling she'd been holding close to her heart all morning. She knew it.

Joss looked at her closely as he pulled on his pants. He had to admire her for not looking away when he was sure she must be horrified by the intimacy of watching him dress. "About last night," he said awkwardly, "about what I did—"

Emmy clasped her hands together to keep them from trembling. "You aren't going to say you're sorry you did it, are you?"

Joss frowned at her. "Well, of course I'm sorry."

Her hands flew to her mouth. "Oh, God. Please don't say that." To her horror, she felt the sting of fresh tears, damn them. How she longed to master the bad habit she had of crying at the most inopportune times.

Joss was instantly alarmed, and confused, by her reaction to his confession. He'd expected her to be upset with him, but hell, he was trying to apologize. "Emmy, wait." He crossed the room in two strides where he settled his hands on her shoulders. "Why are you crying?"

"I'm not," she insisted.

"Yes, you are." Joss felt her shoulders jerk beneath his hands. He had the distinct feeling that she'd just driven a knife through his gut. "God, sweetheart, I know I hurt you last night, but please don't cry. You're going to tear me apart."

Emmy raised her face to look at him through tear-streaked spectacles. "I'm not crying because you hurt me."

"Then why—"

"I'm crying because you said you were sorry."

Joss wrapped his arms around her. Surely she didn't mean what he thought she meant. "I am sorry. I didn't mean to hurt you, Emmy. I didn't want to hurt you."

She shook her head. "Not that you're sorry you hurt me, Josiah, which is irrelevant anyway, because you didn't. I mean not really. It wasn't as though—"

He shook her once to regain her attention. "Emmy, you're babbling. Talk to me."

"I'm crying because you're sorry we . . ." Unable to finish, she buried her face against his chest.

He drew a deep tentative breath as he stepped away from her. He took a moment to dig a handkerchief out of the cedar chest by the bed. Stuffing it into her hand, he pulled her back against him. No man should be given a second chance like this one. Dear God. His own guilt was about to eat him alive. Didn't she have any idea what he'd done to her, how he'd used her? "Emmy," he said cautiously, "I lost control. It was the dream. I, well, I didn't really know what I was doing. I needed someone, something to make me forget, but still, that's no excuse for forcing you."

Her head jerked up in surprise. The wetness in her eyes took on an ominous glitter mere seconds before she pulled her spectacles off. She wiped her wet cheeks with the back of her hand, then gently blew her nose. "You know, this was a perfectly fine morning until you ruined it, Josiah."

He stared at her. "What do you mean?"

"I felt wonderful this morning, despite what you might think, and now you had to go and insinuate that it wasn't me you wanted at all. That you forced me to . . . to . . ." She exhaled an angry breath, then dropped her glasses back on her nose. "Well, where did you come up with a damned fool idea like that?"

Joss blinked. "When did you start using language like that?"

She tapped his chest in absent agitation. "Since I learned it from you. Don't change the subject."

"What subject?"

"The one you brought up. How on earth have you managed to convince yourself that you forced me?"

"You told me no," he said.

She stared at him. "I did?"

Joss nodded. "Last week. On our wedding night. You expressly told me you didn't want me to bed you."

"Last week? You think you forced me last night because I told you no last week?"

Joss dragged a hand through his hair in frustration. She couldn't possibly be saying she'd been a willing participant. Didn't she know he'd rushed her along with no thought whatsoever to her own pleasure or needs? No, he decided, she probably didn't. When he considered the environment in which she'd grown up, he figured she'd probably had no idea whatsoever what to expect from the experience. Despite his lingering guilt, the thought did make him feel better. "My mother told me once that when a lady says no, it always means no. I wasn't aware you'd changed your mind."

Emmy muttered something in disgust. She stepped away from him to scoop up her basket of berries. "Well, you're an idiot then. I told you I didn't want you pretending you had Allyson in your bed." She started to pick up the spilled berries.

"I wasn't—"

"And you sure as hell said my name enough that I was convinced you knew which one of us it was." She went down on her knees to retrieve a berry from under the bed. Joss swallowed at the enticing view he was given of her pale green petticoats.

"Emmy—"

She bent over the long cedar chest to scoop up two fat berries. "I even convinced myself of that after you went to sleep, but here you are big as day telling me it didn't matter who it was."

"Emmy, stop."

"And to think I've been trying to figure you into bed for a week. Evidently I wasn't very good at it." She dropped a handful of berries into the basket.

Joss crossed the room in two strides. He grabbed her upper arms, then shook her once to gain her attention. "Oh, you were good at it all right." He was starting to feel better. He couldn't do much about his guilt over Allyson, but he could at least make things right with Emmy.

Emmy paused in the act of retrieving the scattered berries. "What's that supposed to mean?"

"Only that you've been driving me mad all week with

flashes of your underclothes. Hell, I've chopped enough wood to last through next winter."

"I do *not* flash my inexpressibles."

"Oh, yes you do, and that damned honeysuckle smell you're so fond of was about to drive me insane."

She looked at him skeptically. "What honeysuckle smell?"

"The one that follows you around. I found its source last night right behind your ear." He tapped the spot. "Between that and cleaning acid, you've had me so aroused it's nigh unto a miracle I haven't pounced on you before. Don't you own any white undergarments?" he demanded.

She shook her head. "I made all my inexpressibles from my cousins' discarded dresses."

Joss pushed down a surge of anger at Robert Greene. Damned bastard. "You knew it was driving me crazy, didn't you? That's why you kept hanging it out on the line. You wanted me to think about how you'd look in an orange chemise and petticoats on my way home."

Emmy stifled a pleased giggle. "I—I didn't know." All traces of her tears were gone now. She placed the errant berries in the basket. "If I'd known, I'd have made sure you saw them more often."

He shook his head. "I might not have made it if I'd seen them more often."

When relief swept through her, Emmy wrapped her arms around his waist to hug him close. "I was so afraid, Josiah."

He frowned at that. He settled his hands on her shoulders, tipping her away so he could see her face. "Did I frighten you?"

"Stop that. Have you always been so thick-headed?"

"What are you talking about?"

"You didn't frighten me last night. When you were

so careful not to touch me this week, I was afraid you didn't," she looked away, embarrassed, "want to."

"God, if I'd wanted to any more I would have exploded. I didn't want to want you, I'll admit. I was scared to death of wanting you, but there wasn't a danged thing I could do about it."

The admission had cost him. She knew it, and she knew why. She hugged him closer so she could lay her cheek against his bare chest. His skin felt so pleasantly warm. "I'm not trying to make you forget Allyson, Josiah."

His arms came around her. "I know," he said quietly. He felt another stab of guilt. He should tell Emmy the whole truth about the reasons behind their marriage. But he couldn't bring himself to ruin her growing confidence in herself, and in him, so he decided a few more weeks of guilt weren't going to make things any worse.

Emmy rubbed her cheek against the soft hairs on his chest, oblivious to the battle he was fighting. "What I told you on our wedding day was that I didn't want you pretending you had her back in your bed."

Joss swallowed hard. "That's not the reason I avoided bedding you, Emmy." He rubbed his hand up her spine as he searched for the right words. He had to tell her something. If not everything, then at least something. He owed her that. "The circumstances behind our marriage are—odd. I didn't want you to feel I'd taken advantage of you."

"I don't."

Joss exhaled a long, slow breath. Silently, he admitted the truth. Having touched her once, there was no way on earth he wasn't going to do it again. If he hoped to retain any measure of his self-respect, he damned well better spell out from the very beginning where things stood. "The truth is, Emmy, I was afraid if I made love to you, I'd start to lose sight of Allyson's memory."

She tipped her head back to look at him. "What do you mean?"

Her hair, he noticed, smelled particularly fresh this morning. He twined his fingers into the long, thick braid that hung down her back. "Allyson was the only woman I—"

His voice trailed off. If Emmy hadn't known better, she'd have sworn he was blushing. "You what?" she asked, watching in fascination as the scar on his cheek started to twitch.

"There weren't any women before Allyson," he said. "And none since. Not until you."

Emmy's eyes widened. "Do you mean to say that you never bedded anyone else but your first wife?"

Joss nodded. "Yes. You might not believe me, but it's true. Most men probably wouldn't admit to it, I know, but, well, I could never bring myself to engage in activity like that. My brothers were unmerciful about it, but it didn't matter to me."

Emmy's smile made his heart turn over. "You know, Josiah, I've worn passed-down clothes, and lived in passed-down rooms, and had passed-down belongings my whole life. The nicest dress I ever had was one of the ones my cousin Ruby threw away. It's a very warm feeling to have something that somebody else didn't discard before they gave it to me."

Despite himself, Joss felt something inside him start to thaw. "That's why I was afraid, Emmy. Allyson was the great love of my life, the once in a lifetime kind." Emmy tried to ignore the stab of pain his words caused while she waited for him to continue. "When you came along," he said, "I was worried. It seemed almost wrong that I should want you as badly as I did when my memories of Allyson were still so fresh. I wasn't certain what to do about it. I'm still not."

Emmy drew a deep breath. The pain and indecision in his face made her ache. He had been hurt so deeply, suffered so much. He needed time and love to heal. She could give him both. Laying her palm against his face, she said, "We don't have to solve all the problems at once, Josiah. Can't we conquer them one at a time?"

Joss turned his head to kiss her palm. "You're a fine woman, Emerelda Greene."

"It's Mrs. Josiah Brickston now, and don't you be forgetting it."

Joss hugged her tight. He felt better than he had in weeks, like a terrible burden had been lifted from his shoulders. "You know what this means, don't you Emmy?"

"What?"

"I don't think I can stop touching you now that I've started."

She smiled. "I was counting on it."

It took Joss a moment to absorb her whispered comment, and then, a wicked gleam sprang into his eye. He settled both his hands on her hips to fit her more closely against him. Damn, but the woman pleased him. Her full figure had been just as lush and enticing as he'd known it would be. The sudden temptation to have her apricot-tinted flesh bared to him in the full light of day was enough to make his loins grow heavy.

Emmy must have felt the tight evidence of his growing arousal against her belly. She glanced at him in surprise. "Josiah, it's daylight."

"See what you do to me, wife? One glimpse of those pale green petticoats you're wearing, and I'm obsessed with knowing whether or not the chemise matches."

"What if I told you I wasn't wearing one?"

Joss leered at her. "I'd probably have to find out for myself if you're telling me the truth."

"I won't have time to make your blackberry preserves if you persist with this course of action, Mr. Brickston."

Joss picked up a handful of blackberries with one hand, while his other hand started busily working the buttons of her faded orange blouse. "I have a number of ideas on how we can put these blackberries to good use." He plopped one in her mouth as he spread her blouse open with his free hand.

When she realized his intent, her eyes widened. The blackberry juice was tangy and sweet on her tongue. When his hand settled possessively on her breast, she stared at him in disbelief. "Josiah, what in the name of heaven has come over you?"

He toppled her back on the bed, then came down beside her. He spread a handful of blackberries on her bare stomach. "I've got a week of fantasies to make up for," he said.

"Maybe you'd better chop some more wood."

"Not on your life," Joss growled. "I'm hungry."

# Thirteen

Joss watched from his office window as Emmy lifted two crates and a burlap sack into the buckboard. He frowned at the sight of Avery Brooks and Robert Greene staring at her from the window of the mercantile. When he saw Gray Lawford saunter across the street and lift a flour sack into the wagon for her, his frown turned into a scowl.

"Something wrong, Joss?"

Joss looked at Jim and shook his head. "I'm not sure."

"Your mind's been somewhere else all day."

Joss winced at the extremely just accusation. He'd been forced to call it quits at the survey site by noon when he couldn't keep his mind on the numbers and off the insistent memory of his wife trembling in his arms that morning in bed.

Joss had been woefully unprepared for the effect Emmy would have on him. He kept trying to convince himself it was merely the result of his long abstinence and the week of frustration following their wedding, but it wasn't working. Emmy had lit a fire inside him he couldn't ignore.

Despite whatever feelings of guilt and confusion still lingered, he could no longer deny that he wanted her with a desperation that had him twisted up in knots so bad he could hardly think. He hadn't stopped thinking

about her since he'd crawled out of bed that morning
and left her tangled up in the blackberry-stained
sheets.

She had responded to him with a passion and an
ardor that had robbed whatever pretenses of discipline
he possessed, and when she'd reached her first shattering peak in his arms, with her back arched, and her
head thrown back, and her tumble of red-gold hair
streaming over his arm in a silken cascade, Joss had
known she held an enormous amount of power over
him. In all his born days, he'd never known giving a
woman pleasure could make him that hot. He still
hadn't fully recovered.

In spite of his best efforts to regain his focus, to remember what had brought him to Carding in the first
place, images of her full luxuriant breasts pressed
against his palm, the fire in her tawny eyes, the way her
skin looked flushed and rosy and ready for his hands,
the scent and the taste of her satiny flesh kept intruding on his thoughts. He'd done what he could to push
them aside. It hadn't worked.

Maybe that was why he hadn't quite been able to
dispel the notion that he'd betrayed Allyson's memory.
For the first time since her death, he didn't see her
face clearly. He couldn't precisely remember the place-
ment of her freckles, or the texture of her hair. Emmy
had begun to dim the memories of his family just as
he'd feared. Occasionally, that sick feeling he'd first
felt when he'd awakened in bed and seen the blood
on the sheets would seep back into his body until his
bones hurt. But there was no denying the truth. His
body had been tight and hard since he'd walked out
of the bedroom that morning. It wasn't an image of
Allyson that kept intruding on his concentration. It was
an image of Emmy stripped bare, save for one pale
green petticoat. When he and Jim had stumbled on a

blackberry bush, laden with ripe, sweet fruit, he'd lost what remained of his concentration and been forced to call a premature end to their day.

The notion had left Joss feeling disoriented and frustrated. He was torn between disgust with his lack of discipline, and relief that the long torturous week had come to such a satisfactory close. He wasn't certain how much longer he could have taken his self-enforced celibacy in such proximity to his lusciously attractive wife. One look of her tawny eyes through those cute little spectacles, and his resolve sank into the dust.

Watching her now, with the late afternoon sun casting a shine on her neatly braided hair, and the faded cotton of her yellow and white plaid dress hugging the splendid curves of her figure a damn sight more closely than he thought it should, he seriously considered walking over to the mercantile, giving Gray Lawford a good kick in the butt, and offering to drive her home. And staying for an hour or two.

A fly drifted across his line of sight, then buzzed incessantly around his head. Joss swatted at it with unnecessary vengeance. He was going to have to put things in order. That was that. Too much longer, and he'd lose his damned mind.

"Joss?" Jim was frowning at him.

He realized belatedly that he hadn't answered Jim's question. He cleared his throat, but couldn't drag his eyes from the porch of Avery's mercantile. "Sorry," he mumbled. "I'm just distracted I reckon."

Jim followed the direction of Joss's gaze. He chuckled when he saw Emmy struggling with a sugar keg. "I'll bet," he said.

Joss diverted his attention long enough to give Jim a quick, censorious frown. It irritated him, suddenly, that anyone else should be in such a fine mood when he was waging an internal war. "What do you mean by that?"

"You haven't had your mind on this place since you walked in this morning."

"Of course I have."

"Sure," Jim said agreeably. "That must be the reason the sight of that blackberry bush sent you into a swivet."

Joss propped his booted feet on the corner of his desk. His gaze returned, once more, to the window. Damn, Gray Lawford annoyed him. "I have no idea what you're talking about."

"Yes, you do. And don't think I don't know why you're so eat up today, either."

Joss slid his gaze across the desk long enough to frown at him, then returned his attention to Emmy. "Shut up, Jim."

Jim laughed. "I can see you're going to be real useful today." He looked toward the side window in the cramped office. "Sam," he called.

Sam was balanced on the back legs of his chair, dangling his bare feet out the window. When Jim called his name, he was so startled, his chair tumbled backwards. He fell to the floor with a dull *thud*. Jim laughed harder. "Sam, why don't you take your eyes off Becky Morgan and saunter on over to Brooks's mercantile. Miss Emmy needs help loading the buckboard."

Sam's face turned red as a tomato. He scrambled to his feet, glaring at Jim as he brushed the dust off his britches. "I wasn't watching Becky Morgan."

Joss raised an eyebrow. Joss gave Sam a sympathetic look. Becky Morgan was the fourteen-year-old daughter of the Reverend Elijah Morgan, and Sam had one of the worst cases of adolescent infatuation Joss had ever seen. When the poor boy said her name, it generally came out as a wistful, half-reverent whisper. He felt a sudden burst of sympathy for the poor boy's confusion.

Jim had no such mercy. "You've been watching the grass grow in front of the schoolhouse all afternoon, then. Must be the reason my floor's not swept, and you haven't finished unpacking those boxes we picked up at the landing yesterday."

Sam's blush intensified. The rough twill of his trousers rode up and down his impossibly thin ankles when he scratched his leg. "I wasn't either," he said. "I was watching the folks roaming in and out of Bug Danboat's saloon."

Jim laughed. "And I'm the King of England. Now pull your boots on and get on over to the mercantile before Joss goes crazy looking out that window. We're not going to get a damn thing done as long as she's in sight."

It was Sam's turn to laugh. He sauntered over and peered out the window. "I'm not the only one watching grass grow. I'll tell your though, I wouldn't be any too happy if the marshal was making eyes at Becky like that."

Jim smacked the back of Sam's head with a gentle swat. "I swear, boy. One of these days I'm going to have to teach you some manners."

Joss let the good-natured teasing goad him out of his temper. But he also decided Sam was right. It was definitely time to do something about Gray Lawford. "Drive her home, too, Sam," he said. "I don't want her unloading those supplies by herself."

"Yes, sir." Sam bent to pull his boots out from underneath a heavily laden storage crate.

"And, Sam?"

Sam looked up, his boots in his hand. He pulled a paper wad out of the top of one boot and tossed it to the floor. "Yes sir?"

"When you get back to town, Mr. Pinrose should be just about ready to let his students walk home."

Sam's face crinkled into a grin. "You mean I don't have to come back to work? I thought you wanted to go out to the site again this afternoon. We didn't get hardly nothing done this morning."

Joss ignored Jim's chuckle. "I wouldn't want to deprive a certain young lady of an escort. That walk to the parsonage could be hazardous."

Sam tumbled toward the door, stamping his foot into his boot in a half-run, half-hop that loosely resembled a one-legged chicken. He sent an entire stack of papers scattering across the floor seconds before the door shut on his mumbled apology. Jim looked at Joss with a feigned frown that didn't quite reach his eyes. "If I didn't know better, I'd think you'd gone soft."

Joss strolled across the room to restack the papers, now hopelessly out of order. "Not a chance. I just wanted the boy out of our hair. The way he's mooning over Becky Morgan is enough to turn a man's stomach."

Jim's eyebrows lifted in disbelief. "Ain't it though?"

Joss decided to ignore the pointedly sarcastic comment. "I want to go over those figures for the gradient at the south fork again. Didn't we say six percent?"

Jim mumbled something beneath his breath as he began digging through the papers on his desk. "Since I've already decided you aren't going to tell me what's got you so stirred up today, I think we should talk about Sam."

Joss looked at him in surprise. "What about him?"

Jim pulled a piece of paper out of the stack. "Do you ever get the feelin' that boy's not being honest with us?"

"You mean when he forgets on occasion that he's supposed to be an orphan?"

Jim nodded. "Or when he can't remember how many sisters he claimed he left with that aunt."

"I thought it was an uncle."

Jim laughed. "The first time I heard the story, it was his granny."

Joss dropped the stack of papers on one of the crates. He cleared away a spot so he could sit down. "So what are you thinking?"

"I'm thinking that boy's not an orphan at all."

"That's probably so."

"The way he got all choked up over it, I figure he told the truth about his pa dyin', but his ma's somewhere worried sick to death."

Joss thoughtfully stroked his chin. "I suspect you're right. You did tell me you hauled him out of the river, though."

"That part is true. I was down at the landing picking up some supplies when he came sputterin' in like a half-drowned rat. He told me he'd stowed away on a paddle wheeler, and when the captain caught him, they tossed him overboard. So I dragged him out and brought him to you."

"Where do you think he came from really?"

"Upriver I'm thinking. He usually talks about his home as 'up yonder,' or 'up there.' I don't think he lies good enough to make that up."

"Especially when he can't remember how many sisters he's supposed to have."

"I'm also thinking it's got to be a town 'round medium size. He can't get used to everybody knowing everybody else's business in a town this small."

Joss watched through the window as Sam scrambled about, lifting Emmy's purchases into the buckboard. "If what you say is true, we should find a way to let his mother know he's all right. What do you think we should do about getting him to tell us where she is?"

"Well, I hate to lose him. He's a big help at the site."

"We got by without him before."

"Yeah."

Jim's voice was so harsh, Joss momentarily diverted his attention from the sight of Emmy laughing at something Gray Lawford had said. "We've been over this before, Jim."

"There ain't no good reason you're working this hard, Joss."

"There are plenty of good reasons."

"You could have finished this survey weeks ago and been on to the next place."

"I just got my house settled as it is. Why would I want to move on?" He turned his attention back to Sam. "You haven't answered my question. What do you think we ought to do with Sam?"

"My first inkling is to turn him over my knee and whup the tar out of him till he tells me the truth."

Joss slanted him a wry look. "Do you have a second inkling?"

"You don't think that one'll work?"

"I didn't say it wasn't a good idea, I just don't think you'll get any better answers than the ones you've got now."

"If we can find out where his ma is, we can write her."

"She'll want to come fetch him I'm sure," Joss said.

"But I'd bet you a pint of Bug's best whiskey he ain't told us the truth about his name either. We'll have to get that out of him, too."

"Maybe your first inkling is the best plan."

"I don't think so. It's temptin', I'll tell you. Knowing what that boy is puttin' his ma through. But you're right. He'll just lie some more if I tan it out of him."

"Then what do you suggest?"

Jim nodded his head toward the window. "He seems

awfully fond of Miss Emmy. Maybe you could get her to talk to him."

Joss watched as Sam tied his pony to the rear of the buckboard before vaulting onto the seat. Gray put his hands on Emmy's waist, that ridiculously soft, ridiculously narrow, uncorseted waist, and lifted her up next to Sam. Joss saw the bright smile she gave Gray and ground his teeth. "Maybe I could," he said.

"And while you're at it," Jim drawled, leaning back in his chair, "maybe you could get her to tell you why she's so fond of the marshal."

Joss's breath came out on a sibilant hiss. He glared at Jim. "Gray Lawford has been friends with my wife for quite some time."

Jim nodded. "So has Avery Brooks. There are a few more, too. They don't seem to bother you like the marshal, though."

"I have no idea what you mean."

"If you were frowning any harder, your eyebrows would be touching your chin."

"Just what are you suggesting?"

"I think Gray Lawford gets under your skin like a bad itch."

Joss's frown deepened. "I am not jealous of Gray Lawford if that is what you're getting at."

"Of course not."

"Emmy considers him a close friend."

"Uh-huh."

"He told me the story about the bear."

"Told me too."

Joss ran a finger over the scar on his cheek. It had started to twitch. "Despite what you might think, Jim, Emmy is fond of Gray in the same manner she's fond of you and Sam."

"No doubt."

"And there is absolutely no reason whatsoever to think anything else may be the case."

"Nope."

Joss reached for his hat and crammed it on his head. "Take the rest of the afternoon off, Jim. I've got some business to conduct with the marshal."


Emmy cast another look down the hill for a glimpse of the Diamond Hawk. She had to pull her knees up beneath her skirt for warmth. The days were growing shorter. The cold breezes that swirled about the bluff made her glad they had such a healthy store of wood for the stove.

Taking a deep breath of the still air, heavily scented with sun-warmed earth and late summer wildflowers, she leaned back against the tree to listen to the birds and crickets. A lazy cloud drifted across the darkening sky. The lonesome whistle of a paddle wheeler sounded in the distance, intruding on her concentration.

If the Diamond Hawk didn't show soon, she'd have to leave. She had no idea what time Joss would be home, but she didn't want him to find the watch house empty. Emmy had already determined that she would tell Joss about the Diamond Hawk that night. Perhaps later, when they were in bed. The thought made her skin tingle, despite the growing sense of foreboding she'd had since leaving Avery's store. Indeed, she had been unable to—

"Hello."

The familiar voice startled her. She turned to face him. "Must you insist on creeping up on me like that?"

"It adds to my mystery."

"It makes you annoying." Fifty yards or so behind him, she saw the impressive black horse munching happily on a stand of clover. "How did you approach the bluff from this direction?" She waved a hand in the direction of Carding. "The road runs this way."

"I rode up from the north."

"The north? But that climb is so treacherous. How did you manage it?

"I managed," he said quietly. "I didn't want to be seen approaching the bluff. I feared it might put you in a difficult position."

Beneath the mask, the strong line of his chin seemed to tighten. The action recalled her task. She reached into the pocket of her apron to retrieve the two items she'd tucked there. "I've brought you something to add to your mystique." She extended her hand to drop a long piece of black fringe she'd purchased at Avery's Mercantile onto his gloved palm. "If you stitch that onto your cape, it will give you a bit of added dash."

With a slight laugh, he looped the fringe through his fingers. "I see you are still intent on ridiculing me."

"I think you should make every effort to be worthy of Horace Newbury's adjectives. I'm certain he used 'dashing' not too long ago."

He dropped the fringe into a pocket in his cape. "I shall have to give that some thought, although I'm not sure I want Mr. Newbury to add 'gaudy' to his list."

Emmy then gave him the piece of paper. Her good humor faded with the heaviness of the matter at hand. She had been disturbed about it all afternoon. "You were right about the gems in Avery's store. There are quality fakes among the stones. I've made a list for you."

He took the piece of paper and glanced briefly at it before returning his gaze to hers. "This didn't cause you any trouble I hope?"

She looked away, wondering how much she should tell him. "I . . . I told Avery I was looking for a gift for my husband's sister. That was my excuse for seeing the gems."

He walked up behind her so that his big body protected her back from the cold wind. "And?"

"And, he showed them to me. He was anxious though, almost wary of me."

"If he's selling fake gems as genuine, I can understand why he would be."

She shook her head. "That's the oddest thing. The gems were set by Chandler and Bates. I looked very closely. I'm sure they were in their original settings." Emmy frowned, perplexed as she had been all afternoon.

"Chandler and Bates?"

"They are very credible lapidaries in St. Louis."

"Then they are passing off fake stones."

Again, she shook her head. "Their reputation is above reproach. They would stand to lose their business, possibly even go to prison, if they were caught passing fake stones. The small profit gained from the treachery could not begin to compensate for the loss of their trade."

"Who stands to profit the most from the sale of the stones?"

"The stone handler. Lapidaries like Chandler and Bates are artisans, not gem scientists. While experience would help them recognize a badly flawed stone because of dull fire or streaks, they would probably not know the difference if extremely high quality fakes were substituted into their purchased lot."

"Lot?"

Emmy nodded. "They buy stones in lots, sometimes thousands at a time, from gem handlers. To protect the lapidaries, the handler provides certificates of authenticity for the stones. Only a registered gem scientist can issue a certificate, and it has to be notarized. Generally, the stones are shipped in from the mines. The handlers bid on lots at auction. The mine operators also have to guarantee the authenticity of the stones."

"What happens next?"

"The handler will do one of two things with his lots. He will generally pay his stone cutter to clean up the uncut gems, then cut them to jewelry and ornamental specifications. Then he will sell them to his network of lapidaries. Occasionally, and this is much more rare, he will sell the entire lot of uncut gems to another handler, or perhaps a gem scientist, who is doing a particular type of research."

With his gloved hands on her shoulders, he turned her around to face him. "Say the gem handler was substituting fake gems for genuine before selling to his lapidaries. What would happen to the real gems?"

She shrugged. "He could sell them to someone else."

"At the same profit margin?"

"Higher."

"What do you mean?"

"I told you the stones are guaranteed with a certificate of authenticity. They are also registered by the auction house. With the exception of some very small lots, any large lots are recorded and inventoried when sold. A handler couldn't sell the same lot twice, even if one set of gems was fake. Someone would notice. He would have to sell the second set illegally."

She saw understanding in his eyes. "And illegally obtained gems are quite a bit more expensive than legal ones."

"There's a large market for illegal, unregistered, loose stones. While the handler cannot actually sell them at market value, he can sell them at higher prices individually than he is forced to sell his lots."

The Diamond Hawk studied her for a minute. His eyes glittered behind his black mask. "So what are your thoughts on the fake stones?"

She pushed her spectacles up on her nose. "That perplexes me most of all. As I told you, the gem handler is issued a certificate of authenticity at the time of sale. It is an original document and cannot be duplicated. The handler would have to obtain a second certificate to resell the genuine gems."

He studied her closely. "And to obtain a second certificate, he would need a qualified, registered gem scientist?"

Emmy felt slightly queasy. Avery had been so tense the entire time she was examining the gems in his mercantile, almost as if he'd known she would discover the fake gems. His obvious discomfort had planted some ugly suspicions in her mind. Suspicions she didn't want to admit. "That's right," she said in answer to his question. "There would have to be a second certificate."

"And that certificate would have to be accompanied by a shipment of high-quality fake stones in order to make the substitution."

Emmy nodded.

"Do you know who handles stones for Chandler and Bates?" he asked.

She raised stricken eyes to his. "Jason Carver."

He looked surprised. "The banker?"

Emmy nodded. "Yes. A good number of handlers are also bankers. It makes a certain level of sense when you consider the amount of cash they have to move at any given time."

"The banker," he repeated, reaching up to stroke his chin with gloved fingers. Emmy lowered her gaze to the diamond stickpin in his lapel. The sun glinted colored prisms off the brilliant stone. No fake there, she mentally set its weight at three-quarters of a carat. "I have just one more question, then I will leave you," he said. "I will not bother you again."

She knew what he was going to ask, knew she'd have

to give him the answer. It didn't keep her from feeling sick to her stomach about it, though. "What do you want to know?"

"If Jason Carver is passing fake stones to his lapidaries, where is he obtaining certificates of authenticity?"

Stricken, she met his gaze. "I suspect he obtains them from my Uncle Robert."

"Emmy, what's wrong?" Joss strode up the short climb from the watch house to the tree on the bluff. After his meeting with Gray Lawford, he'd hurried through the rest of his business, hoping to spend a quiet evening with Emmy explaining all that he'd arranged. He'd been surprised to find the watch house empty when he returned home.

She looked at him in surprise. "You're home. I'm sorry. I lost track of time."

He shook his head. "What's wrong, Emmy? Why are you up here by yourself?"

She dropped a pile of weeds and wiped her hands on her apron in nervous agitation. "What makes you think something is wrong?"

He glanced briefly at the piles of weeds. They lay sorted by type in neat piles in a circle around the tree. "Just a hunch," he said dryly as he closed the distance between them. "Are you all right?"

She brushed the dust off his shoulders. "Of course. I'm sorry dinner will be late. I knew you were coming home early tonight. I should have gone in long ago. I'll just hurry back and . . ."

He grabbed her hands and pressed them against his chest. "Emmy, stop prattling about dinner."

"But you must be hungry. It's been a long day for you, I know, and with nothing but jerky and bread at the site, well, you need your supper. I'm sorry. I just . . ."

Joss clamped a hand over her mouth. "Now, if I take my hand away will you answer my question?" She looked at him through worried eyes. "I'll be perfectly content to scrape together my own dinner," he told her. "I want to know what's wrong with you."

When she nodded, he lifted his hand, only to clamp it back down when she opened her mouth to speak. "Promise?" he prompted.

She nodded again. Joss took his hand away to smooth a tendril of her hair off her forehead. "Now. What's wrong?"

"Could we—could we sit first?" she asked, stalling for time.

Joss laced his fingers through hers so he could tug her toward the tree. He toppled her onto his lap, then tucked her head neatly beneath his chin. "Are you comfortable?"

Emmy nodded. She sniffled slightly when a tear slipped from her eye to plop on the faded red chambray of his shirt. "Yes."

A long silence passed between them. "Emmy?" he prompted.

"Yes."

"Are you asleep?"

"No."

She felt him smile against her hair. "I'm waiting."

She rubbed her cheek against his chest. "I'm afraid you'll be angry."

"What if I promise I won't?"

"You can't."

"I can't what."

"You can't promise you won't be angry because you don't know what I'm going to say."

She sounded so miserable, Joss almost laughed. He

rubbed his hand down her back instead. "The sooner you start telling me, the sooner it will be over," he said.

When Emmy sniffled again, he dug in his pocket to hand her his handkerchief. "All right, Em. Get it over with."

In a halting voice, punctuated by occasional sniffles she tried valiantly to suppress, she told him about the Diamond Hawk and how she'd been helping him identify the stones. When she started telling him about her visit to Avery's Mercantile, her tears started flowing in earnest. By the time she got to the encounter on the bluff and voiced her suspicions about her uncle, she was sobbing. "Oh, Josiah, how could he? How could he do that?"

Joss fought back a surge of anger as he hugged her close. "I don't know, Emmy."

Emmy felt him tense. His voice sounded harsh and strained. She tipped her head to look at him, worried that he might have gotten angry after all. Joss's lips were set in a grim line. The scar on his cheek had turned an angry white. Emmy smoothed a finger over it. "Josiah, are you angry?"

He shook his head. "Not at you." He lifted her spectacles off her nose to gently wipe away the tears on her cheeks.

Emmy frowned at him. "But you're angry."

"Yes."

"Why?"

"I'll tell you when the time comes," he promised.

Emmy wavered on indecision. She longed to press the issue with him, but she feared it might set off his temper. There was something cold and dangerous in Joss's gaze that frightened her. So she took the coward's way out and wrapped her arms around his waist. "I want to go home now, Josiah."

Joss set her off his lap without a word. He stood,

then scooped her into his arms and began walking back toward the watch house. She watched his face, hardened into stark lines, and fidgeted in agitation. "Josiah, this isn't necessary. It'll hurt your knees."

It didn't surprise him that she knew, of course. She seemed to notice everything. "My knees are fine."

"I'm perfectly capable of walking."

When he shrugged, she almost fell to the ground. She was forced to grab hold of his shoulder to right herself. She liked the feeling so much, she decided to leave her hand there. "Josiah?" she asked, as he kicked open the door to the watch house.

He set her down in the slat-back rocker before he walked back to bolt the door. "Yes, Em?"

"Do you think Uncle Robert is really doing something illegal?"

He turned to face her. "Yes, Em."

She wrapped her arms around her waist. "I feel rotten," she said quietly.

Joss leaned back against the door and closed his uncovered eye. Emmy anxiously watched him. He seemed to be fighting some deep internal battle. She feared the outcome. When he opened his eye again, he impaled her with an intense stare that made her chest hurt. Slowly, he walked back to her side where he went down on one knee beside her. He threaded his fingers through her hair. "Are you feeling ill?" he asked.

She shook her head. "Not ill exactly." She tapped her finger over her heart. "This kind of rotten."

Joss nestled his hand in her hair as he bent to give her a brief, gentle kiss. "I know."

She thought about his family, about Allyson and Michael and Adam. He did know. On impulse she wrapped her arms around him and buried her face against his neck. "Make it go away, Josiah."

"Em, I can't . . ."

"I want you to put something else there to make it go away. I want you to make love to me."

Joss exhaled a sharp breath. "Emmy, you don't . . ."

"Please, Josiah."

The plea in her voice was all the incentive he needed.


Joss leaned his head against the window in the loft of the watch house and stared at the moon. He was grateful for the cool drafty breeze that whistled through the thin walls and swirled across his bare flesh. Emmy had finally fallen asleep. Her face had been wrinkled into an unhappy pucker after long tearful hours pillowed against his chest. Even their fiery love-making had done little to ease the pain of her uncle's betrayal. It had set flames to his.

When had it all become so blurred, he wondered. He no longer clearly understood his reasons for coming to Carding. He no longer clearly saw his aching desire to find Allyson's killer. Things had gone from black and white to a thousand, indistinguishable shades of gray.

Gray. Joss found his first smile that evening.

The marshal hadn't looked overly surprised when he'd strolled into his office that afternoon, and found Joss sitting in his chair with his booted feet propped on the desk. Gray had clearly expected the confrontation.

Joss felt Emmy's arms circle his waist from behind. He reached to slip his patch over his eye. "I thought you were asleep," he told her.

"I was, I think." She rubbed her cheek against his back. "Your skin is cold."

He could feel the soft flannel of her nightgown and saw the reflection of green sleeves in the glass of the window. He smiled at the incongruous notion of his cold skin and his rapidly heating blood. He turned to gather her into his arms. "Your skin will be cold too if you don't crawl back under the quilts."

She shook her head. "Not when you hold me like this."

Joss rubbed his hand over her spine. The soft, honeysuckle scent of her hair reached him, calmed him. In the wedge of moonlight, her hair glistened. The fiery strands curled about her head like flowering vines. The lyrical thought made him smile. He was an Englishman. He wasn't supposed to be poetical. "Emmy," he said, his voice barely above a whisper, "why didn't you tell me that Gray Lawford was your cousin?"

She leaned her head back to look at him in surprise. "You didn't know?"

Joss shook his head. "No."

"I just assumed you knew. Everyone knows." She frowned at him. "His mother and my mother were sisters. Gray and I are only a year apart."

Joss rubbed his chin on the top of her head. "He told me today. I was—surprised."

She tapped a finger on his chest. "Why did you think I was so familiar with him?"

He raised one eyebrow. "I thought perhaps you had other reasons for being familiar."

"Other reasons? What other reasons?"

"Reasons like attraction."

Her mouth dropped open. "Attraction? Josiah, you didn't think I would act such a way with a man I was attracted to. Why, I entertained the man in my nightdress for heaven's sakes. If he weren't my blood kin, don't you think I'd have raced in the house to dress proper?"

"You entertained me in your nightdress," he said, recalling that morning on the porch.

She shook her head. "I didn't. You rode up, and I

went in to change right off. I would never have behaved like that in front of you. Not when I was thinking—"

Joss felt her blush through the thin flannel of her nightdress. "Thinking what?" he asked, deliberately keeping his expression bland.

Emmy's body temperature rose another two degrees from the heat of her blush. "Nothing."

"Thinking you'd like to have jumped my bones in the dust of your uncle's farm?"

"Josiah, really."

He wagged his eyebrows at her. "Admit it, Miss Em. You wanted my scarred body from the moment I walked into your office with that simpering fool, Avery Brooks."

"I did not."

"Oh, yes you did. What's more, you weren't the least bit shy about it. You started flashing your undergarments at me every chance you got."

She pushed ineffectually at his chest. "I didn't either. I would never do something that unladylike."

"Oh no?"

"No."

"Then tell me for certain you didn't deliberately let me believe you and Gray Lawford were better than friends just to make me jealous."

"Were you?" she asked.

"Was I what?"

"Jealous."

He nodded. "Nearly eat up with it."

Emmy laughed in delight as she rubbed her nose against his chest. "I confess to the whole thing, Mr. Brickston. I deliberately flaunted my familiarity with Gray Lawford. I made a point of dipping my fingers in cleaning acid just to drive you wild, and I flashed my inexpressibles every chance I got."

Joss laughed. It was a rare, rumbling laugh that felt

good, if a little rusty, from disuse. "God, Em," he said as he inhaled a long, deep breath. "You make me feel better than I have in a long time. Do you know that?"

Emmy caught her breath. For Josiah, that was as near a declaration of love as she was likely to get. "I love you, Josiah."

"I know you do," he said, sounding just a little awed.

"I'm sorry if you were jealous of Gray."

He pinched her behind. "You are not."

"No," she agreed with a slight laugh. "I guess I'm not."

Joss fell silent. Emotions waged war in his heart. Emmy's soft warmth had served to ward off some of the familiar chill that had settled in his chest. Even so, he felt melancholy, sad, in a way he had been able to bury beneath angry thoughts since he'd come to Carding. He was losing sight of the anger. The yawning gulf of sorrow was too deep to face without it. The sooner he laid his ghosts to rest, the better it would be for all of them. Emmy's comforting presence couldn't ward them off forever. "Emmy?" he said at last, wondering vaguely how long he'd been silent.

"What are you thinking about, Josiah?"

"The past," he said.

"The murders?"

He nodded. "Yes."

"Will you tell me about it? All of it?"

Joss shook his head. "Not now. I can't."

"I wish I could make the pain go away," she whispered.

"Me, too." He had to fight a familiar knot of tension in his throat. "There is something you can do to help me, though."

She looked at him in surprise. "You know I'll do anything I can."

"I want us to go to the Harvest Festival Masquerade Dance on Saturday."

"What's that got to do with—"

Joss covered her lips with his hand. "I need you to trust me, Em. It just does."

When she nodded, he dropped his hand. She pushed a lock of dark hair off his forehead. She'd waited so long for the right to do that, that the tiny action gave her a warm feeling in her soul. "There's just one problem."

Joss frowned at her. "What?"

"I couldn't go with you to the Slinktons' because I didn't have anything to wear. I still don't. I wouldn't want you to be ashamed of me."

Joss sucked in a breath. God, what a selfish bastard he'd been. She'd been his wife for nearly two weeks, put his life in some semblance of order, worked like a slave for him, and he hadn't even taken the time to see that she'd done something about her clothes. "You haven't ordered anything?"

She shook her head. "No. I—I didn't want to ask you for the money."

Joss groaned. "Dear Lord, I'm sorry. I just assumed you had taken care of it. I thought it was taking a bit long, but I didn't know how long it took to have clothes tailored out here."

"Tailored? My heavens, Josiah, I'd never spend that much money. I wouldn't have done more than order a few bolts of muslin and calico. I can make my own clothes. It will be much less expensive that way."

Joss felt worse. She obviously assumed from the state of his life that he was operating on limited funds. "Emmy," he said cautiously, "I'm the owner of the American branch of Continental Shipping."

"I know," she said, "and I'm sure you want me to be appropriately attired for the Harvest Festival Masquerade Dance. It wouldn't be at all right for me to look out of fashion. There's no cause to worry, though. I'm very good with a needle."

Joss shook his head. "That's not what I mean."

"I wouldn't want you to be ashamed of me."

"I'd never be ashamed of you, Em."

She frowned at him. "Don't you think I can make a dress suitable for the wife of Continental Shipping's American owner and operator?"

"Don't forget," he said dryly, "I've seen your undergarments. You're damned handy with that needle."

"That's right. I'll just slip into town tomorrow and see what I can find at Avery's. And if it's all right, I'd like at least one more piece of calico for a new dress. I know it's an indulgence, but—"

He shook her shoulders. "Emmy, will you look at me."

Her gaze flew to his. "I won't if we can't afford it, Josiah."

He groaned. "I can afford it, Em. Hell, I can afford to buy you every piece of goods in Avery Brooks' store and have more shipped in by riverboat if that's what you want."

Emmy stared at him. "What?"

"I mean I've got enough money to have your whole wardrobe imported from Paris for the winter and replaced the next spring. It never occurred to me you didn't know that."

"Well, of course I didn't. You live so simply, I just assumed your money was tied up in Continental."

Joss gave her a hard, brief kiss. "And I've been too much of a selfish bastard to realize you hadn't yet done anything for yourself. God, I'm sorry, Em."

"Sorry for what?"

"That I've been letting you work like a slave for me,

and I didn't even have the decency to make sure you were taken care of."

"I'm very well taken care of, Josiah. Don't you dare think otherwise."

"I'm taking care of this thing with your clothes first thing in the morning. There's a seamstress in town, isn't there?"

She nodded. "Well, yes. Mrs. Tattingly runs a dress shop of sorts, but she's very expensive."

Joss bit back a smile. He wondered what Emmy would do if she ever saw one of his sisters' dress bills from their London seamstress. Probably faint dead away. "I doubt it," he said. "I want you to go see her first thing in the morning. Order everything, anything, you want. Then see Mr. Whicham."

"The cobbler?"

"Yes, you need some new boots, too. A work pair, and at least one dress pair."

Emmy thought about her clunky work boots. "I can wear my brogans to work in."

"They don't fit right. Don't think I haven't seen the blisters."

Emmy swallowed a tight knot in her throat. "I'm sorry if I've been such an embarrassment to you, Josiah."

"Oh hell," he said, as he wiped a hand through his hair in exasperation. "You're not an embarrassment to me. How can you think that?"

"I know my clothes are worn, and they don't fit right, but you don't have to do all this."

"I want to do this. There's no reason for me not to."

She raised tear-wet eyes to look at him. "Why do you want to spend all this money if you're not embarrassed?"

He looked at her in astonishment before the truth of her statement finally registered. He damned Robert

Greene to hell. "Emmy, I'm not dressing you up as some decoration for me. Is that what you think?"

"I—I didn't think you'd do it just to be kind."

"Well, why the hell not?"

"Uncle Robert always said that it wasn't necessary for me to have new things like my cousins because everyone knew that my father had foisted me on them. It wouldn't reflect poorly on Uncle Robert if I wore castoffs."

Joss swore beneath his breath. "I am not Robert Greene, and don't you dare compare me with him ever again. Do you hear me?"

"Well, I didn't mean—"

"Never."

"All right."

He pulled her tight against his chest. "Emmy, I want you to have nice things because you deserve to have nice things. You're my wife. There's no reason at all for you not to be comfortable, even a bit pampered, if you want."

Emmy had never been pampered in her life. The mere thought of it was startling. "Josiah?"

"What?"

"I—I don't know how. What if I pick the wrong things?"

"Emmy, you're an expert in gem science. You have an eye for color and beauty most women would kill for. Trust me, you won't pick the wrong things."

"But I don't know anything at all about fashion."

"That's Mrs. Tattingly's responsibility. Do you trust her judgment?"

Emmy thought for a minute about Pearl's beautiful clothes, and Ruby's exquisitely tailored dresses, and Jade's fine embroidered gowns. "Yes, I do."

"Then tell her what you like, and she'll see to the

rest. Believe me, this isn't nearly as complicated as de-
termining the density of a calcite deposit."

Emmy stifled a small giggle. "I wouldn't want you to
be disappointed."

Joss leaned her back so he could study her in the
moonlight. "I'll strike a bargain with you. I'll take care
of your gown and mask for the dance, if you'll do the
rest. All right?"

Emmy sighed, feeling much better. After all, if she
chose wrong on a calico dress or two, it wouldn't be
half the disaster of picking the wrong gown. "All right.
Do you have any special requests?"

He thought for a minute. "Just one. Order a corset."

Emmy looked stung. "I know my figure is a bit larger
than is strictly fashionable, Josiah, but I don't think—"

He covered her mouth with a hot kiss. He waited
until she swayed into him before he lifted his head.
"I'm not complaining about your figure. Just the opposite in fact. All these soft curves have been driving
me crazy for days."

Her eyes drifted open. "Really?"

Joss rubbed his thumb over the full curve of her
lower lip. "Really. I want it trussed up in a corset in
case you have to dance with anyone but me."


"Aaaaaagh!" Emmy gripped the bedpost with both
hands, while Joss pulled on the strings of her new white
corset. "Be careful, Josiah, you'll rattle my hair loose."
She reached up to make sure the peach-colored silk
net was still firmly in place.

Joss dropped his knee from the small of her back
with a frown. "It's tight enough. This is ridiculous."

She glanced at him over her shoulder. "You don't
make a very good ladies' maid, Josiah. Mrs. Tattingly
said you'd have to cinch me down two inches, or I won't

fit in the gown you ordered from St. Louis." In truth, she was nearly eaten up with curiosity over the mysterious gown. Joss had ordered it for her from a St. Louis seamstress nearly a week before. It had arrived on one of Continental's cargo runs just that afternoon, and Joss had carried it home with him. Emmy had refused to look at it. She wished to prolong the delicious anticipation she'd been feeling all week.

She'd ordered four new gowns from Mrs. Tattingly, and purchased several more pieces of fabric from Avery's Mercantile. She'd nearly died of embarrassment when she'd had to place an order with Avery for her corset, but Joss had been adamant. She was sharply disappointed that she'd had no say in the color, so she'd consoled herself with a model flounced with a generous portion of lace and white satin ribbons. Strictly speaking, it was a bride's corset, but Emmy had justified the expense to herself with the notion that she would only buy one. It must be fancy enough to wear under her St. Louis gown.

Joss was frowning at her. "I can't understand why it's necessary to wear this damn thing so tight. I used the measurements Mabel Tattingly gave me."

Emmy gripped the bedpost once more. She braced her feet apart, then stared intently at the wall so her shoulder blades would be straight. In truth, the boning was squeezing the breath out of her. She was afraid she wouldn't be able to bend her waist at all once he was done. "The measurements assumed my waist would be squeezed in two inches." She wiggled her behind, then drew in a deep breath. "Now stop dawdling and cinch me up. One more pull ought to do it."

Joss grumbled beneath his breath as he seized the silken cords. "Hold tight." He hauled on the laces with a sharp tug.

Emmy sucked in a shallow breath and gritted her teeth. "I think that should do."

He started deftly stringing the laces through the eyes, mumbling all the while about vanity. Emmy's breath came in small pants. The bone stays of the corset kept her from filling her lungs. Surely that was the reason her heartbeat quickened when she glanced at Josiah.

He looked terribly handsome in his black evening clothes. He'd smoothed his dark hair into a neat queue. A black silk tie circled the collar of his pristine white shirt. "You were the one who told me to buy the fool thing." She tried to sound indignant and not feel scandalously feminine when he rested his hands on her narrow waist. "They don't even come in colors. White was my only choice."

Joss tied off the silk laces in a neat bow at the base of her spine, then turned her around to face him. He stared as all the blood in his body drained to one point south of his beltbuckle. Emmy gave him an anxious look. "Is something wrong, Josiah?"

He shook his head, nodded, then shook his head again. "No." The one word retort sounded strangled.

Emmy felt a flutter of panic. "I know it's lacier than the usual kind, but I didn't think you'd mind. I was disappointed about the color, so I compensated with the lace." He didn't say anything. She tugged nervously at a piece of lace, arranging it in a perfect pleated fan over her left breast. "Is it all right?"

Joss dropped onto the bed where he buried his head in his hands. Dear God. He'd been haunted for days with the notion of how soft she was to the touch. Her ill-fitting, well-worn clothes had hung comfortably on her generous curves. Joss had been able to retain his sanity by not looking too closely. He'd hoped, desperately, that the corset would help take his mind off wanting her. If his hand rested on her waist and found a stiff whalebone instead of a soft curve flaring gently into a perfectly rounded hip, he had assumed his ever-escalating desire for her would be checked.

One look at her laced into that frilly corset had completely destroyed that notion. The thing was seductive, it was true, edged in lace and trimmed in satin ribbons, but that didn't even begin to be the problem. In her pale yellow silk shift, with the corset pushing in and out everything in all the right places, and the lace flounced over the softest parts of her, she looked like a temptress in a nighttime fantasy. It was all he could do not to toss her on the bed then and there. "Later," he mumbled, more for his own peace of mind than her benefit.

"Josiah?"

Emmy was staring at him with a worried look in her tawny eyes. He drew a fortifying breath. "It's fine, Em. I just wasn't prepared for, well, it's rather—" He waved a hand ineffectually, wondering why he'd been chosen to endure this kind of torture. He should have married one of the ugly cousins, he told himself for the umpteenth time. "Oh, hell. We'd better get you into your gown. Scramble into your petticoats, will you?"

Emmy reached for the heavy yellow petticoats and pulled them up around her waist in a quick jerk. Her fingers fumbled with the ties. "Are you certain it's all right?"

Joss picked up the string-tied white box from St. Louis's most exclusive seamstress. "I thought it would make things easier on me. I was wrong." He pulled on the strings until they snapped in two.

Emmy finally understood. The tension left her in a rush. "Josiah," she chided, "you really shouldn't spend so much time thinking about my undergarments. It can't be healthy."

He threw the box top on the floor, then began pulling at the delicate paper. "It's not healthy at all," he grumbled.

When the paper fell away from the box, Emmy gasped at her first glimpse of the gown. Joss froze with his fingers still touching the softest peach-colored velvet she'd ever seen. "What's wrong?" he asked. "Don't you like the color? I thought it would be good for you."

Now he sounded worried. Emmy lifted the fitted peach velvet, lace-trimmed bodice. She ran her fingers in a gentle caress over the luxurious fabric. "It's the most beautiful gown I've ever seen," she whispered.

With a sigh of relief, he lifted the silk skirt out of the box to give it a gentle shake.

The skirt was the softest peach silk she'd ever seen, with wide ivory stripes that ran from waist to hem. It was cut in the very latest fashion, falling straight down in the front and flaring out over petticoats in the back. The hem was edged in ivory lace so fine it was nearly transparent. The same lace trimmed the cuffs and formed a shoulder-wide collar on the fitted velvet jacket. Tiny ivory buttons secured the bodice from throat to waist. It was cut to settle on her hips with two deep points in the front and back. The fitted jacket would make her cinched waist look even smaller relative to the generous flare of her hips and the leg-o-mutton sleeves that ended in tight cuffs at her wrists.

And it looked even better on. Joss made her raise her arms so he could slip the skirt down around her waist. He buttoned her into the jacket, connected the brocade loops of the skirt to hold the bodice in place, then stepped back to admire his handiwork. The fit was perfection. When he saw the two bright tears threatening to spill from her eyes, he dug into his pocket to hand her his handkerchief. "If you don't stop crying, your face will puff up and turn red."

She buried her nose in the handkerchief with a muffled giggle. "Everyone will think my corset's too tight," she said, blowing her nose.

Joss wiped the two tears away from her face. "Are you certain you like it?"

"Oh, Josiah." Emmy threw her arms around his neck. "I've never owned anything like this in my whole life. It's the most beautiful gown in the world and certainly way too fine for me. I feel like a princess."

Joss placed both his hands on her waist only to discover that his fingers now almost spanned the cinched diameter. It was just as unsettling as it had been when she'd worn no corset at all. He set her gently away from him. "We'll never get into town if you don't finish dressing," he admonished as he pushed her gently down on the bed. "Sit down so I can lace your boots."

Emmy watched as he bent to lace the ivory, kid-leather boots with a silver-handled boot hook. There was something wonderfully intimate about the feel of his warm fingers supporting her stocking-covered ankle while he saw to the simple task. Emmy reached out automatically to tuck a strand of his hair back into his queue. When he looked up, his gaze collided with hers. "Is it too tight?" he asked as he tied the leather laces in a bow.

Emmy shook her head. "No. You're very good at this." Joss picked up the second boot. "I was the only one who could get Michael to sit still long enough to lace his boots." He shrugged his broad shoulders.

The innocent comment redirected her thoughts to his strange behavior over the last few days. She wondered if the intimacy they'd shared that evening would allow her a question or two in what was usually forbidden territory. "Josiah?" she said, cautious.

He was deftly wielding the lace hook. "Hmm?"

"Why are you so intent on attending the Harvest Party?"

Joss missed an eye and had to reroute one of the laces. "I thought you would enjoy it."

Emmy paused. "I will, I'm sure, but . . ."

Joss looked up. "But?"

She studied his handsome face. His eye had turned a brooding, purplish blue. "Is that the only reason?"

Joss returned his attention to the laces with a brief shake of his head. "I also thought it was time for Carding to see us together as man and wife."

Emmy studied the crown of his head. She knew he wasn't telling her the whole story, but was afraid to push him for fear she might ruin the easy companionship they'd enjoyed since he'd returned home for dinner that evening. "I see," she said, not really seeing at all.

"I doubt it," Joss answered, tying off the laces of the boot, but not elaborating on the elusive explanation. "Is Sam going tonight?"

Emmy blinked at his abrupt change of subject. "Yes. He was griping this afternoon that his store-bought collar itched."

Joss took both her hands so he could pull her to her feet. "How'd you get him to agree to wear one."

Emmy's smile came easily. "I told him Becky Morgan would think he looked handsome."

Joss reached for the remaining white box. He snapped the strings, then discarded the top. He ignored Emmy's frown when the lid sailed to the floor. "Have you made any progress with him?" he asked.

Emmy shook her head. Joss had spoken with her nearly a week before about his concerns over Sam. She'd been trying to win the boy's confidence, but so far to no avail. "Not yet. I think he's close though. I caught him writing a poem about being homesick the other day."

Joss removed the delicate palatine cape, with its apricot satin lining, from the box and shook out the wrinkles. "He does that a lot, doesn't he?"

"Does what?"

He settled the cape on her shoulders. "Writes."

Emmy waited while Joss secured the frogs. "He's very good too. Some of those poems he's written to Becky Morgan are really quite lyrical."

Joss shook his head as he lifted the hood of her cape. "That boy's got no business frittering away his life cleaning my office."

Emmy laughed while Joss secured the hood with the tiny hair comb at her forehead. "He's much better at writing than he is at cleaning, I assure you."

"I should hope so" He pushed the comb into place in her red-gold hair. He stepped back and swept his eyes over her, all thoughts of Sam suddenly forgotten. "You look beautiful, Emmy. One more thing, and you'll be the belle of the ball." He picked up the last box, untied it, then removed the ornate, gilded mask. With its elegant trim and purple ribbons, it had an opulent look that made Emmy gasp.

"It's beautiful."

He placed it on her face, then reached behind her head to tie the strings. "It pales next to you."

His deep voice sent a shiver up her spine. No one but Joss ever called her beautiful. "I'm thinking I may have to lend you my spectacles, Josiah."

"I'm serious. I wish we had a full mirror so you could see. You look beautiful."

To disguise her embarrassed pleasure, she stepped forward to secure his own black mask. "You look mighty fine yourself, Josiah. I'm certain to have the handsomest escort in town."

Joss captured her hand and pressed it flat against his chest. His gaze became intense. "Emmy, promise you'll stick close to me tonight."

"I'll have to. You'll have every woman in Carding after you."

When he shook his head, his queue brushed against his broad shoulders in a soft swish. "I'm serious now. I want you to make sure you're with me or with Gray all night. Do you promise?"

"Are you expecting some kind of trouble, Josiah?"

He squeezed her hand. "I'm just being careful. Promise?"

She hesitated, not entirely certain what to make of his strange mood. She remembered belatedly her suspicions about Robert. She hadn't seen her uncle since her wedding, and, except for one chance encounter with Jade in town, she'd not seen any of her cousins either. Jade and Alex were supposed to come for dinner soon, but Joss had issued the invitation, and Emmy hadn't spoken with them directly. She wondered if Robert knew he was under suspicion. She wondered if the Diamond Hawk had taken any action yet. She sent up a silent prayer that there wouldn't be a scene. Joss hated scenes.

Perhaps that was why he seemed so odd. Her uncle and her cousins were sure to be at the party tonight. Everyone in Carding would be there. A little flicker of warmth found its way into Emmy's heart when the notion occurred to her that Joss was probably worried she'd be embarrassed or hurt if her uncle caused trouble.

So she nodded briefly. She felt a little like she'd just uncovered one of the secrets of the universe. Happy and pleased, she wriggled her fingers in his. "I do not think it will be such a hardship to stay close to you, Josiah. It isn't as if anyone will actually want to dance with me. By the end of the evening, you'll be ready to pawn me off on the first gent who'll have me."

# Fourteen

Emmy never remembered seeing the small park look so festive, but then, she'd never attended Carding's biggest social event of the year dressed like a queen and escorted by the most attractive man in town. Strictly speaking, she thought, trying her best to be objective, Gray Lawford was probably more handsome than Joss, and Avery Brooks was certainly a good deal prettier than either of them, but there was something seductively attractive about her husband that made her toes curl in the soft leather of her ivory lace-up boots.

Colorful lanterns and garlands festooned the trees. When Joss lifted her down from the buckboard, Emmy sniffed appreciatively at the scent of sugar-roasted pumpkin and caramel-covered apples. She stood for a minute, with his hands spanned around her waist, and her fingers resting on the fine wool of his dark evening jacket. "I'm very happy, Josiah," she said quietly.

"I hadn't realized you minded our relative isolation. I'd have brought you out before."

At that, Emmy barely resisted the urge to kick his shin. "Josiah, you are the most cantankerous old soul. Why must you read things into every word I say?"

"What do you mean?"

"You deliberately interpreted my comment to mean I didn't like spending so much time at the watch house with you. I didn't mean that at all. It's just a lovely night, and a lovely party, and I'm very glad to be here with you."

He had the grace to look nonplussed. "Sorry. I'm a bit out of sorts this evening."

"I wouldn't have known."

Before he could think of an appropriate answer, Sam bounded up beside them. The twinkle in his eyes was unmistakable behind his grey mask. He skidded to a halt, effectively covering his new boots and trouser cuffs in dust. Joss frowned at him, but Sam never took his eyes off Emmy. "Cri-mi-ny, Miss Em," he said, eyes wide, mouth hanging open, "you ain't looked this good ever."

Sam was so genuinely astonished, Emmy started to laugh. Joss's frown deepened. "That's not polite, Samuel."

Sam kept staring at Emmy. "Well, she ain't. Not ever. Not once."

"Sam," Emmy said, still laughing. She laid her fingers on his sleeve. "If Jim were here, he'd give you another lecture on manners, but thank you for the compliment all the same."

Sam nodded. "I meant it, Miss Emmy. There's not a woman here what can outshine you."

"Not even Becky Morgan?" she teased.

Sam's face flushed. "Oh, jeez, I didn't mean, well, you know." He ground his toe in the dirt as he slipped a finger into the store-bought collar. He tugged at it until Emmy was sure it would pop loose.

Joss remembered his own adolescent crushes and took pity. "Where is Jim, Samuel?"

Sam shot Joss a grateful look. "Out sparking with Miss Annie," he said. "Both the banker and his wife are here tonight, so Miss Annie has some time alone." Sam wagged his bushy brown eyebrows. "First time in a long time."

Joss cuffed his ear with a light smack. "Go find Miss Morgan, Samuel, and ask her if she'd like to dance. There's no sense in not putting all those fancy clothes of yours to good use."

With an unabashed grin, Sam gave Emmy an awkward kiss on the cheek. "You really do look pretty, Miss Em. I wasn't horsin' with you."

"I know you weren't, Samuel. Save a dance for me, will you?"

Sam nodded before he went running off in the opposite direction. Emmy noticed the tear in the shoulder seam of his new jacket. She looked at Joss. "He is a bit blunt, I suppose. Sort of reminds me of an uncut gem. He's rough around the edges, but the inside certainly does have fire."

Joss pulled her hand through the bend of his arm as he started toward the crowd. "He's very fond of you, Emmy. You've done an excellent job with him."

She tipped her head against his shoulder as they walked. "I wish I could get him to trust me. When I think about his poor mother, well, she must be worried near to death over him."

Joss lifted her onto the raised platform, not bothering with the steps. "Just a little more time, I think." He leapt up beside her. "You'll get the truth out of him soon."

Emmy spotted Sam at the far end of the platform, with his head bent, listening intently to something Becky Morgan was saying. She nudged Joss's arm and pointed at the pair. "He's going to have a bad case of young love in the morning. He'll probably be sick to his stomach."

Joss captured her hand and squeezed it. His gaze scanned the crowd. "The first party like this I ever went to, I got so ripping drunk, I couldn't stand up straight for two days."

Emmy turned her startled gaze on him. My, but she felt fine standing next to him with his warm fingers laced through hers. "You? You hardly seem the type. You're always so—controlled."

He didn't look at her, but kept his attention focused on the large gathering. "Did I happen to mention I was thirteen at the time?"

"No." She listened, entranced, as always, with one of the rare glimpses he gave her into his life before Carding, Missouri.

Joss still didn't turn his head. "My oldest brother, Jarred, was chasing after Mirabella Adamson."

"Who is Mirabella Adamson?"

"When I was thirteen, I thought she was the most gorgeous girl in London. By some miracle, Mirabella's parents had agreed to bring her all the way out to my father's estate for a ball. I think they were hoping to get a marriage proposal out of Jarred." He stretched his neck to search a darkened corner of the platform.

"Did they?"

"Certainly not. Jarred's intentions didn't run toward marriage. He was only eighteen. My parents were petrified he'd do something foolish and get forced into marrying her."

Emmy started to laugh. "So while your brother chased the lovely Mirabella, and she chased him, her parents schemed, your parents agonized, and you stood in the corner and pined away."

Joss seemed to find what he was looking for. He looked at her with a satisfied gleam in his eye. "I stood in the corner and brooded was more like it. I was so angry, I swiped a flask of brandy from my brother's room and proceeded to drink myself dull."

"Were you sick the next day?"

Joss snorted. "As a swine. The only one who seemed to notice what was going on was my godfather, the Earl of Brandtwood. He and my godmother were out for the weekend house party. He caught me just as I was two-thirds of the way through the bottle."

Emmy stared in half-wonder at her husband who so easily fit into her world when he came from one where earls were casually referred to as godfathers. "What did he do?"

"He made me drink the rest of the bottle just to teach me a lesson. Then he blithely informed my father he was taking me back to London with him to help get his horses ready for the Kensington Cup."

"So your parents never knew?"

Joss shrugged. "Uncle Marcus covered for me as best he could, but I think my mother knew. *My* mother knew everything."

"What happened to Mirabella?"

"She married a pig farmer."

She laughed. "You made that up."

He nodded. "God's truth. Mirabella Adamson is married to a pig farmer, and she weighs four hundred pounds if she's an ounce. We've never let Jarred live it down."

Emmy wiggled her fingers in his hand. She was filled with a budding contentment and a sense of well-being she hadn't known in days. "When we have children, do you think we'll have stories like that to tell?"

The warm light in his gaze went stone cold, gone as surely as it had appeared. His face hardened. Emmy would have sworn a frigid breeze passed between them. "I don't know," he said, his voice sounding gruff.

Emmy realized immediately what she'd done. "I'm sorry, Josiah," she said, and she truly was, for having ruined his warm mood, for having ruined the precious moment, for casting a pall on the evening. Because he couldn't promise her forever. "I misspoke."

Joss shook his head as he straightened her spectacles.

He was terribly out of sorts this evening. He had no business taking it out on her. "I'm the one who's sorry. I've been an abominable nuisance all evening. Dance with me, Emerelda."

It took her a moment to react to the abrupt change of subject, but some of the harshness had disappeared from his voice. His fingers seemed to linger longer than necessary on the skin of her cheek. With a nod, she let him lead her onto the floor.

Her first thought was that her husband was an excellent dancer, which, she decided, should not have surprised her as much as it did. Not only was he naturally graceful, an artist's kind of graceful, but he'd learned to dance in the finest and largest ballrooms in England. A man who'd probably danced the waltz with Queen Victoria herself, wouldn't find the simple tune of Henry Eaker's fiddle, John Reames's banjo, and Walt Kerney's hand organ too much of a challenge. But it was more than that.

With one hand resting at her waist while the other cupped her fingers in a light grip, Joss made her look like a good dancer too. Why, so much so in fact, that she was besieged by invitations to dance the moment the song ended and Joss led her to the small table heavily laden with punch and sweetmeats. And because Joss seemed to expect it of her, she accepted those invitations.

Before long, nearly a half-hour had passed. She'd danced with five different partners and was pleading with the sixth to let her sit out the lively polka.

Across the platform, she saw Joss, his dark head bent, listening intently to something Sam was telling him. He looked up suddenly, as if sensing her gaze, and smiled at her. She smiled back, feeling like he'd kissed her, even all that way away. With Eanis Johnson on one side pressing a glass of punch into her hand, Hardin Willis on the other begging her for a dance, and the smile of the most attractive man alive turning her insides to butter, Emmy had never felt more cozy, more included, in her whole life.

The festive atmosphere disintegrated to a nightmare within a matter of minutes. Robert Greene, all nine children in tow, chose that moment to descend on the Harvest Festival. Though he wore a mask of his own, his wide girth, and flashy clothes, would have marked him anywhere. Emmy watched as Robert stomped onto the platform. His tailored clothes strained at the seams to cover his ever-expanding girth. His children and their escorts surged out around him like a swarm of bees. The first thing Emmy noticed was that they all looked mad as hornets.

Joss heard the disturbance and started shouldering his way through the crowd toward Emmy. He had an inkling of what was coming, and he wanted to make damned sure he was nearby when it did.

Emmy studied her family in open curiosity. They looked the same as she remembered, yet different somehow, not as glamorous. There was an odd tension over the crowd, and Emmy, remembering her suspicions about her uncle, shivered.

Robert didn't see her at first. He began pushing his way through the dense crowd, smiling widely at acquaintances and friends while his children flocked around him. It wasn't until his eyes met hers across the platform that the look on his face turned menacing. He started toward her with purposeful strides. He had the most unpleasant expression she'd ever seen on his thick lips. Everything went absolutely still. The music died. Even the crickets seemed to stop their song.

When Emmy instinctively backed up a step, she bumped into Joss. It felt like backing into a granite wall. His fingers curled on her shoulders, and she sagged into him, watching with something akin to desperation as her family stalked her. Only Jade, she noticed, hung back.

"Well, Emerelda," Robert Greene said. He came to a stop so close to her that his round belly nearly touched her. "You look well."

"So do you, Uncle Robert." She smiled at her cousins. "How are you all?"

With a frown, Ruby grabbed hold of Jefferson Piley's sleeve with long, bony fingers. "As if you didn't know."

Emmy fidgeted nervously. Joss's fingers tightened on her shoulders. "Know what?" She forced a pleasant note into her voice.

Pearl snapped open her fan with a brisk *whap* and started fanning furiously. "Don't be coy, Emerelda. That's an awfully fine dress you're wearing."

Emmy wondered why she'd never noticed how hard the lines of Pearl's face were. Avery Brooks was standing right behind her. Emmy looked him square in his soft, pretty face and felt her lips tug into a slight smile. She was completely unable to resist hurling a small gibe in her cousin's direction. "Yours is rather fine too, Pearl. Isn't it the same one you wore to the Slinktons' ball?"

Pearl gasped in outrage. Her mouth dropped open. "I wasn't aware you'd grown so heartless, Emerelda."

Emmy turned her eyes on her uncle. The feel of Joss's warm strength behind her made her feel bolder. "Why, Uncle Robert, have you closed your accounts in town?"

A loud murmur rippled over the crowd. Robert's face turned redder. "If you hadn't abandoned us when you wed that Englishman, you'd know."

Emmy shook her head. "I didn't abandon you, Uncle Robert. You lost me in a card game. Or did you forget that?"

The murmur got louder. Coral pushed her way forward to glare at Emmy. "What have you got to be so self-righteous about? You haven't any idea what it's been like since you left."

Opal nodded. "That's right, Emerelda. I don't know what you did with the money, but just this afternoon, Pete Fletcher came and took all our horses. Said they weren't paid for."

"They weren't," Pete called from the other end of the platform. He shot Emmy an apologetic look. "Miss Em used to bring me a payment every week. After she got married, the payments stopped."

Emmy resisted the urge to look over her shoulder at Joss. She'd given him the funds every Friday afternoon and asked him to take them to Pete Fletcher. For reasons of his own, he hadn't, but she didn't dare press him on the matter now. She stared at Opal instead. "Where did you think that money came from, Opal?"

"From Papa's book earnings," Gem said. "We all knew that. He told us so."

Emmy shook her head. "Uncle Robert's book earnings were used up at the gambling table. I was doing gem appraisals and cleanings to put food on the table and clothes on your backs."

"That's silly," Topaz said. She stepped from her hiding place behind Jimmy Grafton's wide body. "If you were paying all the bills, why did you always look like the poor relation?"

Pearl's lips curved into a mean little smile. "Yes, Emerelda, you were the one who couldn't go to the Slinktons' ball because you didn't have a gown."

"Emmy's telling the truth." Jade pushed her way through the crowd of her cousins, dragging Grant Lewis with her. Grant grinned at Emmy. Jade walked over next to her and took her hand to give it a comforting squeeze. "I asked Mrs. Tattingly, and Emmy paid our dress bill the morning before the Slinktons' party. That's why she couldn't afford a gown."

"That's right," Mabel Tattingly called out. "She paid me nearly one hundred dollars that very morning."

Carlton Wigger, the blacksmith, yelled, "It was always Miss Em who made sure I got paid for shoeing the horses."

"Emmy brought me the money for the new boots each fall and each spring," said Hank Whicham.

"She paid me for the well I dug," Harley Chippers piped up.

Old Otis Lampton flashed her a toothless grin. "And she always brought me peppermint when she came into town."

Robert was starting to look uncomfortable. He rubbed his hands over the distended fabric of his brocade waistcoat. "I'm sure this has all been a misunderstanding," he said, loud enough for everyone on the platform to hear. "If you will all go back to your party, my niece and I will clear everything up."

"Clear it up?" Garnet shrieked. "What's there to clear up? Since Emmy left we've been nearly starving to death. If Mr. Brooks hadn't advanced us credit, we'd all be dead."

Emmy flinched. Joss held fast and leveled his gaze on Robert. "I think you've got some explaining to do, Robert," he said.

Robert glared at him. "This is all your doing. I don't know why, but you set out to destroy me." He swung his gaze to Emmy. "Do you know he's trying to ruin my reputation with the gemological community? I haven't been able to sell a paper or deliver a lecture in weeks."

Emmy did look at him then. Joss's gaze never left Robert's face. "I just told them the truth," he said.

"You told George Fisk, the *president,* of the American

Geological Society that I hadn't written my own books."

"Did you?" Joss asked.

Robert sucked in a breath. "Do you think for one minute that silly chit could have published or written a word without the power of my name? Of course not. Who was going to take an uneducated mountain man's daughter seriously in the scientific community? It was me. I taught her everything."

Emmy had started shaking. She stared at the sea of angry faces. Joss's fingers had turned to iron clamps on her shoulders. She thought rather vaguely it was a good thing else she might have crumpled to the platform. She drew in a deep breath and turned her gaze to Robert. Her fingers curled into tight fists. "Don't you think I've paid long enough?" she said.

Her voice was so quiet, neither Robert nor Joss heard the question. "What?" Robert said, looking at her in surprise, as if he'd completely forgotten her presence.

Her fingers clenched tighter. "I said, 'Don't you think I've paid long enough?' "

"Paid for what?"

"You always took great pleasure in letting me know I was dumped on you. You didn't want or need the responsibility of another man's child. You didn't want or need the expense. You didn't want or need me. I was extra clutter."

"Emerelda, you're making no sense at all."

She ignored him. "So I worked for you. I learned your trade, I wrote your books, I paid your bills, I cleaned your house, I made sure nothing I had, nothing I was, could ever be in your way. Don't you think I've paid enough now, Uncle Robert?"

Joss drew in a deep breath. He had a sudden insight into Emmy he'd missed before. She was so compulsively neat so she'd never be accused of being under foot.

Of being clutter. He wanted to kill Robert Greene, only this time, he wanted to do it for Emmy as much as he wanted to do it for Allyson.

Robert's face had turned ugly. His thick lips were peeled back into something of a sneer. "Who do you think you are, speaking to me like that, Emerelda?" Robert bellowed, glaring. "This is all lies. You're letting that husband of yours destroy me."

Emmy shook her head. "You destroyed yourself when you started putting your name on those false certificates."

Joss flinched behind her. She ignored him. All the color drained out of Robert's fat face. "I don't know what you mean," he said.

"Yes, you do. You needed money to pay your gambling debts, so you sold your reputation for a few fast dollars. Now, people have died because of it. It may not have caught up with you yet, Uncle Robert, but it's going to."

"Watch your tongue, Emerelda."

"Don't threaten me," she said.

Robert sneered at her. "Why the hell not?"

"Because," Joss drawled, "when you threaten my wife, you threaten me."

His voice sounded so rock-hard, so sure, so menacing that the crowd gasped. Jade's fingers tightened on Emmy's. Emmy continued to stare at Robert. "It's the truth, isn't it Uncle Robert?"

"You don't know what you're talking about."

"I do. You signed those certificates. People died and you are too much of a coward to admit that you did it."

Robert's face screwed into a mask of fury. "You've pushed me too far, Emerelda."

"What's the matter, Uncle Robert? Don't you want

your children to know what a deceitful, lying coward you've turned into?"

Ruby sucked in a breath so loud it was audible above the animated silence of the large crowd. Robert's face turned white, then red. His eyes glittered dangerously. His whole body drew up tighter than a bowstring. Before Joss or Emmy could react, he swung a beefy fist and backhanded her across the jaw.

Pearl fainted against Avery. Garnet screamed. Ruby gasped. Joss growled something dangerous. Sam started barreling across the platform at a dead run.

And the earth opened up, and hell gushed forth into Carding, Missouri.

Joss immediately thrust Emmy behind him to protect her, then drove his fist into Robert's fat belly with such force, that the man went flailing backwards into the crowd. Sam launched himself into the air with a whoop. When he landed on Robert's back, he wrapped his scrawny legs and arms around the man's wide body.

Sam started pounding on Robert's head with his fist, while Joss delivered another solid punch to his midsection. When Robert spun around, trying to shake Sam off his shoulders, Sam's feet connected with Jimmy Grafton's groin. Topaz screamed and grabbed hold of Jimmy just as he dove for Sam. She knocked him off balance. He stumbled into Eanis Johnson. Eanis slugged Jimmy. Jimmy jumped on Eanis, and they started rolling on the wood platform.

Eanis's cousin Eddy saw the commotion from across the platform and started in, only to have his progress arrested by Wes Schenk, Jimmy's brother-in-law. Wes hit Eddy. Eddy swung at Wes, missed when Wes ducked, and his fist connected with Clovis Tattingly's head.

Sam was still holding on to Robert's shoulders, hollering for all his worth, and before long, every man on the platform was either swinging fists or running for cover. Things didn't get really bad, though, until Avery took a menacing step toward Emmy. Old Otis Lampton picked up a pumpkin and crashed it down on Avery's head, knocking him out cold. Pumpkin shards and Avery collapsed to the platform. Somebody started hurling muffins and candy apples through the air. The bowl of punch ended up poured over Pearl's head. Joss drove his fist into Robert's belly again just as Carlton Wigger's knuckles connected with Joss's good eye. With a yell, Sam slammed his fist down on Robert's head. All the women were screaming, or swooning, or staring with mouth's aghast, except for Mabel Tattingly who had an apron full of candy apples she was throwing into the crowd.

Emmy and Jade stood at the edge of the platform watching the commotion in frozen horror. A pumpkin muffin whizzed past Emmy's ear. She turned to find the culprit at the same moment Gray Lawford rode his palamino mare onto the platform. He fired two shots into the air. Joss decided that was as good a time as any to get as far from the chaos as possible. Without sparing Gray so much as a second look, he dove for Emmy. He had her over his shoulder and was striding for the steps of the platform with Jade trailing along behind, before Gray fired his third shot.

Grant Lewis was sitting in the buckboard grinning at him. He leapt down and tossed him the reins. Joss dumped Emmy into her seat. "Thanks, Lewis," he said.

Grant tipped his hat, then took Jade's hand. "I thought you might be looking for a means of escape before matters got really sticky."

"Emmy. Emmy." Alex was running toward them with little Tommy Wigger behind her. She was biting on a candy apple.

"Alex," Emmy called. "Stay with Jade, darling. Grant will look after you."

Alex skidded to a stop in front of Jade. Tommy slammed into the back of her. "I miss you, Emmy."

Emmy caught her breath. Joss was climbing into the driver's seat of the buckboard. "I miss you, too, Alex," she said.

Joss stamped on the brake. "Jade," he called.

"Yes, Mr. Brickston?"

"Please don't forget you're scheduled for dinner at our house one night next week. Emmy has been looking forward to it."

Despite the sinking sensation in the pit of her stomach, Emmy had to suppress a smile. Only Joss could be that civilized in the midst of such an unmitigated disaster. Several more shots sounded amid the confusion on the platform. Jade gave Emmy's hand a quick squeeze. "Yes, yes. I won't forget."

"Bring Alex," Emmy said.

Jade nodded. "We will. Take care, Emmy."

"You too, Jade."

Joss snapped the reins to send the horses galloping into the autumn night.

They traveled in silence almost all the way to the bluff. Emmy twisted her hands in her lap while Joss drove the horses along the darkened road with only the moonlight for guidance. They were within sight of the watch house when he reined in beside a small clearing and turned to look at her.

Emmy sat beside him, her head bowed, her hands clasped together in her lap, clutching the gilded mask. Even in the dim moonlight he could see the lines of worry on her face. She was fighting tears. He would have sworn it. At just that instant, he saw a large, glistening drop form at the corner of her eye and slide down the soft skin of her cheek. Joss sucked in a sharp breath as he stomped his foot on the brake.

The moment the buckboard stopped, Emmy jumped

down from her seat and ran for the trees. She collapsed with a sob onto the soft grass. Joss swung down from the buckboard and went after her where he knelt beside her on the damp earth. He stripped his own mask from his face. Her shoulders were shaking with the force of her sobs. He laid his hand on her back. "Let's talk, Em," he said quietly. She ignored him. "Please," he implored.

"Go away," she said. "Please just go away."

"Emmy, please listen to me."

She shook her head. "You couldn't understand. I don't want to—to talk about it." Her voice broke on a sob. Joss felt it all the way down to his bones.

"Emmy, I'm not going to leave you up here like this."

She raised her head. "Why do you care, Josiah? You've never cared about me, did you? If you had you wouldn't have used me like this."

"Emmy . . ." He looked at her helplessly. "Emmy, you have to let me explain."

She raised tear-soaked eyes to look at him in the moonlight. "You did this on purpose. You knew what would happen tonight and it did. What's there to explain?"

Shucking off his jacket, he laid it carefully around her shoulders. "Please, Em. Just let me talk to you."

She sniffed miserably and sat up. Carefully, she spread her skirts around her. "My gown is ruined." She showed him a large tear in the skirt.

"I'll buy you another one. I promise."

"I liked this one." She sounded more melancholy than distressed.

He covered her hand with his and gave it a gentle squeeze. "Perhaps you can use the material for a new corset."

That won a strangled sound from the back of her

throat that Joss decided could have been called a laugh if he stretched his imagination. She met his gaze and wiped at her cheeks with the back of her hand. "I need your handkerchief."

Joss felt a great tide of relief. He dug in his pocket and handed her the white cotton square. "One day soon, I'm going to have to procure you a passel of your own."

Emmy gently blew her nose. "It's only because you make me cry, Josiah. If you didn't make me cry, I wouldn't need one."

When he sensed her slight change of mood, he dropped down beside her to capture the handkerchief in his large hand. Carefully, he wiped the tears from her cheeks, then bent to softly kiss each eyelid. "Better?" he asked.

She nodded. "How's your eye?"

"My eye's fine. Don't worry about it."

"I saw Carlton Wigger hit you. Are you certain you're all right?" Despite her best efforts, her voice wavered on the last word. She was afraid she'd start crying again.

Joss took both her hands in one of his. "You're the one I'm worried about." He used his other hand to poke at the red place on her fist.

She batted his hand away. "That hurts."

Joss's breath came out on a hiss. "God, Em. I'm so sorry."

"It was bound to happen sooner or later."

Joss lost his patience and pulled her onto his lap. She struggled briefly, but he held fast. "Now, be still and listen to me. I want to explain."

"What's there to explain?" She still couldn't bring herself to look at him.

"Why I wrote George Fisk that letter and didn't tell you. Why I haven't let you visit your family. Why I've kept you isolated at the watch house. Why I didn't give the money to Pete Fletcher, or any of the others, like you asked me. Why I married you."

"Oh. That."

Joss kissed her right palm and pulled her close against him. "Yes, that. Sweetheart, it isn't at all like it seems."

Emmy pillowed her damp cheek against his chest. She found comfort in the steady thrum of his heartbeat. "Then explain it to me, please, Josiah. Because at the moment, it's very much like it seems."

He leaned his head back against the tree. "At first, it was true, I had no other intention than destroying your uncle. Surely you've guessed by now he had something to do with Allyson's death."

Emmy nodded. "Yes. I know."

Joss's breathing turned harsh. "I came to Carding intent on finding who had murdered my family. I was consumed with it. It didn't take long before I discovered Robert's involvement, and once I saw how dependent he was on you, well, I knew I needed you."

"What you told me that day in your office," she said, tracing an absent circle on his chest, "it was true. Wasn't it?"

"About why I married you?" he guessed. She nodded. "No," he said. "I wanted it to be true. I didn't want to feel anything for you. I didn't want to feel anything ever again. Not after what I'd been through, but I couldn't stop it."

Emmy tipped her head back to look at him. His face had drawn taut. His scar had whitened and started to twitch. She traced a finger over the line of his patch. "Josiah?"

"Yes?" his voice sounded raw.

"What are you going to do to Uncle Robert?"

Joss's breath came out in a long rasp. "I don't know,

Em. I can't do anything until I know who else he's working with."

"Did you really think you'd gain anything by marrying me?"

"I gained a lot. I knew you were the key to Robert's existence when you detected the fake pearl I'd substituted in the sapphire earrings I brought you the first day we met."

"You did that on purpose?"

"Um-hmm. I had no idea you were tending to business for your uncle until after I came to Carding and heard your name a few times. I needed to know how good you were. After the episode with the pearl, and then later when I saw you writing that treatise, well, I knew for sure."

"Why didn't you just tell me the truth?"

"I needed you to recognize it on your own. If I told you, you wouldn't have believed me. It would have been asking too much of you to choose sides. When you saw the gems in Avery's store, it was enough for you."

Emmy sighed. "Now that you know he's guilty, what are you going to do?"

"I can't do anything yet. I don't have any proof for one, and I don't know who else is involved for another. I want them all, Emmy." His voice took on a sharp edge. "I have to know who was there that afternoon."

She looked at him closely. "How long are you going to live your life in the past, Josiah?"

His gaze met hers. "As long as it takes."

"And where does that leave me?"

Joss hesitated. "I don't know," he said honestly. "I can't let Allyson's death go unanswered. It's a matter of honor, of living, for me. I couldn't live with myself if I turned my back on it. After that, I don't know. There hasn't been a future for me for a long time."

Emmy sighed, saddened, but not really surprised by

his answer. "Do you at least have suspicions about who else might be involved?"

"Yes, a few. Nothing I can act on yet."

"Do you think Avery's involved? I asked the Diamond Hawk, but he wouldn't tell me."

"Do you think he is?"

"I don't know," she admitted. "It's hard to imagine that Avery would actually do something illegal, but then, I couldn't have imagined it about Uncle Robert either."

"Emmy, I know you have feelings for Avery Brooks, but you have to consider the possibility. It's a good possibility. You said yourself he was anxious the day you looked at the gems."

"I do not have feelings for Avery Brooks."

"You did once."

"Before," she said quietly. "Before you."

Joss sighed, shaken. He didn't want her to care for him like that. And he sure as hell didn't want it to matter. "Sometimes you scare the hell out of me, Emmy."

She waited, hoping he'd say more. When he didn't, she prodded him with another question. "But do you really believe Avery is capable of anything illegal?"

Joss nodded. "Greedy men are capable of a lot of things. I know for a fact that Avery has been making some very large bank transactions over the past few months."

"They could be business transactions."

"They could be."

"But you don't think so."

"No. I don't."

"Have you discussed this with Gray Lawford?"

"Yes. The same day he told me he was your cousin." Emmy hesitated. "Josiah?"

"Hmm?"

"Why didn't you take the money to Pete Fletcher like I asked you?"

Joss exhaled a slow breath. "I didn't mean to deceive you. All that money's in the vault in my office. You can have every cent of it back."

"But why didn't you take it to him?"

"Because I knew Robert wasn't going to act again unless he got desperate for the money. He was already scared to death of being caught. I was afraid he'd back out if I didn't force him to do it. If he didn't agree to sign another round of certificates, the whole scheme would have fallen through."

"Did he do it?"

"Not yet."

"Did I ruin your chances by confronting him tonight?"

Joss shrugged. "Maybe. I don't know. I knew Robert would be furious when he saw you. Things have been difficult for him lately. The gossip in town is fairly intense. Folks are losing their patience."

"That's why you wouldn't let me visit them, isn't it."

"Partly. I was worried, though. I had no way of knowing what Robert would do, and I wanted to make sure I was around when he moved on you."

"Why did you pick tonight?"

Wavering on indecision, he rubbed his palm up and down her back in long, soothing strokes. "Two reasons. I didn't think Robert would be able to resist going after you, especially not with this business with George Fisk hanging over his head."

"And?"

He sighed. "And, in light of our, uh, changed circumstances in this marriage, I wanted to get things moving again. I wouldn't be doing right by you if I didn't settle matters as soon as possible."

A long silence passed between them. Emmy absently

stroked her hand over the soft lawn of his white shirt. "You never planned for us to have a real marriage, did you?"

He shook his head. "It wasn't fair to you. If we'd never consummated the marriage, well, you could have gotten it annulled later. I didn't marry you for the right reasons, and I didn't want you to be bound to me for the wrong ones."

"I'm not sorry, Josiah. I love you."

"I know, Em. God help me, I know. I've made a horrendous mess of everything, and now I don't know what to do."

She shivered. "What do you want to do?"

"I can't think beyond finding the man who killed Allyson and Adam and Michael. When that happens, I just don't know. I can't let them walk away from it, Emmy. I can't."

"I know," she said quietly.

"But after that, I, well, I can't think that far. I've spent nearly two years promising myself I wouldn't think any farther than the next day."

"Does your family know?" she asked.

"Know what?"

"How your wife and sons died?"

He shook his head. "No one knows. Not really. I've never told anyone the whole story."

"What did you tell them?"

"I wrote home and told them there had been an accident. My mother made my father buy passage on the first ship across the Atlantic. When they got here, I was a mess. I hadn't bathed or eaten hardly at all for weeks. It took nearly three months before my health was restored, and I could get Mama to go home. Even then, I had to make my father nearly drag her to the ship."

Emmy squeezed him tight. "You should have told them, Josiah. You needed them then."

"I couldn't, Emmy." He paused. "I was too ashamed."

She looked at him in surprise. "It wasn't your fault. You mustn't ever believe it was your fault."

His eyes were sad, haunted. He let out a long shaky breath. "I gave up trying to convince myself of that a long time ago."

She saw something in his gaze that she didn't like. She rubbed her finger over his scar. "I'm afraid," she said.

"I won't let anything happen to you."

"You're so sure you caused their deaths, you're nearly determined to die too. Jedediah used to say, 'If a man's already decided he's going to die the next day, he'll probably find a way to make it happen.' If something happens to you, I won't have anything left, Josiah. What will I do?"

"That's one of the reasons I wrote George Fisk. You should be established on your own without needing Robert's name anymore."

"It won't matter. I'd rather have you than all the esteem and reputation in the world."

Joss exhaled a deep breath. It wasn't right that a man should be loved like this twice in one lifetime, especially a man no more deserving of it than he was. He might not be able to make many promises to Emmy about the future, but he could at least give her the security of knowing she'd always be well cared for. Almost surprising even himself, he said, "Emmy, I want you to go to St. Louis with me."

She looked at him in surprise. "What do you mean?"

"Right now," he said. "Will you?"

"Right now this minute?"

He nodded. "There's a Continental riverboat leaving

the landing in less than a half hour. If you'll go with me, I want to show you my life, what I came from. I want you to understand. Nothing's going to happen to you. I swear it."

She stared at him for long seconds, watching as the moonlight cast haunting shadows over the strong planes of his face. He looked haggard, tired, like a man who'd fought too many demons for too long, and needed rest and a safe haven. Like a man who needed to face the past and be done with it. She could help him do that, she realized, if she loved him enough. He wasn't just asking her to go to St. Louis with him, he was asking her to see his past. He was asking her to share the private hell he'd kept locked away and reserved for himself alone.

She hesitated only briefly before she nodded. "I'd follow you anywhere, Josiah."

# Fifteen

Neither of them had slept on board the *Empress*. After a quick conversation with the captain, Joss had procured them a stateroom, then left Emmy alone, suggesting she get some rest. She'd stared out the porthole during the three-hour voyage, listening to the lap of waves and the churn of the paddle wheel, while he'd stayed on deck and watched the stars.

When they reached the landing in St. Louis, Joss hired a carriage to take them to his home. Emmy sank onto the soft leather seats with something akin to dread. Since they'd left the bluff, even before they'd boarded the *Empress*, Joss had become more withdrawn. She sensed she was losing him. When he sat beside her, she grabbed his hand. His fingers were like ice. "Josiah?" her eyes met his in the darkness, "you're leaving me behind."

Joss gave her a blank look. "What?"

"You've been distant, withdrawn, since we left the bluff. You're going somewhere without me."

With a shake of his head, he folded her hand in his. "I'm sorry, Emmy. I—" he stopped to clear his throat. "It's hard."

"I know. That's why I want to share it with you. You don't have to do it alone."

He squeezed her fingers until they hurt. She didn't care. The carriage rolled on in silence until they stopped in front of a large, comfortable-looking brown-stone town house. "It's big," she said wishing she didn't sound like such a dimwit.

He waited until the driver opened the carriage door before he climbed down so he could lift her onto the pavement. "Didn't you expect it to be big?"

She shook her head. "Not like that. I mean, you seem so comfortable just being simple." She stared up at the big wooden door. "This seems almost out of place."

Compared to the watch house, the place was a mansion. Joss was starting to feel some hefty pangs of guilt when he realized Emmy truly didn't know anything about his financial background. He'd been so wrapped up in his own thoughts, he hadn't given notice to how hard she'd been working to save money at every turn, while still trying to make the watch house feel like a home. It was no wonder she'd been so surprised by the gown he'd ordered for her. He straightened her lace collar. "I'm sorry if you think I misled you. I thought you understood Continental Shipping's position."

She kept staring at the door. "Well, I did. I mean, I knew Continental was doing very well, but I, oh, I don't know. You just seem different here." She finally looked at him. "More like the English lord you are, and less like the map maker I'm married to."

Joss took her hand to lead her up the steps. "I'm both, Em. I'm just having more trouble than I thought balancing the two."

Emmy waited while he rapped sharply on the door. Nothing happened. After several seconds, he knocked again. Still nothing. Joss started pounding on the door with his fist. There was a terrific noise from inside the house. Then the metal bolt slid free, and the large door swung open.

"What in bloody hell—Mr. Joss?"

Emmy found herself face to face with the oddest-looking man she'd ever seen. Small in stature, not even five feet tall, she guessed, he was so wiry she might have mistaken him for a boy if it hadn't been for his shaggy, long white beard and even longer hair. He was chewing on an enormous cigar, but he'd clearly forgotten to put his teeth in. His lips were turned in at the sides. He was standing in the doorway staring at Joss, wearing nothing but a blue dressing robe. Beneath the hem, Emmy could clearly see where one of his legs had been replaced by a wooden peg at the knee. Beyond his shoulder, the shattered vase on the floor explained the loud crash she'd heard before he'd opened the door. The large black dog beside him thumped his tail as he licked Joss's hand with ardent glee.

Joss looked at her apologetically. "Emmy, this is Mr. Pinkus Seaton. He's my," Joss paused, "my man," he said rather lamely.

Pinkus Seaton frowned at him as he plucked the cigar out of his mouth. "Not lately I'm not. Where the bloody hell have you been? Why the hell hasn't your eye healed yet?" He looked at Emmy. "Who the hell is that?"

"Pinkus." Joss's voice held a note of warning. "Emerelda is my wife."

The man's toothless jaw dropped open. "Your wife?" Emmy imagined she must look very out of place standing on the stairs of the big house with her hair mussed and her gown torn.

She opened her mouth to introduce herself to the strange little man, but Joss interrupted her. "Yes," he said. The simple retort brooked no more questions. He pulled her inside, then shut the door before he squatted down next to the dog. "How are you, Archimedes? Is Pinkus keeping you fed?" The dog began licking Joss's face with unsuppressed exuberance.

"Damn mongrel eats more than I do."

Joss slanted Pinkus a wry look. "Which isn't saying much. You're wasting away again, Pinkus. I'll have to speak to Mrs. Gronheim about you."

Pinkus snorted. "Blasted woman's always trying to force food down my throat."

Joss's eyes met Emmy's. "Mrs. Gronheim is my cook. She's six feet tall and weighs three hundred pounds." Emmy looked at him, skeptical. "It's true," he said. "I hired her to take care of Pinkus."

Pinkus grumbled a few more choice curses beneath his breath as he waddled over to the door. He stretched up to slam the bolt into place. "Well, welcome back. 'Bout time you dragged yourself home. Your mama's been nearly frantic with worry sending letters across the ocean trying to find your sorry backside." He looked at Emmy. "You, too. Guess the house is yours now. I'll pack up and leave in the morning if you want."

Emmy started to tell him she wanted no such thing, but Pinkus pivoted on his peg and waddled off in the opposite direction, ignoring the broken vase. Joss gave Archimedes a final pat. He stood, sending the dog racing after Pinkus. "I'd forgotten," he said, "what it felt like here."

"What does it feel like?"

"Pinkus has been with me a very long time. He lost his leg dragging me out of a fire when I was fourteen, and most of his teeth scrapping with other servants on my behalf. He cared for my family a great deal. It's been very hard on him."

Emmy wrapped her arms around Joss's waist and squeezed hard. "It hurts so much doesn't it, Josiah?"

"Almost too much," he said. He held her for long minutes as he scanned the dim interior of the foyer. Everything was as he remembered it. The long banister Michael used for sliding, the wide oak staircase, the thick carpet and large windows, the imported crystal chandelier. Nothing had changed, and yet, everything had. Allyson wouldn't come gliding out of the drawing room door at the sound of his voice with a handful of cut flowers she was arranging. Michael wouldn't call to him from the top of the staircase before making the long slide down and flying off the end, always certain Joss would be there to catch him. Adam wouldn't toddle out from behind his mother's skirt and tug on Joss's trouser legs with his pudgy fingers, demanding his attention.

Joss felt a tremor begin in the region of his belly. His voice was hoarse when he spoke. "I think it will be best if you look around. I'll wait for you in the library."

Emmy looked up at him. "Josiah, I—"

He dropped a soft, gentle kiss on her lips. "Please, Em. I need some time."

Emmy hugged him tight once more before she stepped out of his arms. "Which one's the library?"

He pointed to the door. "That one. Take as much time as you want, all right?"

"All right." She stood in the foyer and wrung her hands while she watched him stride to the library. When the door shut behind him with a soft *click,* Emmy wrapped her arms around her waist feeling suddenly alone, and very, very afraid.

As if on cue, Archimedes came bounding out from behind the staircase. He bumped her hand with his head. She scratched his ears, finding a strange sort of comfort in his affection. "Would you like to show me the house, Archimedes?"

He bumped her hand with his nose again, and Emmy looped her fingers through his leather collar. "All right. Let's look upstairs first."

The dog bounded ahead of her. Emmy clung to his collar as she hurried up the long staircase. At the top,

Archimedes pulled her to the left. So Emmy followed, stopping in front of the first door. "This one, Archimedes?"

The dog panted. Emmy turned the knob. The door opened silently into an enormous boudoir. She searched until she found the gaslights. Once the room was lit by the warm, yellow glow, she stared at it in wonder. Never in her life had she seen such a place. She was almost afraid to touch anything.

Beneath the chair rail, dark cherry paneling covered the walls. The rich polish gleamed in the gaslight. Mauve silk covered the walls to the ceiling. Blue and mauve curtains hung loose over enormous windows all along the far side of the room. The carpet was thick and lush, unlike any she'd ever seen. On impulse, she stooped down and threaded her fingers through the deep pile. That was when she saw the painting.

Above the mantel, hung a portrait that Emmy knew immediately was Allyson. She was seated with Michael and Adam in a garden, laughing while Michael pressed a rose into her hand and Adam tried to catch a butterfly with his fingers. Emmy crossed the room to stare at it. She almost expected the lovely woman in the picture to ask what she was doing snooping about the house.

Allyson had, indeed, been lovely, with hair the color of corn silk, and eyes the deepest blue Emmy had ever seen. In the painting, she wore the purple sapphires Joss had brought to Emmy's office that morning. Her face was turned easily in its laughing smile, as if laughter were a common thing for her.

Emmy stared at the painting a long time. She memorized the details of Michael's dark hair and Adam's blond curls, of Allyson's sparkling eyes and laughing smile. She didn't even realize she was frozen to the spot until Archimedes nudged her hand again. "Did she always laugh so much, Archimedes?"

She would have sworn that he nodded. Grabbing the dog's collar, she said, "I think I've seen enough of this room, Archimedes. Perhaps you'd better show me another one."

Emmy spent nearly an hour looking from room to room, absorbing the intimate details of Joss's life. She found the suite of bedrooms he'd shared with Allyson. She stared at it for long minutes, feeling out of place, and somehow slightly foolish. The large four-poster bed with its crocheted canopy and spread dominated one of the bedrooms while the other had evidently been used as a parlor.

The parlor was lined with enormous wardrobes full of clothes—more clothes than Emmy had ever seen in one place before. She thought of the brief conversation she'd had with Joss over her own wardrobe and flushed in embarrassment. He must have thought her a fool for her concerns over the cost of her simple calico dresses and cotton skirts. She fingered the soft velvet of a blue gown with a feeling of despair. How could she ever hope to belong in this part of his life? Archimedes rubbed against her legs until she followed him from the room.

In Michael's room, she saw the maps and paints and drawing pencils strewn haphazardly across the small desk. She pictured the little head bent over one of his father's maps in rapt concentration. There was a rocking horse in the corner, and a chest piled high with boyhood treasures like toy boats, and rocks and sticks, and a clump of dead flowers. Emmy automatically moved to straighten the desk. She fingered each of the paints with a delicate touch for fear she'd intrude on the little boy's privacy.

In the nursery, Adam's toys awaited him in his crib.

It looked untouched, as if no one had entered since the night of his death. The blankets were turned back in preparation. Emmy remembered Joss telling her they'd been traveling at night when Allyson had been killed. Adam's bed was still waiting for him. One of the blankets had fallen to the floor. Emmy folded it carefully over the railing of the crib. Archimedes decided it was time to go.

By the time she reached the library, Emmy was exhausted, drained, from the emotional upheaval of seeing Joss's house. At times, she had felt his family's presence so acutely, it wouldn't have surprised her if one of them had rounded a corner and said hello to her. Adam's high chair still sat in the dining room where, evidently, the family had taken meals together despite modern day customs of feeding the children in the nursery. The drawing room was filled with Allyson's feminine affectations. Mementos of England lay about, carefully mixed with childhood art and treasured gifts.

Emmy paused outside the library to scratch Archimedes' ears. "Thank you for your help, Archimedes," she whispered. As if sensing his duty was done, the big dog bounded off toward the stairs. Drawing a deep breath, Emmy reached for the doorknob.

The library door swung open. She paused, transfixed by the sight of Joss at the far end of the room, his good eye closed, playing the enormous piano. His fingers were moving over the keys in a soft, haunting melody that was filled with something so intense, so deeply painful, Emmy felt almost like an intruder.

An untouched glass of brandy sat on the edge of the piano. Joss had lit the fire in the large room, but not the gaslamps. There was something very unreal about watching him from across the room in the eerie orange glow of the fire. Emmy nearly turned around and left, but he stopped playing abruptly and opened his eye. She felt strangely impaled on his gaze. So she stared at him, torn between a desire to rush across the room and comfort him, and an equally strong desire to flee.

"What did you find?" he asked. The raw note in his voice proved to be her undoing.

Emmy all but ran across the room to the piano. He caught her close to him, nearly squeezing the breath out of her, but she didn't mind. "I found the happiness you lost, Josiah, and I want to help you get it back."

His gaze met hers. He rested his hands on either side of her waist with a slight shake of his head. "I don't know where to start."

She threaded her fingers through his hair. The soft waves twined around her fingers. "Why don't we start with the nice things and see where that takes us?"

Joss leaned his forehead against her breast. A shudder racked his large shoulders. "I don't deserve you, Emerelda."

His voice was a harsh whisper. Emmy kissed the crown of his head. "Just start at the beginning, Josiah. I'll be right here if you need me."

He drew in a shaky breath. "I met Allyson when I was twenty-one years old. I had just completed my cartography studies at Cambridge. She was enjoying her debut Season in London."

Emmy shifted so she could sit beside Joss on the piano bench. "How did you meet her?"

His eye took on a far away look. "Everyone knew her. She was one of the Incomparables that Season. Every man in London wanted her."

"But she fell in love with you?"

His brief exhalation was almost a laugh. "She didn't know I existed. Her mother had died years before, and her father, the Earl of Castehaven, had asked his aunt to serve as Allyson's chaperon and social guide. The earl was determined to procure the best possible marriage proposal for his daughter. The third son of a duke, even an important duke, couldn't hope to compete."

"What did you do?"

"My Aunt Caroline had invited Allyson to a ball, and I managed to meet her that evening."

"You fell in love instantly?" Emmy asked, ignoring the slight twinge of jealousy.

"Sooner. God, Em, you can't imagine what she looked like that night. I couldn't breathe I was so awestruck." He cast Emmy a rueful smile. "It sounds silly now."

She shook her head, remembering how she'd felt the morning he'd walked into her office. "I don't think it sounds silly at all. Did she fall in love with you right then too?"

Joss shot her a self-deprecating smile. He stood from the piano bench, then reached for her hand. "Hardly," he drawled as he led her to the more comfortable sofa. He sat so he could drape his arm around her shoulders. "I didn't rate more than a passing glimpse and a notice of my title, or lack thereof."

Emmy thought Allyson sounded rather shallow. "Was Allyson very interested in titles?"

"Not really. She was heavily reliant on her aunt, though, and Dowager Bess, as my brothers and I called her, wasn't going to settle for less than a ducal coronet."

"So how did you manage to win her?"

Joss stared at the fire. "I have my mother to thank for that. I was never certain how she knew which way the wind was blowing, but I imagine she decided to take matters into her own hands after I mooned about for well over a fortnight, I had been playing polo with my friends one afternoon, when I arrived home around four-thirty. I was barely through the door when I was told my mother required my presence in her sitting room immediately. I assumed, of course, that something was dreadfully wrong, and all but ran up the stairs to see her. I was covered in dirt and sweat, and urgently in need of a bath when I burst in on them."

"Allyson was there?"

Joss nodded. "My mother had invited her and her aunt to tea. My brother Jarred, was, after all, considered one of the finest catches in London, and there was no way Dowager Bess was going to miss an opportunity like that."

Emmy trailed her fingers over his thigh to smooth a wrinkle from his elegant trousers. "What happened?"

"My mother, of course, was delighted with the entire scenario. She made a great show of telling Allyson and her aunt how surprised she was to see me, and made me sit down and take tea with them. After they left, Mama gave me a good lecturing, and told me if I really wanted Allyson, she believed I could win her, but I'd have to sink my teeth into it and stop moping about like a love-starved calf."

"Did you?"

"I made the biggest possible bother of myself, all but camping on Allyson's doorstep to be noticed. I knew she was receiving all the usual fripperies London gents offer when they're courting, so I set out to make certain I stood out from the crowd.

"I found out through a friend," he continued, "that Allyson was afraid of horses and preferred walking instead. So I walked in the Park every morning until I learned her schedule. I was always standing beneath the same tree at the same time every day. I discovered that she liked dogs, and I bought a puppy and started taking him to the park with me."

"Archimedes?" Emmy guessed.

Joss nodded. "Yes. I also found out Allyson was fluent in ancient Greek, of all things. Hence, the poor pup's name. I suspect he would have preferred something more dignified like Wolf, or Bear."

"He seems quite content with it to me."

"Yes, well, I used him shamelessly that Season. The first day Allyson and her aunt stopped to talk to me about Archimedes, I nearly fainted."

"I doubt that."

"Don't. I made a top-rate fool of myself. I went to every ball, every dinner party, every conversazione, in London and turned up at her elbow like a bad headache that wouldn't be forgotten. Allyson didn't like champagne, so I made sure I had a glass of lemonade always at the ready. I maneuvered myself onto her dance card. When I found out she enjoyed opera, I made a point of introducing her to several composers who are friends of my family. I became such a confounded nuisance, she told me one evening I was like a splinter under the skin. No matter how much she tried to ignore me, I kept turning up to annoy her at the most inopportune times."

Despite herself, Emmy had to smile. The image of Josiah pining away was almost comical in light of his cool reserve and casual elegance. "Not a very good beginning," she teased.

He shook his head. "I was beginning to attract her, though. I knew it. She didn't ignore me anymore, and, once or twice, I caught her watching me from across the room."

"It sounds very tedious."

"It was. Had I not been so completely enamored, I would have likely given up."

"But you didn't?"

"No. In fact, I owe my success to the stress of the situation. It was the evening of the Duchess of Hawthorne's annual Season ball. Regina Hawthorne was one of the most respected and feared hostesses in London right up until her death a few years ago. Everyone who received an invitation to her annual ball attended. If you had plans, you changed them. No one ever missed an event at Hawthorne House."

"Allyson was there?"

"Yes. It was packed that night. The room was so crowded, hardly anyone was dancing, and it was stiflingly hot. The heat from the candles turned the place into a near inferno, and I was feeling particularly uncomfortable. I had never really enjoyed the demands of social life in London. I had been to so many balls and parties over the last few weeks, I was exhausted. Allyson was standing in the center of a ring of suitors, when I finally found her in the crush. I suddenly had such an acute need for privacy, I slipped out the ballroom door and walked down the hall to the duchess's music room.

"I had been to Hawthorne House on numerous occasions, and knew from experience that the music room had two doors that opened onto the terrace. As I suspected, it was empty. So I slipped inside and locked the door, opening both terrace doors and all the windows to let the cool air in. The light from the ballroom was so bright, I didn't even need to light the candles in the music room. I sat down at the piano and started to play, just as a means to calm my spirit."

"I didn't know you played the piano until I heard you tonight," Emmy said.

"Of all my brothers and sisters, I was the artist. Mama had composers give me music lessons, and painters give me drawing lessons while my brothers were learning to ride and shoot and any number of other fun things."

"Did you mind?"

"I never thought about it really. It just seemed right,

somehow, that I should learn those things. I would not be able to draw maps as I do, had I not been allowed, and encouraged, to create as a child."

Emmy led him back to the story. "You were in the music room," she prodded gently.

"Yes. I was playing Franz Schubert's *Winter Journey*. I'd learned the piece from the composer himself shortly before his death. I knew that night that Allyson was meant to be mine, and I hadn't just been imagining the entire thing. She'd been suffering from the heat and had stepped out onto the terrace when she heard the music. She followed the sound until she stepped into the music room and found me playing the piano.

"She said later that she stood there for nearly a quarter hour listening to me play before I felt her presence and turned around. It was like something out of a dream, Emmy. The light in the room was dim. The candles in the ballroom and the glow of the full moon were the only light we had. We sat in the music room and talked for what seemed like hours. I felt as though I'd known her my entire life."

Emmy ruthlessly pushed aside the sharp pain in her heart. "And she fell in love with you right then."

"Right then," Joss said. "Although it wouldn't really have mattered. She'd been gone so long that her aunt came looking for her. When we were caught in the darkened music room behind a locked door, well, I would have been forced to marry her whether I wanted to or not."

"But why?"

"Because the English are the most prudish people on earth. As far as they're concerned, there's only one possible explanation for a gentleman and a lady to be alone together."

"Did she mind?"

"No indeed. She confessed to me later that she'd

deliberately stayed in the room with me, hoping we'd be found out. Her father was not very happy about it. He was already giving serious consideration to a marriage proposal from the Prince of Thuringia, but at that point there was nothing we could do."

"What about your family?"

"Oh, my family is completely oblivious to scandal. My mother practically thrives on it, in fact. They were waxing ecstatic by the end of the evening, but to placate the earl, my father suggested we should be wed right away. I wasn't about to argue with that course of action, you understand, and Allyson became my wife a few weeks later."

"You loved her very much, didn't you, Josiah?"

"Madly," he said. "Almost obsessively, I'd say. The kind of love only very young people can have. We were very different in what we wanted, and in how we viewed things, but I'd have cut my right arm off if she'd asked it of me. In reflection, I never really respected Allyson enough for what she sacrificed on my behalf."

At that, Emmy sat back and looked at him for the first time since he'd begun the story. "What do you mean by that?"

Joss rubbed his hands on his knees. They'd started to ache while he was standing on the deck of the *Empress*. The throbbing had only grown more intense in the ensuing hours. "Had she been given her choice, Allyson would have stayed in London, with the life she knew. She didn't have much of a heart for adventure, or change, and the decision to come to America wasn't an easy one for her. I'd already purchased my way into Continental when I married her, though, and the only reason I'd stayed in London was because of her."

"Didn't she want to come with you?"

He shrugged. "No, not really, but it wasn't a matter of want. She was my wife, and that was where life was taking us. We left for Boston as soon as the weather was warm enough to travel. Once we arrived, she settled in all right. It was hard though, making friends. The English aren't very popular, in case you hadn't heard."

Emmy nodded. "You did fight two wars with us, Josiah. Americans don't normally just forget things like that."

He smiled at her ruefully. "We lost two wars, too. Brits don't normally forget things like that. Anyway, we arrived in Boston in the summer of 1843, and I opened Continental's American office. It took a long time, and a lot of hard work, to build the business. We were hard-pressed for money at first, and Allyson wasn't used to living that way. We couldn't afford to retain anyone but Pinkus. I think, at least at first, Allyson was a little afraid of him.

"It took almost a year before she really began to adjust, and then she became pregnant with Michael the following autumn. Michael changed everything. I was obscenely, almost ridiculously happy. It just didn't seem possible that one man could have so much. Once he was born, Allyson became much more content with the long hours she was forced to spend alone. I worked nearly eighty hours a week in those days. When I wasn't at the office, my mind was buried in the books."

"But you built Continental into an empire in a very short period of time, Josiah. That was a monumental task."

He nodded. "I wanted out of Boston. Unlike Allyson, I hadn't been raised in the city. I was obsessed with getting Michael out into the open. The city had become so congested and crowded, that I wanted desperately to bring my family west."

"When did you decide to expand Continental's operation into river traffic?"

"The day Samuel Morse telegraphed his first message from Washington to Baltimore. I knew then it was only a matter of time before the entire west opened up. Morse's communication system, along with the innovations in railways and steam engines, meant the population would be shifting. If Continental Shipping helped move all those goods, and all those people, we'd become the dominant force in the United States."

"And you did it."

He nodded. "Yes. I borrowed every cent I could against the business, and persuaded my Uncle Marcus to become an investor. I bought as many riverboats as I could afford, hired the best man I could find to run our Boston office and oversee our transatlantic business, and then Allyson and I came to St. Louis."

Emmy suspected he was being a bit modest about the magnitude of the task, but decided to let it pass. "How old was Michael then?"

"Just a year and a half. He didn't really know what was happening, so it didn't bother him too much. Allyson was really distressed, though. We didn't know it at the time, but she was pregnant when we started the move. After Michael was born, her monthlies were very irregular. If we'd known, we'd have waited."

"She was pregnant with Adam?"

Joss shook his head. "She lost that baby during the move. We got caught in a bad storm one night and the wagon upset. Allyson bled for two days before she told me about it." He raked a hand through his hair with a heavy sigh. "God, I was frantic. We were miles from nowhere, and I didn't even begin to know how to find a doctor. When we finally figured out she was losing the baby, it was too late to do anything about it."

"Oh, Josiah, it must have been awful."

"It was. She became very despondent after that. It was as if she just started to fade mentally away. I was afraid I was going to lose her. That's when Michael started having nightmares."

Emmy reached out and took his hand, sensing immediately his change in mood. The story was darkening now. "Michael was terrified of the dark. I think the trauma of the storm, and the tension of the following days, were more than his little mind could handle. He'd wake up screaming in the night, and I'd have to calm him down. After a while, I always said the same thing. I'd tell him he got his name from the archangel Michael, and since Michael was the strongest angel, nothing could ever hurt him. The angel Michael would take care of him, and so would I. It became almost a ritual for us, and soon, Michael turned it into a game we played every night before he went to sleep."

Emmy softly stroked his hand as she studied his face in the firelight. "Did you make it to St. Louis without any more trouble?" she asked.

He nodded. "Yes, and we were hardly settled in before Allyson was pregnant with Adam. It was like a miracle. She'd told me while we were traveling that she wanted to try right away to have another baby. I didn't know if we would be able to, and I was scared. I wasn't sure what would happen if she lost another one, but Adam was determined to make it into the world.

"The business was growing quickly, and I was able to spend more time with Allyson and Michael than I had been in Boston. By the time Adam was born, Continental was well on its way to controlling most of the river traffic on the Mississippi. So we moved into this house, and those became the happiest two years of my life. I'd never felt so blessed, so fulfilled as I did here. We laughed all the time. Michael and Adam were such happy little boys."

Emmy brushed a lock of hair off his forehead. "I saw the portrait upstairs," she said quietly.

Joss nodded. "I had that painted when Adam was a year old. I never wanted us to forget how happy we were then. No matter what happened, I knew we'd always have that."

Emmy waited for long seconds while she watched the play of emotions across his face. She knew that in his mind, he was in the carriage the night of the accident. She saw his scar begin to twitch. "What happened the night of the murders, Josiah?"

He shuddered and lifted her onto his lap so he could bury his face in the side of her neck. "A business associate of mine owned the bank in Jefferson City. Allyson and I took Adam and Michael to visit Gordon and his wife for a holiday. On the return trip, Gordon asked if I would carry along a bank transfer he was making to St. Louis. Allyson didn't want me to."

"But you did?" she prodded, afraid he'd stop talking.

Joss tipped his head back against the sofa, his eye clamped shut, his forehead drawn. "I did. It was a large sum of cash, and several jewel cases, but I knew we'd travel on Continental ships downriver. It couldn't have been safer. There was a riverboat accident the night we should have arrived in St. Louis, so we were forced to disembark at Soldan and travel the rest of the way by coach."

"And you were stopped?"

He nodded. "I know now that they arranged the riverboat accident to force us to approach the city by coach. We were just north of St. Louis when I heard the shots. It was late, and Michael and Adam were sleeping. There were four men, and they stopped the carriage on the northern road and murdered my driver."

Joss crushed Emmy against him as his mind slipped back into the darkened carriage. He could still see the

terrified look Allyson had given him just before the
door was ripped from the hinges. "They tore the door
off and shot me in both legs before I had a chance to
react. I was so terrified they were going to hurt Allyson
or the boys, I didn't dare move. The boys woke up at
the sound of the shots. Allyson and I were trying to
keep them quiet. I kept getting faint from the pain in
my legs.

"One of their men mounted the driver's box, and
they drove us at least a mile off the road before anyone
said anything."

Emmy heard the raw note in his voice. She wrapped
her arms around his waist, hugging him tight. She
waited in silence until he spoke again. "They stopped
the carriage finally, and two of them came around to
the side to jerk Allyson out of the door. That's when
Adam started screaming. He was terrified. I couldn't
get him to stop, and I couldn't move because of the
pain in my legs. I was holding Michael out of the way,
and he was sobbing, trying to crawl inside my coat he
was so frightened. Adam started toddling across the
carriage after Allyson. One of the men told her to make
him quit crying."

He rubbed a hand over his eyes. "She tried. God,
Em, she tried, but he was terrified. She couldn't get
him to stop. When he wouldn't quit screaming, they
shot him."

Emmy flinched and raised her head. "Oh, Josiah."

When he opened his eye, his gaze was haunted, exposed. "He was just a baby, Emmy, and they shot him.
God, I thought I was going to explode. I tried to get
out of the carriage, but my left knee was almost completely shattered. I fell on the floor when I tried to
move. Allyson went crazy. She started scratching and
fighting the man who was holding her. She kept trying
to get to Adam.

"He was so quiet. His little body was lying right there beside me, and he was so quiet. The next thing I knew, one of the men started yelling at Allyson to shut up. She kicked him in the groin. That's when they shot her, too."

Emmy felt the tears start to flow down her cheeks. She reached up to wipe them away. "Oh, God."

Joss swallowed, his face a rigid mask of pain. "They threw her on the ground. Two of the men started hauling the boxes off the top of the coach. Michael was crying so hard, his body was shaking the carriage. I tried to hold onto him, but I was already faint from the bullet wounds. Somehow, he squirmed free of me and started running for Allyson."

"Oh, Josiah, no."

"They didn't have to shoot him, Em. He couldn't have done anything. None of them could have. He was so upset, and so frightened. All he wanted was to make sure his mother was all right. He was just out of the carriage when the same man who'd shot Allyson and Adam beaded in on him and shot him in the stomach. Michael screamed."

Joss's body started to shake. "I'll never forget that scream, Emmy. He just fell down in the dirt and screamed. It turned to whimpering fast. He couldn't take that much pain and he passed out. I pulled myself out of the carriage and started crawling toward him, when the man kicked me in the face. His boots had metal tips, and he got me right in the eye. That's when I fainted."

Tears were streaming down his face now. They even poured from beneath the black patch. Emmy kept trying to wipe them away with her hands. "By the time I came to, they'd set the carriage on fire. Allyson and Adam were already dead, and somehow, I managed to pull Michael away from the fire so we wouldn't be burned alive. He was barely breathing."

"Oh, Josiah. Oh, dear God, I'm so sorry."

He didn't seem to hear her. "For two days we lay there in the dirt. I kept praying somebody would find us. Every now and then, Michael would regain consciousness. He was so scared. He hurt so much, and there was nothing I could do for him. Every time he woke up, he wanted to play the game. So I'd tell him about the angel Michael, and promise to protect him, and hold him, and try to crawl toward the road.

" 'Daddy, I'm scared.' He kept saying it over and over. I didn't know what to do. I needed him so much, Emmy. I was terrified. I kept talking to him, hoping I could keep him alive by desire. I'll never forget the way it felt to hold his little body and feel the way he would shudder every now and then.

"He was bleeding so much, it had soaked all the way through the blanket I'd used to wrap him up. He had this awful cough. I kept telling him I loved him. I kept telling him everything would be all right, and he kept holding on to me and begging me to play the game with him."

Emmy was sobbing in earnest now. His pain set off an explosion in her heart. She collapsed against his chest. "Oh, dear Lord. Oh, my love."

Joss's body shuddered several times. "Every time he coughed, I felt it all the way down to my bones. I'd have given anything to take his pain away, but I couldn't even walk. I was so scared that I'd faint again and not be there when he needed me. Finally, he just seemed to stop fighting it. He rubbed his face on my shirt and told me he wasn't scared anymore. He said he could see angels, that he'd stopped hurting, that everything was going to be all right."

Joss clutched Emmy close to him. She felt his tears

drop onto her face. She stroked his cheek. Joss's voice was empty when he finally spoke again. "And then he died too, Em. The whole time I was telling him I'd take care of him, and he died anyway. That was when I lost my soul."

*Sixteen*

They sat on the sofa for long minutes while Joss clung to Emmy. Remembered flashes of pain made his body shudder. She held onto him as she tried to absorb some of the anguish. It seemed like hours before he raised his damp cheek from the top of her head and managed to meet her gaze. He ran the callused pad of his thumb over her cheek to catch a few stray tears. "You're crying," he said.

She wiped away the lingering tears on his face. "I'm always crying, Josiah. How can you have failed to notice?"

His hand trembled when he smoothed her damp hair back. "I didn't mean to make you cry, Emmy."

"That's part of love, Josiah. I hurt because you hurt."

He hugged her close to him. "You really do love me, don't you?"

She rubbed her cheek against the soft wool of his evening jacket. "Yes. I understand now why you can't love me back. I would never try to replace Allyson in your heart." Even as she said the words, she felt more miserable than she had in her life. The role Allyson Brickston had played in her husband's life had been easier for Emmy to ignore when the woman had been an unknown entity. Now that she had been in her house, heard her story, and felt the pain of Joss's loss, Emmy felt alone, desolate.

Joss stared at the fire as he thought about Emmy's words. She did love him, amazing though it seemed. He had treated her badly, taken advantage of her physically, deliberately used her as a weapon against her own family, and yet, she'd wept over his pain with no thought at all toward her own.

Emmy sat in his lap with her arms wrapped around his middle. He inhaled the soft honeysuckle scent of her hair. He was exhausted, it was true, from reliving the memory of the accident, but there was something about the feeling of holding her in the soft glow of the firelight, of knowing that she loved him that salved his wounds.

He thought about the tender touches of warmth she'd given the watch house, things she'd done to make him more comfortable, more content. He thought about the cozy atmosphere she'd struggled so hard to create for him, and the hours of hard work she'd given to putting his life in order. When he'd met her, he had been living for one purpose. He had wanted only to find Allyson's murderer. If Joss had died in the process, he would have welcomed an end to the pain.

But Emmy had changed that. Days passed, not often, but sometimes, when he didn't think of the murder. There were times when the memory of Allyson's face was not as clear as it had once been. Lately, he had been able to watch Emmy with Sam and not feel like he'd been kicked in the stomach. The sight of children no longer made him feel faint. The dull ache that had become a permanent fixture in his heart had given way to moments he would almost call contentment.

There had been smiles, and even laughter in his life in recent days, and once or twice, he'd thought beyond Carding, Missouri to the life he could live after his business there was complete. And those thoughts always included Emmy.

He realized it then. It was so painfully apparent, he couldn't imagine why the thought had never dawned on him before. Emmy had worked her way into his heart, and he was falling in love with her. Oh, it hadn't been the same breathtaking feeling it had been with Allyson. That had been almost like a hurricane. Falling in love with Emmy Greene reminded him of a changing season. The passage from the spring of his life had taken him through a long, difficult summer, filled with violent storms and long, hot, endless days. But autumn had come.

With a slow, peaceful change in the weather, autumn had come. The love he'd had for Allyson had, indeed, been young and wild and free, but with Emmy, it was different. He was different. Pain had changed the idealistic young man who had chased Allyson Caste all over London. The man he was now needed a quiet, gentle kind of love. The kind he had for Emmy.

On the heels of that realization came another even more shocking one. He had feared from the beginning that Emmy would make him forget Allyson, but suddenly, he realized he would not have to. To love Emmy would not mean he was betraying Allyson. Indeed, Allyson would want this for him as much as he would have wanted it for her. Joss stared at Allyson's portrait over the mantel. Her eyes smiled at him in silent understanding. He felt as though the burdens of the world had just been lifted from his shoulders.

With a slight smile, he leaned Emmy away from him, realizing he still had not responded to her statement about replacing Allyson. He nearly blurted out right then that he loved her, but he decided he'd better ease her into the revelation. It had not come easily to him, and he wasn't certain she would be able to accept the notion without some means of an explanation. He didn't want her to think the emotional turmoil of the last few hours had clouded his judgment. When he told her what was in his heart, it would be real. He wanted to make sure she understood.

A sudden memory of a conversation he'd once had with his father flared in his mind. It was such a simple concept, one he'd learned over and over again, he found it hard to imagine the thought hadn't occurred to him before. "Emmy," he said, his voice a hushed whisper in the still quiet room, "did I ever tell you about the conversation I had with my father when my sister Katy was born?"

With a curious look, she shook her head. Joss arched his neck to kiss the tip of her nose. "I was the youngest child before Katy, you know? I had been Mama's baby for nine years when she became pregnant with my sister. I wasn't very happy about it."

"We went through that with Garnet. She was five when Gem was born, and she was horribly jealous."

"Jealous is the best word, I think. I was afraid too. I didn't think my mother and father would love me as much when the new baby was born."

Emmy's lips curved into a half smile. "You must have learned that lesson with Adam, though. You don't love one child more than the next."

"That's right. It was my father who told me that for the first time. I was upset, angry upset, and he came to my room and asked me to walk with him for a while. There was a tree on the estate where my father always took us for the really important, father kind of talks. He met my mother there the first time, and despite what he likes everyone to believe, he really is sentimental."

Emmy leaned back against Josiah's chest. She pictured him as a boy walking hand in hand with his father across the lawn of their estate in England. "Did he take you there for whippings too?"

Joss laughed softly. "No. We got those whenever, and wherever, the time was right. The tree was for really important things. You always knew it was going to be profound when Papa came to take you walking."

"What did he tell you?"

"We talked for a long time about my fears about the new baby. I didn't want to tell him at first. I was embarrassed. I knew my brothers would tease me if they knew what I was thinking, but I enjoyed being my mother's youngest, and I didn't want to lose the privilege. That's when I had my first conversation with my father about the meaning of love."

"He told you that he loved all his children equally, and the new one wouldn't be any different. Didn't he?" she asked.

"Not precisely. He told me he'd been terrified when my sister, Cana, was born. She was the first child, and he loved my mother so obsessively that he was afraid there wouldn't be room in his heart for the baby, and that he wouldn't be able to love her like he should."

"Really?"

"Yes. I was glad he was so honest. It gave me dignity about feeling so afraid."

"Then how did he resolve it?"

"After my sister was born," Joss continued, "Papa said he found out that he just had that much more love to give. He didn't have to love Mama less to love Cana as much. It was such a startling revelation to him, he was almost afraid to test it when my brother Jarred was born, but it happened again. He quit being afraid then."

Emmy's eyes widened. "Why are you telling me this, Josiah?"

"Because you told me you knew you could never replace Allyson in my heart, and that's true." He rubbed his thumb over the soft, full curve of her lips. "But I have only just realized that my father was right."

Something fluttered deep in her heart. She swallowed hard, not daring to take her eyes off him. "What are you saying?"

"I mean, that I have been rather slow about it, love, but I finally recognize what's had me in such a stir for the past few weeks. I was afraid, and I told you so, that you'd make me forget Allyson. I was afraid that if I married you, cared for you, I'd betray her memory. But my father was right. I don't have to stop loving her to love you, Emmy. All I have to do is say good-bye."

Emmy's hand flew to her mouth. She stared at him in the firelight. "Josiah, are you saying that—" she lost her nerve halfway through the question.

"I am saying that I love you, Emerelda."

Emmy dropped back against his chest with a muffled sob. "Oh, Josiah. You don't. You can't."

"I do, and I can, Emmy. It hasn't been a particularly easy revelation for me," he nestled his fingers in her hair. "I'd like to know you are taking it seriously."

"I'm taking it very seriously. It's just that I . . ." she trailed off again.

"You what?"

"I'm afraid."

"I've told you before that you don't need to be afraid. I'm not going to let anything happen to you."

Emmy lifted her head and met his gaze. "You don't understand. When I loved you, and you didn't love me back, there were no choices for you. All you had to do was concentrate on Allyson. It's different now."

He drew his brows together in confusion. "Different how?"

"You're not going to give up until you find Allyson's killer. Are you?"

Joss shook his head. "I can't. But I've already explained that to you. Just because I loved Allyson, still do in a way, doesn't mean I don't love you, too."

"But you'll have to choose now, Josiah. You came to Carding to kill the man who murdered your family. You told me so."

He nodded. "Yes. It's a matter of honor for me. I can't simply turn my back on it."

"I know," she said. "But you said yourself that there was no future for you after that. If there's no future for you, there's no future for us. I can't make you choose that, Josiah. I can't."

"Emmy," he said cautiously, not certain what to make of her mood, "I've faced a lot of demons tonight."

"I know."

"I've been living in the present for almost two years now."

"I know."

"I can't go any farther than this right now."

Emmy shook her head. "I don't want you to. I can't make you choose. You have to do it on your own."

Joss exhaled a deep sigh. "For tonight, can't you just accept that I love you. It's a lot for me, Em. Something I couldn't have given anyone else."

"Oh, Josiah, I'm just so afraid. I couldn't bear it if you thought I was forcing you to pick between us."

"God's going to force me to choose. He decided that when He put you in my path and made me feel again. I don't know right now what that choice will be. I can't promise you anything, especially not a future."

"I know you can't."

"But I can at least let you know that I love you. You brought me back to life, Emmy. I'd still be half a man if you hadn't made me whole again."

"Oh, Josiah."

"Do you know no one in the world but you and my mother calls me Josiah?"

"It means 'God Supports,'" she said. "Did you know that?"

"Yes. That's why my mother picked it. She had a difficult pregnancy with me, almost lost me mid-term. It's one of the reasons I was so spoiled, and had such a hard time accepting Katy. My mother used to say she named me Josiah because I'd only made it into the world with God's support."

Emmy pressed her hands to his face, threaded her fingers into the soft hair at his temples. "I knew when I met you how special you were, Josiah. There was something in the way you looked at me. I fell in love with you right then, that day you told Pearl you admired my orderly office."

"I admired a lot more than that."

"There I was, standing in my trousers and work shirt, and you made me feel like the Queen of England."

The fire had dimmed to a dull glow and was casting a red light on soft hair. He reached up and twirled his fingers in the curls. "I remember thinking you had the most extraordinary hair, like spun birch honey. I hadn't even noticed a woman since Allyson's death, and from the moment I met you, you had me reeling."

She shook her head. "Do you see what I mean, Josiah? My hair's the color of pigweed. Only you would think of something so ridiculous as birch honey."

"Spun birch honey," he corrected, "the soft buttery kind that melts on your tongue. The sun was shining through your window. You were looking at me through these cute little spectacles with those tawny eyes."

"They're yellow. Like jaundice."

"Tawny." Joss removed the spectacles and dropped them on the sofa. He traced his finger down her nose.

"I had this insane urge to remove your spectacles and find out if there were freckles underneath."

"There are. I spend too much time in the sun."

His finger followed the delicate arch of an eyebrow. "I've always liked freckles. Between your freckles, and the notion that your figure was probably full and round and soft, I nearly pounced on you right there in your office."

"My figure's a good bit too full and round and soft, and you know it. I have far too much of everything to look like a lady."

He gave her waist a gentle squeeze. "It's perfect."

"Only you think so, Josiah. That's why I knew."

"Knew what?"

"I knew that day I was going to love you. I knew it from the look in your eyes."

"To think I was lusting over you, and you were seeing something entirely different the whole time."

She poked his shoulder. "You were not."

"Wanna bet?"

Emmy kissed his chin. "You're incorrigible. I'm trying my best to have a very sentimental moment, here. You have, after all, finally told me you love me."

Joss nodded, all traces of humor gone from his eyes. "I do, Emmy. I really do."

She looked at him in wonder. "I know, and I love you too. You do know that, don't you Josiah."

"Yes. I didn't want you to, Emmy, I told you that, but knowing that has become a part of me now. It's unbelievable that one man should be loved by two such extraordinary women in his lifetime. Especially a man like me."

"Everything's going to be all right, Josiah. I know it is."

"I hope so," he said, and realized with something of

a start that, for the first time in two years, he really, really did.


"Isn't that Gray's horse?" Emmy asked as they drove up the bluff in the buckboard late the following afternoon.

Joss squinted against the setting sun. Sure enough, Gray Lawford's mare was hitched to the post in front of the watch house. "Looks like it."

Emmy felt a slight tremor of fear. By unspoken consent, she and Josiah had decided to return to Carding today. They both knew the past would have to be laid to rest before they could turn their thoughts to the future. They had ridden the paddle wheeler upriver, and just arrived back in Carding. She had hoped for a brief respite before trouble started, but the sight of Gray's horse confirmed her worse fears. Trouble had already come to visit. "What do you think he wants?"

Joss nudged the horses into a faster trot. "I don't know. Everything seemed quiet enough when we came through town."

They pulled up in front of the watch house where they found Gray, reclined back in a rocker on the porch with his booted feet propped on the railing. "Afternoon, Joss," he said. He nodded at Emmy. "Em."

Joss jumped down from the driver's seat then rounded the back to lift Emmy down. "What brings you out here, Gray?"

"Been missing you folks. Where ya been?"

Emmy smoothed her hands over the skirt of the green dress she'd borrowed from Allyson's closet. "We've been in St. Louis, Gray."

Gray shoved his hat back on his head. His feet dropped to the porch with a heavy *thunk*. "That so?" He looked at Joss.

Emmy nodded. "Yes. Joss had business to see to in St. Louis. We've been there since last night."

"What sort of business."

Emmy narrowed her eyes. "Business business. You know Continental is headquartered there."

"Yeah, I know."

Joss studied Gray's stony profile. "What's wrong, Gray?"

"If you've been in St. Louis, I reckon you wouldn't know anything about Jason Carver's murder then?"

Emmy stared at Gray. "Murder?"

Gray's eyes never left Joss. "Yeah. Murder."

Joss slipped an arm around Emmy's waist. He led her toward the house. "No, we don't know anything. I think we'd better all go inside."

"I suppose you must have seen a few folks in St. Louis?"

"Of course," Emmy said, walking with Joss.

"They'd be able to verify that you were there, then?"

Emmy glared at Gray. "What exactly are you trying to say?"

Gray looked uncomfortable. "I've got a murder to investigate, Em. It's a bit strange that the banker got murdered the night of that scene at the Harvest Party, and you two were nowhere to be found."

Emmy's face started to turn pink. "Gray, you do not think Joss killed Jason Carver."

Joss tightened his grip on her waist. "Emmy—"

Gray interrupted him. "I don't know what to think. Despite what he might have told you, Joss came to Carding with blood lust in his heart." He shot a cold glance at Joss. "Now, I've got three deaths on the north road, some unidentified character riding about the countryside in a black costume stirring up trouble, and Jason Carver's murder on my hands. What would you think if you were looking at this rationally?"

Emmy stepped away from Joss and planted her fists on her hips. "I am thinking rationally, and I'm thinking you're about to push me too far, Gray."

"I think we should go inside," Joss said again, watching Emmy thoughtfully.

"I don't want to go inside." She didn't take her eyes off Gray. "How long have you been sitting here in wait? I can tell from your beard you that haven't shaved in at least a day and a half."

"I've been here since Rosalynd Carver came and got me, and I found Jason hung up in his own living room."

"And you immediately knew Joss must be guilty, so you raced up here to wait for us while the real killer got away?"

Joss leaned back against the door frame to watch the angry confrontation. Gray shook his head, saying through clenched teeth. "No, Em."

"Then you explain it."

Stalking forward, he grabbed her elbow, then dragged her toward the door. Joss swung it open and let them enter ahead of him. He paused to drop his hat on the hook. Gray plunked her down in a chair while Joss walked to the pantry in an unhurried stride. He poured her a glass of brandy. "Well," he heard her demand.

He walked back, brandy in hand, to find Gray looming over her. "I think you'd better drink this." He handed her the glass.

"I don't want it." She tried to bat his hand away.

He extended it to her again. "Humor me."

Emmy took the brandy and downed an enormous gulp. Joss started pounding her back when she came up sputtering, her eyes watering. "What are you trying to do to me," she gasped, her voice breathy and hoarse, "strip my gut?"

Gray shot Joss a meaningful look. "Maybe you'll stop screeching long enough to listen to me now, Em."

She glared at him. "I don't want to listen to you. All you've done so far is accuse my husband of murder."

"I'm not accusing anyone of anything. Stop glaring at me like you want to claw my eyes out."

"I do."

Gray yanked his hat off. He strode across the watch house to jam it down on a hook. "Damn it, Em, I'm doing my job. All I've been trying to do throughout this whole thing is my job."

Joss squatted down next to Emmy and took her hand. "It's all right, Emmy. Gray has a right to be concerned."

Gray nodded. "Damn right I do."

"And stop talking like that," Emmy said. "I don't want you cursing like that in my house."

Joss looked at Gray apologetically. "We have a lot to discuss, Gray. I'll tell you about our trip to St. Louis, and you tell me about the murder. Do you want to stay for dinner? You look like you could use a good meal."

"He's not invited," Emmy said.

Joss squeezed her hand. "Of course he's invited, sweetheart."

Gray exhaled a brief, irritated sigh. "Stop frowning at me like that, Emmy. If you want me to go, I'll go."

Emmy started to say she wanted him to go very much indeed, but his silver eyes implored her to hear him out. The fact that Joss truly didn't seem to be upset swayed her. "All right," she said, reluctantly, "he can stay."

Gray rolled his eyes. "So gracious. How do I know I won't be poisoned?"

"Am I being accused of murder now too?"

"Damn it, Em." Gray wiped a hand through his black hair.

Joss started to laugh. "I'll taste everything first, just to be sure." Standing, he squeezed Emmy's shoulder. "Do we have enough on hand to make dinner?"

"I suppose so. At least bring my bag in so I can change out of my nice gown."

Gray leapt at the opportunity. "I'll get it. You look nice, Em. Real nice."

She frowned at him. "You can contact Josiah's housekeeper in St. Louis if you need another witness to our whereabouts."

Without comment, he headed for the door. When it clicked shut behind him, Joss pulled her to her feet. "Don't you think you were a bit rough on him?"

"He accused you of murder, Josiah."

"He did not."

"Near about. Close enough," she amended. "Gray should know better."

"He just wants answers, Emmy."

"Well, so do I, but I don't run around accusing people like that."

"Emmy, Gray's your friend. He's my friend. Don't lose sight of that."

She looked at him closely. "What do you think this means?"

"I don't know. I'll have to talk to Gray."

"It's time we put things in order, Josiah. This won't be over until we do."

He nodded. "I know."

Gray came back in the house carrying the valise and the small trunk from the buckboard. They had gone to St. Louis with nothing but the clothes on their backs. All they'd brought back were the few personal effects and clothing items Joss had wanted to bring to Carding. "Where do you want this?" he asked.

Emmy took the valise from him. "The trunk has Joss's papers in it. It goes in the loft. If you'll give me a minute to change, you can use our bathing closet to shave before dinner."

Gray looked relieved. He accepted her olive branch without complaint. Joss suspected he'd had no intention of shaving, but he was smart enough not to argue with Emmy. "Thanks, Em." He hoisted the trunk onto his shoulder and headed for the ladder.

Joss looked at Emmy. "Do you need any help?"

She shook her head. "I can manage. Would you bring in one of the salted hams and start the fire?"

"Of course."

Emmy walked back to him and kissed his chin. "And tell me everything's going to be all right."

He rested his hands on her shoulders. "It is, Em. You'll see."

She waited while he exited out the back before making her own way into their small bedroom. The watch house was so dramatically different from Joss's large, elegant town house in St. Louis. She felt more at home here, like it belonged to her too, but there was also an underlying tension in the air. Jason Carver's murder opened a new chapter in Joss's reasons for being in Carding. She shivered as she hurried out of her traveling gown and into a familiar faded-green calico gown.

She found Gray seated in the slat-back rocker, waiting for her. Caution filled his silver eyes. "Through?" he asked.

"Yes. The bathing closet's back that way. You can use Joss's razor."

"Emmy, about before—"

She shook her head. "Don't apologize, Gray. You're just doing your job." She hadn't realized the house had a chill in it before. She started rubbing her upper arms to warm them. "I'm just scared is all."

He levered out of his chair and crossed the room in

two long strides so he could pull her into his arms for a tight hug. "You really care for him, don't you?"

She nodded, embarrassed when she felt the tears start to slide down her cheeks. "Yes."

Gray tipped her away with a gentle smile. He reached in his pocket for his handkerchief. "Lord, Em, you cry more than any woman I know."

She accepted the handkerchief with an admonishing glance. "I do not."

Gray waited while she blew her nose. "Whatever you say."

"I don't."

"I'm not picking another argument with you tonight. I damn near got my head bit off last time."

Emmy wiped her eyes and tucked the handkerchief into her apron pocket. "Go shave, Gray, and wash your hands while you're in there."

"Yes, ma'am."

Emmy poked his ribs. "Insolent yip. I've a good mind to poison your food after all, just to put you out of our misery."

Joss came in through the back door, arms laden with wood, a smoked ham dangling from his fingers by its binding string. "If you keep threatening Gray like that, he won't come back." He dropped the ham on the table as he strolled into the living room. "You'd better do as she says all the same, Marshal. I wouldn't want to be explaining why your lifeless body was found in my house."

With a laugh, Gray headed for the bathing closet. Joss dropped down on one knee and started to lay the fire. He'd shucked his black jacket, and Emmy stood back and admired the way his white lawn shirt emphasized the breadth of his shoulders and the narrow taper of his waist. He looked over his shoulder with a slight smile. "I'm sorry it's so cold in here," he said. "Hopefully the fire will warm it quickly."

"Hopefully."

He set a match to the dry kindling, then blew gently through cupped hands until the fire flared into life. The sound of splashing water and an off-key whistling came from the bathing closet. The acid taste and smell of smoke peppered the air. Emmy wished she could stop and savor the quiet, homey atmosphere. She headed for the pantry instead. "Will ham biscuits be all right for dinner, Josiah?"

He looked over his shoulder. "Yes, whatever. Don't fret over it."

She picked up the ham and disappeared into the kitchen.

Gray joined Joss by the fire, dabbing at his wet face with a clean towel. Joss waited until the marshal sat across from him. "Feel better?"

Gray draped the towel over his leg. "I hadn't planned on shaving."

"You were wise not to argue."

"One time was enough, thanks. What have you done to that girl, Joss? She's turned into quite the little tiger."

Joss laughed. "I haven't done anything to her."

"For her then," Gray said. "She looks good. Real good."

Joss leaned back in his chair and crossed his ankles out in front of him. "If I didn't already know you were Emmy's cousin, I'd take offense at that."

"I know you'll never believe I didn't mislead you on purpose."

"The hell you didn't. You stood right there on her porch and told me that story about the bear with the straightest face I've ever seen. You never once mentioned you were her cousin."

"So maybe I goaded you a little."

"Yeah. A little. Now shut up and tell me about Jason Carver."

"I'm sorry about the way I presented things before, Joss, but you did disappear kind of sudden and—"

Joss held up his hand. "Don't worry about it. I'll give you a list of people you can contact and check our whereabouts just to put your mind at ease. What happened?"

"Rosalynd found him strung up like a butchered calf in their living room."

"Anything stolen?"

"No. I ruled out a robbery as soon as I saw the door wasn't tampered with. Whoever it was, Jason let 'em in the house before they killed him."

"Got any theories?"

Gray exhaled a long breath. "A few." Gray dug in his pocket and pulled out a small leather bag. "I found these in Jason's office when I went through his effects."

Joss lifted his eyebrow in query and accepted the bag. He pried open the strings and poured the contents onto his palm. They appeared to be diamonds. "Emmy," he called.

She came tumbling out of the kitchen. Gray shot her a wry glance. "Listening at keyholes, Em?"

She glared at him. "Certainly not."

Joss held out his palm. "What do you think?"

She walked over to him so she could sort through the pile with her fingers. "Fakes mostly. Like the ones the Diamond Hawk brought me before."

"The *same* ones?" Gray asked.

Emmy shook her head. "I don't think so. These are larger."

"Why do you think Jason had them?" Gray asked.

Joss stared at the fake diamonds in his palm. "Maybe he didn't know."

"Maybe," Emmy said, "but I doubt it."

Joss and Gray looked at her in surprise. "Why?" Joss asked.

"Because Jason Carver routinely handled small split-lots for area lapidaries. Many small bankers do that. They don't have the cash flow or the contacts to bid on large lots, so they buy marked-up splits from large dealers.

"Once they have the split lot, they sell it to smaller, less prestigious lapidaries who can't afford to buy large quantities of gems. If Jason were a regular handler, he'd know the procedure for authenticity. Those gems would need a new certificate from a registered gemologist, and Jason would generally only accept the gems once he'd seen the original certificate from the auction house. Then he would take them to a secondary gemologist to have a certificate issued."

"Someone like Robert Greene?" Gray asked.

Emmy looked at Joss and nodded. "Yes, someone like Robert."

Emmy was sitting in the washroom with her feet dangling in a tub of warm, sudsy water when she heard him call her name. She didn't bother to open her eyes. "I was wondering if you'd show up today."

The Diamond Hawk strolled into the room. "Why today, especially?"

"Well, in light of those fake diamonds Gray Lawford found in Jason Carver's desk, it just seemed natural that you would."

"I came earlier."

"And I wasn't here."

He propped his broad shoulder against the door frame. "The gems were fake, weren't they?"

"Yes. They were the same quality as the ones you showed me before."

"What do you think that means?"

Emmy finally looked at him. "I think it means that Robert was issuing the certificates for the fake gems, and Jason Carver was providing the cash flow for their purchase and distribution."

"Then did Robert murder Jason?"

Emmy shook her head. "No. I don't think so. Neither does Joss." She looked at him closely. "Do you?"

"No. You know that I'm wanted for his murder, as well as the murder of the two men on that road."

Emmy pulled her feet out of the sudsy water. She reached for a towel. "Yes, I know. You didn't do it, though."

"How do you know that?"

"I just do." She finished drying her feet, then pushed the fabric of her faded yellow dress into place over her green petticoats. "Do you know who killed him?" she asked.

His eyes narrowed behind the mask. "I think so."

"Are you going to tell me?"

He shook his head. "No."

"Then why are you here?" She scooped up a basket full of clean, wet clothes and headed for the door. He swung it open for her, then followed her out into the sunlight. "As I said, I'm fairly certain I know who killed Jason Carver, but I needed to know something."

She dropped the basket. One by one, she pinned Joss's shirts on the line. "What?"

"If Jason Carver and Robert Greene were selling fake gems and stealing real ones, they'd still need at least one more person. Am I right?"

She clipped a shirt onto the line, then reached for another. "Yes."

"Why am I right?"

Emmy looked at him, two clothespins between her teeth. "Don't you know?"

"I think so, but I want to hear it from you just to be sure."

She started pinning the wet shirt. "Jason Carver had the necessary cash and the experience to steal the gems and sell them on the secondary market. He'd handled enough gems to have the proper contacts for that. Robert, of course, was the needed expert. If Jason brought pressure to bear on Robert about outstanding bills, debts, and obligations, he could have convinced him to sign the certificates."

"But?"

Emmy hesitated. "Well, I'm not sure you understand."

He nodded. "I understand."

"I haven't even told Joss this because I'm afraid he'll overreact."

"Told him what?"

"Well, Joss knows Robert has been signing the certificates. He and Gray both suspect that the fake gems in Jason's office point to Jason's corruption, but they haven't figured out the source of the fake gems yet."

"You think you know."

She clipped another shirt onto the line. "Yes."

"And you think that person killed Jason Carver?"

Emmy looked at him. "That's hard to say. It's possible, I guess. Especially if Jason was losing his nerve."

"Who is it, Emmy?" he asked quietly.

She raised stricken eyes to his. "This is tearing me apart."

"I know that."

"I don't want it to be true."

"I know that too."

Emmy sighed. "To manufacture fake gems of the

quality you've shown me, a person would need several things. Fine sand, extremely high-priced paste, an excellent furnace system, crystal cutting tools, and several minerals to give the stones their shine; manganese, copper salt, zinc-oxide, and brissilum. They are mostly mined minerals, and derivatives, but nothing that is readily available."

"How would Jason and Robert have procured them?"

"Well, as one of the safeguards against this type of thing, you can't just start buying large quantities of these items all at once, or someone's bound to get suspicious. So they'd have to buy the items from several different sources, then find an expert to manufacture the stones."

"How?"

"They'd likely use someone with a lot of contacts around the country. Someone who routinely purchases a variety of items in large quantities. Someone who is used to doing business on a very big scale." She finished clipping the last of the shirts to the line before she looked at him. "Avery Brooks would be a very good candidate."

She saw the tightening of his jaw. "What if I told you that Avery Brooks and Rosalynd Carver were, ah—"

"Lovers?" Emmy asked.

"Yes."

Emmy shrugged. "Most folks in Carding are aware of Avery's indiscretions. I would say it wouldn't surprise me."

"But what if I told you that he was using Rosalynd to tamper with the bank books."

Emmy picked up her basket and balanced it on one hip. "I would say that you don't know Avery Brooks like I do. He might have been asking Rosalynd to tamper with the books to keep her out of the way. He might have been asking her to do it just to see if she would, but with Avery, business is business. He would no more mix business and pleasure than he'd sacrifice himself on someone else's behalf. Avery might have been using Rosalynd for a lot of things, but it didn't have anything to do with selling fake gems."

# Seventeen

Emmy was only mildly surprised when Sam knocked on the door of the watch house at six-thirty that evening. She was in the loft, cleaning a sapphire necklace and brooch for a client, when she heard him rapping on the door.

"Hi, Miss Em." He flashed her a sheepish grin.

"Hello, Samuel. What brings you up here?"

"Mr. Joss sent me." He handed her a small box and a folded piece of paper. "Told me to tell you that he was working late trying to catch up from last week."

Emmy accepted the parcel. Joss had lost a lot of time with the survey because of the chaos surrounding the Harvest Party and Jason Carver's murder. He'd left the watch house hours before dawn that morning. She'd not really expected him home until late. She motioned Samuel inside, certain Joss had used this errand as an excuse to give her some time with the boy. "Why don't you come in, Sam? I've got supper almost ready, and I'd rather not eat alone."

Sam twirled his hat in his hand. "Are you sure it's all right?"

"Of course it's all right." She opened the note and scanned the brief explanation for Joss's absence that evening. Slipping the note in her apron pocket, she began pulling at the strings on the parcel. In his note, Joss had said he'd sent her something she needed very badly. "How are things going at the site, Samuel?" she asked.

He picked up an apple, took a bite, then wiped the juice from his mouth with the back of his sleeve. "Good, I think. Jim says we should be ready to clear a new plot by early next week. What's in the box, Miss Em?"

She pulled back the paper and lifted the lid. The contents made her laugh. "Josiah was right. It was something I needed." She held up the box so Sam could see the rows of neatly folded, brightly colored silk handkerchiefs.

Sam frowned. "What did he send you that for?"

"It's a jest between us, Samuel."

"Wouldn't you rather have gotten something useful—like a good hunting knife?"

With a chuckle, Emmy motioned for Sam to follow her into the kitchen. "Believe me, Sam. The handkerchiefs are very useful. Besides, if you were picking out a present for Becky Morgan, would you buy her a hunting knife?"

Sam blushed. "I bought her a book yesterday. 'Cause she told me she wanted it."

"See." Emmy picked up a plate and dished out two pieces of roast and a spoonful of carrots, potatoes, and onions. She handed it to Sam. "There's milk in the icebox if you want it, or pump water."

Sam carried his plate to the table, then went to fetch two glasses out of the pantry. "Do you want milk, Miss Em?"

"Yes, please."

He poured out two glasses while she fixed her own plate. Once they were seated, Emmy had Sam say grace over the meal. They started to eat in companionable silence. Sam wolfed down half his food before he took a long drink of milk. "It's good, Miss Em. You're as good a cook as my ma."

She swallowed a bite of hot-buttered biscuit as she met Sam's gaze across the table. "Don't you mean as your mother was, Samuel?"

He stared at his plate where he'd begun to push a potato around with his fork. "I've been meaning to sort of talk to you about that, Miss Em."

She handed him a buttered biscuit. "About what, Sam?" she asked gently.

"About my ma." He took a healthy bite of the biscuit, but still refused to meet her gaze.

"You miss her a lot, don't you?"

Sam raised his gaze to hers. "Yes, ma'am."

"Sam," Emmy pushed her chair back so she could walk around the table to sit next to him, "do you know what happened to Josiah's family?"

Surprise flickered in his bright blue eyes. "Some I do. I know his wife and two kids got killed."

"That's right. Haven't you noticed how sad he is sometimes?"

"There've been times when I swore he was fixin' to start crying."

"Do you know why?"

"He misses 'em I guess."

"That's right. But he also knows they're never coming back. But your ma doesn't know that about you, does she, Sam?"

He looked down at his hands. "How'd you know my ma was still alive, Miss Em? I told everyone she died."

Emmy ruffled his reddish brown curls. "You're a good storyteller, Sam, but you're not a very good liar. Don't you think it's time you went home?"

He looked at her, stricken. "But I don't know if she wants me back now. That was an awful thing I did."

"What exactly did you do, Samuel?"

"I think Ma thought I was dead. After my pa died, she apprenticed me to Mr. Charles Garrison. He's a printer in Hannibal, where we live. It's just upriver about an hour from here."

"I know the place. Did you run away, Sam?"

"More or less."

"More? Or less?"

"More, I guess. Ma and I were traveling downriver to St. Louis to visit my Aunt Gertie Jo when I jumped ship. Ma didn't know I'd learned to swim. I'm sure she thought I drowned."

"How deep was the water?"

"Twelve feet. I jumped when I saw the twain marker giving the depth."

Emmy nodded. "So your poor mama's been grieving away thinking she lost her only boy, while you've been having a holiday here in Carding."

Sam's face crumpled. "It wasn't like that at first, Miss Em. I just wanted so much more than Hannibal had for me. I want to be a riverboat pilot, and sail up and down the Mississippi, not be stuck in Mr. Garrison's print shop."

"Sam," Emmy said, "if you want to be a riverboat pilot, you have to have all kinds of schooling for it. You're a smart boy. You ought to be doing a lot more than cleaning out Continental's site office."

Sam looked miserable. "I wrote her a letter, Miss Em."

She looked at him in surprise. "Your mama?"

"I mailed it two days ago. I told her I was sorry, that I wanted to come home if she'd have me. I told her you and Mr. Joss and Jim were taking real good care of me, though, so she didn't have to take me back unless she wanted to." He started to cry then. "What if she don't want me anymore?"

Emmy pulled him into her arms to hug his thin

shoulders. "She'll want you, Samuel. How could she not?"

Sam rubbed his wet face against her neck. "I don't know, Miss Em. I was awful rotten to her."

Emmy stroked his soft hair. "Mothers have a way of overlooking things like that, Samuel. I'm not saying it'll be easy, and if she's smart, she'll make you pay for putting her through so much, but I suspect she'll forgive you soon enough."

Sucking in a breath, he leaned back in his chair. "I hope so, Miss Em. I really hope so. I want to go home."

"Everything is going to be all right, Sam. You'll see."

"Is there enough food left for me?" Joss asked from the doorway.

Emmy looked up in pleased surprise. She'd been so absorbed with Sam's story, she hadn't heard Joss come in. He was leaning casually against the door frame, but she could tell by the gruff note in his voice, and the odd look in his eye, that he'd witnessed the emotional scene. "Of course, Josiah." She walked across the room to push his oilskin coat from his shoulders. Despite Sam's presence, she stretched up on tiptoe to kiss him. "Sam was just clearing the table, weren't you Sam?"

Sam jumped up and started stacking dishes. He seemed grateful for the reprieve. Emmy suspected he wasn't at all comfortable with the notion that Joss might have seen him crying. She waited while Joss hung his coat on the hook by the door. He removed his hat so he could rake his fingers through his hair. "It's starting to get rough out there. I think we're due for a storm," he told her.

Emmy dropped his hat on a hook before she turned into his arms. "Perhaps Sam had better stay the night."

Joss lightly kissed her. "I'm sorry I'm so late."

She shrugged. "It gave me a chance to talk to Sam."

"I was hoping it would."

Emmy snuggled close to him. The sound of Sam rattling the dishes in the kitchen carried on the still quiet of the room. If she pretended very hard, it was easy to picture this scene with children of their own. "Thank you for my present. I adore them."

"I was just being practical. I kept losing all of mine."

"You were not." She poked his ribs. "You were being sentimental."

"I am never sentimental."

Emmy leaned her head back. "No, of course not. You are undoubtedly the most coldly unsentimental man I have ever known."

With a slight growl, Joss kissed her once more, then whispered in her ear, "I'll show you tonight how cold I am."

Laughing, Emmy stepped away from him. "Sit down, Josiah. I'll get your dinner."

Joss sat and stretched his arms out with a loud yawn just as Sam came out of the kitchen carrying a glass of milk for him. He plunked it down on the table. "Milk all right?" he asked.

Joss nodded. "Fine. Go in there and carry the plates for Em. Will you, Sam?"

Sam scurried back into the kitchen. He almost collided with Emmy on his way through the door. Joss indicated the chair across from him. "Sit down, wife. If the boy's staying the night, make him earn his keep." Emmy took the seat, then picked up a stack of napkins to refold. Joss decided then and there that he was sick to death of watching her wait on him. She looked tired, worn out, like the strain was starting to get to her. He knew she was still upset over Jason Carver's murder, and even more upset over what the implications might be. If he hadn't been such a selfish bastard, he'd have seen it days ago. What kind of man was he to let his wife work her fingers to nubs on his behalf? He could have afforded to hire someone to do most of the labor. Hell, he could have hired half of Carding if he wanted to. Instead, he'd sat back and let Emmy run circles around him. It had to stop. He reached across the table to squeeze her hand. "Emmy?"

Her hands stilled on a napkin and she met his gaze. "Yes, Josiah?"

"Are you all right?"

She hesitated. "Yes. I'm a little scared is all."

"I know. It's almost over. Just a little longer, all right?"

She would have asked him what he meant, but Sam came in carrying an enormous plate of food. So she said, "All right," instead.

The conversation turned to simpler things. Joss and Sam talked about the site, answering Emmy's questions while Joss ate. By the time he'd finished his meal, the wind was howling outside, and the shutters were rattling. Joss picked up his plate and glass to carry them into the kitchen. Over his shoulder he said, "Sam, you'd better plan on staying the night. We'll set you up in the loft."

"I can make it back to town, all right," Sam protested.

Joss stopped in the doorway. He didn't miss the pleading look Emmy shot his way. "You go and you'll worry my wife. I won't have it."

Sam glanced between them as he yawned. "We did start awfully early this morning. Even my bones are tired from lugging that equipment up to the site."

Emmy patted his arm as she stood. "That's settled, then. I'll go and get you blankets and a pillow, Samuel. You can sleep on a pallet in the loft."

Joss disappeared into the kitchen. Automatically, he washed his plate and glass, then added them to the clean stack next to the sink. There was no sense in

making Emmy do it later. With a weary sigh, he dried
his hands on one of the fresh towels before he strolled
back into the living room. He lowered his tired body
into the slat-back rocker by the fire. He stretched out
his legs, then crossed one ankle over the other, leaned
his head back, folded his hands on his chest, and sat
contentedly listening to Emmy and Sam rustling about
in the loft.

When Emmy had the sheets and blankets spread
neatly on the floor, she handed Sam a pillow. "There,"
she said, "I think you should be comfortable now. I've
put two extra blankets on the desk in case you get cold
in the night."

Sam sat down to start unlacing his boots. "Thanks,
Miss Em."

"Is there anything else you need, Sam?"

"No, ma'am. I'll be fine. Are you sure you don't
mind my staying in your house and all. I could sleep
in the barn."

"Don't be silly, Sam. You're like part of our family."

When Sam finished unlacing his boots, he slipped
them off. They dropped to the floor with a loud *clunk*.
He gave Emmy an embarrassed smile. "Thanks for
everything. I mean, about my ma and all."

Emmy kissed his forehead, completely ignoring his
awkward blush. She smoothed a lock of his hair off his
face. "Just promise you won't forget us when you're
home in Hannibal, Sam."

"I won't, Miss Em. I'll even write."

"I'd like that." She started to climb down the ladder.
She paused as Sam slipped beneath the blankets.
"Sam?" she asked.

"Yes, ma'am?"

"Did you lie about your last name, too?"

He yawned. "Yes, ma'am. Langhorne's my middle

name, not my last. My full name's Samuel Langhorne Clemens."

"Well, Sam Clemens, it's been a very great honor to have you in my house."

He gave her a shrewd look. "You're a lot better liar than I am, Miss Em. I'm sure Mr. Joss will take every ounce of that honor out of my hide tomorrow."

Emmy climbed down the ladder to find Joss staring at her with a strange expression on his face. Tentatively, she crossed the room to stand in front of him. "Are you all right, Josiah?"

He nodded. "Yes."

He didn't sound all right. "You seem—preoccupied."

Without preliminaries, Joss pulled her onto his lap to bury his face in the bend of her neck. He was silent a long time while she held him, rubbed her hands over the broad expanse of his shoulders. "Emerelda?" he finally said, not lifting his head.

"Yes, Josiah?"

"You'd be a wonderful mother. You ought to have half a dozen kids running around your house."

At last she understood the source of his odd mood. She wove her fingers into the hair at his temples, then tipped his head back so she could look at him. "You heard Sam telling me about his mother, didn't you?"

"And other things. I've seen how you are with them. The children in town adore you. Alex hangs on every word you say like it's the gospel truth. Even nail-tough Sam is under your spell. You were meant to be a mother, Em. I wish I could give you that."

Emmy wished it too, but she didn't say so. She sensed his melancholy mood and sought to pull him out of it. "Weren't you the one just an hour or so ago telling me we were almost done with this rotten mess?"

Joss nodded. "Almost."

His voice sounded haunted. Emmy snuggled closer to his chest. "If that's all the future you can give me for right now, it's enough."

"I don't deserve you."

She gently kissed his forehead. "Probably not, but you're stuck."

His sigh came out as a shudder.

Sam and Joss headed for town before dawn the next morning. Emmy awoke to find herself alone in the house. Joss had built up the fire before he left, and the heat from the hearth knocked the chill off their room. She looked outside the small window to find that the night before had brought the promised rain. In the dim morning light, a fine, wet mist continued to fall. The earth was soaked and muddy puddles stretched across the sloping grass that led to the bluff. Emmy traced the path of a raindrop on the windowpane with her finger as she thought about Joss.

Deep in the night, she'd rolled over to touch him, only to find their bed empty. Disoriented, and unaware of the time, she'd assumed it was morning, that he'd left for the site already. But she heard him come inside long minutes later. He'd stripped off his wet clothes and crawled into bed beside her, barely making a sound.

"What time is it?" she'd mumbled.

"Late. Go back to sleep."

Emmy had rolled over to burrow against his chest. His skin was cool and damp from the rain. "Are you all right?"

"Yes." He held her close. "Just go to sleep, Em."

And she had, without giving the episode another thought. Now though, in the weak morning light, it seemed strange, almost frightening. She had sensed in

the two days since their return from St. Louis that she
was losing him again. He was bogged down at the office, it was true, but Emmy knew the trip to St. Louis
had awakened a host of conflicting emotions in him.
She wished she could help. She wished she could set
everything aright.

With a sigh, she turned from the window and started
to dress. She may not have much control over some
things, but there were other areas in Joss Brickston's
life that she intended to resolve. Her talk with Sam the
day before had taken care of one. Today, she would
see to the other.

She plaited her hair and dressed quickly, deciding
she would wear one of the two gowns she'd brought
with her from St. Louis. It took a bit of ingenuity to
get herself into the corset, but she finally decided that
if she left the laces a bit loose, she could fasten the
front hooks, then tighten the laces at her waist. She
had to struggle a good bit, but she finally got her waist
cinched down enough to fit in the skirt. She was thankful that the waistband was larger than the gown he'd
ordered for the Harvest Festival, but even so, the dress
was so tailored that it looked better with the corset
underneath.

Her husband had excellent taste, she thought as she
smoothed the lines of the gown over the whalebones.
The ocean-green brocade suited her perfectly. She adjusted her bodice, then slipped her feet into her work
boots. She refused to ruin the new tobacco suede dress-
boots she'd ordered from Mr. Whicham. Taking Joss's
extra oilskin coat from the hook by the door, she
shrugged into it. The hood pulled securely over her
hair. Both of his oilskins were bulky and enormously
cut, but because he'd had them made for use in the
field on rainy days and in inclement weather, Emmy
knew the coat would keep her dry all the way into town.

She struggled to hitch the horses to the buckboard
in the rain. The wooden tongue kept slipping from her
fingers, but finally, she managed it. She mounted the
driver's box with a strong sense of purpose. The rain
had slowed to fine drizzle. The clouds appeared to be
struggling to hold back the sun. With any luck, the rain
would stop completely by midday.

When she reached Carding, the streets were already
a quagmire from the previous night's rain and the
morning's carriage traffic. Maneuvering the buckboard
through the mud and slosh proved to be no easy feat.
With a little luck, and a good deal of forbearance, she
made her way through town to stop in front of the
Express building that housed Joss's office. Joss came
charging out the door just as she prepared to climb
down. "Emmy. What are you doing out in this?"

She held her arms out to him. "Are you going to lift
me down, or not?"

He lifted her off the driver's box, but didn't put her
down until he set her feet firmly on the wooden porch.
"Wait there." He headed back through the mud to
hitch the horses.

Emmy watched while he saw to the task. The sight
of his tan trousers buried calf-deep in mud made her
wince. He trudged back to her side, stepped up on the
porch, then wiped his feet on the sharp edge. "I'd have
hitched the buckboard for you this morning if I'd
known you were coming into town," he said. "I didn't
think you'd want to be out in this mess."

"I thought you'd be at the site today."

"Too muddy. We tried this morning, but there wasn't
enough solid ground to keep the transit level." Joss
pushed the hood of the oilskin back. "You dry in there?"

"As a tinder box. Warm, too. You have a nice coat,
Josiah."

Joss started unbuckling the coat. "This thing swallows you whole. I'll have to order a smaller one if you're going to insist on running about in the rain."

"Just today." She waited while he slipped the coat from her shoulders and tossed it over his arm. "It's a special occasion."

Joss was too busy admiring the way she looked in the ocean green gown to pay much heed to what she said. He rested his hands at her waist. The feel of the corset warmed his blood. "How'd you get yourself trussed up in this thing?"

"It's not nearly as tight as it's supposed to be," she said. "I had to do a great deal of twisting about to get the thing laced."

He decided he didn't even want to think about that. If he started imagining her twisting about in her chemise, he might embarrass himself. He reached around her to push open the door to the Express office, saying, "After you, madam."

Joss stopped long enough to check the post. He scanned the addresses of both letters, then slipped them into the back pocket of his trousers. "Up you go," he said to Emmy. He pressed a hand at the back of her waist to guide her toward the stairs. "I do assume you'll at least consent to visit us while you're in town?"

Emmy preceded Joss up the stairs. "What was in the post, Josiah?"

"Letters," he said, noncommittal. He opened the door to his office and let Emmy enter first.

As she'd expected, she found Jim seated at his desk tinkering with a piece of equipment while Sam stared out the window. "Good morning, Jim. Sam."

Jim glanced at her with a broad smile. "Well, mornin', Miss Em. Didn't expect to see you here on a dismal day like this."

Sam nodded. "Yeah. I figured all this mud must give you the fits something fierce."

Emmy laughed. "Well, it's not my favorite type of weather, I'll admit, but I've got some business to conduct in town." She glanced at Joss. "If you don't mind, may I have the money I gave you for Uncle Robert's bills out of the vault?"

Joss raised an eyebrow, but didn't comment. He laid her oilskin on his desk, then reached into his back pocket. "Here. Read these while I open the safe."

She took the letters. To her surprise, both were addressed to her. "Well, who in the world?" she mumbled. When she slit open the smaller letter, a two-dollar Missouri bank note fluttered out. Emmy caught it as she scanned the first page of the letter. Her eyes began to sting.

"Lord Amighty, Miss Em," Sam said, scurrying across the room. "You look like you're going to cry. What's wrong?"

Joss's head snapped up from his concentration on the safe. "Emmy?"

Jim looked at her in concern. "You all right?"

Emmy glanced at each one in turn. "Oh, I'm fine. I'm just fine." Two large tears spilled down her cheeks. "Could I possibly borrow your handkerchief, Josiah?"

Pulling it from his pocket, he crossed to her in two quick strides. He stuffed it into her hand as he snatched the letter from her to read it.

Sam frowned at her. "He just gave you a whole box full of those, Miss Em. What do you need his for?"

She mopped her eyes. "I forgot to carry one."

When Joss finished reading the letter, he gave her a light kiss. "Samuel," he said, handing Sam the letter. "You'd best start packing your bags."

"What in crickets is going on?" Jim asked.

Joss let Sam read the letter before he explained the

situation to Jim. "My wife has just received a letter from Mrs. Jane Clemens saying that her youngest daughter is too ill with influenza for her to come to Carding and fetch her son, Sam. She expects the child to recover completely," Joss affectionately smacked Sam's head, "but she wants us to use the enclosed bank note to send Sam home on the first riverboat."

"Oh, Sam," Emmy hugged him. "Isn't it just wonderful?"

Sam looked embarrassed. He gave Emmy an awkward pat on the back that looked more like an assault on her shoulder blades. "It ain't nothing to cry about, Miss Em."

She kissed his cheek, then hugged him again before she let him go. "Of course it is, Samuel. Your mother must be so happy."

Sam ground his toe on the floor as he tucked the two-dollar note into his trousers. "I guess I'd better see about buying a ticket on the next boat upriver."

Joss wrapped his arm around Emmy's waist. "Wouldn't you like to go home in fashion, Samuel?"

"Fashion?"

Jim started laughing. "He means he owns more than half the boats going up and down that river every day. He can probably do better for you than a two-dollar ticket."

Emmy turned imploring eyes to Joss. "Can we book him the stateroom, Josiah?"

Joss nodded. "I believe I can arrange that."

Sam shuffled his feet on the wooden floor. He looked from Emmy to Joss to Jim. "I—I'd better go pack my things. But, well, I just want you to know, I'm not ever going to forget you, not any of you. You're the best friends a fellow ever had."

Emmy sniffled as she leaned into Joss. Clearing his throat, Jim stood. "I reckon I better walk him down to the landing," he said. "Make sure Laphete puts him in the right cabin. You know how squirrely that bas—" he looked at Emmy, "—man can be." As he walked by Sam, he swatted the back of his head. "Hurry up, boy. Quit dragging your feet."

Sam loped off in the direction of the back room with Jim pushing him from behind. Emmy looked up at Joss. "Oh, Josiah, I'm so glad it worked out for him."

"Have I told you yet how beautiful you look this morning?" he asked her.

She shook her head. "No. I was thinking maybe you'd finally realized I'm not beautiful at all. Sometimes, I think your eyesight's worse than mine."

He gently tweaked her nose. "Read the other letter, love. I'll finish getting your money."

Emmy ripped open the other letter while Joss returned to the safe. When she read the first paragraph, her hand flew to her mouth. "Saints a mercy."

He swung open the door of the safe. "Good news or bad?" He started to count out bills.

"Josiah, you really did send that letter to George Fisk, didn't you?"

"What letter?" He hesitated. "Emmy, do you want the small bills you gave me or larger ones?"

She looked up from the letter. "Umm, large. The letter, Josiah. The one Uncle Robert said you sent to George Fisk."

He turned back to the safe and started counting again. "Oh that letter. Yes, I really sent it."

"Do you know what this is?" She walked to his side.

He finished counting bills, then slammed the door shut. He gave the handle a good, hard spin. "A response from George Fisk?" he guessed.

Emmy stared at him through her spectacles. "It's an invitation to present a paper on my theories on industrial uses for diamonds to the American Geological Society. The *American* Geological Society, of all places."

"How wonderful." He waved the bills in front of her nose. "Here's your money, Em. What are you going to do with it?"

"Josiah." She planted her hands on her hips. "You told George Fisk about that, didn't you?"

"I told George you had some very interesting theories I thought should be aired. From an engineering perspective, I think they could be invaluable." He grabbed her hand and stuffed the bills into it. "Three hundred, forty-two dollars," he picked up her other hand and filled it with coins, "and twenty-seven cents."

Emmy stared at the money, then back at him. "Josiah, I cannot possibly write a paper for the American Geological Society."

"Of course you can. Do you want to count that money?"

"No, I don't—stop changing the subject." She pulled open her reticule and dropped the money in it. "You can't possibly expect me, *me,* to write this paper."

Joss took George Fisk's letter from her, scanned it, folded it neatly, then slipped it into his back pocket. "Suppose we talk about this later, and you tell me now what you're going to do with that money."

"But—"

"Don't worry about it, Em. If you don't want to write the paper, don't write the paper."

"Well, of course I want to write it."

"So do."

She glared at him. "It's not that simple."

Joss sat down on the corner of his desk to casually swing one leg back and forth. "Like I said, I don't see any pressing need to finish this conversation right now. I'll be glad to discuss it with you, but I don't think it'll do any good until we have time to analyze it properly.

We've got to get Sam on the boat. Jim and I have work to do. We can talk about this later."

She looked like she wanted to argue, but she pressed her lips into a tight line. "All right, but don't think for a minute I am letting this subject drop."

"I would never make a mistake like that. Now, about the money."

"What about it?"

"What do you need it for?"

Emmy hesitated. She didn't want to lie to him, but she didn't want to tell him either. "It's my money, Josiah. I earned every penny of it from publishing treatises. Most of it came from the work I completed on coral before we were married."

"I know."

"You can't tell me how to spend it."

"I'm not going to." He didn't budge from the corner of the desk.

Emmy could tell he still wanted an explanation. She toyed with the strings of her bag. "Since you didn't give it to Uncle Robert's creditors, I thought I'd put it to good use." Joss narrowed his gaze. "I explained why I didn't—"

"I'm not upset with you over it," Emmy rushed out. "I completely understand why you didn't, now."

"It's all there. You can count it if you like."

She shot him a scathing look. "As if I believe you'd steal money from me, Josiah. Lord, you are the most obstreperous one man."

He braced his weight on the desk with his hands to bring his face close to hers. "I just want to know what you're going to do with it."

A partial truth, she supposed, was better than no truth at all. "The house needs some work, the big kind of work, like scrubbing the windows inside and out and polishing all the floors. You said it would be all right if I hired somebody to help me."

Joss blinked. "Of course it's all right. You don't have to use that money for that, Em. I'll pay for whatever, anything you think you need. All you have to do is let me know."

She shook her head. "No. I want to use my money."

"But, Emmy, that's ridiculous. I thought for sure you were going to buy yourself something nice." He grabbed her hand. "You earned that money. There's no reason on earth for you to spend it having my house cleaned."

"You buy me something nice, Josiah. I'll take care of the house." She kissed him before he could argue with her, thinking it would be best if she distracted him. As it was, she was the one that ended up being distracted. Joss's hands closed around her corseted waist. He deepened the kiss almost immediately, stroking the inside of her mouth with his tongue. She stepped into the V of his legs so she could wrap her arms around his neck.

With a groan, Joss lifted his head. "Lord, Em, have you got any inkling what you do to me?"

Her eyes drifted open. She felt languorous. "I've got a very good idea." She moved intimately between his legs. His breath caught, and he would have kissed her again except that Sam and Jim chose precisely that moment to come out of the back room.

Sam let out a long whistle. His bag dropped to the floor with a *clunk*. Jim grumbled something under his breath as he shoved Sam into the room. Joss ignored Emmy's embarrassed flush and looked over his shoulder. "All packed, Sam?"

Sam nodded. "Yes, sir."

Joss set Emmy away from him, then paused to straighten her bodice. "Then I reckon we'd better

head down to the landing. I think I'll go along in case
Laphete gives you any guff." He kissed Emmy's forehead. "Want to come along?"

She shook her head. "I have business to conduct."
Ignoring Joss's frown, she walked over to Sam to adjust
his collar, and retie his kerchief. "Now, Samuel, you
make sure you apologize to your mother when you get
home."

"Yes, ma'am."

She settled his lawn shirt squarely on his shoulders.
"And don't you be pulling anything like this again."

"Yes, ma'am, I mean, no, ma'am."

Emmy brushed his hair back from his forehead.
"And you'd better write me at least as often as you
write Becky Morgan."

Sam's face flushed scarlet. "Aw, Miss Em."

When she kissed his cheek, his blush heightened.
"Good-bye, Samuel."

"Bye, Miss Em. Maybe Joss'll bring you to Hannibal
in the spring."

"Maybe," she agreed, not daring to look at Josiah.
She'd never thought as far as spring before.

Jim gave Sam a good-natured shove in the direction
of the door. "The boat's leaving in ten minutes. If you
don't hurry, you'll have to swim home."

Joss let Jim and Sam precede him out of the office.
He waited, his hand on the knob, his eyes on Emmy.
"I meant what I said about the money, Emmy."

"I know you did."

He studied her a few seconds more. "Don't go causing any trouble while I'm at the landing."

"I know how you hate public spectacles."

He seemed satisfied. "I'll be back in fifteen minutes
or so. I suppose you can't get in too much trouble
between now and then."

# Eighteen

"Miz Emmy, you can't be here." Annie Evans cast an anxious look over her shoulder at the kitchen door of Rosalynd Carver's house. She clutched her broom with both hands.

"It's all right, Annie." Emmy leaned on the Dutch door as she talked to Annie from the garden. "I need to speak with you." After Joss had left for the landing, Emmy had hurried over to Rosalynd Carver's house, hoping to take care of her business before he returned. She knew quite well that he and Jim both wouldn't approve of what she was going to do. The very best thing was to have done with it and let them be angry later.

"No, Miz Emmy, please. You gotta go."

Emmy studied the worried expression in Annie's expressive brown eyes. "Annie, are you afraid of something?"

"No, ma'am." she said, a bit too quickly. "But Miz Carver ain't gonna like me talking to you."

"Rosalynd Carver isn't going to have much to say about it when I'm done with her."

"Miz Emmy, I don't know what you're about, but I can't let you stand here and talk to me. I gotta get back to my work."

"Listen, Annie, I know Jim's been saving money to buy your papers."

Annie cast another glance over her shoulder. She

turned sad eyes back to Emmy. Emmy had always
thought the young woman was exceptionally pretty, and
didn't like the look of fear she saw in her eyes that
morning. "That's so. It'll be a long while yet. I don't
think Miz Carver's gotta mind to let me go."

Emmy squeezed Annie's callused, work-roughened
hand. "Josiah offered to give Jim the money, even lend
it to him, but he wouldn't take it."

"No, ma'am, he wouldn't. My Jim's prouder than
most."

"It's been my experience, Annie, that male pride is
a strange thing. I don't think I'd let something like
pride stand in the way of my doing something so important."

Annie shrugged. "That's the way he is. He's had to
fight so hard his whole life to be who he is, Miz Emmy.
A lifetime of fighting makes a man sturdy."

"But how do you feel about it?"

Annie sighed. She set her broom aside and met
Emmy's gaze. "God's truth, Miz Emmy, I wisht he would.
I know he'd never take the money flat out, but we could
work it off. Every penny of it. Mr. Joss is a good man,
and he's been good to Jim. I know he'd let us."

Emmy dropped her voice to just above a whisper.
"What if you took the money?"

"Me?"

"Um-hmm."

"Miz Emmy, I don't think you understand."

"I want to strike a bargain with you. Just between
you and me. I need some help working on our house.
I figure I need about three hundred, forty-seven dollars
and twenty-eight cents worth of work."

Annie's eyes widened. "But, Miz Emmy—"

"So I'm thinking maybe I'll pay you to do that work
with me." Annie started shaking her head. Emmy ignored her. "Now I know Rosalynd's not likely to let

you come up to the watch house with me, so I thought maybe I'd just give her the money, and see if she's more amenable. What do you think?"

At the mention of Rosalynd's name, Annie cast another fearful glance over her shoulder. "Miz Emmy, please. I appreciate your being so kind, but you don't understand. I can't—"

"What's going on in here?" Rosalynd Carver shouted as she burst through the kitchen door. "Annie, why are you dawdling about when I told you—" When she saw Emmy, she abruptly stopped.

Rosalynd was dressed in black mourning clothes. Emmy thought that she resembled a locomotive with a full head of steam. "Good morning, Rosalynd," she said.

"Emerelda." Rosalynd's acknowledgment sounded more like a rebuke. "I don't know why you feel you need to hang about the back of my house and converse with my slave. You could call at the front like decent folks."

"Annie's my friend, Rosalynd. I needed to speak with her."

Rosalynd cast Annie a scathing look. She waited until the young woman picked up the broom, then she brushed past her to stomp out into the garden. "You've no business speaking with my kitchen help, Emerelda. What do you want?"

Rosalynd's tone had turned waspish. Emmy looked at her in surprise. "I was saying good-morning to Annie, then I was coming to see you."

"You have my attention now, although God knows I cannot spare the time for you. I'm tremendously busy with the details of Jason's death."

"I'm sure you must be, but I've business to conduct with you."

"What business?"

In her agitation, Rosalynd's voice had risen to a loud pitch. Emmy noticed, with absentminded interest, that several passersby had stopped to gape at them. Rosalynd's back was to the street, however. Emmy suspected the woman was unaware that she was drawing a crowd. "I've come to buy Annie."

Rosalynd was clearly taken aback. She flashed Annie an angry look, then returned her gaze to Emmy. "What?"

"I need Annie's help. I'm willing to give you two hundred fifty dollars for her." It was a sound offer, Emmy knew. Domestic help like Annie usually sold for less than that. While she could afford to go higher, she didn't want to tip her hand.

"She's not for sale," Rosalynd bit out.

She would have stalked back into the house, but Emmy stopped her with a hand on her shoulder. "Wait."

"Who do you think you are, Emerelda?"

"I'm a businesswoman just like you. I don't know why you're so irritated, Rosalynd. This should be a simple transaction."

"There's nothing simple about it, and you know it. Don't even think I don't know what you're about."

"I haven't got the slightest idea what you mean, Rosalynd."

"Oh, yes you do." She was shouting now. A sizable crowd had gathered at the small white fence. "You know good and well. You may have put on airs for marrying Mr. Brickston, but don't think I've forgotten what you came from."

"I'd never think something like that," Emmy said, not quite masking the sarcasm that crept into her tone, "but I'm very determined about this. I'll raise my offer to two hundred seventy-five."

"No." The brief retort brooked no arguments.

Emmy took a deep breath. She was sure Annie was valuable to Rosalynd Carver, but if she knew one thing about the former banker's wife, she knew she was greedy. Something else had to be making her resist. If circumstances were normal, Rosalynd would have been delighted with the generous offer. Emmy knew she'd have to find another way around the tree if she wanted to succeed. "Listen, Rosalynd, two hundred seventy-five dollars is very generous. You could replace Annie for a little more than half the amount."

Rosalynd shifted from one foot to the other as she cast an anxious glance at an upstairs window. She returned her gaze to Emmy. "I said no. I meant no. Now get off my property before I'm forced to call the marshal."

The marshal, Emmy noted, was now one of the crowd of people standing around Rosalynd's fence. Gray was looking at her through angry silver eyes. Emmy flashed him a brief, I-have-everything-under-control smile. "All right, Rosalynd, what's your price?"

"I don't have a price," Rosalynd shrieked.

Emmy planted her hands on her hips. She ignored the frantic glances Annie was giving her from the Dutch door. She had no idea why the confrontation had turned so volatile, but she wasn't leaving until she had Annie's papers in her hand. "I don't know what's gotten into you, Rosalynd Carver, but I'm not leaving here until you sell me those papers."

Rosalynd's face turned red. "You listen to me, little mountain girl, I don't know who you think you are, but—"

"Who I am has nothing to do with this, Rosalynd. If I were you I'd be careful how I went about casting stones."

"What the hell do you mean by that?"

When Rosalynd cursed, several of the ladies in the now-substantial crowd began nervously to fan themselves. Emmy wondered what the woman would do if she knew she was creating such a scene. "I mean," she said, "you may be fooling the rest of this town with your show of mourning for your dead husband," Emmy jerked her thumb in the direction of the large black swag over the door, "but you're not fooling me."

"Oh Lord Amighty," Annie mumbled.

Rosalynd's mouth dropped open in an outraged gasp. "After the scene your despicable family caused at the Harvest Party, it's a wonder you'd show your face in town. You're the laughing stock of Carding, Emerelda."

"No one's laughing any harder at me than they are at you." Annie looked vaguely like she might faint. The color in Rosalynd's face mottled into splotchy red patches. The crowd at the fence leaned closer to hear better. Emmy barely noticed. She was now focused on Rosalynd. For the life of her, she couldn't figure why what should have been a simple business transaction had turned into such a fiasco. She drew a deep breath. In a tone she hoped was at least partially conciliatory, she said, "Listen, I don't know why you're so angry. I just want to make a simple business transaction with you. Suppose I increase my offer to three hundred dollars?"

"How dare you?" Rosalynd bit out with the kind of ire only a very self-righteous woman can muster. "How dare you come into my home and insult me like this, acting like I don't know what you're about? You're the one making a fool out of yourself, Emerelda. Don't you think everyone in this town knows about you. Your husband hired that Negro just to spite us. Now you see how it turned out. What he's doing with you is no better. Why the way that man dressed you up and paraded you in front of us like some china doll, it was despicable."

Emmy lost the slender rein she had on her temper. "At least I'm not the one pretending to mourn over my husband while the whole town knows I've been having an affair with Avery Brooks."

A collective gasp sounded from the crowd at the fence. Emmy didn't pay them any heed. Her gaze was riveted on Rosalynd. She expected steam to start shooting out of her ears at any moment. Rosalynd opened her mouth, but nothing came out. Her eyes turned ice-hard. Her face screwed into a mask of fury. She would have slapped Emmy hard across the face except that Joss Brickston's fingers clamped around her wrist in midair. "Problem?" he said smoothly.

Emmy didn't know if she'd ever been as glad to see anybody in her life. She'd been so absorbed in watching Rosalynd, she hadn't even noticed that Joss and Jim had shouldered their way through the crowd. Gray Lawford was standing just behind Joss. Jim was looking at Emmy in shock. Joss looked furious, it was true, but she had no doubt that he'd make sure she got her way. "I'm glad you're here, Josiah," she said. "I'm having considerable trouble conducting my business with Mrs. Carver."

"What in blazes is going on?" Jim said. Annie was looking at him fearfully from behind the Dutch door. He didn't look very happy about it.

Joss dropped his hand from Rosalynd's wrist, but kept her impaled with his frosty gaze. "Emmy, tell me what's going on, please."

She took a deep breath. "You told me I could hire someone to help at the watch house, and I decided to hire Annie."

Rosalynd glared at her. "She wants to buy Annie's papers."

Joss still didn't look at Emmy. "Is that true?"

"Yes," Emmy said quietly.

"Did she make you a fair offer?" he asked Rosalynd.

"It was more than fair, Josiah," Emmy rushed out.

"Rosalynd?"

Rosalynd straightened the bodice of her gown with a sharp tug. "Your wife insulted me."

"With her offer?" he asked.

"No," Rosalynd bit out. "I know exactly why she wants Annie's papers." She turned an icy glare on Annie. "And so do you."

Jim started forward, but Gray restrained him with a hand on his shoulder. Annie rushed out of the house to throw herself against Jim. "Please, Jim. Please don't say nothing. It'll get worse."

Emmy was confused, and starting to feel a little afraid. She slipped her hand into Josiah's. His fingers closed on hers in a bruising grip. "Mrs. Carver," he said slowly, "I'm certain you misunderstand my wife's motives. She wants Annie's papers so she can set her free. Jim and Annie want to get married."

Rosalynd cast a scathing look in Jim's direction. For the first time, she seemed to notice the large crowd. She stared at Gray Lawford for a long minute, then turned her attention back to Joss. "The girl's not for sale."

"I'll pay you twice what she's worth," he said.

Rosalynd shot a quick glance at the window again. "She's not worth anything, Mr. Brickston, and neither is that Negro you keep in your employ."

Jim's hands tightened on Annie's shoulders. Joss gave Emmy's fingers a tight squeeze, warning her to keep quiet. "What do I have to do to get the papers from you, Mrs. Carver?"

Rosalynd looked at him narrowly. Her full lips thinned into a tight line. "Perhaps there is something we can arrange."

"Joss," Jim said, his voice held a note of warning.

Joss shook his head almost imperceptibly. "What do you want, Rosalynd?"

A satisfied smile curved her lips. She looked at

Emmy. "You know, Emerelda, despite your loose tongue, I really should thank you for this. You've saved me a great deal of trouble."

"What do you want, Rosalynd?" Joss bit out before Emmy could respond.

"I'll give you Annie's papers for three hundred dollars," she said. Emmy sighed in relief. Rosalynd turned around and looked at Gray Lawford. "But I want you to arrest Jim Oaks for the murder of my husband."

Emmy held Annie's hand in a tight grip. She studied Joss's profile as he drove them up the bluff. He hadn't said more than two words to her since Rosalynd had delivered her outrageous demand. Her accusation had whipped Carding's population into such a furor, Gray had been forced to put Jim in jail for his own protection. Emmy had finally managed to coax a sobbing Annie into the buckboard, where they'd waited while Joss made the necessary transactions with Rosalynd Carver.

He reined in the horses in front of the watch house then leapt down. He rounded the wagon to lift Emmy and Annie to the ground. "Take Annie inside, Emmy." He set her feet firmly on the muddy ground. "Don't leave here unless the house is on fire, or some other disaster, and don't let anyone in. Do you understand me?" He lifted Annie down before he turned his attention back to Emmy.

"Josiah, I . . ."

"Please, Emmy. Just do as I ask. Don't ask questions."

"I—I'm so sorry."

He leaned over to kiss her briefly. "It was probably inevitable. I'm going back to town to talk to Gray."

Annie laid a hand on Joss's sleeve. "He didn't do it, Mr. Joss."

He smiled at her gently as he gave her hand a reassuring squeeze. "I know he didn't, Annie."

"If there's a trial," she said, her eyes brimming with tears, "they'll hang him sure. No way somebody's gonna believe Jim over Miz Carver."

"Everything's going to be all right, Annie. Gray's a fair man. He's not going to let anything happen to Jim."

Emmy laid her arm across Annie's shoulders. "We'll talk everything over while Josiah returns to town, Annie. Don't worry, we'll figure something out."

Annie nodded. "My Jim says you're the finest folks he's ever known. I'm starting to understand why."

Joss stepped back into the driver's seat. He picked up the reins. "Remember what I said, Em."

"I will, Josiah. Please be careful."

Joss started back down the bluff. With her arm around Annie's shoulders, Emmy waited until he disappeared around a bend in the road. "Let's go inside, Annie. You must be cold."

It only took Emmy a few minutes to have the fire blazing again. Annie found the coffee tin in the kitchen and put the kettle on to boil. By silent agreement, neither of them spoke again until they were both seated in front of the fire, with heavy wool shawls wrapped around them, and mugs of steaming hot coffee in their hands. Annie smiled shyly at Emmy. "I ain't never done this before, Miz Emmy."

"Please, Annie, I'd much rather be your friend than your employer. Can't you just call me Emmy?"

Annie looked at her for several minutes. "I reckon I could. It feels strange, you know. I never let myself think much about owning my papers. That was always something Jim and I talked about in dream whispers."

Emmy tilted her head. "Dream whispers?"

"You and Mr. Joss must have 'em. All lovers do. The things you talk about and don't tell no one else."

Emmy thought about the way Joss had discussed his dreams for the railways, and the future of Continental shipping; about the way he'd believed in her when she'd told him her theories about diamonds. They did indeed share dream whispers. She smiled. "Yes. We do."

Annie nodded. "Owning my papers was a dream whisper for me and Jim." She met Emmy's gaze. "Only now that we do, they're gonna hang him."

"They are *not* going to hang Jim," Emmy said, more emphatic than she had been about nearly anything in her life. Rosalynd Carver had falsely accused Jim to protect someone. Emmy suspected it was Avery Brooks. She also suspected that the Diamond Hawk knew the truth. "Annie," she squeezed the young woman's hand, "do you know why Rosalynd accused Jim?"

Annie shivered. "She told me she would if I caused any trouble over what I saw that night Mr. Carver died."

Emmy set her mug down on the low table in front of the fire and concentrated all her attention on Annie. "What did you see, Annie?"

"I don't know if I should say."

"Annie, Josiah is going to do everything he can to help Jim, but if you know something, you must tell me. I promise Rosalynd can't hurt you now."

"What if she makes things worse for Jim?"

Emmy didn't really think that was possible, but refrained from saying so. "Why don't you just tell me what you saw? If we think it will hurt Jim, we'll agree not to tell anyone else."

Annie seemed satisfied. "All right," she hesitated, "Emmy."

Emmy gave her hand another reassuring squeeze. "Did you see Jim the night that it happened?"

"Yes. It was the evening of the Harvest Party. I was so happy that Jim and I were getting to be alone. I hadn't seen him in such a long time."

"Sam mentioned that to Josiah and me when we arrived at the party. He said you and Jim were spending the evening together."

"That's right. Jim waited round the back of the house until Mr. and Miz Carver left for the Party. I made a new skirt from some scraps Miz Carver had tossed out so it would be real special. Jim was all dressed up like a Thanksgiving turkey. He'd borrowed one of Mr. Joss's boiled shirts and a store-bought collar. It was almost like we were going to the party like regular folks."

"Next year you will," Emmy predicted.

Annie swallowed a sip of her coffee. "We walked over to the Fletcher's livery, across from the park. We could hear the music from there. We danced awhile, just being quiet and together, and then we stretched out in one of the hay piles and watched the stars." Annie's expression turned pensive. "Jim told me he was expecting another year at most before we could be together all the time."

Emmy remembered the disastrous events of the Harvest Party. She shot Annie a wry smile. "It sounds like you had a much nicer time that I did that evening."

"We could see most of the goings-on from the livery. I saw your gown. It was the handsomest gown I ever saw and that's a fact."

"Yes. It was rather wonderful. I must admit, I was having a lovely time until my family showed up."

Annie laughed softly. "I wish you could have seen the look on Jim's face. He was spitting mad, Miz Emmy. When that puffed up puke lit into you, it was all I could do to keep him from stalking over there and whomping him."

Emmy wondered what Robert Greene would do if he heard Annie's accurate, if exceedingly disrespectful, description. "I'm very glad you did. The very last thing we needed was another set of fists in that brawl."

"That's what I told Jim. He was firing mad, though. I thought for sure he was gonna split a gullet he was fuming so bad. As soon as Mr. Joss carried you off the platform, Jim was hell-bent to make sure you was all right. We were going to try and catch you on the edge of town, but that's when he saw young Sam."

"Sam?"

"Sam was still right in the middle, holding onto your uncle's neck, when Marshal Lawford started to break things up. Your uncle tossed the poor little thing on the platform like a sack of beans."

"I didn't know Sam got hurt that night."

"He didn't. Not bad, anyway, but little Miz Becky was powerful impressed with him."

"I'll bet she was."

"She went running out on the platform, and started pittling all over that boy like he was a war hero. Jim started laughing so hard at the way young Sam was acting sick, I had to whomp him to make him stop. Miz Becky helped Sam off the platform, with him looking like he'd swoon any minute, and they started walking to her house."

"That certainly sounds like Sam's shenanigans."

"Jim didn't think it'd be right for us to let 'em alone, with Sam being fifteen and Miz Becky being the Reverend Morgan's youngest."

"That was probably wise."

"Jim likes that boy a lot. He decided Mr. Joss could take care o' you, but he better keep Sam out of trouble."

"Did you follow them?" Emmy pulled her shawl tighter around her shoulders.

"Yes. Followed them all the way back to Reverend Morgan's house. Everyone in town was at the party, and I reckon poor Sam thought he could have Miz Becky all to hisself."

"I imagine he wasn't very happy when you and Jim came strolling up to the house."

Annie laughed. "Oh Lord, no ma'am. You ain't never seen a boy frown like that."

Emmy started to laugh, too. "I wish I'd been there."

Annie shook her head. "It was a sight, that's for sure. Jim made Sam say good-night to Miz Becky, and the whole time that boy was scowling at him like he'd wished he could rip the skin right off his back. And then Jim made Sam walk with us back to the Carvers'. Told him the cold air would help his dizzy feelin'."

"Sam didn't like that one bit, I'm sure."

"He did it, though. Jim tol' him he'd give him a reason to be dizzy if he didn't. When we got to the Carvers', the house was dark, and I said good-night to Jim. I wished he could o' stayed a while, but I knew the party would end soon, and Mr. and Miz Carver would be coming on home."

"Do you know where they went after that?"

"Jim and Sam?" Annie asked. Emmy nodded. "Jim tol' me later that he took Sam back to the office and made him work off sweat by chopping firewood out the back."

"That's supposed to be a very effective remedy," Emmy said, thinking of the enormous supply of chopped wood outside the watch house. "Was that the last time you saw Jim that evening, Annie?"

Annie shook her head. The fearful look came back into her eyes. "I went after him when Mr. and Miz Carver started fighting."

"They had an argument that evening?"

"They was always having arguments, but this one was

worse than most. Mr. Carver had found out that Miz Carver was running about with Mr. Brooks."

Emmy drew in a sharp breath. "He didn't know before?"

Annie shrugged. "Hard to say. We all knew, o' course. Everyone in the house that is. It weren't no great secret, but Mr. Carver, well, maybe he'd been looking the other way for a good long while and didn't want to do it any more. I don't know."

"Is that all they fought about?"

"I didn't hear much. I went running for Jim as soon as Mr. Brooks got there."

"Avery? Avery was there that night?"

"He came in shortly after they started hollerin'. They were talking about money and the bank, and things were getting nasty. I went to fetch Jim 'cause I was scared."

"What happened?"

"Jim was at the shipping office with Sam. By the time we got back to the Carvers', Mr. Carver was dead already. Hung up in his own house."

"Did you see anything? Do you know who did it?"

Annie shook her head. "I was the only one of the slaves in the house that night. There's only three of us, any how, and Maybelle is off visitin' her sick mama. That leaves me and Johnny Dittle. Johnny don't stay in the main house overnight. He sleeps in the livery. Like I said, when Jim and I got there, Mr. Carver was already dead."

"And you didn't see anyone?"

"Miz Carver and Mr. Brooks was gone. Jim didn't want me to stay, but I was afraid what would happen if they didn't find me in my bed case they came lookin'. I didn't want nobody to know I'd seen Mr. Brooks."

"Jim went back to the office?"

"Yes. I went on to bed, though I didn't like the

thought of staying in the house with his body there, and all, but I was so scared."

"When did Rosalynd threaten to accuse Jim?"

"Not 'til the next mornin'. I was in the kitchen making breakfast when she came in and started asking me about the night before. I told her I'd seen Jim in the early part of the evenin'. It seemed right to tell the truth 'bout at least part. Then I said I went to bed early, like always, so I could get up at dawn and start my chores."

"Did she believe you?"

"I don't think so. I don't lie too good. She just told me if anybody asked, that I was to tell 'em the same story. That's when she said if she heard any different, she'd accuse Jim. I was so mad at that I told her nobody would believe Jim'd do such a thing as that."

Emmy saw the quick flash of anger in Annie's brown eyes. "What did she tell you, Annie?"

"She said they'd believe it if she tol' him Jim had caught Mr. Carver grabbin' at me and killed him for it. Nobody was going to take a Negro's word over hers." Annie met Emmy's gaze. "And that's a fact. Nobody's going to."

"I'm going to. Joss is going to. Gray is going to. Don't worry Annie. We'll get Jim out of this."

"I'm afraid, Miz Emmy. I'm afraid of losing Jim."

That was a feeling Emmy could easily understand. "I know, Annie, but you and I will find a way out of this. I have a good feeling in my heart. If you'll help me. I'll help you."

He sat astride his dark horse, ignoring the cold, driving rain that had started to fall. It smote his face in icy shards, but he paid it little heed as he focused his attention on the long, sloping road that led to the bluff.

He had to be right. He was counting on being right. If his instincts were on target, they would be riding by at any moment. When they did, he'd be ready.

The Diamond Hawk let out a long breath and watched as it formed a plume of mist in the wet air. What an ungodly mess this had all become. Jim Oaks was in jail for a murder he didn't commit. Few people knew, he suspected, that Avery Brooks had watched from Rosalynd Carver's upstairs window as the whole sordid scene had unfolded that afternoon. Lack of evidence wasn't going to do Jim much good. The only hope he had was irrevocable proof that someone else killed Jason Carver.

Another twenty minutes passed before he heard the hoofbeats in the distance. He was beginning to grow stiff from too many hours outside in the cold. He cast a grateful glance down the slope, thankful it would soon be over. It was late, almost midnight. Avery's men had taken longer than he'd thought to make their move.

There were six of them. The Diamond Hawk counted heads as they came bobbing over the hill. His gloved fingers tightened on the length of rope he held coiled in his hand. They rode abreast, charging up the hill with no thought at all to their safety or strategy. Avery Brooks would have to learn to hire smarter men in the future.

He wrapped the rope around his knuckles more securely, then waited until their horses were within a hair's distance. With a sharp tug, he brought the rope up tight. The startled horses charged into the line, tumbling forward, tossing riders into the mud. Startled curses filled the night. Just two riders managed to maintain their seats. Four men lay crumpled in the mud while their horses, frightened and disoriented, charged back down the hill.

The Diamond Hawk wasted no time. Every second could prove fatal. He uncoiled the long whip from his belt and flung it out to knock a fifth rider from his horse. There were several gunshots. A musket ball whizzed past his ear. The last rider was charging at him, pistol drawn. The Diamond Hawk snapped the whip across the man's hand to send the pistol flying into the darkness. With a gasp of pain, the man raced forward, shouting obscenities.

The Diamond Hawk cracked the whip again, its report as loud as a strike of lightning. He knocked the final man from his horse. When all six riders stood calf-deep in the muddy road, he reined in his horse to stare down at them. "Are you all willing to die for this cause?" he asked quietly.

They looked properly impressed by their adversary, the imposing man dressed all in black. The one with the wounded hand rubbed at his wrist and shook his head. "It's not you we're after," he growled.

"If you have business on the bluff, you have business with me." The force of the storm had picked up. He had to shout to be heard over the driving rain. "I will kill any one of you who tries to go further."

They looked at each other in consternation, mumbling amongst themselves. As he suspected, their loyalty didn't extend past the paltry amount of gold they'd been promised to complete their task. None was willing to die in the process. "Turn back now," he shouted, "and I'll let you all go."

Four of them started to run down the hill. The man with the wounded hand, and one other, held fast. In the distance, the terrified whinny of the frightened horses carried on the wind. "What will it be?" the Diamond Hawk asked them, his voice tight, controlled.

"If I go back, I'll likely get killed anyway."

"If you stay, you'll certainly get killed."

The fifth man began pulling at his companion's shirt. "Come on, Tom. We ain't getting paid enough for this."

The wounded man batted him aside. "Run, then, you coward. I'm not through up here."

"But, Tom—"

"Go on. Run." He turned his attention back to the Diamond Hawk. "I think you broke my wrist."

"Perhaps."

The man continued to stare at him, as if trying to read his expression through his concealing mask. Tom jerked his own kerchief off his face. The Diamond Hawk recognized him instantly, but didn't budge. "You seen my face now," Tom said. "You could report me to the marshal."

He nodded. "Yes. I could."

"But you ain't gonna."

"Not if you leave this bluff, I'm not."

"How come?"

"Because I have one goal in mind. Marshal Lawford can tend to his own problems."

"Who are you?" Tom asked, wiping a hand over his wet brow. "Why're you doing this?"

"I'm going to be the last man who sees you alive if you don't leave this bluff."

Tom started to fidget. He was still rubbing at his wrist. "All right, I'll go, but you ain't heard the last of this."

"I'm sure I haven't. As long as it's the last for tonight, I'll be satisfied."

Tom's feet sloshed in the mud when he turned. The Diamond Hawk felt his tension begin to ebb. The entire confrontation had not been nearly as bad as he'd feared. He made a near fatal error, then. He allowed himself to think ahead, past the present moment. In so doing, he diverted his attention from the man on

the road. Before he had time to react, he saw Tom
pivot in the mud with a revolver in his hand. The shot
sounded in the darkness. The spark from the flint lit
Tom's face for the briefest flash. A musket ball whistled
through the rain. The Diamond Hawk jerked to the
side just in time to avoid taking the shot in his temple,
but he could not avoid it altogether.

The musket ball ripped through his shoulder and
lodged in his flesh where it caused a searing pain to
spread through his chest. He felt the warm, sticky flow
of blood begin seeping through his shirt front. His
horse, startled by the shot bolted even as Tom began
running frantically down the hill to escape the charging horse.

The Diamond Hawk managed, by some miracle, to
regain control of his frightened mount. He jerked on the
reins with his good arm, trying to ignore the pain in his
chest and shoulder and his sudden light-headedness.
He had to make it to shelter, or the elements and the
wound would kill him. Drawing several steadying breaths,
he slumped over his horse's neck and began the torturous ride toward the watch house. Emmy would know what
to do, he thought, even as he felt a wave of nausea well
up inside him. He slipped slowly, inexorably into unconsciousness.

Emmy didn't begin to seriously worry about Joss until after eleven o'clock that night. Annie had been exhausted by the time she'd finished telling the story.
Emmy had helped her fix a pallet in the loft where the
young woman had almost immediately collapsed.
Emmy, however, was far too anxious to sleep.

She had known Joss would be with Gray Lawford well
into the evening. Neither of them would rest until they
felt certain they'd devised a plan to help Jim, but when

eleven o'clock came and went, self-control alone kept her from saddling her mule and riding into town to find Joss. His grave warning about not leaving the house still rang in her ears. She wondered just what kind of trouble he was expecting.

Emmy paced about in front of the fire until her feet hurt, listening to the relentless ticking of the clock. Eleven-thirty passed with still no sign of him. Her stomach was tied in knots, her nerves drawn taut as a bowstring. Where could he be? Why hadn't he at least sent her word that all was well.

Twice, she reached for her oilskin cloak. Twice she put it back. Her shoulders ached from the tension. Wearily, she dropped into the rocker to stare at the fire as she replayed Annie's story in her head. Sam could vouch for Jim's whereabouts that night, of course. She was certain Joss would send for him if need be, but Jim had been at the Carver's house. That fact was irrefutable, and, Emmy knew, could be damning. If the judge allowed Annie's testimony at the trial, it would help. Particularly if the story matched Jim's, Sam's and Becky Morgan's, but nevertheless, Rosalynd Carver had been right about one thing: not many folks were going to take the word of a Negro over the word of the banker's wife.

When Emmy heard what sounded like a commotion outside, she jerked her head up. It could have been a trick of the storm, but she was sure she'd heard shouting. She sped to the door and grabbed her oilskin coat. Joss did say she could leave if there was an emergency.

Outside, the rain bit at her face, as the wind lashed it against her skin and whipped her hair into her eyes. Roiling clouds completely obscured the moon. She could hardly see in front of her to pick her way across the yard. The sound of the shouting was clear, though, as was the sharp, insistent crack of a whip. She ducked her head against the rain and stumbled forward, holding the edges of her coat.

The noises from the road suddenly ceased. She looked up, straining her eyes for some glimpse of the trouble ahead. The briefest spark clearly lit young Tom Gabernick's face when the shot fired. Emmy watched in horror as the musket ball cut a visible path through the rain and slammed into the Diamond Hawk.

With a startled cry, she jerked up her skirts and started running in his direction. By the time he managed to pull his horse around, Emmy was gasping for breath from the stitch in her side. She forced her feet to keep churning through the mud, even though it sucked at her boots to slow her progress and make her swear in frustration. A crack of lightning briefly lit the road. She saw him slump low over the neck of his horse. She pushed forward, determined to reach him, and did, the instant he toppled from the saddle and knocked her to the ground.

"Oh, God." Emmy clutched at him, trying to shake him awake. "You can't die, do you hear me? You just can't."

The horse, still frightened from the earlier commotion, had bolted the moment his rider slid from the saddle. Emmy stared helplessly at the retreating animal, wondering how she would manage to pull her wounded burden back to the house. She looked over her shoulder, barely making out the dim light from the watch house in the distance. It was at least fifty yards away, mostly uphill. She wasn't sure how she would ever manage.

He coughed suddenly, and she bent forward to shield his face from the rain and listen to the sound of his breathing. It was steady, but shallow. She pressed her lips to the cool skin of his face where her tears

mingled with the rain. "Please, please," she whispered.
"I will help you. I swear I will."

Another flash of lightning split the night. The lines
around his mouth were drawn tight. She smoothed
them with her finger before working her way around
to cradle his head in her lap. She slipped both hands
beneath his wide shoulders as she tried to ignore the
stab of fear she felt when she encountered the sticky
patch of blood on his back. She pulled with all her
might. His body moved an inch.

Emmy gasped for breath, then pulled again. Two
more inches. She kept tugging at him, until her arms
ached with the strain and her back throbbed from the
effort of dragging his big body through the mud. She
kept glancing at the watch house, wondering if they
would ever make it. Briefly she considered what would
happen if she ran back and got the mule. She could
never lift him onto it. Even if she could, the mule was
too temperamental to be counted on in this weather.
She pulled again, moving her burden perhaps another
six inches.

He started to cough then, and Emmy tried to hold
his shoulders still. She feared he'd do himself more
harm if the coughing fit jerked his body. All the while,
she kept talking to him. When she ran out of things
to say, she started talking about gemstones, telling him
the precise equation for density measurements. She
covered the proper procedure for measuring calcimite
deposits, and inch by precious inch, she pulled him
closer to the house.

She was about to give up, about to fall down in the
mud next to him and beg his forgiveness for failing to
get him to shelter, when she felt a hand on her shoulder. Annie stood behind her, wrapped in one of the
heavy wool shawls. Without speaking, she bent down
and slipped both her hands under one of his shoulders.

Emmy took a deep breath and grabbed the other shoulder, the wounded side, and together, they managed to drag him back to the watch house.

They crashed through the door, gasping for breath. Annie rushed over to the fire saying, "We have to get him warmed up before you can do anything about that wound. If he gets pneumonia, he'll be too ill to heal proper."

Emmy slammed the door shut and dragged him farther into the room. She raced into the bedroom to fetch a pillow and three quilts. Annie stoked the fire into a roaring blaze while Emmy started tugging his clothes off. "If you die on me now," she said, "I'll never forgive you, do you hear me?"

She ripped open his shirt, and gasped at the sight of the ugly wound. "Oh dear Lord."

Annie came over to kneel next to her. "What are you going to do, Miz Emmy?"

Emmy covered him with the quilts, then pushed the pillow under his wet head. "First I'm going to dig that musket ball out of his shoulder," she said, leaning down to kiss him lightly on the mouth. "And then I'm going to kill him for putting me through this."

She reached up to jerk the mask off his head. She ignored Annie's small gasp. Emmy laid her hand against the cool plane of his face and said, "And don't you even think about dying and depriving me the pleasure, Josiah Brickston."

# Nineteen

The fiery liquid burned like a river of lava down his throat and Joss coughed, momentarily disoriented by the cloudy feeling in his head and the searing pain in his shoulder. He opened his eyes, trying to focus on the red-haloed angel kneeling over him. She looked remarkably like his wife. "Emmy." His voice was a whispered sigh.

The angel frowned at him. "Shut up, Josiah, and drink this," she snapped.

He wasn't sure, but he didn't think angels talked like that. He swallowed another sip of the brandy. "Where—" his voice failed him, so he took a deep breath and tried again. "Where am I?"

She laid his head back down on the pillow. "You're on the floor of our house, that's where you are. I couldn't drag you any farther than the front door, so you're just going to have to lay here a while." Despite her waspish tone, she reached out and smoothed a lock of his hair back from his forehead. "You scared me, you big clod."

Joss's mind scrolled through the events of the evening. The fight on the road. The gunshots. His eyes widened. It was indeed his wife kneeling over him and not some angel of mercy. He was alive. He tried to sit up. Emmy pushed him back to the floor. "Lie still. I have to dig the musket ball out."

Joss reached up and rubbed a hand over his face. The mask was gone. "You know." he said.

Emmy wiped a smear of mud off his cheek, knowing instantly that he was referring to his identity as the Diamond Hawk. "I've known for the longest time, Josiah. Now be quiet. I have to get the ball out of your shoulder."

He waited while she laid out several thick towels and carried a pan of boiling water in from the kitchen. She set the items down on the floor next to him and sank down to her knees. "I wish you'd stayed unconscious. This is going to hurt."

Emmy was looking anxiously at the blade of the knife, her eyes filled with concern. Joss grabbed her hand. "It's all right, Em."

"I've never done this before."

He shook his head on the pillow, trying to clear it. She'd fed him so much brandy, he felt stuffed with cotton. He knew he'd be glad for it in a minute though. Not only was it warding off the chill, but it would dim the pain when the time came. "I don't think the wound's very deep," he said, trying to reassure her with his slurred words. "You shouldn't have much trouble."

Emmy frowned at him. "There wouldn't be a wound at all if you hadn't put yourself in the way of that musket ball. Tom could have killed you."

Joss would have shrugged, but it hurt too much. "They were after Annie."

"I know. She told me what happened the night of the murder."

"I talked to Jim about it," Joss said. Emmy was cleaning the knife in the boiling water. He watched while she carefully wiped the blade dry.

"What did he tell you?" She carefully tore open his shirt, trying not to disturb the wound. The flesh was torn and bleeding, and Emmy swallowed, staring at the angry gash in his shoulder. "It's in your shoulder," she said, before he answered.

Joss nodded. "I know. It's not so serious that way, Em." She frowned at him again, and he thought maybe he'd better keep her talking. "Jim didn't know much. Annie had been afraid to tell him the whole story. All he knows is that Rosalynd and Jason had an argument the night of the murder." He gasped when Emmy touched the hot blade to his skin.

"I don't think I can do this, Josiah."

"Yes you can. Just tell me what Annie told you. We'll go from there."

Emmy started working at the wound, probing for the musket ball. She couldn't look at his face. "She told me the same thing," she said, wincing when she felt the tip of the knife strike metal and heard Joss's gasp. "Do you want some more brandy?"

He shook his head. She saw the sweat that had broken out on his forehead. "Do you have something I can bite on?" he asked.

She leaned back. "Wouldn't you just rather scream?"

He managed a weak smile. "Men don't scream."

"Of all the ridiculous—"

"Emmy," he interrupted softly, "there's a piece of leather in my desk drawer. I use it for grinding down pencils. That'll do."

She hesitated briefly before she scurried up the ladder to the loft and fetched the hardened piece of rawhide. When she returned to his side, Joss was sweating profusely. "Are you sure you're all right?"

He took the leather. "Just keep telling me about Annie." He wedged the thick rawhide between his teeth.

Emmy picked up the knife again, sterilized it as best she could in the hot water, and turned her attention back to his shoulder. "Did Jim also tell you Avery Brooks was there that night?"

Joss jerked and she couldn't tell if it was the mention of Avery's name or the pain that caused the reaction. She kept probing for the musket ball. "That's what Jason and Rosalynd were fighting about. Jason told Rosalynd he knew she was running about with Avery and he wouldn't have it. Annie said things got really ugly when Avery showed up at the house."

"What happened?" he asked, the words slurred around the rawhide he held clenched between his teeth.

"Jim was with Sam. Annie went to fetch him because she was scared. By the time they returned to the house, Jason Carver was already dead." The tip of the knife struck the musket ball, and Emmy gritted her teeth and ignored the sharp expletive Joss muttered beneath his breath. "I already sent Annie to fetch Sam back. I gave her passage on the *Salimar*. I knew that was the next ship upriver."

Joss nodded, his eyes glazing over slightly as Emmy worked the knife beneath the musket ball. "Leaves tonight," he gasped.

"Left already," she said, barely stifling the urge to scream in frustration when the ball lodged deeper in his skin. She kept working at it. "Annie should be back with Sam late the day after tomorrow. I wish the boats ran more often." She managed to get the knife beneath the ball. "Hold still, Josiah, I've almost got it."

His spine arched and he sucked in a deep breath when she slid the ball free. Emmy tossed it to the floor and picked up one of the towels, pressing it to his shoulder to stop the bleeding. "It's out," she said. "I got it out."

Joss nodded and fell into unconsciousness once more.

\* \* \*

When he awoke, a thin, watery streak of light was shining across his face. He still lay on the floor, covered in a mound of quilts. Emmy was curled up in a ball at his side with her face pillowed on his stomach. He lifted his hand to tangle it in her soft hair. Thin lines of fatigue and worry etched her face. A smudge of mud covered one cheek, and what looked like dried blood, his blood, speckled her forehead. Her eyes were still red around the rims from crying. Her dirty, blood-stained hands were tucked beneath her cheek. She looked beautiful to him. "Emmy," he whispered. He got no response. He gave her shoulder a gentle squeeze. "Sweetheart, wake up."

Emmy started awake. She felt confused and sore. She stretched her aching muscles and looked at Joss a full ten seconds before she remembered the events of the previous night. She scrambled to her knees as she reached to touch his forehead. He didn't appear to have a fever. "Are you all right?" she asked.

"Just weak. The wound feels fine." He bent his right elbow. "Everything appears to still work."

Emmy brushed his hair back from his forehead. "If you ever scare me like that again, I'll kill you myself, Josiah."

"I believe you threatened to do that during the night."

Her hand shook. "I was so frightened. What if you had died? Just a few more inches down or over, and that musket ball would have killed you."

He turned his head to kiss her palm. "But it didn't. Thanks to you."

"What if I hadn't found you? What if you'd lain out there all night in the rain?"

"Emmy, it didn't happen. You're getting worked up over this."

Emmy shivered. "But it could have happened."

Joss folded her hand in his. "Yes, it could have, and I'm sorry if it frightened you. I had to protect you and Annie." He glanced around. "Where is she?"

Still shivering, she peeled back the bandage to check his wound. "On her way to fetch Sam." She waited for his nod of comprehension. "It was a long night." The wound looked clean. The neat stitches she'd made held the puckered skin in place. She was glad she'd poured the brandy on it. She remembered the night her father had been attacked by a bear, and her mother had treated the wounds with brandy, claiming it would stave off infection. "Do you think you can get to the bed?" she asked. "I hate to leave you here on the floor."

"I think so. If you help me."

They struggled for several minutes while Joss tried to get to his feet. By the time he was on his knees, he was already gasping for breath. "You lost so much blood, Josiah. I know how weak you must be."

"Can you get me a chair to pull myself up with?"

Emmy hauled one of the sturdy chairs over to his side. Using it for support, he levered himself up with his left arm so he could drape his wounded arm over Emmy's shoulders. She took as much of his weight as she could, and tried to keep him balanced as he walked to the bed. When they reached the bedroom, Joss collapsed across the bed with a low groan. He was shivering from the exertion and the chilling effect of his still damp clothes. "Are you all right?" Emmy asked.

He took several deep breaths. "I will be in a minute. Do you think you could bring me some coffee?"

She hurried to the kitchen where she decided she'd heat him some milk instead. After she set the pan on the stove, she went back to the bedroom. "I put some milk on to heat for you. While we're waiting, I have to get your clothes off, Josiah. You could catch your death of cold."

He managed a weak smile. "You're always trying to strip me naked, wife."

Emmy felt a wave of relief wash over her. He was teasing her. Everything would be all right. Somewhere during the long anxious night, she'd begged God to let Josiah live. Evidently, her prayers had been answered. She started pulling at his trousers, trying not to jostle him any more than necessary. By the time she had him undressed and tucked beneath a mound of quilts, his milk was heated. She poured it in a mug and dropped in two squares of chocolate and enough sugar to sweeten it. She stirred until the chocolate completely dissolved. When she carried it back to the bedroom, she found him propped against the pillows, watching her through half-hooded eyes. "Here's your chocolate." She sat as she handed him the mug.

Joss took it and swallowed a grateful sip. He never took his gaze from hers. Emmy was still not used to seeing him with both eyes uncovered. She fought the urge to fidget beneath the impaling intensity of his gaze. "Why are you looking at me like that?"

"Why haven't you asked me why I deceived you about being the Diamond Hawk?"

She diverted her gaze. "I've known for a long time. I think almost from the very beginning." The look she gave him was sheepish. "It was one reason I couldn't help goading you just a bit."

Joss swallowed another sip of his chocolate and gave her a mocking glance over the top of the cup. "A lot, you mean. You had no respect for my aura at all."

Her eyes filled with amusement. "Your aura, indeed. It wasn't nearly so daunting when I knew who you were."

"How did you guess?"

"I'm not an idiot, Josiah. There were several things. Your voice, for one. You do still have a trace of an accent, you know. There's not a man alive who says 'schedule' and makes my blood race like you do."

"I shall remember to whisper it in your ear more often."

"Then there was the way you moved. You're a very graceful man, especially for your height. I noticed it right off. I'll admit that your eye patch did throw me a bit, but you couldn't have disguised the intensity of your eyes no matter what you'd done. That's what gave you away. I suspected it at first, but after the second or third time I saw you, I was sure."

He looked at her thoughtfully. "Why didn't you confront me about it?"

"I was going to, but I kept telling myself you must have a reason for your secrecy, or you would tell me yourself." Emmy met his gaze. "You do have a reason, don't you?"

Joss nodded. "Several reasons. As the disguise goes, it was the best way I knew to find out what I wanted. Thieves move about at night on darkened highways. The best way to watch their activities is to spend time on the same highways. I couldn't very well stroll about at night by myself without some means of protection. The disguise allowed me nearly uninhibited freedom of movement."

"But had you planned on developing such a reputation?"

"In part." He pushed a tendril of hair off her dirty face. "It helped, you know, to have them afraid of me. I must admit Horace Newbury's newspaper was an unexpected bonus."

Emmy's laugh was soft, gentle. "Do you know, I privately thought most of what he said was true."

Joss eyed her cynically. "This from the woman who bought me a piece of black fringe for my cape."

"I couldn't resist the urge to goad you at least a little,

Josiah. I mean, I knew it was you under there, and it didn't seem fair that you were deceiving me."

"If you knew, then I wasn't deceiving you at all."

"Now you are splitting hairs with me. Besides, you must admit you were terribly dramatic about the entire thing. You were always dropping in windows and swinging about in the dark." She paused while he finished his chocolate and set the mug down on the chest by the bed. "And that diamond stickpin," she prodded. "Surely that wasn't necessary."

He took her hand in his. "That was Allyson's. I didn't want to forget," he said, his voice soft.

"You are the most wonderfully romantic man I know, Josiah."

He looked embarrassed. "Romantic or not, it worked very well. I came to Carding and began living in the watch house a full month before anyone knew I was in town. That gave me the freedom to move about once I officially arrived without arousing any suspicion. Once I overheard Avery's name in conversation between two thugs on the road, I followed that lead until I knew Avery was working in conjunction with Rosalynd Carver."

Emmy's eyebrows drew together in confusion. "How did you know that?"

Joss hesitated. He didn't really want to share the sordid details of room eight in the Carding hotel with her. It seemed too harsh for her ears, and unfair that she should know something so ugly. Avery's betrayal had hurt her. She'd trusted him once. Joss saw no reason to inflict still more damage. Instead, he lifted her hand to place a tender kiss in the center of her palm. "Don't ask, darling," he pleaded.

Understanding dawned in her eyes. "Oh."

"Yes, oh."

She looked very vulnerable to him with her dirty,

tear-stained face, and with her eyes still a bit puffy. She wasn't wearing her spectacles, and her hair lay in disarray around her shoulders. He felt a stab of guilt as he realized the extent of her exhaustion from the strain and worry of the previous night. He wished he felt strong enough to pull her into his arms and comfort her. "Josiah?"

"Yes?"

"Do you think Avery murdered Jason Carver?"

"Yes."

"Do you know why?"

"I think so."

Emmy frowned at him. "This is all tied into Allyson's murder, isn't it?" She didn't miss the flash of pain that flared in his eyes.

"I didn't even put all the pieces together until you said what you did about Avery and Rosalynd. It never occurred to me that Jason would be giving Avery the cash, when, er, considering the circumstances."

"Do you have any proof that's what happened?"

"It all hinges on Annie now. I suspect Jason started to get nervous. We were bringing so much pressure to bear on Robert, he was starting to crack. Gray was pressing Jason fairly hard to make the bank records available, and while we knew Rosalynd was tampering with the accounts, we couldn't figure out where the cash was coming from. Stupid, I guess."

"You gave Avery too much credit for being a decent sort of man. He was just trying to keep Rosalynd out of the way."

"So it seems."

His voice sounded tight, withdrawn. "What are you going to do, Josiah?"

"I don't know. I still don't know who pulled the trigger that night and killed my family."

"You can't go out as the Diamond Hawk again. It's

too dangerous. You're wanted for the murder of Mace Johnson, and Gray would be forced to arrest you."

His eyelids had begun to droop. He leaned back against the pillow. "I'm glad you believed me when I told you I didn't kill him.

"Of course I believed you." She walked into the bathing closet to wet a cloth under the pump. She carried it to him to wipe away the lingering sweat and dirt and blood on his face. "How are you feeling?"

"I'm exhausted, Em. Come lie down with me for a while."

She stretched out beside him and curled her fingers into his big hand. "I'm glad you're all right, Josiah. I couldn't bear it if I lost you."


Emmy stretched her sore muscles and burrowed her head against Josiah's chest, hoping to drown out the insistent pounding. Joss squeezed her shoulders. "Emmy, love, someone's at the door."

She sat straight up in bed. "The door. What time is it?" She glanced at the small clock on the mantel. "It's afternoon already."

Joss nodded. The pounding sounded again, this time accompanied by Gray Lawford's voice calling her name. "It's Gray." She moved to the side of the bed. "What if something's wrong with Jim?"

Joss leaned back against the pillows. A sharp twinge of pain made him wince. "He'll want to see me. It's all right, Emmy."

She stared at him. The thought just occurred to her that she'd have to explain Joss's injury to Gray. Joss gave her a reassuring nod. "It's all right," he repeated. "Let him in."

She walked slowly to the door to tug it open. Gray's fist was still poised in midair, ready to strike the door again. He stared at her. "You look like hell, Em." He pushed past her into the house.

Frowning, she slammed the door. For the first time she realized that she still wore what was left of her olivine gown from the previous morning. The skirt was torn about the hem. Dirt and Josiah's dried blood stained the fabric. There was a tear in the bodice. She knew her hair and face must look a fright. "Thank you, Gray. It's lovely to see you too."

He glared at her. "Where's Joss?"

"Why do you want to know?"

"Damn it, Emmy, don't play games with me. Tom Gabernick came slinking into my office this morning to confess the entire thing from last night. He told me he shot the Diamond Hawk." He lowered his voice. "Where is Joss?"

"I'm in here, Gray," Joss called from the bedroom, "though you'll have to come see for yourself, I haven't got the strength to walk out there."

Gray shot Emmy a quelling glance as he stomped into the bedroom. He took one look at Joss, at the discarded pile of black clothes by the bed, and swore beneath his breath. Gray pulled his hat off and ruffled his hair with his fingers. "Damn," he said. "Damn."

Emmy moved between Gray and Joss to sit on the bed. "Watch your language, Gray."

He glared at her. "I'm in one hell of mess now. You do realize that don't you?"

"Josiah did not shoot Mace Johnson, or any of those other men," she insisted.

"I know that," he bit out. "But there's still a warrant on his head." He looked past her to meet Joss's gaze. "There's still a warrant on your head. I told you if you got involved in this, somebody was going to get hurt. Damn."

Joss shrugged. He ignored the pain it caused his

shoulder. "You wouldn't have known about Avery's role in this if I hadn't gotten involved."

"There still isn't any proof, nothing solid I can show a judge."

Emmy toyed with the soiled fabric of her gown. "Surely there must be traces of mismanaged funds. If you checked the bank records carefully, you could determine where the money was coming from, and who was making deposits. If Avery was setting up the sells and buys, his name must be linked somewhere with the lapidaries. Why don't you check there?"

Gray nodded. "That would be enough to convict Avery and Robert and Jason on swindling, but Joss won't be satisfied with that."

Joss rubbed his hand up her spine. "I want them for murder, Em."

She turned tearful eyes to him. "They'll go to jail. Why can't it be enough? Is it worth dying for, Josiah?"

"I'd have died for my family when they were killed. I'll do it now."

She felt suddenly very cold and very depressed. There was a note of inflexibility in his voice that she recognized. Emmy wiped at her eyes with her hands. The grime on her face yielded to the salty tears. She frowned at the smudges on her fingers. Joss took her hand to kiss her fingertips. "You'll feel better if you have a bath, Em. I know you're exhausted."

Emmy shook her head. "I don't want a bath." She completely missed the concerned frowns Gray and Joss exchanged. Standing, she headed for the kitchen. "Would you like something to eat, Gray? I'm going to fix Josiah some soup."

Joss tried to catch her hand. "Emmy, I—"

She eluded him. "There's no sense arguing with me. Gray?"

He nodded. "I haven't eaten since yesterday. I'd appreciate the food."

Emmy left them alone. Gray pulled a chair over to the side of the bed. "How serious is that wound?"

"Not bad. Emmy got the ball out all right. He hit me in the shoulder."

"Tom thinks he killed you."

"Good for Tom. Why did he confess?"

"I'm not sure. I'm fairly certain Avery told him he was going to kill him for failing to get Annie. Tom figured he was safer in my jail than he was a free man."

"You're getting quite a crowd in there."

"If I haul your sorry hide in, I'll have one more to brag about."

"You're not going to do that, Gray."

"You sure as hell aren't making this easy on me."

"Have you suspected I was the Diamond Hawk all along?"

"Right from the start. I saw you in St. Louis, remember. Even in the state you were in, there was this half-crazed look in your eye. When you arrived in Carding just a few weeks after the raids started, well, I was almost positive. The day you upended Gentleman Mack, I was sure. There were too many connections between the jewel thefts and your wife's murder to be strictly coincidental."

Joss leaned back against the pillows. "So what do you want to do now?"

"First thing is get Jim out of jail. If this goes to trial, they'll hang him."

Emmy walked back into the room with two bowls of soup. She handed one to each of them, then sat on the side of the bed. "We've already sent Annie after Sam. Sam can testify for Jim's whereabouts the night of the murder."

Joss looked at her closely. "Aren't you eating?"

"I'm not hungry." She looked back at Gray. "They should be here by tomorrow afternoon."

Gray swallowed a spoonful of soup. "That'll help, but it's going to be Sam's word against Rosalynd. That'll be tough to stand on."

"That's not true," Emmy said. "Sam and Jim and Annie walked Becky Morgan home that night. She can testify, and so can her father for that matter."

"Reverend Morgan was just called out of town on a family emergency," said Gray. "Damned convenient, isn't it?"

"You can't let them hang Jim, Gray. You can't," she said.

"Nobody's getting hanged." Gray lifted his bowl to his lips and took a long swallow. "But it's not going to be easy."

Exhausted, Joss tried to focus his thoughts. He was worried about Emmy. She was acting odd. Normally, she would have leapt at the opportunity for a warm bath, cleanliness being high on her list of recuperative procedures. She wasn't eating. She looked tired and pale. She hadn't even changed out of her ruined gown and into more comfortable clothes. The thought occurred to him that she had been soaked through when she'd dragged him into the house. The fact that she'd never changed out of her sodden clothes made him frown. He placed a hand on her forehead. She looked at him in surprise. "Josiah?"

"I thought you might have a fever," he said.

"I'm fine." She pulled away from him. "I'll be more fine if we find a solution to all this."

Joss watched her, speculating. Finally, he turned to Gray. "There's every chance that Rosalynd and Avery are making plans to leave town with the money. They have a temporary respite now that Jim's in jail, but they know you don't think he's guilty. They aren't stupid enough to stay in town when the whole thing could come crashing in around them."

Gray nodded. "Do you think they're still in tight with one another?"

"Did you happen to notice Avery standing in the upstairs window of Rosalynd Carver's house during the confrontation yesterday?" Joss asked.

Emmy stared at him. "Avery was there in her house?"

Joss nodded. "She kept glancing up at him. I didn't doubt for a minute that Avery was making the decisions."

Gray uttered a curse. "I'll keep a close eye on them, see if I can determine what they're up to. Are we agreed that they'll probably betray Robert to save their skins?"

"Yes," Joss said. "And they won't think twice about it. He's got to be nervous. He might turn on them."

"Annie will be back with Sam by tomorrow afternoon," Emmy said. "Surely nothing will happen before then."

Gray looked at Joss. "Avery already went after Annie once. If he finds out she's gone, he might guess where. How's she traveling?"

"Continental riverboat," Joss answered. He knew without asking that Emmy would have arranged the woman's passage. "They'll be safe until they step off the boat at the landing. You'd better be there to meet them."

"I will." As he stood, Gray picked up Joss's bowl to stack it with his own. "I'd best be heading back to town. I don't want to leave the jail unattended for too long."

Emmy jumped up to grab the two bowls from Gray. "Let me send some soup back with you for Jim." She raced out of the room toward the kitchen.

Gray frowned at Joss. "Is she all right?"

"I'm not sure."

"She's all the family I got, Joss. See that you take care of her."

Joss stared at the door, thoughtful. "She's upset, and tired. It's more than the accident, though."

"Keep an eye on her. Things are very tense right now, and there's no telling what anybody might do. Avery's getting desperate."

Joss nodded. "I know. Nothing's going to happen to Emmy. I won't let it."

Gray picked up his hat from one of the chests and settled it on his head. "I hope you're feeling better. I'm glad you weren't too seriously hurt."

"Thanks, Gray."

Gray hesitated. "Joss—"

Joss met his gaze and held it. "Yes?"

"Think real hard before you do anything else." He cast a quick glance in the direction of the kitchen. "You have a lot to lose now."

Emmy walked back into the room carrying a leather bag. "I lidded the pail and wrapped it in towels to stay warm." She handed the bag to Gray. "There are some biscuits in there, too."

As he took the parcel, Gray leaned down to kiss her forehead. "Get some rest, Em. You look exhausted."

"I will. Thank you, Gray, for—" her voice broke.

He hugged her close. His eyes met Joss's across the room. "Promise you'll take care of yourself. All right?" Gray urged.

She nodded, sniffling as several tears slipped down her dirty cheeks. "All right."

Gray shot Joss a final stern look. "Don't forget what I told you."

"I won't." Joss's gaze rested on Emmy.

Gray left the room without another word. Emmy shifted, uncomfortable beneath Joss's intense gaze.

"I'm still not used to seeing you with two eyes, Josiah. It makes me feel—transparent."

He held out his hand to her. "Come here, Em."

She walked slowly across the room to slip her fingers into his. "Are you feeling all right? Is there anything I can get you?"

He tugged at her hand until she sat down next to him. With his thumb, he wiped at the smudges on her face. "You're not transparent at all. If you were, I could tell what's wrong."

"Nothing's wrong."

Joss laid his palm against her face. "Tell me, sweetheart. Let me fix it."

"You can't." Several more tears slipped down her cheeks.

"I'm going to be fine," he said. "Is that what has you so worried?"

She shook her head. "I know you're all right now."

"Gray's not going to let anything happen to Jim."

"I know that too."

Joss slipped his hand to the back of her nape to urge her down against his chest. "Then tell me what's wrong, love. Just tell me."

"Oh, Josiah," she wrapped her arms around his waist. "This is all my fault."

"What's your fault?"

"Everything." Emmy rubbed her cheek against his bare chest. "It's all my fault."

"Sweetheart—"

"No. Please don't try to deny it. I meddled when you told me not to. I pushed you into telling me what happened to Allyson and Michael and Adam. I manipulated Sam into writing his mother and now he's not here to help Jim. I confronted Rosalynd Carver, and that's why she accused Jim. That's why Avery sent those men after Annie." She raised stricken eyes to him. "That's why you got shot."

Joss stared at her. "Emmy, none of this is your fault. You were trying to help me."

She shook her head. "No I wasn't. I was trying to help myself. I was afraid of being more clutter, Josiah. There were so many things demanding your attention. I was afraid you'd think I was too much to trouble with, so I started trying to set things aright."

"Emmy—"

"It's true. I wanted to take care of Sam because it was unfinished business. I knew you were worried about him. I wanted to take care of Jim and Annie for the same reason. But that was all clutter you picked. You chose to take on Sam. You chose to help Jim. You got stuck with me."

Joss exhaled a deep sigh as he shifted her slightly against his chest. He was starting to understand. "Emmy, I want you to listen to me."

"It's all true, isn't it?"

"No. It is not true. Nothing that happened is your fault, and in case you hadn't noticed," he said, casting a wry look around the now spotless bedroom, "I'm not particularly adverse to clutter." He threaded his hands into her hair. "Emmy, I love you. I told you I do."

"I know."

"Don't you believe me?"

"Yes."

She didn't look very convinced. Joss decided he'd better do something, fast. There was at least one way, he knew, to calm her fears, to show her how much he did love her. He kissed her temple. "Love," he said quietly, "I think I need a bath."

Emmy stared at Joss. "A bath?"

He nodded. "I'm still covered in dirt and blood from last night. I think I need a bath."

She drew a quick breath, feeling instantly contrite. "Oh, Josiah, I'm so sorry. I should have thought of that." She rolled off the bed to hurry toward the bathing closet. "I'll heat the water for you."

He leaned back against the pillows, listening while she fussed about in the bathroom. What he really wanted to do was go to sleep, but Emmy needed this from him right now. If he could coax her into his bed, content her with his lovemaking, make sure she knew she was wanted, she would feel better. He was sure.

He waited while she hung the kettle of water in the fireplace grate. "It will only take a few minutes," she told him as she walked back to the bed. She peeled back the bandage and checked his wound. "This looks good."

"You did a beautiful job."

"I hope I did it right. I stitched Gray up once, but I never had to remove a musket ball before."

Joss was beginning to feel a languorous heat seep through his body. The delicious anticipation of touching her was driving away the last vestiges of his fatigue. Emmy always did that to him. "Next time I'm shot, you'll be more prepared."

She clung to his hand. "There's not supposed to be a next time."

Joss gently kissed her palm. "I'm teasing you."

"It isn't funny. I was afraid. I'm sorry I'm such a coward."

"Only stupid people are never afraid, Em. Doing what you did while you were afraid doesn't make you a coward. It makes you strong."

She stood there for several minutes, just watching him. Her lip quivered occasionally, as a new flood of tears threatened to burst forth, but she held them at bay. Instead, she clung to his hand and found solace in the warmth of his gaze. It took nearly fifteen minutes for the water to boil. Joss made her sit on the side of the bed and talk to him about nonsensical things while they waited. "Do you think Jade is going to marry Grant Lewis?" he asked, searching about for a safe topic of conversation.

She hesitated before she sank down on the side of the bed with a shake of her head. "No. Jade's not really interested in Grant. He's just a nice boy. I've been trying to make her realize how handsome Gray is, but I'm not having very much luck."

Joss ran his fingers over her collarbone and along the collar of the olivine bodice. "I like Jade," he said. "She's the only one of your cousins I can tolerate besides Alex, and Alex is simply too young to have turned into a hellion."

Emmy's smile was sad. "That's not all true. Alex has a sweet disposition. Jade was just like her at that age."

"Tell me." He circled the top button of her bodice with his index finger.

"Jade is just genuinely kind at heart. She'd never hurt a soul. She likes everyone, and everyone likes her." Emmy started telling him a story about the time Jade had noticed Otis Lampton hadn't been in town for three days. She'd skipped school one day and made the long walk to Otis's house, only to find out he was laid up with croup. Jade had spent every day of the next week and a half taking care of Otis. By the time Robert and Clare Greene found out Jade had been absent from school, the teacher had been ready to fail her. Only when Otis showed up at the schoolhouse and argued on her behalf was Jade allowed to continue in her grade and advance to the next.

Emmy was so involved in the story, she didn't even notice that Joss had unbuttoned half the buttons of her bodice. He worked his way down the tiny buttons at her neck, carefully spreading the fabric back from her throat. He didn't stop until his fingers encountered the lace-trimmed edge of her corset. He caught a glimpse of peach and white stripes. His mouth went suddenly dry. "I think the water's boiling," he said in a tight voice.

Emmy looked at the kettle in surprise. "Yes. I suppose it is." She hurried over to the fire and wrapped a towel around the handle to lift the heavy kettle. Joss was afforded an enticing view of her bosom, and the outline of the corset he now knew was definitely crafted from the ruined peach and white silk skirt she'd worn to the Harvest Party. When a wash of desire flooded his limbs, he wondered how he'd make it through the bath.

It wasn't easy. Emmy filled the tub, using the boiling water from the kettle to heat the cold water from the pump. When she returned to the bed, he'd swung his legs to the side where he waited for her to assist him. He hoped she wouldn't notice his growing arousal. With no small amount of relief, he saw the soap flakes that she'd put in the water. The tub was filled with bubbles. When he sank down in the steaming bath, his lower body was completely obscured from view. Emmy handed him a cloth. "Is there anything else you need?" she asked.

He realized for the first time that she intended to leave him alone in the bathing closet. He leaned back against the tub with a dramatic sigh and allowed his eyes to drift shut. "I'm feeling weak, Emmy." He extended the cloth to her. "I think you'd better do it."

She frowned at him in concern. "Are you certain you're all right, Josiah? Perhaps I should have Gray send for a doctor. There's one in Smithton. That's only a twenty-minute ride."

Joss shook his head. "I'm sure it's just from blood loss. If you'll just see to my bath, I'll go straight back to bed." He opened his eyes to give her a pleading look. "Promise."

She knelt by the tub and took the cloth. Joss waited in breathless anticipation while she rubbed it over his chest. When she neared his wound, he decided that was excuse enough to flinch. He did so, and splashed a healthy amount of water on her. "Sorry," he mumbled, giving her what he hoped was a pained look. He was having trouble concentrating while she was running her hands over his chest.

She brushed idly at a spreading water stain on her bodice. "It doesn't matter. The gown was ruined anyway."

"Why don't you take it off, Emmy. It's not good for you to be wearing wet clothes. You might catch cold."

"It doesn't matter."

"What will I do if you get sick?" he persisted. "I'm too weak to take care of myself."

She yielded, then. With a shrug, she stood to shed her gown. Joss watched through half-closed eyes, trying his best to act disinterested. He decided that the efficient way Emmy dispatched with the gown was a hell of a lot more tempting than any seductive strip-tease could have been. His body started to shake when she dropped the bodice on the floor. He got his first good glimpse of the peach and white corset. Well, great God in Heaven, he thought, just what was she trying to do to him?

Emmy unbuttoned her skirt and stepped out of it and her petticoats. She tossed them in a heap on the floor. She stood before him wearing her corset, pantaloons and shift. Her hair felt matted and dirty, suddenly, so she undid the pins and shook it free. When she ran her fingers through the tangled mass of red-gold curls, Joss sank deeper into the tub.

Emmy returned to his side and picked up the cloth again. "Feeling better?" he asked.

With a nod, she continued wiping the traces of dirt and blood from his skin. "I hadn't realized how grimy I felt."

Joss took the rag and gently wiped her face until all the dirty streaks were gone. "You'd feel better if you had a bath."

"I will later. Are you ready to go back to bed?"

Joss thought about telling her he'd never been so ready in his life, but decided against it. The sight of her clad in that erotically enticing corset, with her faded orange pantaloons and shift, had caused his loins to tighten almost unbearably. He wondered how he'd make it out of the water without hauling her in to the tub and ravaging her. Standing, she handed him a towel. He took it gratefully, wrapping it around his lower body as he rose from the tub.

Emmy supported him with an arm about his waist as he walked back to the bed. He felt stronger than he had since he'd awakened on the floor that morning. The force of desire caused his adrenaline to accelerate, sent strength roaring through his blood. Nevertheless, he fell across the bed, using it as an excuse to pull her down with him. She sat up, watching him, looking concerned. "I don't think you should still be this weak, Josiah. I'm worried."

"There's nothing wrong with me a day or so in bed won't cure," he drawled, any pretense of weakness gone. His eyes smoldered as he took in the enticing way the corset pushed at her full breasts. He ran his finger over one rounded, creamy curve.

Emmy stared at him. "Are you certain?"

Joss used his other hand to tug away the towel and give her a clear view of his full arousal. "Positive," he said.

Emmy's eyes widened as comprehension dawned. "Josiah, you can't mean to—"

"Oh, I mean to all right," he growled. He pushed her back down on the bed, then threw a heavy leg over both of hers. "I've been meaning to all morning."

"But your shoulder." She shivered when he rubbed his rough, unshaven chin against her neck.

"We'll be careful." He pulled at the neckline of her shift until it tore free. The exposed curves of her full breasts mounded above the top of her corset.

"I don't think we should."

Joss's laugh was soft, warm. He bent his head and nuzzled the fragrant valley between her breasts. "If we don't, I think I might die after all."

When his lips touched her nipple, Emmy arched into him. "Oh, Josiah."

He sensed her surrender. A rush of desire shot through him. "Let me show you how much I love you, Em. Just let me love you."

Emmy grabbed his head and clung to him. "I love you, Josiah. With all of me, I love you."

"I love you, too." He slipped one large hand inside the bodice of the corset to free the heavy weight of her breast. Bending his head, he flicked the nipple with his tongue until the peak hardened. Only then did he take the tight little nub between his teeth and begin to suckle.

Emmy threaded her fingers through his hair as she moaned her pleasure. "It's incredible what you do to me, Josiah."

"What do I do to you, Em?" he whispered against her breast. "Tell me."

"You make me feel so beautiful, so alive." She gasped when he licked his way across the curve of her breast until his lips settled on the other peak, already begging for his touch.

"You like this, don't you?" He laved the peak with his tongue. There was no demand in the question, just the gentle insistence of a lover seeking to give pleasure.

Emmy twisted beneath him as she struggled to free her arms from the confining sleeves of her torn shift. He held her still. "Yes." The word came out on a hiss. "Yes, I do."

"Tell me what else." He gently bit her nipple.

She moaned again. "That, too."

Joss's hand slid to her waist where the corset had cinched it in. "I love this thing you're wearing. It's so decadent."

She wriggled again. "You told me to make a corset out of it when the skirt got ruined."

"Wise suggestion on my part. Sometimes my brilliance amazes me." He kissed her again, deeply, thrusting his tongue in and out of her mouth while one hand stayed firmly at her waist. He tangled the other in her hair. When he raised his head, they were both breathing heavily. Joss smiled at her as he began spreading her hair with meticulous care over the pillow. "Do you know what the sight of your hair does to me? I've always loved your hair."

She could no longer stand the constriction of her torn shift. She tugged her arms free, luxuriating in the freedom to spread her hands over the naked flesh of his back. Droplets of water beaded the light spattering of curly hair on his chest. She arched her neck to lick them away with her tongue. Joss gasped as a tremendous shudder ripped through him.

Emmy trailed her fingers lightly beneath the line of the white bandage, down his waist, and over the sharp curve of his hipbone. "I like this too," she murmured. "I like the way your body responds when I touch you."

Joss took her hand and guided it to his arousal. He curved her fingers around the smooth, hard length of him. The exquisite torture of her touch made him ache. "Then do it," he whispered hoarsely. "Touch me all over."

Emmy ran her fingers along his hardened shaft. She sucked in a pleased breath when she felt his body jerk at her touch. His hands tugged at her pantaloons, pulling the waistband free from beneath her corset. He pulled them off and tossed them to the floor with a groan. "Emmy." His voice caught when she rubbed her thumb over the tip of his arousal. "Sweetheart, if you don't stop that, I'm not even going to have time to get your corset off. I'm on fire."

She squeezed him. "So am I," she whispered. "I want you inside, Josiah."

He buried his lips on hers while he threaded his fingers through the soft hairs at the apex of her thighs. When he found her wet heat, he lost what remained of his resolve. "Oh, my love. Hold onto me. Take me inside."

Emmy spread her legs wide and guided him to her. She cried out in pleasure when he entered her in a smooth stroke.

Joss ground his teeth against the exquisite sensation as he waited for her to adjust to the full feeling of his weight sheathed in her tight warmth. Emmy rotated her hips against his. The restricted feel of the corset, pressing at her pelvis, making her feel even more full and tight and stretched where he was buried inside her, was incredibly arousing. "Please, Josiah, now."

"I don't want to hurt you."

She arched against him. "You won't. You can't."

When she swiveled her hips, a ragged groan tore from his throat. He thrust into her, fully embedding himself. She threw her head back on the pillow and shuddered. "Now, Josiah. Please now."

He shouted her name as he moved into her with

frenzied thrusts until she hurtled over the edge, drawing him right along with her.

He collapsed on top of her. She'd drained him completely. His exhaustion, he knew, owed far more to the force and power of their lovemaking than the lingering effects of his wound. Emmy's fingers trailed lightly over his sweat-dampened skin. She held him close with her legs wrapped tightly about his thighs.

Joss softly kissed her. He lingered over her full mouth with heart-breaking tenderness. "I love you, Emmy," he whispered. "I'll always love you."

"I love you more than I thought was possible, Josiah." *That's why I'm so afraid of losing you*, she thought. *I've already lost so much.*

He hugged her close and would have withdrawn, but she stayed him with her thighs. "Stay please."

"Inside of you?"

"I like having you here. I feel safe."

"Don't you want me to take your corset off?"

"Only if you don't have to pull away."

Joss's smile was very gentle. He kissed her with slow, lazy possession. "I think I can manage," he whispered against her lips.

He did. And when she was free of the rest of her clothes, he made love to her again until he became big inside of her, and he carried her once more to a place where she could forget that her world was crashing down around her. She fell into a deep sleep at last, held securely against his chest, with a prayer on her lips that somehow, everything really would be all right.

But when she awoke, the afternoon sun was high in the sky, and Josiah was gone.

# Twenty

Emmy looked at the clock with a flutter of panic. It was after three. She knew as surely as she knew her own name that Joss had gone into town to meet the *Salimar* and ensure that Sam and Annie arrived back in Carding safe and sound. She jerked back the covers to scramble out of bed.

The room was in perfect order. Joss had collected their ruined clothes and disposed of them. He'd stretched the wet towels over the side of the tub to dry. Her corset was hung on a hook inside the upended crate she used for a wardrobe, and the rest of her undergarments were folded neatly in a pile on top of her trunk. She felt a cold sliver of dread work its way into her heart. Josiah had started clearing away clutter.

She dropped down on the side of the bed to rub her throbbing temples. What a disaster this all was. Joss had no business being out of bed in his state, much less taking on Avery Brooks, and yet, Emmy was certain Avery would try to get to Annie. Her testimony would be damning. She could prove that Avery had lied about his whereabouts on the night of Jason Carver's murder. She could testify that Rosalynd and Jason had quarreled about Rosalynd's scandalous relations with Avery. If that happened, Gray would have enough cause to call in a bank examiner. Once the evidence was found in the bank's book, Avery wouldn't be able to escape.

Thrown into the whole horrid equation was Robert's involvement in the mess. There was simply no telling what he might do if he felt trapped. If Gray found evidence of Robert's guilt, as surely he would, Robert was prone to do just about anything. She ran through all the details in her mind, trying to think what on earth she could do to protect Josiah from the inevitable. There was only one place where he was vulnerable, and Emmy suspected that Avery knew it.

The Diamond Hawk was wanted for murder. If Avery exposed Joss's identity, Gray might be forced to arrest him. That left one option, and one option only. Emmy raced to Joss's trunk and began to dress.

By the time he reached the landing, Joss was nearly doubled over his horse's neck in pain. His shoulder ached like it was on fire. Try as he might, he couldn't seem to make his legs feel any more solid than jelly. He still felt weakened from his loss of blood, but damned if he'd let Annie and Sam walk into a trap. He dismounted when he reached the landing. The sharp ache that ran down his arm made him wince. With a swift economy of motion, he hitched his horse and started through the afternoon crowd.

The recent rains had coated the landing with a layer of mud and soggy debris, but the usual level of activity was unaffected. Everywhere, shoremen swung heavy crates and cargo kegs onto the dock. Street vendors moved in and about the milling crowds, crying above the din, peddling their wares. In the distance, a riverboat whistle carried on the cool wind. Joss spotted Gray's dark head above the throng of people, and began picking his way along the landing.

Gray looked at him in surprise. "What are you doing out of bed?"

"I thought you might need some help."

"You're sure to be useful. You look pale as a ghost.
I see you've got the patch back on."

"It's part of the disguise. You don't want a blood-
thirsty crowd on your hands demanding my arrest, do
you?"

With a frown Gray turned his attention back to the
*Salimar.* The large boat was pulling into the landing.
"Are you sure they'll be on this one?"

"Unless something happened in Hannibal. Emmy
sent word to my pilot to put 'em in the stateroom and
not let them leave until they reached Carding."

Two crewmen leapt down to grab the mooring ropes
so they could secure the large boat to the massive brass
anchors. The plank was lowered, and the passengers of
the *Salimar* started to disembark. Joss scanned the surrounding crowd as he and Gray started. He found what
he sought and jabbed Gray in the ribs. "What?" Gray
asked.

"To the left," Joss said not looking around. "There
are three men next to the fur boxes. Do you see them?"

Gray glanced sideways toward the boxes. "Yes."

"They were on the road to the bluff last night."

Gray nodded. "I'll put myself between you and them.
You meet Annie and Sam."

Joss left Gray's side and headed toward the gang
plank. Annie and Sam appeared at the railing. Sam saw
Joss and waved his hat. Annie looked scared. Joss shouldered his way through the crowd, trying to protect his
injured arm.

Sam called to him. "Mr. Joss. We're over here. Is Jim
all right? They still got him in jail?"

Joss reached the gangplank where he lifted his hand
to assist Annie. No sooner did she place her gloved
hand in his than he heard the commotion at the end
of the landing. "Marshal Lawford." It was Avery

Brooks's voice. "Marshal Lawford, I demand that you arrest that man."

Gray flashed a brief look at Avery. He was pointing the end of his walking cane right at Joss. Rosalynd Carver stood at his side. "Hold on, Avery," Gray said, trying to defuse the situation. From the corner of his eye, he saw the three men Joss had indicated begin to move into position. He spun around and drew his revolver, holding them in his sights. "I want all of you over there with Mr. Brooks where I can keep an eye on you."

The crowd parted on a startled gasp to line up on either side of the brewing confrontation. Joss still stood at one end of the muddy landing with Annie and Sam behind him. Avery stood at the other end, watching Gray Lawford with a menacing eye. "Really, Marshal," he drawled. "All these dramatics are not necessary." Avery lifted his hat to wipe a gloved hand through his shock of blond curls. "I have come to inform you that Josiah Brickston is the Diamond Hawk, and I demand that you arrest that man."

The crowd gasped. Joss noticed that the throng on the landing was growing. Children were squeezing their way through the adults for a better look. Along the slope that led into Carding, more folks were coming as the news spread. Gray didn't take his eyes off Avery. "I got a man in my jail who says he killed the Diamond Hawk last night, Avery," Gray said. "He also says you paid him to do it."

Another collective gasp. The crowd all turned to look at Avery. His face turned an angry, blotchy red. "I've been an upstanding citizen in this town for years, Marshal. You have no reason to doubt me." He pointed the cane at Joss again. "There's your man. He murdered Mace Johnson, and those other two men, and I'd wager he killed Jason Carver, too."

"Mr. Joss didn't kill nobody," Sam said, leaping down from the *Salimar*. Joss restrained him with a hand on his shoulder.

The crowd turned to look at Joss. "It's true," he said. "I didn't kill anybody. Mace Johnson died because Avery's own men shot him."

The crowd looked at Avery. His eyes were glittering with rage. "That's preposterous. That man is the Diamond Hawk, I'll tell you, and if you'll just arrest him, I assure you that you'll find he's wounded."

Gray still held the gun on Avery. "How would you happen to know that, Avery? Unless, of course, you really did hire Tom Gabernick to kill him, and Tom failed. Is that what happened?"

The crowd looked back to Avery. "Of course not. I heard the news this morning, like everyone else, that the Diamond Hawk had been killed." He glanced briefly at the three rough-looking characters Gray had motioned to stand behind him. "I believe these three ruffians were among those spreading the rumors."

They glared at Avery, their expressions menacing. Avery ignored them. From the corner of his eye, Joss saw Robert Greene join the throng of people on the landing. He was flanked by several of his children. Joss drew a deep breath, knowing the entire situation was about to escalate out of control. He turned his gaze to Annie. "Get back on the boat, Annie. You're not safe here. Jim needs you alive."

"There," Avery shouted. "You see. He's in league with that woman, that Negro. Everyone knows she's responsible for Jason Carver's death." Rosalynd did her best to contribute to the situation by pretending to swoon into Pete Fletcher's arms.

"That's not true," Sam shouted.

Joss tightened his grip on Sam's shoulder. "Keep still, Samuel." He leveled his gaze on Avery. "You aren't fooling anybody, Brooks. You were in Jason Carver's house the night of the murder, and Marshal Lawford already knows it."

The crowd gasped again. Every eye focused on Avery. He was starting to look pale. "That man's wanted for murder, Marshal," he said. "You have a warrant for his arrest. It's your duty to put him in jail."

"It's his duty to arrest the Diamond Hawk," a voice called from the opposite end of the landing. The crowd parted to make way for the massive black horse and rider, garbed in a hastily altered version of the now infamous costume. Emmy rode up to Gray. "Joss Brickston is a free man."

Avery gaped at her. "Emerelda, what are you doing in that ridiculous costume?"

"It's my disguise, Avery. Didn't you know?"

"Cri-mi-ny," Sam muttered. Joss started forward, but Sam grabbed hold of his arm.

Gray shot her a quelling glance. "Get down," he ordered.

"No," she said, returning her gaze to Avery. "It's true. I'm the Diamond Hawk. You know, Marshal Lawford will confirm, that all the thefts were jewel thefts. There's no one else in this town more qualified for that than I am. Joss Brickston doesn't know the first thing about gemstones."

The crowd murmured agreement. Emmy didn't dare look at Joss. "This is ridiculous," Avery said. "It's obvious she's just protecting him. The man's her husband, for God's sake."

Emmy shook her head. "No. It's not obvious. I took the gems. I analyzed them and resold them on the market. Only I had the contacts to do that. Only I had the knowledge and the ability. No one else could have issued the certificates and found secondary markets for the stones."

Avery's eyes shot blue fire at her. "You are in over your head, Emerelda."

"No. If you are demanding the arrest of the Diamond Hawk, you are demanding my arrest."

Avery looked at Joss. His cool eyes took in the sight of Annie still aboard the *Salimar*. Emmy noticed a flicker of panic on his too-pretty face. "That is not true, Emerelda. I had hoped to spare you this, as we have been such good friends, but I see I have no other choice." He turned to stare at Robert Greene. Robert's fat face drained of color. "What you say about the gems is true. There were secondary markets. There were false certificates, but you didn't issue them." He lifted his cane and pointed at Robert through the crowd. "He did."

Robert gaped at him. The crowd parted again. They gave Robert a collective shove forward. "It's not true," Robert spluttered. "It's not true."

Emmy still couldn't look at Joss. "Isn't it?" she asked Robert, her voice deadly calm.

He glared at her. "Get down from that horse, Emerelda. How dare you embarrass your family like this? Look what you've done."

"I've embarrassed no one. You're the one who has been illegally issuing certificates for Avery and Jason Carver. People have died for this, Uncle Robert. How could you?"

"No one was supposed to die," Robert said. "It was the money."

"Shut up, Robert," Avery snapped, turning back to look at Gray. "He's confessed. What more proof do you need?"

Gray didn't lower his revolver. "I want to know why you tried to have Annie killed last night."

"I did no such thing," he said.

"Annie's story is true." Elijah Morgan pushed his

way through the crowd. "Jim Oaks and Annie did walk
my Becky home from the Harvest Party. Just this morning, I received notice that a member of my family in
St. Louis had fallen ill. I got halfway there when a courier from Continental Shipping chased me down and
brought me back."

Avery was starting to look vaguely like a caged animal. The crowd was gaping at him in stunned silence.
Emmy dismounted and tossed the reins of the enormous horse over the hitching post. Gray said, "I sent
that courier. I'd already heard Annie's story and knew
you could confirm it, Reverend."

Avery drew himself up to his full height. Rosalynd
had revived from her swoon. She now clung to his arm.
She stepped in front of Avery to glare at Gray. "Are
you going to take the word of that, that slave woman,"
she flicked her hand in disdain toward Annie, "over
mine?"

Gray found his first smile. "As a matter of fact, I am,
and given your reputation, I'm sure as hell going to
take Reverend Morgan's."

Rosalynd gasped. Her hand flew to her throat. It was
then that Emmy saw the ruby necklace. "Wait," she
cried. "The necklace."

Gray looked at her in surprise. "What about it?"

Emmy ripped the black mask from her head and
threw it to the ground. "It's not the same one I cleaned
for her. I mean, it's the same necklace, but the stones
have been replaced."

Avery turned pale. Gray kept looking at Emmy.
"What does that mean?"

"When I cleaned the necklace, most of the stones
were either fakes, or poor quality. They have been replaced with genuine rubies." She looked at her Uncle
Robert. "Uncle Robert will confirm that the stones are

real." She cast a brief glance at Josiah. "Josiah was there when I gave Avery my analysis of the necklace."

Gray looked at Robert Greene. "Are they genuine?" he asked.

Robert, knowing that he'd been betrayed by Avery already, seized his chance. He bent low and peered at the stones. "Yes, they are. Very high quality."

"What does this mean?" Gray asked Emmy.

"Avery replaced those stones himself. If you look at the back, I assure you you'll find only one lapidary mark. They originally were set at Fieldler's in Chicago. Jason bought them on a business trip. Avery told me so when he brought them to me to clean."

Gray walked over and lifted the necklace from Rosalynd's bosom. He glanced at the back. "An *f,*" he said.

Emmy nodded. "That's Fieldler's mark." She slipped the diamond stickpin from her lapel and held it out to Gray. "See, here's the horseshoe and cross used by Chandler and Bates. Every lapidary has one."

Gray looked at the pin before he gave it back to her. "There's only one mark on the back of the necklace. You're right. So what?"

"So," Emmy said, starting to feel like her heart was being gripped by ice, "A lapidary didn't replace those stones. He would have added his own mark. The only person who handled that necklace besides me was Avery Brooks."

Avery glared at her. "What are you trying to say, Emerelda?"

"When I gave you that necklace, I told you the stones were poor quality. You told me not to tell anyone. You then replaced the stones with genuine rubies, *stolen* rubies, and returned it to Rosalynd. You had already taken the real stones and sold them, using the fakes to replace them in the necklace. That's why it needed cleaning."

"This is all conjecture, Emerelda. You cannot prove any of it."

"But a look at the bank books will." Emmy turned her gaze on Rosalynd. "Did you know Avery was getting the necessary cash for this venture from Jason? Did you know he was just using you so you'd stay out of their way? He knew you handled the books anyway. Jason and Avery had a good long laugh over the notion that you had no idea what they were doing."

Rosalynd turned on Avery. "Is that true?"

He glared at her. "Calm yourself, Rosalynd. You might say something you'll regret."

"Emmy," Gray said, his voice quiet, hard. "What does all this mean?"

"It means two things, Gray. First, it means that Avery was involved from the very beginning with the thefts, the swindling, everything. What Josiah said was true. Avery had those men killed."

"What else?" Gray prompted.

Emmy took a deep breath and looked at Joss. "There's only one place Avery could have gotten stones as high quality as those rubies. I remember discussing this with Uncle Robert when it happened. There was a shipment stolen two years back just north of St. Louis."

Joss's whole body had started to shake. He was staring at Avery. "It was you," he said, his voice barely above a whisper.

Avery met his gaze. "What are you talking about?"

Joss ripped the patch from his eye and threw it to the ground. He pulled the revolver out of his gun belt. "On the road. It was you. You're the one who killed my family."

Avery seemed to sense that the battle was lost. Like a trapped animal, he attacked. "Yes, Brickston, I was the one. I see I made a mistake by not putting another bullet into you. I'd left you for dead on that road."

Joss took another step forward. "You murdered them. Right there in cold blood."

Emmy looked frantically at Gray. "Do something," she said.

"Joss," Gray took a step forward. "If you kill him, I'll have to arrest you."

Joss shook his head, but never took his gaze off Avery. "I've waited for this for two years, Brooks. I lay there in that carriage and watched while you shot my wife through the head. You killed my son Adam. You shot my son Michael. Do you honestly think I'm going to let you live?"

Avery looked at Gray. "You cannot let him kill me, Marshal. It's your job to stop him. You can see he means to shoot me."

"Oh, I mean to all right," Joss said.

Emmy thought he sounded lethal. "Joss," Gray interrupted, "this won't bring them back."

"He murdered them, Gray. You can't deny my right to kill him."

"I can't let you, Joss."

Joss looked at Gray, his purple eyes ice hard. "You can't stop me either. What are you going to do? Kill me? It won't be any worse than what that son-of-a-bitch has put me through for the last two years."

Emmy felt panicked. Joss was going to kill Avery, and Gray was going to kill Joss. "Josiah, wait," she called.

He looked at her with haunted eyes. "Please wait," she said. "Gray's right. You can't bring them back. Do you think Allyson would have wanted you to die trying to avenge their murders?"

"I would have died trying to save them. I should have."

Avery sneered at him. "You were too weak to do anything about it then, and you're too weak now."

"Shut up, Avery," Emmy shouted, not looking at

him. "If you value your life, you damned well better shut up." She reached out an imploring hand to Joss. "He's already taken so much from you. Are you going to let him take your life too?"

"He'll go to jail, Joss," Gray said. "If we convict him for Allyson's murder, he'll hang. If you kill him, I'll have to hang you, too. I don't want to do that."

Joss's hand was shaking, but he held the revolver leveled at Avery. "It's a matter of honor, Emmy," he said. "I've told you that."

"What honor is there in killing him, Josiah? Is there honor in your dying? Is there honor in your letting Avery Brooks turn you into less of a man than you are? If you kill him, you won't be any better than he is."

Joss looked at her. "You don't understand."

"And what about me," she pleaded. "Am I supposed to be widowed, to sacrifice everything because of your damned honor? What will happen to me if you die?"

"Emmy—"

She shook her head. A steady stream of tears wetted her cheeks. "Am I supposed to keep myself warm at night knowing your honor is intact? Am I supposed to find comfort in the knowledge that I'm alone but you have your honor? I won't do it, Josiah."

"Emmy, you can't—"

"I won't let you do this. If you do, you'll be telling me and everybody else in this town that Emmy Greene was just another piece of clutter in your life like everything else. You discarded me with the rest of the garbage because of your damned honor."

Joss stared at her while images of Allyson, of Michael and Adam floated through his mind. They were slowly replaced by the softness in Emmy's gaze, the warmth of her touch, the depth and intensity of her love for him. When he looked back at Avery, his eyes narrowed to slits. Could he just let him go? Could he forget what he'd done to his family and turn him over to the law? Joss thought of the pleading look in Emmy's eyes, of the way the tears were streaming down her cheeks and falling onto the black silk of her shirt.

And he leveled the gun on Avery, watching as he cowered. He could pull the trigger and be done with it. He could avenge Allyson's death. He would know that Michael and Adam were at peace. A sudden memory of Michael, dying in his arms, telling him he saw angels, flashed into Joss's mind. They *were* at peace, he realized. He was the one who wasn't. Slowly, he raised the pistol above his head and fired a shot into the air. "Arrest him, Gray," he choked. "Get him out of my sight."

The crowd roared to life. Shouts and sobs mingled with the mournful whine of the riverboats. Avery crumpled to the ground. Gray took two strides and knocked him flat on his stomach. He pulled a piece of rope from the back of his trousers and tied Avery's wrists. Emmy sagged back against the horse, too weak, too exhausted to move.

"Emerelda," Joss called in a voice loud enough to be heard above the din of the crowd. A hushed silence fell once more.

She met his gaze and held it. "Yes, Josiah?"

"I hate public spectacles."

She felt a wave of relief wash through her. "I know."

"There's something you said that has me worried, though."

"Only one thing?" she asked, feeling almost intoxicated she was so light-headed.

"We'll settle the rest later." A hint of a smile tugged at his lips. "It's this issue about your name?"

"My name?"

"You said I'd be proving to the world that Emmy Greene was nothing but clutter in my life."

"I did?"

"You did. You're not clutter, Emmy. You've never been clutter."

"I'm not?"

"No, you're not."

"I'm sorry I misunderstood."

"I suppose it was understandable, given the circumstances."

"But what's wrong with my name?" she asked.

"There's nothing wrong with it," he said, and suddenly, Joss felt all the strain and weariness of two years drain out of him. He felt well. He felt alive. "It's just not right."

"Not right?"

He shook his head. "It's not Emmy Greene."

Emmy understood. He knew by her smile. "Then what is it?"

"It's Mrs. Josiah Brickston now, and don't you be forgettin' it." Before he got all the words out, Emmy started running across the platform. She launched herself at him so hard, they fell backwards onto the dirty hardwood planks.

"Your arm," she protested when he hugged her tight.

"Damn my arm. Just kiss me, Emerelda."

Emmy didn't even care that they were lying in the mud, or both of them were soon covered in it. The dirt was the last thing on her mind. She rained kisses over his face, crying all the while. "Oh, Josiah, I do love you."

With a laugh, he wrapped her in his arms. He hardly even noticed the pain in his shoulder. He rolled her to her back and kissed her soundly, not even caring that they were creating possibly the worst public spectacle in the history of Carding, Missouri.

# Epilogue

*September, 1854*

"Are you certain I look all right, Josiah?" Emmy stood in front of the mirror in the luxurious traveling car. She tugged on the sleeve of her new apricot silk gown as the private train Joss had hired for them sped toward London.

Joss came up behind her. He wrapped his arms around her waist. He wondered how it was possible to feel so content. After all that he'd shared with Allyson, the joy of their years together, it didn't seem fair that he should be so richly blessed a second time. "You look beautiful as always, love. Why are you so nervous?"

She shifted anxiously while he nuzzled her neck. "I can't help it. I've never met your family before, and I want them to like me, especially Katy." She fidgeted while she pleated the green lace trim of her bodice.

"Katy likes everyone. That's the trouble."

Emmy frowned at him. They had not intended to travel to England until the following spring, when their six-week-old daughter Alayne was older. But word had come from Josiah's father, requesting them to hurry home. It seemed the duke was tremendously concerned over his youngest daughter's recent escapades, and felt she would benefit from returning to St. Louis with Joss and Emmy. "Now, Josiah, you don't know anything about this situation. I don't think you should be passing judgment on your sister before you hear her side of the story. She might be completely innocent."

"Not Katy," he assured her. "She's going to love you." He stilled her fingers where she was busily retying the green silk frogs on her bodice. "There's nothing to be nervous about, Emmy. They will love you because I do."

Emmy turned around to face him. He rested his hands at her waist, smiling a secret smile when he thought of her lush curves beneath the saffron-yellow corset he'd ordered specially made for her from Paris. Emmy was watching him through worried eyes, and he removed her spectacles. He slipped them into his pocket. "Josiah, I need my spectacles, or I can't see."

"It's easier to kiss you without them, sweetheart," he murmured as he bent his head and took her lips in a long, satisfying kiss.

"Daddy, Daddy," Tyler Grayson Brickston's three-year-old voice came from the door of the traveling car as he came toward them in his usual full-run.

Joss groaned against Emmy's mouth, then raised his head. He handed her the spectacles with a look that said "later." He bent down and picked up Tyler, ruffling his red-gold hair. "Yes, son?"

"Alayne gots milk on her dress. Aunt Jade said don't tell Mama."

Joss shot Emmy a knowing look. Emmy rolled her eyes as she dropped her spectacles on her nose. "She is definitely her father's child," she said. She headed for the door of the traveling coach. "Josiah, would you please tuck Tyler's shirt in, and try your best to convince him it's supposed to stay that way?"

When she opened the door of the coach, Jade walked in, carrying Alayne. "Don't panic," she said, giving her cousin a sharp look. "I've already changed her. I hope this dress is all right."

Emmy reached out to smooth a lock of the infant's ridiculously curly brown hair. Soft purple eyes twinkled at her from the rosy little face. "It's fine, Jade. Thank you." She took Alayne. "I'm not sure what I'd do without you, sometimes. I'm so glad you were able to come with us."

Jade nodded. "So am I." She walked over to the window where Joss was showing Tyler the city as the train chugged into the outskirts of London. "Are we almost there?" she asked him. "I'm so excited."

Joss nodded. "Almost. We should be pulling into the station in another few minutes."

"Will your entire family be there, Joss?" Jade asked.

"Well, not all of them, I suspect, but a good number at least."

Emmy sucked in a breath as she tried to quell her rising panic. She folded Alayne's blanket over her tiny head three different ways before she realized what she was doing.

"There it is," Jade said, pointing out the window. "I can see the station from here." She patted Tyler's head. "Isn't this exciting, Ty?" Tyler gave her an adoring look.

Joss looked over his shoulder at Emmy. He motioned for her to join them. Jade let out a startled gasp. "Saints a mercy, Joss. Are all those people your family?"

Curiosity got the better of Emmy. She joined Joss at the window. He nodded in answer to Jade's question. "There are a few more than I'd anticipated."

Emmy stared in horror at the well-dressed, exceedingly elegant crowd on the railroad platform. "Josiah, there must be fifty people there. You said there'd be a small gathering. Just your parents and a few close relatives."

"Well," he hedged, "I was afraid if I told you the entire lot would show, you would be too nervous."

"Nervous?" Emmy's voice came out on a squeak. "My Lord, I'm scared to death."

"Don't be silly, Emmy," Jade said. "I think they look very nice."

"Where's Grandpa?" Tyler pressed his nose to the window, seeking his first glimpse of the man who sent him what Emmy called "just because" gifts. Tyler didn't even have to wait for holidays to open them.

Jade tapped on the pane. "I'll bet he's the tall one with the walking cane and the imposing look in his eyes."

"Oh, Lord." Emmy sank down in a chair. "Oh my Lord."

Joss started to laugh. "Emerelda, stand up. They're just people. Stop worrying."

"But Josiah, what can we possibly talk about? They'll think I'm uneducated, and uncultured, and un, un— well any number of things I'm not that I should be."

As the train chugged to a halt, Joss pulled her to her feet. "Aren't you the same woman that was just honored by the American Geological Society for a paper you wrote *three years ago* that inspired the invention of the diamond rock drill last month?"

She nodded. "Yes, but—"

"And aren't you the same woman who discovered the method for measuring double refractive indices that has now become standard in the United States?"

"Well, yes, but, Josiah—"

"And aren't you the same Emerelda Brickston who has been invited by the London Geographic Society to present your thoughts on the classification of gemstones by their crystal systems at a symposium next week?"

She met his gaze. "Only because your father insisted."

"Only because you know more about it than they do."

Emmy leaned into him. "But nobody wants to know about those things, Josiah. It's the important things I don't know. Things like art and literature and fashion."

He dropped a brief kiss on her lips. "The really world-changing things, you mean."

"You know what I mean."

Joss looped his fingers under her elbow. "Come on, Emmy, my family is waiting to meet you."

Handing Tyler to Jade, Joss jumped down from the train. From behind the gate on the platform, a woman Emmy knew must be his mother called out to him. Emmy waited while Joss lifted her down. He made sure Alayne was securely wrapped in her arms before he set her down, then he reached up to assist Jade and Tyler.

His family rushed forth. They poured onto the platform in a sea of interested faces and inquiring eyes. Emmy covered her nervousness by concentrating on Alayne. Joss set Jade's feet on the platform, then took Tyler in his arms while a swarm of children in all ages and sizes crowded around his legs and pulled at his trousers. His mother pushed her way through the crowd to throw her arms around him. She hugged him fiercely while Emmy watched, feeling more than just a little left out.

It was Josiah's godfather, the Earl of Brandtwood, the same man Emmy had heard so many stories about, and wondered about so often, who set her at her ease. She recognized him instantly from Joss's description of his Uncle Marcus and the startling, almost shocking, green eyes that met and held her gaze. She gave him a tentative smile. Without comment, he lifted Alayne from her. He paused to let the infant wrap her tiny fingers around one of his large ones, then he smiled at Emmy. "They're a bit overwhelming, aren't they?" he said, nodding his head in the direction of Joss's family, all clamoring for his attention.

"Yes."

"I was more than a little intimidated the first time I met them, too," he assured her.

Emmy doubted that Marcus Brandton was intimidated by anyone, but she didn't say so. She reached out and tucked Alayne's blanket away from her face, to give the earl an ample view of Alayne's expressive little purple eyes. He winked at her. Alayne gurgled, clearly enchanted. "Joss," Marcus called, his voice demanding.

When Joss turned his head, Marcus said, "Introduce your wife around so I can carry this charming infant off and spoil her while her mother's not watching."

Joss pulled Emmy against his side. Tyler squirmed out of his father's grasp to wrap his chubby arms around his mother's neck. "This," Joss said, almost as if he were introducing the Queen of England, "is Emmy."

The chatter started again, as Joss's whole family began asking questions and talking at once. And suddenly, something in the sea of people caught her eye. Emmy stared, certain she must be imagining things. But no, her first thought had been correct. She went up on her tiptoes and whispered in Joss's ear. "Josiah, someone really should tell your sister-in-law that the third emerald from the center on that necklace is paste."

Joss laughed, a full, rich laughter, that made the entire family stop and stare at him. They all knew what had happened to Allyson. They all knew how he had suffered, the state he'd been in when his mother and father had returned to England from their visit following the funeral. Yet his laughter rang out, smooth and content. And suddenly, Emmy was engulfed in the crowd of his family. She was a part. She belonged.

Dear Friends,

Even as a kid, I was in love with Zorro. I mean, after all, what could be sexier than this guy who could do anything, sneaking about in that oh-so-handsome costume? The superhero myth has endured for centuries, and, as any woman could explain, its no wonder. MATTER OF HONOR was born out of my enchantment for Zorro. It was a long-held infatuation that I was finally able to put on paper.

But, as happens with every book, this one held many surprises. Each and every book has special meaning for authors. There's a reason why we refer to them as our children. MATTER OF HONOR was no exception. From page one of this book, I was captivated by its heroine. Emmy Greene was just the kind of woman I admire; courageous, strong, compassionate, giving, she lets nothing stand between her and the ones she loves. She was the perfect match for a man like Josiah Brickton. While the infamous Diamond Hawk fascinated and amused her, she had little patience for his histrionics. Instead, her grief-ridden husband turned her head, and captured her heart.

Frankly, I always thought that Doña Elena was a fool for not realizing that Don Diego was Zorro. Emmy Greene, I vowed, would out smart them all.

I can't tell you how much I loved writing this book. Carrying on the stories I began in my first historical romance, THE PROMISE, then continued in my second, BEYOND ALL MEASURE, was especially satisying. That's why I'm pleased to let you know that the tale isn't done. As I was finishing MATTER OF HONOR, Marcus Brandton stepped off the railway platform, with his striking green eyes and undeniable charm, and demanded his own story. I told it in UNTAMED. I hope you'll look for it in 97. As always, I love to hear from readers. You can reach me at 101 E. Holly Avenue, St. 3; Sterling, VA 20164.

Sincerely,

*Mandalyn Kaye,* aka Neesa Hart

P.S. I also write contemporary romance as Neesa Hart. My next two releases are ALMOST TO THE ALTAR, a January 97 release, A PLACE CALLED HOPE, coming in May, and SEVEN REASONS WHY, scheduled for September. Enjoy!